D1008192

The band of cowboys charged down upon them.
[Frontispiece]

A Tale of the Western Plains

G. A. Henty

With Illustrations by
Alfred Pearse

Dover Publications, Inc.
Mineola, New York

Bibliographical Note

This Dover edition, first published in 2006, is an unabridged republication of the work originally published as *Redskin and Cowboy: A Tale of the Western Plains* by Blackie & Son, Ltd., Glasgow, 1892. The original running heads have been modified to include the book title and chapter titles only.

Library of Congress Cataloging-in-Publication Data

Henty, G. A. (George Alfred), 1832–1902.
    [Redskin and cow-boy]
    A tale of the western plains / G. A. Henty ; with illustrations by Alfred Pearse.
       p. cm.
    Originally published: Redskin and cow-boy: a tale of the western plains.
London : Blackie & Sons, 1892.
      Summary: In 1859, sixteen-year-old Hugh travels from England to the American West and finds work on a cattle ranch, where he struggles with the elements, fights Indians, and chases kidnappers.
    ISBN 0-486-45261-1 (pbk.)
    [1. Cowboys—Fiction. 2. Frontier and pioneer life—West (U.S.)—Fiction. 3. West (U.S.)—History—19th century—Fiction. 4. Interpersonal relations—Fiction. 5. Adventure and adventurers—Fiction.] I. Pearse, Alfred, ill. II. Title.

PZ7.H4Tan 2006
[Fic]—dc22

2006040331

Manufactured in the United States of America
Dover Publications, Inc., 31 East 2nd Street, Mineola, N.Y. 11501

PREFACE

There are but few words of preface needed to a story that is not historical. The principal part of this tale is laid among the cowboys of the Western States of America, a body of men unrivalled in point of hardihood and devotion to work, as well as in reckless courage and wild daring. Texas, which twenty-five years ago was the great ranching state, is no longer the home of the typical cowboy, but he still exists and flourishes in New Mexico and the northern States and Territories. The picture I have given of their life can be relied upon, and its adventures and dangers are in no degree coloured, as I have taken them from the lips of a near relative of my own who was for some years working as a cowboy in New Mexico. He was an actor in many of the scenes described, and so far from my having heightened or embellished them, I may say that I have given but a small proportion of the perilous adventures through which he went, for had I given them in full it would, I am sure, have seemed to you that the story was too improbable to be true. In treating of cowboy life, indeed, it may well be said that truth is stranger than fiction.

G. A. HENTY.

CONTENTS

ILLUSTRATIONS

I. AN ADVERTISEMENT

Cedar Gulch was, in 1851, a flourishing camp. There had been some good finds by the first prospectors, and a rush had of course followed. In many cases first discoveries proved illusive, but it was not so at Cedar Gulch. The ground turned out well, and although no extraordinary finds were made, the average was good all over the bottom, and there were few who were not doing fairly well.

The scene was a busy one. Several hundreds of men were hard at work on the flat, which in winter was the bed of a wide stream, but which in summer was a mere thread of water among the rocks, scarce enough for washing purposes.

Everywhere were piles of stones and rubbish that had been brought up from the shafts; men toiled at windlasses; others emptied the buckets as they came up into swinging troughs or cradles; others again kept these supplied with water, and swung or rocked them, taking off the large stones that the motion brought to the surface, while the slush and mud ran out at the lower end. Newcomers moved about watching the work with eager eyes, wishing that they had had the luck to get there among the early arrivals, and to take up a claim, for every foot of ground far down the valley had already been occupied, and there was now no getting into a claim except by purchasing a share or altogether buying out the present holders.

One of the claims that was doing best was held by three men who had worked in partnership for the last two years, and who had been among the first to arrive at Cedar Gulch. They were known among the others as English Bill, Sim Howlett, and Limping Frank. Sim Howlett was perhaps the leader of the

1

party. He had been one of the earliest gold-diggers, and was a square, powerfully built man. He was a man of few words, but the words when spoken were forcible. He was by no means quarrelsome, but was one whom few cared to quarrel with, even in a place where serious quarrels were of constant occurrence, and where revolvers cracked so often that the sound of a fray excited but little attention.

English Bill was a tall wiry man, hot of temper, but a general favourite. Generous with his money, always ready to lend a helping hand to anyone who was down on his luck, he also was a capital worker, and had, in spite of his rough clothes and the use of language as rough as that of his companions, a certain air which told that, like many others in the diggings, he was a gentleman by birth. Why these two men should have taken up with Limping Frank as a comrade was a matter of surprise to those who knew them. They were both men in the prime of life, while he was at least ten years their senior. His hair was already white; his face was that of a student rather than a miner, with a gentle and almost womanly expression. His frame was slight, and looked altogether incapable of hard work, and he walked with a distinct limp, the result of a bullet wound in the hip. And yet there were men in the gulch who, having known the trio at other diggings, declared that they would rather quarrel either with English Bill or Sim Howlett than with Limping Frank, and as some of them were desperate fellows, and noted pistol shots, their report was quite sufficient to secure respect for a man who otherwise would have been regarded with pity or contempt.

Very little of the hard work of the partnership fell upon Frank. He cooked, looked after the shanty, did what washing and mending to the clothes was necessary, and occasionally came down and assisted to work the cradle and sort the stuff. They generally addressed him as doctor. Not that he made any profession of medical knowledge; but he was always ready to give his services in case of sickness, and many a miner had he pulled through fevers which, had it not been for his nursing and care, would have proved fatal.

"I can't make out what yer mean by saying I had best not

quarrel with that little old atomy you call Limping Frank," a big, powerful fellow who had recently arrived at the camp said to one who had been talking over with him the characteristics of several of the miners. "I ain't very pertiklar who I quarrels with; but what on arth there can be in that little chap to make one keep clear of him beats me. Can he shoot?"

"You bet," the other replied. "He could put a bullet plumb between your eyes ten times following, the length of the long saloon up there. There ain't no better shot nor quicker anywhere on the slopes."

"But he don't look as if he could speak up for himself," the other said.

"No; and he doesn't speak up for himself, though his mates would be ready enough to speak up for him if anyone said anything to him. There is nothing quarrelsome about him. He is always for peace and order. He is a sort of Judge Lynch all to himself. He has cleared out one or two camps I have been at. When a chap gets too bad for anything, and takes to shooting over and above what is usual and right, 'specially if he draws on quiet sort of chaps and becomes a terror, then Limping Frank comes out. I was down at Dead Man's Gulch when there was a gang of three or four men who were a terror to the place. They had stretched out seven or eight between them, and Texan Jack, as the worst of them was called, one day shot down a young fellow who had just come into camp, for no reason at all, as far as anyone knew.

"I happened to be in the saloon five minutes afterwards, when Limping Frank came in. Texan Jack was standing drinking there with two of his mates, laughing and jawing. You would scarcely have known that little chap if you had seen him then! He had been nursing a mate of mine only the night before, and as I had been sitting near him I thought what a gentle sort of face he had—more like a woman's than a man's. But now his eyes were wide open and his lips closed, and there was just a set look in his face that I knew meant mischief—for I had seen him once before when his dander was up—and I put my hand into my back pocket for my pistol, for I knew there was going to be a muss. He stopped in the middle of the room, and he said in a loud, clear voice that made everyone look sharp round, 'Texan Jack, murderer and villain, we have borne with you too long. If you are a man, draw.' Texan Jack stared with astonishment.

"'Are you mad, you little fool?' he said.

"'Draw, or I will shoot you down as you stand,' Limping Frank said, and the Texan saw that he meant mischief. Frank had no weapon in his hand, for he was not one to take an advantage. The Texan carried his weapon up his sleeve, but quick as he was with it, Frank was as quick, and the two pistols cracked pretty well at the same moment. Frank got a ball in the shoulder, but the Texan fell dead with a bullet in the centre of his forehead. His two mates drew in a moment, but Frank's revolver cracked twice as quick as you could count them, and there were just three bodies lying dead in a heap. Then he put up his pistol, and said in his ordinary quiet voice, 'I don't like these things, but we must have peace and order. Will some of you tell the others that they had better git.' And you bet they did git. Limping Frank never said another word about it, but got his arm in a sling, and half an hour afterwards I saw him quietly cooking his mates' dinner while they were both standing by blowing him up for starting out without them to back him."

"What did he say?" the newcomer asked.

"I heard him say, 'It is no use your going on like that, mates. If you had gone down he would have got his friends, and then there would have been a general fight, and several would have got hurt. When you have murderers like these you don't want a fight—you want an execution; and having a sort of natural knack with the pistol, I took it upon myself to be executioner.'

"There was another case, although it didn't happen at the camp I was at, in which a woman was murdered by a half-breed Mexican. I did not hear the circumstances, but it was a shocking bad case. She left a child behind her, and her husband, a little German, went clean off his head.

"Next morning Limping Frank was missing. All that was known was that he had bought a horse of a man who had come in late the night before, and was gone. His two mates looked high and low for him, but said at last they guessed he would turn up again. It was wellnigh two months before he came back. He brought back with him a watch and some trinkets that had been stolen from the murdered woman, and it seems that he had followed the fellow right down into New Mexico, and had shot him there. The man who told me said he never made any talk about it, but was at work as usual the morning after he came back. I tell you I would rather quarrel with Sim Howlett and English Bill together than I would get that little man's dander up. He is a peacemaker too, he is, and many a quarrel he has smoothed down. At one camp we were in we made him a sort of judge, and whenever there was a dispute about claims, or tools, or anything else, we went to him and he decided, and no judge could have gone into the case fairer or given a better judgment; and though, in course, those he decided against were not pleased, they had to put up with it. In the first place, the camp was with him; and in the second, there ain't much use disputing with a judge who can shoot as straight as he can, and is ready to do it if necessary."

The three partners had finished their day's work, and sat down to a meal of tea, steak, and corn-cakes that Limping Frank had prepared for them.

"We shall have to be moving from here soon," the Englishman said. "Another week and our claim will be worked out. We have not done badly, on the whole. The question is, had we better buy up somebody else's claim and go on working here, or make a start for some fresh field?"

"I vote for a move," Sim Howlett said. "I don't say the claim hasn't panned out well, but there is no excitement about it. The gold lies regular right through the gravel, and it is almost as bad as working for wages. You can always tell within an ounce or so what there will be when you come to clean up the cradle. I like a bit of excitement. Nothing one day and eight or ten ounces the next."

"It comes to the same thing in the long run," the Englishman said. "We don't get very much forwarder. Grub costs a lot of money, and then what there is over and above slips through our fingers somehow. The gambling-tables take a large share of mine; and your weakness for champagne, Sim, when you break out about once a month, makes a hole in yours; and as to Frank's, he spends half his in getting meat for soups and wines and medicines for his patients."

"What is one to do?" Frank said apologetically. "One cannot see people die for want of ordinary necessaries. Besides, Bill, you give away a lot too."

"Only my money is not so well spent as yours, doctor."

"Well, no, I don't think it is."

"I suppose it comes to the same thing in the end. I don't want to lay by money. What should I do with it if I had it?"

"You don't want to lay by money, because you are strong, and can go on earning it for years yet; and you both know very well that if you had a hundred thousand dollars you would chuck it all away in six months."

Sim Howlett laughed aloud.

"Perhaps you are right, doctor," English Bill said. "But if your argument means anything, it means that we are fools for working as hard as we do."

"Not at all," the doctor said gently. "You don't earn more than you want, as is shown by the fact that you lay by so little, and that we haven't more than enough dust in our sack to keep us for a month or two if we don't happen to strike it in the next claim we take up. No; I think we earn just enough. If you earned three times as much you would go three times as often to that cursed gambling-table, and it would be bad for your temper. If Sim earned three times as much he would go on the spree three times as often, and it would be bad for his health. If I were to earn three times as much, I should have three times as many patients to attend to, and I couldn't stand such a strain; so you see we are just right as we are," and he nodded pleasantly to his two comrades.

"You are the most perplexing beggar I ever came across, doctor," the Englishman said, "and I have seen some rum specimens during the twenty years I have been knocking about in the States."

The little man nodded as if it had been a compliment.

"I know, Bill. That is what I think myself sometimes; there is a tile just a little loose somewhere."

"Not at all, not at all," Bill said hotly; while Sim Howlett growled that he would like to hear anyone else say so.

"Not off, you know," Frank said, "but just a little loose. I know, dear boys. You see my machine gets muddled up. It may work right enough sometimes, but the chances are that a cog has got bent, or that there is a little twist in a crank, and the thing never works quite even. It just catches, you know—rattles now and then. You may look it all over as much as you like, but you cannot spot where it is. You say it wants grease, but you may pour bucketfuls over it and it makes no difference. There"—and he broke off—"they are at it again up in that saloon."

Two or three pistol-shots rang out in the evening air.

"Things are not going on as they ought to," he went on quietly. "That is another machine that wants regulating. There are more bad men in this camp than there ought to be."

"Don't you worry yourself," Bill said hastily. "You cannot expect a mining camp to be a sort of paradise, doctor, and all the bad men kept outside. Things have been going on pretty smooth of late. It has been quite a peaceful camp."

"I don't like the ways of that man Symonds the gambler," the doctor said meditatively, with his head a little on one side.

"He is a bad lot," Sim Howlett agreed; "but he is going. I heard tell yesterday that he said he was going down to Frisco at the end of the week; and if he doesn't go, Bill and I will get a dozen other fellows to go with us and tell him that he had better git, or the air of this camp is likely to be unhealthy for him."

"Well, if that is so we need not think any more about it," the doctor said. "I dreamt last night I saw him with a bullet mark in the centre of his forehead; but perhaps that was a mistake, or the mark will not come at present. It will come sooner or later," he added musingly, "but perhaps not for a good time yet."

"Well, well," Sim Howlett broke in, "we are wandering about like green hands lost in a sage-bush. We started by talking about whether, when we have worked up our claim, we shall stop here or foot it."

"If we foot it, where do you propose to go, Sim?"

"I heard this morning that they are doing well in that new place they call Gold Run. Then, again, you know we have always had a fancy for a month's prospecting up at the head of the Yuba. The gold must come from somewhere, though nobody has ever hit the spot yet."

"I am ready to go where you like, Sim," the doctor said; "but as I have often told you before, you miners are altogether wrong in your notions, as anyone can see with half an eye by the fact, that whether you are down here in the bottom of a gulch, or whether you are up on those flats, 2000 feet above us, you always find gravel. Now those flats were once the bed of a great river, that was when the mountains round were tens of thousands of feet higher than they are now; they must have been all that or there would never be water enough for such a river as that must have been. That river must have rolled on for thousands of years, for the gravel, which you can see in some places is 500 feet thick, is all waterworn; whether it is big boulders or little stones, it has all been rolled about.

"Well, in time these mountains were all worn away. There wasn't water then for the big river, and the water from the hills, as you see them now, began to cut fresh channels, and this Yuba, which is one of them, lies a thousand feet below the old gravel bed. In some places it has crossed the old bed, and the gold that came down from the former mountains into the gravel has been washed down into these valleys. You will never find, as you all dream of doing, a quartz vein stuck full of gold. There may have been veins like that in the old mountains, but the quartz veins that you find now, and lots of them have been assayed, are all very poor; they have got gold in them, but scarce enough to pay for working even when they get the best machinery. I fancy gold goes off with depth, though why it should I cannot say, and that these quartz veins which near the surface had big nuggets, and were choke-full of small stuff, just pettered away to nothing as they went deeper. That is why I think, Sim, that you will find no quartz reefs worth working anywhere now, and why you are less likely to find much pay dirt in the upper gorges, because the water there has not gone through the old gravel fields as it has in its windings lower down."

"But according to that, doctor, we should find it richest of all if we were to sink in the bed of the river down by the plains."

"Not at all, not at all, Bill. From the point where the Yuba's course leaves the old gravel bed of the big river and makes its own way through hills down to the plains it has picked up no more gold. As you know the big nuggets are generally found pretty high up, as was natural they should be, for as soon as the new river washed them out of the old bed they would sink down in some convenient hole; and as in the course of ages the Yuba cut down deeper and deeper, they would go down too. Their weight would prevent their rolling far; the light stuff would wash down, moving onwards with the sands and gravel. And so, as you search lower down, you get better surface washings, but find less coarse gold."

"I dare say you are right, doctor," Sim Howlett said, yawning, "so we won't go prospecting up in the hills, though some nice little finds have been made up there in spite of what you say. I vote we leave it open until we have cleared up, and then look round. A new rush may be started before a week is over, and if we are ready to move at once we may manage to take up claims in the thick of it; if one isn't pretty early at a new place, one may just as well stay away altogether. There is the horn. The mail is late to-night. I will go out and see if I can get hold of a Sacramento paper—one sees all about the new places there. Not that one need swallow all they say, for the lies about what is being got are tremendous. One fellow strikes it rich, and then they put it in that every fellow in the camp is making from four to ten ounces a day. I believe most of these lies come from the store-keepers. Of course, it is to their interest to get up a rush to places where they have set up their stores, and if a newspaper man comes along they lay it on thick. Well, here goes"; and throwing on his wideawake, Sim Howlett sauntered off.

In a quarter of an hour he returned with a newspaper. "Here you are, Bill, you may as well do the reading. I am out of practice, and the doctor is not to be depended upon, and will miss the very bits we want to know."

Taking the paper, the Englishman read the columns devoted to reports from the mining camps. A stranger would have thought from the perusal that every miner on the Pacific slope must have been making a fortune, so brilliant were the accounts of the gold that was being obtained in every mining camp. *"John Wilkins and party obtained at their week's clear-up 304 ounces of gold, including many fine nuggets. Many others have met with almost equal good fortune; the sand on the shoulder is panning out very rich."*

Such was a sample of the descriptions. The three men were unmoved by them. They knew too well how untrustworthy were the reports. Many were, as has been said, the work of the store-keepers; others were the invention of miners desirous of disposing of their claims to newcomers, and shifting to more promising regions. Little was said of the fabulous prices of provisions, of the fever that decimated some of the camps, of the total abandonment of others; and yet even the miners, although knowing by frequent experience that no dependence could be placed on these reports, were prone to cling to the hope that this time they were correct, and the roads were thronged by parties who, having failed at one camp, were making their way to a distant location of which they had heard brilliant reports, and who were met, perhaps, on their way by parties coming from that very camp to the one they had just quitted.

"It sounds well," the doctor said with a quiet smile when the reading was concluded.

"Sounds be blowed!" Sim growled. "They are thundering lies. What do they say of this camp?—read it again, Bill."

"It is difficult to get at the exact state of things at Cedar Gulch. Men who are doing well are always reticent as to their earnings; but there is little doubt that all are doing well, and that while those working in companies are obtaining very large results, the average through the camp is not less than from two to three ounces a day."

"The camp is not doing badly," Sim remarked. "There are

mighty few here who ain't earning their grub. I don't believe there is one who is making from three to four ounces a day, not regular. Of course if he comes on a pocket, or strikes the bed rock, he may earn a good bit over that, ten times as much perhaps in a day; but take it all round, an ounce, or at most an ounce and a quarter, would be the outside."

English Bill nodded. "I should say an ounce at the outside. There are scores who ain't earning half an ounce regular, and there are a few who have to run into debt for their grub. Well, there is nothing very tempting in that lot of notices. We have tried a good many of them in the last two years, and at any rate we have got another week before we need make up our minds. I expect it will come again, Bill, to what it has come to half a dozen times before. Write all the names on a piece of paper, put them into a bag, let the doctor draw one, and go for it. It is as good a plan as another, and the doctor's luck has always pulled us through."

Sim and the Englishman stretched themselves upon their blankets and lay there smoking, while Limping Frank squatted down by the side of the solitary candle and began to look at the small portion of the paper devoted to general news. This was soon finished, and then he ran his eye over the advertisements. These principally related to articles in demand by miners— patent rockers and cradles, picks and shovels, revolvers and bowie-knives, iron houses for stores, tents, clothing, waterproof boots, and flannel shirts. Then there was a column of town lots in Sacramento, notices of steamers starting for San Francisco, notices of stolen horses, offers of rewards for the capture of notorious criminals, and advertisements for missing friends.

"Bill," he said presently.

"Hello!" said the Englishman with a start. He had just laid his pipe down and was already dozing.

"Didn't you once say your name was Tunstall?"

"Yes, that's it, though I have pretty well forgotten it. What is it?"

"Well, there is an advertisement here that may relate to you."

"What is it, say? I haven't been running off with a horse, or shooting a sheriff, so I don't know why they are advertising for me."

"Five hundred dollars reward. The above sum will be paid by James Campbell, attorney, San Francisco, to anyone who will give him information as to the whereabouts of William Tunstall, who was last heard of four years ago in California. The said William Tunstall is entitled to property in England under the will of his brother the late Edgar Tunstall of Byrneside, Cumberland."

"That's me," the Englishman said, sitting upright and staring at the doctor. "Well, well, so Edgar has gone, poor lad! Well, I am sorry."

Sim Howlett had also roused himself at the news. "Well, Bill, I was going to congratulate you," he said; "but that doesn't seem the light you take the news in."

"No, I am not thinking of money," the other said. "I could have had that long ago if I had chosen to take it. I was thinking of my brother. It is twenty years since I saw him, and I don't suppose I should have ever seen him again anyway; but it is a shock to know that he has gone. It never was his fault, and I am sorry now I held off so. I never thought of this. It has come to me sometimes that when I got old and past work I might go back to the old place and end my days there; but I never thought that he would go before me. I am sorry, mates, more sorry than I can say."

"How was it, Bill?" the doctor asked. "Don't tell us if you don't like; it is no business of ours. Here in the diggings there are few men who talk of old times. Their eyes are all on the future, and what they will do with their wealth when they gain it; but no one asks another as to his past history. The answer might sometimes be a pistol-shot. Here we three have been living together for more than two years, and not one of us has wanted to know what the others were before we met. It is quite an accident that I know your name. You gave it when you gave evidence as to the murder of that old German that we hung Red Hugh for. It struck me it was an odd name then, but I never thought of it again until I saw it in the paper. And you said once—it was Christmas Day, I remember—you said there was a home for you in England if you liked to go to it."

"I will tell you the story," the Englishman said. "I would have told it to you long ago, only there was nothing in it to tell you. It was just what has happened ten thousand times, and will happen as often again. My father was one of the largest landowners in Cumberland. I was his eldest son. We never got on well together. He was cold and haughty, a hard landlord, and a despot at home. We should have quarreled earlier than we did; but I was sent to Rugby, and often did not even come home for the holidays, for I had a good many friends in those days. I went back when I was eighteen, and was to have gone to college a month or two later. I made a fool of myself, as boys do, and fancied I was in love with one of our tenants' daughters.

"Some meddling busybody—I always thought it was the parson's wife, for she drove along one evening just as I was saying goodbye to the girl at the stile—told my father about it, and there was a frightful row. For once he got in a passion, and I lost my temper too. It was really a harmless flirtation, I think, and would have died out when I went off to college. However, when my father swore that if I ever spoke to her again he would turn me out of the house, I said he might do as he liked, and that I would marry her when I came of age. He ordered me to leave the house and never see his face again; said that I was no longer his son, and might go to the devil, or words to that effect. So, being just as obstinate in my way as he was in his, I went, and never did see him again. Of course, I went first to see the girl. She was frightened out of her life when she heard of what had happened, said that her father would be turned out of his house, and all sorts of things, and at any rate she would have nothing more to say to me.

"So I walked to Liverpool, and took my berth in the first sailing ship to the States. My brother Edgar, who was two years younger than I, was away at the time. We had always been capital friends. Ten years later, when my father died, he advertised for me, and, the name being an uncommon one, someone pointed it out to me, and I answered. He wrote most affectionately, and lamented that our father had died without forgiving me, and had not only cut me entirely out of his will, but had, knowing his affection for me, inserted a clause that should he endeavour to alter the purport of the will, or to hand over by deed or otherwise any part or share of the estates to me, the property should revert at once to a distant relative. Edgar said, however, that he had consulted his lawyers, and they were of opinion that this clause in no way affected his power to dispose of his income drawn from the estate, and that he proposed to share this equally with me.

"I wrote back that while I was obliged to him for his offer I should not accept it, for, as the property was not entailed, our father had a perfect right to leave it as he liked. He had left it to him, and there was an end of it. We exchanged several letters, but I was just as obstinate as my father had been. I was too busy or too lazy for letter-writing. Somehow no one writes here, and then one is constantly on the move. Anyhow, I had one or two letters from him which I never answered. The last was three or four years ago. And now he is dead, and I suppose has left me some of the property I would not take during his lifetime. Of course I was a fool, and an obstinate fool, all along, but one never acknowledges this until it is too late."

The others made no remark for some time.

"Well, anyhow, Bill, you ought to go down to Frisco and see this lawyer."

"I will think it over," the other said as, after relighting his pipe, he lay back on the blankets again; "there is no hurry for a day or two."

No further mention was made of the matter until the claim was cleared up, but that evening Bill returned to the subject. "I have thought it over, and I suppose I had better go down to Frisco. I don't think I shall take this money. I should be like a fish out of water in England, and should be miserable there. If I take anything it will be a thousand pounds or so. I should sink that in buying a snug little place on the foothills, and I should put somebody on to work it and plant it up with fruit trees or vines, or that sort of thing, and then some day when I get too old for knocking about I shall settle down there; and I needn't say that my home will also be yours, mates. I sha'n't be much more than a week away. I shall come back here, and if you hear of anything before I return leave a line with the store-keeper telling me where you are off to. I have my kit packed, and if I start in half an hour I shall catch the night coach as it comes along past the top of the gulch."

Sim Howlett made no comment, but simply observed, "I expect you will find us here." But just as Bill was starting the doctor put his hand on his arm and said, "Don't do anything hasty, mate. You see you made rather a mess of your life by putting your foot down before when it seems there was no occasion for it. There is never any good comes of making up your mind in a hurry when there is no need for it. When you see a man slipping his hand round towards his back trouser-pocket, I allow that is not the time for thinking. You have got to act, and to act mighty sharp too, or you will get a bullet in you before you have drawn; but in a thing of this sort it makes no difference whether you decide now or six months hence. You need only write and say that you are found, and ask for particulars and so on, and when you have got them you can take your time about giving an answer. Many men before now have refused a good thing and been sorry for it afterwards. Your brother, according to your own account, has acted kindly and well towards you. Why should you refuse what he wished you to have, merely because you think that it ought to have come to you in the first place? That is all I have to say, Bill"; and he walked slowly back to the tent, while Bill started at a steady pace up the long steep hill from the gulch to the plateau above, along which ran one of the principal roads from Sacramento through the mining district.

"We shall miss him, Sim," Limping Frank said as he and his mate lighted their pipes after their meal that evening. "It seems kinder lonely without him after sitting down regularly for two years now."

"He ain't gone yet," Sim growled, "and I don't think as he is going. What Bill said he will stick to, you bet."

"Oh, yes! he means what he says, Sim. Bill has gone away from here with the fixed idea of going down there, writing a letter or two, coming back here, waiting for his money to come over, investing it in a farm, and going on working with us just as before; but, bless you, it is one thing to make up your mind and another to carry it out."

"What is to prevent his carrying it out, doctor?"

"Lots of things, Sim. When a man once gets mixed up in a will, or in any kind of law business, he ceases to be a free agent."

"Ceases to be what, doctor?"

"Well, he ceases to be his own master. Bill thinks he has only got to go into a lawyer's office, and say,—'Here I am, I am the chap mentioned in that advertisement. I dare say my brother has left me a good lot, but I don't want it. Just write and tell them to send me on five thousand dollars, that's all I want out of it. I am going back to Sacramento to-morrow. When the money comes pay it into the bank there for me.' Then he thinks that he will have a day's spree at Frisco, and come back by steamer next day."

"And why shouldn't he? What is to hinder him?"

"Well, it won't be like that, Sim, at all. When he goes in and says 'I am William Tunstall,' the lawyer will say, 'I am heartily glad to see you, sir. Allow me to congratulate you'; and he will shake Bill by the hand, and Bill will say to himself, 'This is just as it should be. Five minutes will do this job. I will go out and look up two or three friends who are in from the mines, and we will have a bottle of champagne apiece over this business.' Just as he has thought that over the lawyer will say to him, 'Of course you are in a position to prove that you are the Mr. Tunstall advertised for.' Bill will say, 'Oh, yes! here are my brother's letters.' Then the lawyer will smile and nod and say 'Most satisfactory,' and then he will add, 'Of course, you are in a position to prove that you are the person to whom these letters were sent? Of course, I don't doubt it for a moment, but letters do get lost, you know, and fall into other people's hands. In a matter of this kind we must proceed in a legal and business way.' Then Bill will say, 'Of course, I can prove that. There is Sim Howlett and

Frank Bennett, my mates. They know I am Bill Tunstall.' 'They knew you before you came out here, I suppose?' 'Oh, no! but they have known me for two years.' 'Known you as William Tunstall?' 'Yes, of course,' Bill will say, beginning to get riled. Then the lawyer will point out to him that we can only say that he called himself Will Tunstall, and that as the last of these letters he has got is dated earlier than that, it comes to the fact that there is only his word to go upon, and that the law requires very much stronger proofs of identity than this. Then Bill will get mad, and will say the money can go to the deuce, and that he sha'n't trouble any more about it."

"What then, doctor?" Sim Howlett asked as his companion stopped.

"Ah! well, that I cannot say. He may come straight off without doing anything more, or the lawyer may get him to talk it over. As to that I cannot say; but you may be quite sure that if Bill is to touch a penny of the money left to him he will have to go back to England to prove who he is, and it is like enough he may not succeed when he gets there. By what he says he was only at home just occasionally during his school holidays. He was little more than a boy when he left, and after twenty years' knocking about on the plains and here it is like enough he may not be able to find a soul to recognize him."

II. TERRIBLE NEWS

William Tunstall returned to Cedar Gulch the very day upon which his mates began to expect him. Having finished up the work in their claim on the previous day, they strolled up the hill to meet the coach on the chance of his coming.

"Well, mate, how goes it?" Sim Howlett asked.

"Well, it doesn't go at all, Sim."

"How is that?"

"Well, the lawyer was civil, and all that, but if I had let him he would have made me believe that I was not Will Tunstall at all. I showed him my brother's letters, which ought to have satisfied anyone, and he hinted that these might have come into my possession anyhow, that Tunstall might be dead, or that his kit, with these letters in it, might have been stolen."

"That is the very thing the doctor said he would be after," Sim Howlett exclaimed in great admiration at the latter's perspicacity.

"I suppose he didn't say he thought so, Bill?" the doctor asked.

"No, he knew better than that, doctor. He kept on saying that he was quite satisfied, but that other people wouldn't be satisfied. Then he asked about references, who could I refer to? Could I refer to anyone who had known me as William Tunstall before the date of these letters? I said that I had been knocking about on the plains and doing trapping and Indian fighting for years, and that I was known as English Bill, and that I did not suppose there were half a dozen fellows ever did know my name, and that, for aught I knew, they had all been scalped, shot, or hung long ago. He said, in that case I should have to go to England to prove my claim. I said I would see the claim at the bottom of the sea first, and then I left him.

"I met some fellows, and made a night of it, but in the morning the lawyer turned up at the hotel just as I had finished breakfast. I had told him the hotel where I was staying. He said it was no use being hasty. I said I wasn't hasty, and we were near having a row again. Then he said that he had only had instructions to find me, and did not know how much was left me under the will, or anything about it, except what he had put in the advertisement. At any rate he would write to the people who had instructed him in England and tell them that a gentleman representing himself to be William Tunstall had called, and that he possessed letters from the late Mr. Edgar Tunstall. That in the present state of affairs I declined to make the voyage to England for the purpose of proving my identity, but that he had my address, and could communicate further with me upon receiving instructions from them.

"I told him to say that I didn't want the money, and was not going to put myself out one way or the other about it. He listened, and shook his head, just the way the doctor does when he don't agree with you. Then he remarked that he would not do anything rash if he were in my place. I told him it was no odds to me whether he would or would not, and as I had just time to catch the steamer I wasn't going to waste any more time jawing over it, so off I came, and here I am. Well, what is doing here? Has there been any fresh rush?"

"Nary one. The doctor and I think we cannot do better than stay here. I was talking with Halkett and his partners this afternoon. They don't get on well together. Halkett said they would sell out if they could get a fair price. They are getting out about six ounces a day. No great thing, but they are only halfway down at present. It is in four shares, for two of the gang are on day wages. Of course, I said that it wasn't much of a thing to buy, as they were only getting an ounce apiece, and besides, the shaft is badly timbered. Still, if they would say what they wanted for it we would talk it over with you when you got back. Halkett was evidently anxious to sell, and said they would take a hundred ounces for it right out. Of course, I said that was too much, but I think it is a bargain, so does the doctor. They have got through

the worst half, and there is the best behind. It don't always turn
out rich on the bed-rock here; it didn't with us. Still, there is the
chance of it; and if it only keeps as it is now, and we take on a
couple of men to work with us, we should, after paying them
and keeping ourselves, be making three ounces a day anyhow,
and it will take us a couple of months to get to the bottom, and
perhaps more."

"How do we stand after the clear-up, doctor?" for Frank was
the treasurer of the party.

"We got twenty ounces at the last clear-up, and we had eighty-
nine before, so if we give him his price we should have nine
ounces left."

"It will take fifty or sixty dollars," Sim Howlett said, "to make
that shaft safe. Halkett is the only one of the lot that knows anything about that, and it has been done in a very slovenly style. I
shouldn't like to work down there until we have strengthened it
all the way down. I told Halkett the other day that if he didn't
mind it would be caving in. I think that is partly why they are
selling."

"Well, I think we couldn't do better than take it, Sim; but you
must get them to knock a few ounces off, otherwise we sha'n't
have enough to repair the shaft, and from what you say we must
do that before we go to work in the bottom. Let us go and make
a bargain at once."

"That will never do, Bill," Sim Howlett said; "that would look
as if we had made up our mind to take it, and they wouldn't
come down an ounce. No, no, we will have our meal, and wait
an hour or two, then I will stroll round to Halkett's tent, and say
that as we calculate it would cost a heap of money to make the
shaft safe we do not see our way to it, though we might otherwise have taken to the job. Then you will see to-morrow morning, when they knock off for breakfast, Halkett will come round
here and make some proposal."

So indeed it turned out. Soon after breakfast Halkett came to
the tent door. "Look here, boys," he said, "I want to get out of
this lot. The men I am working with ain't worth shucks. The
three of them don't do a fair man's work, and I am sick of it. But

I have been talking to them, and they won't take less than twenty-five ounces a share, and they have been talking to some men who have pretty well made up their minds to give it. If I had the dust I would buy the others out, but I haven't. If you will buy the other three out at their terms I will keep my share and work partners with you. I have got enough dust to pay my share of retimbering the shaft. What do you say?"

The doctor had gone off to take some broth to two of his patients. The other two looked at each other, and then Sim Howlett said: "Well, this is how it stands, Halkett. My mate here and I would have no objection to work with you; but it is this way: we and the doctor have chummed together, and have never taken anyone else in with us, partly because we are quite content as it is, and partly because the doctor can't do his share of the work—he hasn't got it in him. We don't want to go away from here now, and we have dust enough to buy your three partners out. I suppose we should want to work four at that shaft. I don't know what you have been working six for, except that three of your lot are of no use."

"That is about it," Halkett said.

"So you see we should have to take on a man to do the doctor's work."

"Well, you would have to do that if you worked it yourselves."

"So we should," Sim Howlett assented. "What do you say, Bill?"

"Halkett's proposal seems a fair one, Sim; it seems to me we can't do better than accept it. We must consult the doctor, Halkett. He is sure to agree, but we should not like to do it without speaking to him; that would not be fair. But you may consider it a bargain."

"Very well, I will go back and tell them I have made the agreement with you. Then I will come back and bring you fifteen ounces of dust, which is all I have got; I don't want them to know that I am going to stop in it. If I do, like enough they will cut up rusty, so I want you to make it up and hand the hundred ounces over clear; then they will hand me my share, and I can give you the other ten ounces. They will leave the camp as soon as they get their money. Somebody has been blowing to them about a find he has made prospecting among the hills, and I fancy they mean going off with him, and it would be no use letting on that I am going to stop in the partnership until they have gone. They are just the sort of fellows to think that I had been somehow besting them, and if they said so there would be trouble, and I don't want to do any of them harm."

The doctor on his return fell in, as a matter of course, with his mates' arrangement.

At dinner-time Halkett and his partners came in, and the dust was weighed out and handed over to them. Sim Howlett and Tunstall spent the afternoon in making a careful examination of the shaft, and in deciding upon the best plan for strengthening it. Halkett's former partners left a couple of hours after they got the money, and on the following morning the new proprietors of the claim set to work. The first step was to make an arrangement with a man who had horses, to haul timber from a little sawmill that had been erected two miles away, and as soon as this began to arrive the work of strengthening the shaft was set about. It took the three men, and another whom they had taken on at daily pay, a week, and at the end of that time it was pronounced safe against any pressure it was likely to have to bear.

The advertisement in the Sacramento paper had been noticed by others than by those for whom it was intended, and there happened to be among the miners who had worked at various times in the same diggings with William Tunstall another who had been on the jury when he had mentioned his name. He did not, however, notice the advertisement until a day or two after the newspaper had arrived in camp.

"There," he said to some mates who were sitting round the fire, "that is just like my luck; there is five hundred dollars slipped clean through my fingers because I did not happen to see this here paper before."

"How is that, Jones?"

"Why, here is five hundred dollars offered for information as to the whereabouts of William Tunstall."

"And who is William Tunstall? I never heard of him."

"Why, English Bill; that is his name sure enough; he gave it on a jury we served on together. I told him then I had never heard the name before. This is how I came to remember it."

"Well, why are you too late? Why don't you write off at once and say he is here, and claim the money?"

"Because he is gone, mate. Sim Howlett asked Black Johnson yesterday, when I was standing by, if he knew of a good man he could take on for a week's work, as he was singlehanded, for of course Limping Frank don't count in the way of work. I asked him if English Bill was laid up, and he said, No; he had gone the night before down to Frisco. I wondered then at his starting just before they had cleaned up their claim. Now it is clear enough, he had seen this advertisement."

"Bolted?" one of the other men asked.

"Bolted! no," Jones said in a tone of contemptuous disgust. "You don't suppose English Bill has been cutting anyone's throat, do you? or robbing some digger of his swag? No, he has gone down to Frisco to see the chap that put this into the paper. Why, look here," and he read the advertisement aloud; "he has come into a fortune, I expect. They would never have taken the trouble to advertise for him if it hadn't been a big sum. You bet English Bill has struck it rich; like enough it is a thundering big ranche, with two or three hundred thousand head of cattle."

"They don't have estates like that in England," another digger put in. "I was chatting with an Englishman at Holly Creek. He said land was worth a heap there, but it was all cultivated and hedged in, and he didn't suppose as there was a man in the whole country who had got as much as five thousand head of cattle. However, cattle or not, I expect it is a big thing English Bill has come in for, and we sha'n't see him in here again."

The news spread quickly through the camp. It was discussed by the men as they worked the rockers, by the gamblers up at the saloon, and in the tents when the work was done. Sim Howlett was soon questioned, but was surly, and little could be got from him. Limping Frank was no more communicative. He was accosted frequently, as he went from the tents with his soups and medicines, with "Well, Frank, so I hear your mate has come in for a big thing, and gone down to Frisco. Jack Jones saw the advertisement for him in the paper."

"If Jack Jones saw it, of course it was there," the doctor said with his quiet smile, "couldn't have seen it otherwise, could he? Yes, Bill has gone off. I am glad to hear that it is a big thing; hadn't heard it before. It will be a surprise to him, for he didn't expect it would be a big thing. Didn't think it would be worth troubling about, you see. However, I dare say he will be back in a week or two, and then no doubt he will tell you all about it."

Cedar Gulch was greatly disappointed when English Bill reappeared in his ordinary red shirt, high boots, and miner's hat, and went to work on the following afternoon as if nothing had happened. There had been a general idea that if he came back he would appear in store-clothes and a high hat, and perhaps come in a carriage with four horses all to himself, and that he would stand champagne to the whole camp, and that there would be generally a good time. He himself, when questioned on the subject, turned the matter off by saying he had not thought the thing worth bothering about; that he could not get what there was without going to England to fetch it, and that it might go to the bottom of the sea before he took that trouble.

The only person to whom he said more was the man who ran the gambling-table. Things had been lately going on more quietly there, and the gambler had postponed his departure to San Francisco. Bill Tunstall spent, as the doctor said, no inconsiderable portion of his earnings at the gambling-tables, and had struck up an acquaintance with Symonds. The latter was, like many of his class, a man of quiet and pleasant manners. For his profession a nerve of iron was required, for pistols were frequently drawn by disappointed miners, flushed with drink and furious at their losses, and the professional gambler had his life constantly in his hands. The accusation, "You cheated me!" was the sure signal for one or two pistol shots to ring out in sharp succession, then a body would be carried out, and play resumed.

Symonds bore no worse reputation than others of the class. It was assumed, of course, that he would cheat if he had the chance; but with a dozen men looking on and watching every movement of the fingers, even the cleverest gambler generally played fair. These men were generally, by birth and education, far above those with whom they played. They had fallen from the position they had once occupied; had, perhaps, in the first place been victims of gamblers, just as they now victimized others; had been cast out from society as detected cheats or convicted swindlers; but now, thanks to nerve, recklessness of life, and sleight of hand, they reaped a fortune, until the bullet of a ruined miner, or the rope of Judge Lynch, cut short their career.

Symonds was not unpopular among the miners. He was liberal with his money, had many times spared men who, according to the code of the diggings, had forfeited their lives by an insult or a shot that had missed its aim. He had often set men on their legs again who had lost their all to him; and if there was a subscription raised for some man down with fever, or for a woman whose husband had been killed in a shaft, Symonds would head the list with a handsome sum. And yet there were few men more feared. Magnanimous on some occasions, he was ruthless on others. He was a dead shot, and handled his pistol with a lightning speed, that in nine cases out of ten enabled him to fire first; and while he would contemptuously spare a man who was simply maddened by ruin and drink, the notorious bully, the terror of a camp, a man who deliberately forced a quarrel upon him, relying upon his strength or skill, would be shot down without hesitation.

Thus in nine cases out of ten the feeling of the communities among whom he plied his vocation was in his favour. While he himself was a dangerous man, he rid the camp of others who were still more obnoxious, and the verdict after most of these saloon frays was, "Served him right"; but as a rule men avoided discussing Symonds or his affairs. It was dangerous to do so, for somehow he seemed always to learn what was said of him, and sooner or later the words were paid for.

Will Tunstall knew that he was a dangerous man, and had no doubt that he was an utterly unscrupulous one, but he himself never drank while he played, and was never out of temper when he lost, therefore he had no reason whatever to fear the man, and Symonds had always been civil and pleasant with him, recognizing that there was something in him that placed him somewhat apart from the rough crowd. He met him one afternoon soon after his return.

"Is it true all this they are saying about you, Bill?" Symonds asked.

"Well, it is true enough that I was advertised for, and went down to Frisco to see a man there about it. Of course it is all nonsense as to what they are saying about the value of it. It is some family property that might have come to me long ago if I hadn't kicked over the traces; but I am not going to trouble about it. I shall have all the bother and expense of going to England to prove who I am, and I wouldn't do it if it were ten times as much."

"Come and have a glass of cham, Bill. My own story is a good deal like yours. I dare say I might be master of a good estate in the old country now, if I hadn't gone a mucker."

"It is too early to drink," Will said; "if I did drink it would be just a cocktail. The champagne you get is poison."

"Just as you like. By the way, if I can be of any use to you let me know. It is an expensive run home to England from here, and if you have need for a thousand dollars, I could let you have them. I have had a good run of luck this last six months. It would be a business transaction, you know, and you could pay me a couple of hundred for the use of it. It is of no use losing a good thing for the want of funds."

"Thank you, Symonds. I have enough to take me home if I have to go; but I am very much obliged for the offer all the same."

"It is business," the other said carelessly, "and there are no thanks due. If you change your mind let me know; mind I owe you a cocktail next time we meet in the saloon."

The gambler went on. Will Tunstall looked after him with a little wonder at the offer he had made. "It is a good-natured thing to offer, for, of course, if I went to England he could not make anything out of me beyond the interest of the money, and he would get more than that putting it on house property in

Frisco. He is a queer card, and would look more at home in New York than in Cedar Gulch!"

The gambler's dress, indeed, was out of place with the surroundings. Like most of his class he dressed with scrupulous neatness; his clothes were well made, and fitted him; he wore a white shirt, the only one in the camp, and abstained from the diamond studs and rings, and heavy gold watch chain that was generally affected by professional gamblers. He was tall, as tall as Tunstall himself, though not so broad or so strongly built; but his figure was well knit, there was in his walk and action an air of lightness and activity, and he had more than once shown that he possessed an altogether unusual amount of muscular strength.

"It is a pity that the fellow is what he is," Will Tunstall said when he turned away; "what a soldier he would have made, with his strength, and pluck, and wonderful coolness!"

This little conversation was followed by several others. Somehow or other they met more frequently than they had done before, and one evening, when there was no play in the saloon, Symonds asked him to come in and have a chat with him in his private room at the hotel. For some time they chatted on different subjects. Symonds had brought out a box of superb cigars, and a bottle of such claret as Will Tunstall had not drunk for years, saying carelessly as he did so, "I always carry my own tipple about with me. It would ruin my nerves to drink the poison they keep at these places."

After a time he brought the subject round to the legacy. "I have been thinking over what you said about not going back, and I think you are wrong, if you don't mind my saying so. What have you got to look forward to here? Toil and slave year after year, without ever getting a step farther, living all the time a life harder than that of the poorest labourer at home. It is well enough now, I suppose. You are seven or eight and thirty, just about my own age; in another ten years you will be sorry you let the chance slip. Of course it is different with me. As far as money goes, I could give it up now, but I cannot go back again. Men don't take to my sort of life," he said with some bitterness, "unless they have got a pretty bad record behind them; but I shall give it up before very long, unless I am wiped out first. Then I'll go and settle in South America, or some place of that sort, buy an estate, and set up as a rich and virtuous Englishman whose own climate doesn't agree with him."

Then he carelessly changed the subject again, but it was reverted to once or twice in the course of the evening, and before Will left he had said enough to enable his companion to gather a fair estimate of the value of the property, and the share he was likely to have of it.

The new claim turned out fairly well, improving somewhat in depth, and yielding a good though not an extraordinary profit to the partners. Some four months after Will Tunstall had been down to San Francisco, he received a bulky letter from the attorney there. It contained an abstract of his brother's will. This left him half the property, with a statement saying that he considered it to be his brother's by right, and enclosed with it was a copy of a letter written a few days before his death. It ran as follows:—

"My dear Will,—You have wandered about long enough. It is high time for you to come back to the old place that you ought never to have left. I shall not see you again, for I have long been suffering from heart disease, and the doctors tell me the end may come any day. I have had the opinion of some of the best authorities, and they all say that, thanks to some peculiar wording in the will, which I don't understand in the slightest, the prohibition to divide with you is only binding during my lifetime, and that nothing is said that restricts my right to leave it as I please. I don't suppose the contingency of your surviving me ever entered into our father's mind, and probably he thought that you would never be heard of again. However, you see it has turned out otherwise. You have wandered and roughed it, and gone through dangers of all sorts, and are still, you tell me, strong and healthy. I have lived quietly and comfortably with every luxury, and without a day's trouble, save my terrible grief when my wife died, and the ever-constant regret that you were not here beside me; yet I am dying, but that enables me at last to redress to some extent the cruel wrong you have suffered.

"I have left you half the estate, and it makes me happy to think that you will come back again to it. I have appointed you sole guardian of my boy. He is only twelve years old, and I want you to be a father to him. The estate is large enough for you both, and I hope that you may, on your return, marry, and be happy here; if not, I suppose it will all go to him at your death. In any case, I pray you to come home, for the boy's sake, and for your own. It is my last request, and I hope and believe that you will grant it. You were always good to me when we were boys together, and I feel sure that you will well supply my place to Hugh. God bless you, old fellow! Your affectionate brother,

"EDGAR."

With these documents was a letter from the solicitors to the family saying that they had heard from their agents at San Francisco that he had presented himself in answer to their advertisement, and had shown them the letters of the late Mr. Edgar Tunstall. They therefore forwarded him copies of the will, and of Mr. Tunstall's letter, and begged him to return home without delay, as his presence was urgently required. They assumed, of course, that they were writing to Mr. William Tunstall, and that when he arrived he would have no difficulty whatever in proving his identity.

"I think I must go, boys," he said as, after reading his brother's letter three or four times, he folded the papers up, and put them in his pocket. "My brother has made me guardian of his boy, and puts it so strongly that I think I must go over for a bit. I don't suppose I shall have to stop; although the lawyers say that I am urgently required there; but, mind, I mean to do just what I said. I shall take a thousand pounds or so, and renounce the rest. A nice figure I should make setting up at home as a big land-owner. I should be perfectly miserable there. No, you take my word for it, I shall be back here in six months at the outside. I shall get a joint guardian appointed to the boy; the clergyman of the place, or someone who is better fitted to see after his education and bringing up than I am. When he gets to seventeen or eighteen, and a stanch friend who knows the world pretty well may be really of use to him, I shall go over and take him on his

travels for two or three years. Bring him out here for a bit, perhaps. However, that is in the distance. I am going now for a few
months; then you will see me back here. I wish I wasn't going; it
is a horrible nuisance, but I don't see that I can get out of it."

"Certainly you cannot, Bill; it is your plain duty. We don't go
by duty much in these diggings, and it will be pleasant to see
somebody do a thing that he doesn't like because it is right. We
shall miss you, of course—miss you badly. But we all lose
friends, and nowhere so much as here; for what with drink and
fever and bullets the percentage wiped out is large. You are
going because, in fact, you can't help yourself. We shall be glad
when you come back; but if you don't come back, we shall know
that it was because you couldn't. Yes, I know you have quite
made up your mind about that; but circumstances are too strong
for men, and it may be that, however much you may wish it, you
won't be able to come. Well, we shall be clearing up the claim in
another two or three days, so it could not come at a better time
if it had to come."

The work was continued to the end of the week, and then, the
last pan of dirt having been washed, the partners divided the
result. Each week's take had been sent down by the weekly con-
voy to the bank at Sacramento, for robberies were not uncommon, and prudent men only retained enough gold dust by them
for their immediate wants. But adding the dust and nuggets
acquired during the last and best week's work to the amount for
which they had the bank's receipt, the four partners found that
they had, after paying all their expenses, two hundred and fifty
ounces of gold.

"Sixty-two ounces and a half each," the doctor said. "It might
have been better, it might have been worse. We put in twenty-
five each four months ago, so we have got thirty-seven ounces
each for our work, after paying expenses, and each drawing half
an ounce a day to spend as he liked. This we have, of course, all
of us laid by."

There was a general laugh, for not one of them had above an
ounce or two remaining.

"Well, it isn't bad anyhow, doctor," William Tunstall said.

"Sixty-two ounces apiece will make roughly £250, which is as much as we have ever had before on winding up a job. My share will be enough to take me to England and back."

"Yes, provided you don't drop it all in some gambling saloon at Sacramento or San Francisco," the doctor said.

"I sha'n't do that, doctor. I have lost big sums before now in a night's play, I confess; but I knew I could set to work and earn more. Now I have got an object before me."

That afternoon English Bill went round the camp saying goodbye to his acquaintances, and although it was very seldom that he drank too much, the standing treat and being treated in turn was too much for his head, and it was with a very unsteady step indeed that he returned late in the evening to his tent. Sim Howlett, who had started with him, had succumbed hours before, and had been carried down from the saloon by a party who were scarcely able to keep on their own legs.

When Will Tunstall woke in the morning he had but a vague idea of the events of the latter part of the evening. He remembered hazily that there had been many quarrels and rows, but what they had been about he knew not, though he felt sure that there had been no shooting. He had a dim recollection that he had gone into Symond's room at the hotel, where he had some champagne, and a talk about his trip to England and about the people there.

"What the deuce could have set me talking about them?" he wondered in his mind. He was roused from these thoughts by the doctor.

"If you are going to catch this morning's coach, Bill, you must pull yourself together."

"All right!" he said, getting on to his feet. "I shall be myself when I have put my head in a bucket of water. I'm afraid I was very drunk last night."

"Well, you were drunk, Bill. I have never seen you drunk but once before since we were partners; but I suppose no one ever did get out of a mining camp where he had been working for some time, and had fairly good luck, without getting pretty well bowled over after going the rounds to say goodbye. Now, then,

Sim, wake up! Bill will be off in a quarter of an hour. I have got breakfast ready."

Sim Howlett needed no second call. It was no very unusual thing for him to be drunk overnight and at work by daybreak the following morning. So after stretching himself and yawning, and following Will's example of having a wash, he was ready to sit down to breakfast with an excellent appetite. Will, however, did poor justice to the doctor's efforts, and ten minutes later the trio started off to meet the coach. There were many shouts of "Goodbye, mate! good luck to yer!" from the men going down to the diggings, but they were soon beyond the camp. Few words were said as they went up the hill, for the three men were much attached to each other, and all felt the parting. Fortunately they had but two or three minutes to wait before the coach came in sight.

"Just you look out for me in about six months' time, mates; but I'll write directly I get home, and tell you all about things. I shall direct here, and you can get someone to ask for your letters and send them after you if you have moved to a new camp."

With a last grasp of the hand, Tunstall climbed up to the top of the coach, his bundle was thrown up to him, the coachman cracked his whip, the horses started again at a gallop, and Sim Howlett and his mate went down to Cedar Gulch without another word being spoken between them.

Three days later, as they were breakfasting in their tent, for they had not yet made up their minds what they should do, a miner entered.

"Hello, Dick! Back from your spree? How did you get on at Frisco?"

"Yes, I have just got off the coach. I have got some bad news to tell you, mates."

"Bad news! Why, what is that, Dick?" Sim Howlett asked.

"Well, I know it will hit you pretty hard, mates, for I know you thought a heap of him. Well, lads, it is no use making a long story of it, but your mate, English Bill, has been murdered."

The two men started to their feet—Sim Howlett with a terrible imprecation, the doctor with a cry like the scream of a woman.

"It is true, mates, for I saw the body. I should have been up yesterday, but I had to wait for the inquest to say who he was. I was going to the coach in the morning when I saw half a dozen men gathered round a body on the footway of a small street. There was nothing unusual in that at Sacramento. I don't know what made me turn off to have a look at the body. Directly I saw it I knew who it was. It was English Bill, so I put off coming, and stopped to the inquest. He hadn't been killed fair, he had been shot down from behind with a bullet in the back of his head. No one had heard the shot particular. No one thinks anything of a shot in Sacramento. No one seemed to know anything about him, and the inquest didn't take five minutes. Of course they found a verdict of wilful murder against some person unknown."

Sim Howlett listened to the narration with his hands clenched as if grasping a weapon, his eyes blazing with fury, and muttering ejaculations of rage and horror. The doctor hardly seemed to hear what was said. He was moving about the tent in a seemingly aimless way, blinded with tears. Presently he came upon his revolver, which he thrust into his belt, then he dropped his bag of gold dust inside his shirt, and he then picked up his hat.

"Come along, Sim," he said in hurried tones, touching his companion on the arm.

"Come along!" Sim repeated. "Where are you going?"

"To Sacramento, of course. We will hunt him down whoever did it. I will find him and kill him if it takes years to do it."

"I am with you," Sim said; "but there is no coach until to-night."

"There is a coach that passes through Alta at twelve o'clock. It is fifteen miles to walk, but we shall be there in time, and it will take us into Sacramento by midnight."

Sim Howlett snatched up his revolver, secured his bag of gold dust, and said to the man who had brought the news, "Fasten up the tent, Dick, and keep an eye on it and the traps. The best thing will be for you to fix yourself here until we come back."

"That will suit me, Sim. I got rid of all my swag before I left. You will find it all right when you return."

They had but four hours to do the distance across a very broken and hilly country, but they were at Alta a quarter of an hour before the coach was due. It taxed Sim Howlett's powers to the utmost, and even in his rage and grief he could not help looking with astonishment at his companion, who seemed to keep up with him without difficulty. They ran down the steep hills and toiled up the formidable ascents. The doctor's breath came quick and short, but he seemed almost unconscious of the exertions he was making. His eyes were fixed in front of him, his face was deadly pale, his white hair damp with perspiration. Not a word had been spoken since that start, except that, towards the end of the journey, Howlett had glanced at his watch and said they were in good time and could take it easy. His companion paid no attention, but kept on at the top of his speed.

When the coach arrived it was full, but the doctor cried out, "It is a matter of life and death; we must go! We will give five ounces apiece to anyone who will give us up their places and go on by the next coach."

Two men gladly availed themselves of the offer, and at midnight the two companions arrived at Sacramento. The doctor's strength had given way when the necessity for exertion was over, and he had collapsed.

"Perhaps someone has got a flask with him?" Sim Howlett suggested. "My mate and I have just heard of the murder of an old chum of ours at Sacramento, and we are on our way down to find out who did it and to wipe him out. We have had a hard push for it, and, as you see, it has been too much for my mate, who is not over strong."

Half a dozen bottles were instantly produced, and some whisky poured down the doctor's throat. It was not long before he opened his eyes, but remained for some time leaning upon Sim Howlett's shoulder.

"Take it easy, doctor, take it easy," the latter said as he felt the doctor straightening himself up. "You have got to save yourself. You know we may have a long job before us."

There was nothing to do when they entered the town but to find a lodging for the night. In the morning they commenced

their search. It was easy to find the under-sheriff who had con-
ducted the inquest. He had but little to tell. The body had been
found as they had already heard. There were no signs of a
struggle. The pockets were all turned inside out. The sheriff
supposed that the man had probably been in a gambling-house,
had won money there, and had been followed and murdered.
Their first care was to find where Will Tunstall was buried, and
then to order a stone to be erected at his head. Then they spent
a week visiting every gambling-den in Sacramento, but
nowhere could they find that anyone at all answering to their
mate's description had been gambling there on the night before
he was killed.

They then found the hotel where he had put up on the arrival
of the coach. He had gone out after breakfast and had returned
alone to dinner, and had then gone out again. He had not
returned; it was supposed that he had gone away suddenly, and
as the value of the clothes he had left behind was sufficient to
cover his bill, no inquiries had been made. At the bank they
learned that in the course of the afternoon he had drawn his portion of the joint fund on the order signed by them all. At another
hotel they learned that a man certainly answering to his description had come in one evening a week or so before with a gentleman staying at the house. They did not know who the gentleman
was; he was a stranger, but he was well dressed, and they thought
he must have come from Frisco. He had left the next day. They
had not noticed him particularly, but he was tall and dark, and so
was the man who came in with him. The latter was in regular
miner's dress. They had not sat in the saloon, but had gone up to
the stranger's bedroom, and a bottle of spirits had been taken up
there. They did not notice what time the miner left, or whether
the other went out with him. The house was full, and they did not
bother themselves as to who went in or out. It was from a
German waiter they learned all this, after having made inquiries
in vain two or three times previously at this hotel.

As soon as they left the place the doctor seized Sim's arm.
"We have got a clue at last, Sim."

"Not much of a clue, doctor; still there is something to go upon. We have got to hunt out this man."

"Do you mind going back to the camp to-night, Sim?"

"No, I don't mind; but what for, doctor?"

"You go and see whether Symonds is still there, and if not, find out what day and hour he left."

"Good heavens! you don't suspect him?"

"I feel sure, Sim, just as sure as if I had seen it. The description fits him exactly. Who else could Bill have known dressed like a gentleman that he would have gone up to drink with when he had £250 about him. You know he had got rather thick with that villain before he left the camp, and likely enough the fellow may have got out of him that he was going to draw his money from the bank, and thought that it was a good bit more than it was. At any rate, go and see."

Two days later Sim Howlett returned with the news that Symonds had left two or three hours after Tunstall had done so. He had said that he had a letter that rendered it necessary that he should go to Frisco, and had hired a vehicle, driven to Alta, and caught the coach there. He had not returned to the camp.

"That settles it, Sim. When I find Symonds the gambler, I find the murderer of Bill Tunstall. I have been thinking it over. It may be months before I catch him. He may have gone east into Colorado or south into Mexico, but I am going to find him and kill him. I don't think it is any use for us both to hunt; it may take months and years."

"Perhaps he thinks he is safe, and hasn't gone far. He may think that poor Bill will be picked up and buried, and that no one will be any the wiser. We would have thought that he had gone off to England; and so it would have been if Dick hadn't happened to come along and turn off to look at the body. Like enough he will turn up at Cedar Gulch again."

"He may," the doctor said thoughtfully, "and that is the more reason why you should stop about here. You would hear of his coming back to any of the mining camps on the slopes. But I don't think he will. He will feel safe, and yet he won't feel quite safe. Besides, you know, I dreamt that I should kill him. However, if he does come back anywhere here I leave him to you, Sim. Shoot him at sight as if he were a mad dog. You don't want any fair play with a fellow like that. When you tell the boys the story they will all say you did right. I will write to you from time to time to let you know where I am. If you have killed him let me know. I shall come back to you as soon as I have found him."

And so it was settled; for, eager as Sim Howlett was for vengeance, he did not care for the thought of years spent in a vain search, and believed that his chance of meeting Symonds again was as good among the mining camps as elsewhere.

III. THE WANDERER'S RETURN

Had the circumstances of William Tunstall's leaving his home been more recent, or had the son of Edgar Tunstall been older, the news that William Tunstall had returned and had taken up his residence at Byrneside as master of the portion of the estate left him by his brother, and as guardian to the young heir to the remainder, would have caused a good deal of interest and excitement in the county. The twenty years, however, that had elapsed since Will Tunstall had left home, and the fact that when he went away he was but a lad quite unknown personally to his father's acquaintances, deprived the matter of any personal interest. It had generally been thought that it was hard that he should have been entirely cut out of his father's will, and the clause forbidding his brother to make any division of the property was considered particularly so, especially as it was known that Edgar was attached to his brother, and would have gladly shared the property with him.

But William had been away twenty years, and no one had a personal interest in him. Ten years had elapsed since he had been finally disinherited by his father's will. Beyond a feeling of satisfaction that justice had been done, and that there would not be a long minority at Byrneside, the news that the eldest son had returned created no excitement.

Messrs. Randolph & Son of Carlisle, who were business agents for half the estates in the county, reported well of the newcomer. They had never seen him as a boy, but they expressed themselves as agreeably surprised that the long period he had passed knocking about among rough people in the States had in no way affected him unfavourably. His manners were particularly good, his appearance was altogether in his favour, he was a true Cumberland man, tall and powerful like his father and brother, though somewhat slighter in build.

He was accompanied by his wife. Yes, they had seen her. They had both dined with them. They had not been previously aware that Mr. Tunstall was married. Their client, Mr. Edgar Tunstall, had not mentioned the fact to them. They were not prepared to give any decided opinion as to Mrs. Tunstall. She had spoken but little, and struck them as being nervous; probably the position was a novel one for her. There were, they understood, no children.

Messrs. Randolph, father and son, oldfashioned practitioners, had from the first considered the scruples of their agents in San Francisco to be absurd. Mr. Tunstall had presented himself as soon as they had advertised. He had produced the letters of his brother as proof of his identity, and had offered to bring forward witnesses who had known him for years as William Tunstall. What on earth would they have had more than that? Mr. Tunstall had had reason already for resentment, and it was not surprising that he had refused to set out at once for England when he found his identity so absurdly questioned. So they had immediately sent off the abstract of the will and a copy of Edgar Tunstall's letter, and were much gratified when in due time Mr. Tunstall had presented himself at their office, and had personally announced his arrival.

It was indeed a relief to them; for, had he not arrived, various difficulties would have arisen as to his moiety of the estate, there being no provision in the will as to what was to be done should he refuse to accept it. Moreover, application must have been made to the court for the appointment of fresh guardians for the boy. Altogether they were glad that a business that might have been troublesome was satisfactorily settled. Mr. Tunstall, after introducing himself, had produced the letters he had received from his brother, with the abstract of the will and copy of the letter they had sent him.

He had said smilingly, "I don't know whether this is sufficient, gentlemen, for I am not up in English law. If it is necessary I can, of course, get a dozen witnesses from the States to prove that

I have been always known as William Tunstall; though I generally passed, as is the custom there, under a variety of nicknames, such as English Bill, Stiff Bill, and a whole lot of others. It will naturally take some little time and great expense to get witnesses over, especially as men are earning pretty high wages in California at present; but, of course, it can be managed if necessary."

"I do not see that there is any necessity for it," Mr. Randolph said. "Besides, no doubt we shall find plenty of people here to identify you."

"I don't know that, Mr. Randolph. You see I was little more than a boy when I went away. I had been at Rugby for years, and often did not come home for the holidays. Twenty years have completely changed me in appearance, and I own that I have but a very faint recollection of Byrneside. Of course I remember the house itself, and the stables and grounds; but as to the neighbours, I don't recollect any of them. Neither my brother nor myself dined in the parlour when my father had dinner parties; but it seems to me that, after all, the best proof of my identity is my correspondence with my brother. Certainly, he would not have been deceived by any stranger, and the fact that we exchanged letters occasionally for some years seems to me definite proof that he recognized me as his brother."

"Undoubtedly so," Mr. Randolph said. "That in itself is the strongest proof that can be brought. We mentioned that in our letter to Mr. Campbell in San Francisco. His doubts appeared to us, I may say, to be absurd."

"Not altogether absurd, Mr. Randolph. California has been turned pretty well topsy-turvy during the last four or five years, and he was not to be blamed for being suspicious. May I ask you if you have come across my letters to my brother among his papers?"

"No, we have not done so. In fact, your brother told us that he had not preserved them, for as you were wandering about constantly the addresses you gave were no benefit, and that beyond the fact that you were in California he had no idea where you could be found. That is why it became necessary to advertise for you."

"It is unfortunate that he did not keep them, Mr. Randolph, for in that case, of course, I could have told you most of their contents, and that would have been an additional proof of my identity."

"There is not the least occasion for it, Mr. Tunstall. We are perfectly and entirely satisfied. Mr. Edgar's recognition of you as his brother, your possession of his letters, the fact that you answered at once to the advertisement in California, your knowledge of your early life at Rugby, and so on, all tend to one plain conclusion; in fact, no shadow of doubt was entertained by my son or myself from the first. I congratulate you very heartily on your return, because to some extent the very hard treatment which was dealt to you by your father, Mr. Philip Tunstall, has now been atoned for. Of course you only received a short abstract of your brother's will; the various properties which fall to you are detailed in full in it. Byrneside itself goes to his son; but against that may be set off a sum invested in good securities, and equal to the value of the house and home park, so that you can either build or purchase a mansion as good as Byrneside. We may tell you also that the estates were added to in your father's time, and that other properties have been bought by your brother, who, owing to the death of his wife and the state of his health, has for some years led a very secluded life, investing the greater part of his savings in land. So that, in fact, your moiety of the estates will be quite as large as the elder son's portion you might have expected to receive in the ordinary course of events."

"What sort of boy is my nephew, Mr. Randolph?"

"I have seen him two or three times when I have been over at Byrneside. Of course I did not notice him particularly, but he is a bright lad, and promises to grow into a very fine young man. I fancy from something his father let drop that his disposition resembles yours. He is very fond of outdoor exercises, knows every foot of the hills round Byrneside, and though but eleven or twelve years old he is perfectly at home on horseback, and he is a good shot. He has, in fact, run a little wild. His father spoke of him as being warm-hearted and of excellent impulses, but lamented that, like you, he was somewhat quick-tempered and headstrong."

"Edgar ought not to have selected me for his guardian, Mr. Randolph."

"I said almost as much, Mr. Tunstall, when I drew out the will; but Mr. Edgar remarked that you had doubtless got over all that long ago, and would be able to make more allowance for him and to manage him far better than anyone else could do."

"I shall try and merit Edgar's confidence, Mr. Randolph. I have suffered enough from my headstrong temper, and have certainly learnt to control it. I shall not be hard upon him, never fear."

"Are you going over to Byrneside at once, Mr. Tunstall?"

"No; I shall go up to London to-morrow morning. I want a regular outfit before I present myself there for inspection. Besides, I would rather that you should give notice to them at Byrneside that I have returned. It is unpleasant to arrive at a place unannounced, and to have to explain who you are."

"Perhaps you would like to see the will, and go through the schedule?"

"Not at all, Mr. Randolph. There will be plenty of time for that after my return."

"You will excuse my asking if you want any money for present use, Mr. Tunstall?"

"No, thank you; I am amply provided. I was doing very well at the diggings when your letters called me away, and I have plenty of cash for present purposes."

"You will, I hope, dine with us to-day, Mr. Tunstall."

"I thank you. I should have been very happy, but I have my wife with me. I have left her at the 'Bull'."

"Oh, indeed! I was not aware——"

"That I was married? Yes, I have been married for some years. I did not think it necessary to mention it to Edgar, as he would only have used it as an additional argument why I should accept his generous offers."

"We shall be very glad, Mrs. Randolph and myself, if you will bring Mrs. Tunstall with you."

And so Mrs. Tunstall came. She was a dark woman, and, as Mr. Randolph and his wife agreed, was probably of Mexican or Spanish blood, and spoke English with a strange accent. She had evidently at one time been strikingly pretty, though now faded. She had rather a worn, hard expression on her face, and impressed Mr. Randolph, his wife, son, and daughter-in-law less favourably than the lawyer had thought it right to say to those who made inquiries about her; but she had, as they said, spoken but little, and had seemed somewhat nervous and ill at ease.

Mr. Tunstall did not appear for some time at Byrneside. He went down to Rugby to see his nephew, who had, in accordance with his father's wish, been placed there a month or two after his death. The holidays were to begin a week later, and Hugh was delighted when his uncle told him that he and his aunt were thinking of going to the Continent for a few months before setting down at Byrneside, and would take him with them.

Hugh was very much pleased with his new relative. "He is a splendid fellow," he told his schoolboy friends. "Awful jolly to talk to, and has been doing all sorts of things—fighting Indians, and hunting buffalo, and working in the gold-diggings. Of course he didn't tell me much about them; there wasn't time for that. He tipped me a couple of sovs. I am sure we shall get on first-rate together." And so during the summer holidays Hugh travelled with his uncle and aunt in Switzerland and Italy. He did not very much like his aunt. She seemed to try to be kind to him, and yet he thought she did not like him. His uncle had taken him about everywhere, and had told him lots of splendid yarns.

At Christmas they would be all together at Byrneside. His uncle had been very much interested in the place, and was never tired of his talk about his rambles there. He remembered the pool where his father had told him they both used to fish as boys, and about Harry Gowan the fisherman who used to go out in his boat, and who was with them when that storm suddenly broke when the boat was wrecked on the island and they were all nearly drowned. He was very glad to hear that Gowan was still alive; and that James Wilson, who was then under stableman and used to look after their ponies, was now coachman; and that Sam, the gardener's boy who used to show them where the birds' nests were, was now head gardener; and that Mr. Holbeach the vicar was still alive, and so was his sister Miss Elizabeth; and that, in fact, he remembered quite well all the people who had been there when he was a boy. Altogether it had been a glorious holiday.

His uncle and aunt returned with him when it was over, the former saying he had had enough of travelling for the present, and instead of being away, as he had intended, for another couple of months, he should go down home at once. They went with him as far as Rugby, dropped him there, and then journeyed north. On their arrival at Byrneside, where they had not been expected, Mr. Tunstall soon made himself extremely popular. Scarcely had they entered the house when he sent out for James the coachman, and greeted him with the greatest heartiness.

"I should not have known you, James," he said, "and I don't suppose you would have known me?"

"No, sir; I cannot say as I should. You were only a slip of a lad then, though you didn't think yourself so. No, I should not have known you a bit."

"Twenty years makes a lot of difference, Jim. Ah, we had good fun in those days! Don't you remember that day's ratting we had when the big stack was pulled down, and how one of them bit you in the ear, and how you holloaed?"

"I remember that, sir. Mr. Edgar has often laughed with me about it."

"And you remember how my poor brother and I dressed up in sheets once, and nearly scared you out of your life, Jim?"

"Ay, ya; I mind that too, sir. That wasn't a fair joke, that wasn't."

"No, that wasn't fair, Jim. Ah! well, I am past such pranks now. Well, I am very glad to see you again after all these years, and to find you well. I hear that Sam is still about the old place, and is now head gardener. You may as well come out and help me find him while Mrs. Tunstall is taking off her things."

Sam was soon found, and was as delighted as James at Mr. Tunstall's recollection of some of their bird-nesting exploits. After a long chat with him, Mr. Tunstall returned to the house, where a meal was already prepared.

"You need not wait," he said, after the butler had handed the dishes. "I have not been accustomed to have a manservant behind my chair for the last twenty years, and can do without it now."

He laid down his knife and fork with an air of relief as the door closed behind the servant.

"Well, Lola," he said in Spanish, "everything has gone off well."

"Yes," she said, "I suppose it has," in the same language. "It is all very oppressive. I wish we were back in California again."

"You used to be always grumbling there," he said savagely. "I was always away from you, and altogether you were the most ill-used woman in the world. Now you have got everything a woman could want. A grand house, and carriages, and horses; the garden and park. What can you want more?"

She shrugged her shoulders. "I shall get accustomed to it in time," she said, "but so far I do not like it. It is all stiff and cold. I would rather have a little hacienda down on the Del Norte, with a hammock to swing in, and a cigarette between my lips, and a horse to take a scamper on if I am disposed, and you with me, than live in this dreary palace."

"Baby! you will get accustomed to it in time; and you can have a hammock here if you like, though it is not often that it is warm enough to use it. And you can smoke cigarettes all day. It would shock them if you were an Englishwoman, but in a Mexican they will think it right and proper enough. And you have got your guitar with you, so you can have most of your pleasures; and as for the heat, there is sure to be some big glass houses where they grow fruit and flowers, and you can have one of them fitted up with Mexican plants, and hang your hammock there; and it won't need a very long stretch of imagination to fancy that you are at your hacienda on the Del Norte."

"If you can manage that it will be nice," the woman said.

"Anything can be managed in this country when we have got money to pay for it."

"At any rate it will be a comfort to know that there is no fear of your being shot here. Every time you went away from me, if it was only for a week or two, I knew I might never see you again, and that you might get shot by some of those drunken miners. Well, I shall be free of all that now, and I own that I was wrong to grumble. I shall be happy here with you, and I see that it was indeed fortunate that you found those papers on the body of the man you came across dead in the woods."

She looked closely at him as she spoke.

"Well, that is a subject that there is no use talking about, Lola. It was a slice of luck; but there is an English proverb, that walls have ears, and it is much better that you should try and forget the past. Remember only that I am William Tunstall, who has come back here after being away twenty years."

She nodded. "I shall not forget it. You know, you always said I was a splendid actress, and many a fool with more dollars than wit have I lured on, and got to play with you in the old days at Santa Fé."

"There, there, drop it, Lola," he said; "the less we have of old memories the better. Now we will have the servants in, or they will begin to think we have gone to sleep over our meal." And he struck the bell which the butler, when he went out, had placed on the table beside him.

"Have you been over the house?" he asked when they were alone again.

"Not over it all. The old woman—she called herself the housekeeper—showed me a great room which she said was the drawing-room, and a pretty little room which had been her mistress's boudoir, and another room full of books, and a gallery with a lot of ugly pictures in it, and the bedroom that is to be ours, and a lot of others opening out of it."

"Well, I will go over them now with you, Lola. Of course I am supposed to know them all. Ah! this is the boudoir. Well, I am sure you can be comfortable here, Lola. Those chairs are as soft and easy as a hammock. This will be your sanctum, and you can lounge and smoke, and play your guitar to your heart's content. Yes, this is a fine drawing-room, but it is a deal too large for two of us; though in summer, with the windows all open, I dare say it is pleasant enough." Having made a tour of the rooms that had been shown Lola, they came down to the hall again.

"Now let us stroll out into the garden," he said. "You will like that." He lit a cigar, and Lola a cigarette. The latter was unfeignedly delighted with the masses of flowers and the beautifully kept lawns, and the views from the terrace, with a stretch of fair country, and the sea sparkling in the sunshine two miles away.

"Here comes the head gardener, Lola, my old friend. This is Sam, Lola," he said, as the gardener came up and touched his hat. "You know you have heard me speak of him. My wife is delighted with the garden, Sam. She has never seen an English garden before."

"It is past its best now, sir. You should have seen it two months ago."

"I don't think it could be more beautiful," Lola said, "there is nothing like this in my country. We have gardens with many flowers, but not grass like this, so smooth and so level. Does it grow no higher?"

"Oh, it grows fast enough, and a good deal too fast to please us, and has to be cut twice a week."

"I see your are looking surprised at my wife smoking," William Tunstall said with a smile. "In her country all ladies smoke. Show her the greenhouses; I think they will surprise her even more than the garden."

The long ranges of greenhouses were visited, and Sam was gratified at his new mistress's delight at the flowers, many of which she recognized, and still more at the fruit—the grapes covering the roofs with black and yellow bunches; the peaches and nectarines nestling against the walls.

"The early sorts are all over," Sam said; "but I made a shift to keep these back, though I did not think there was much chance of any but the grapes being here when you got back, as we heard that you would not be home much before Christmas."

"We changed our mind, you see, Sam, and I am glad we did, for if we had come then, Mrs. Tunstall would have been frightened at the cold and bleakness. I'll tell you what I want done,

Sam. I want this conservatory next the house filled as much as possible with Mexican and South American plants. Of course, you can put palms and other things that will stand heat along with them. I want the stages cleared away, and the place made to look as much like a room as possible. Mrs. Tunstall will use it as a sitting-room."

"I think we shall have to put another row of pipes in, Mr. William. Those plants will want more heat than we have got here."

"Then we must put them in. My wife will not care how hot it is, but of course we don't want tropical heat. I should put some rockery down the side here to hide the pipes, and in the centre we will have a fountain with water plants, a foot or two below the level of the floor, and a low bank of ferns round. That is the only change, as far as I can see, that we shall want in the house. I shall be going over to Carlisle in a day or two, and I'll arrange with somebody there to make the alterations."

"Very well, Mr. William, if you will get some masons to do the rockery and fountain, I can answer for the rest; but I think I shall need a good many fresh plants. We are not very strong in hot subjects. Mr. Edgar never cared for them much."

"If you will make out a list of what you want, and tell me who is the best man to send to, Sam, I will order them as soon as you are ready to put them in."

And so, when Hugh returned at Christmas for the holidays, he was astonished at finding his aunt swinging in a hammock, smoking a cigarette, slung near a sparkling little fountain, and surrounded by semi-tropical plants. The smoking did not surprise him, for he had often seen her with a cigarette during their trip together; but the transformation of the conservatory astonished him.

"Well, Hugh, what do you think of it?" she asked, smiling at his surprise.

"It is beautiful!" he said; "it isn't like a greenhouse. It is just like a bit out of a foreign country."

"That is what we tried to make it, Hugh. You see, on the side next to the house where there is a wall, we have had a Mexican view painted with a blue sky, such as we have there, and mountains, and a village at the foot of the hills. As I lie here I can fancy myself back again, if I don't look up at the sashes overhead. Oh, how I wish one could do without them, and that it could be covered with one great sheet of glass!"

"It would be better," Hugh admitted, "but it is stunning as it is. Uncle told me, as he drove me over from Carlisle, that he had been altering the conservatory, and making it a sort of sitting-room for you, but I never thought that it would be like this. What are those plants growing on the rocks?"

"Those are American aloes, they are one of our most useful plants, Hugh. They have strong fibres which we use for string; and they make a drink out of the juice fermented—it is called pulque, and is our national drink, though of late years people drink spirits too, which are bad for them, and make them quarrelsome."

During the holidays Hugh got over his former dislike for his aunt, and came to like her more than his uncle. She was always kind and pleasant with him, while he found that, although his uncle at times was very friendly, his temper was uncertain. The want of some regular occupation, and the absence of anything like excitement, told heavily upon a man accustomed to both. At first there was the interest in playing his part: of meeting people who had known him in his boyhood, of receiving and returning the visits of the few resident gentry within a circuit of ten miles, of avoiding mistakes and evading dangers; but all this was so easy that he soon tired of it. He had tried to make Lola contented, and yet her lazy contentment with her surroundings irritated him.

She had created a good impression upon the ladies who had called. The expression of her face had softened since her first visit to Carlisle, and the nervous expression that had struck Mr. Randolph then had disappeared. Her slight accent, and the foreign style of her dress, were interesting novelties to her visitors, and after the first dinner party given in their honour, at which she appeared in a dress of dull gold with a profusion of rich black lace, she was pronounced charming. Her husband, too, was considered to be an acquisition to the county. Everyone had expected that he

would have returned, after so long an absence, rough and unpol-
ished, whereas his manners were quiet and courteous.

He was perhaps less popular among the sturdy Cumberland
squires than with their wives. He did not hunt; he did not shoot.
"I should have thought," one of his neighbours said to him, "that
everyone who had been living a rough life in the States would
have been a good shot."

"A good many of us are good shots, perhaps most of us, but it
is with the pistol and rifle. Shot-guns are not of much use when
you have a party of Redskins yelling and shooting round you,
and it is not a handy weapon to go and fetch when a man draws
a revolver on you. As to shooting little birds, it may be done by
men who live on their farms and like an occasional change from
the bacon and tinned meat that they live on from year's end to
year's end. Out there a hunter is a man who shoots game—I
mean deer and buffalo and bear and other animals—for the
sake of their skins, although, of course, he does use the meat of
such as are eatable. With us a good shot means a man who can
put a ball into a Redskin's body at five hundred yards certain,
and who with a pistol can knock a pipe out of a man's mouth ten
yards away, twenty times following; and it isn't only straightness
of shooting, but quickness of handling that is necessary. A man
has to draw, and cock, and fire in an instant. The twinkling of an
eye makes the difference of life or death.

"Oh, yes! I am a good shot, but not in your way. I went away
from here too young to get to care about tramping over the country all day to shoot a dozen or two of birds, and I have never been
in the way of learning to like it since. I wish I had, for it seems an
important part of country life here, and I know I shall never be
considered as a credit to the county unless I spend half my time
in winter riding after foxes or tramping after birds; but I am afraid
I am too old now ever to take to those sports. I heartily wish I
could, for I find it dull having no pursuit. When a man has been
earning his living by hunting, or gold-digging, or prospecting for
mines all his life, he finds it hard to get up in the morning and
know that there is nothing for him to do but just to look round the
garden or to go out for a drive merely for the sake of driving."

When summer came Mr. Tunstall found some amusements to his taste. If there was a wrestling match anywhere in the county or in Westmorland he would be present, and he became a regular attendant at all the racecourses in the north of England. He did not bet. As he said to a sporting neighbour, who always had a ten-pound note on the principal races, "I like to bet when the chances are even, or when I can match my skill against another man's: but in this horse-racing you are risking your money against those who know more than you do. Unless you are up to all the tricks and dodges, you have no more chance of winning than a man has who gambles with a cheat who plays with marked cards. I like to go because it is an excitement; besides, at most of the large meetings there is a little gambling in the evening. In Mexico and California everyone gambles more or less. It is one of the few ways of spending money, and I like a game occasionally." The result was that Mr. Tunstall was seldom at home during the summer.

When Hugh came home his aunt said: "I have been talking to your uncle about you, and he does not care about going away this year. He has taken to have an interest in horse-racing. Of course it is a dull life for him here after leading an active one for so many years, and I am very glad he has found something to interest him."

"I should think that it is very dull for you, aunt."

"I am accustomed to be alone, Hugh. In countries where every man has to earn his living, women cannot expect to have their husbands always with them. They may be away a month at a time up in the mountains, or at the mines, or hunting in the plains. I am quite accustomed to that. But I was going to talk about you. I should like a change, and you and I will go away where we like. Not, of course, to travel about as we did last year, but to any seaside place you would like to go to. We need not stop all the time at one, but can go to three or four of them. I have been getting some books about them lately, and I think it would be most pleasant to go down to Devonshire. There seem to be lots of pretty watering-places there, and the climate is warmer than in the towns on the east coast."

"I should like it very much, aunt; but I should like a fortnight here first, if you don't mind. My pony wants exercise terribly, Jim says. He has been out at grass for months now; besides, I shall forget how to ride if I don't have some practice."

So for the next fortnight Hugh was out from morning until night either riding or sailing with Gowan, and then he went south with his aunt and spent the rest of his holidays in Devonshire and Cornwall. He had a delightful time of it, his aunt allowing him to do just as he liked in the way of sailing and going out excursions. She always took rooms overlooking the sea, and was well content to sit all day at the open window; seldom moving until towards evening, when she would go out for a stroll with Hugh. Occasionally she would take long drives with him in a pony-carriage, but she seldom proposed these expeditions. As Hugh several times met with schoolfellows, and always struck up an acquaintance a few hours after arriving at a place with some of the boatmen and fishermen, he never found it dull. At first he was disposed to pity his aunt and to urge her to go out with him; but she assured him that she was quite contented to be alone, and to enjoy the sight of the sea and to breathe the balmy air.

"I have not enjoyed myself so much, Hugh," she said when the holidays were drawing to a close, "since I was a girl."

"I am awfully glad of that, aunt. I have enjoyed myself tremendously; but it always seems to me that it must be dull for you."

"You English never seem to be happy unless you are exerting yourselves, Hugh; but that is not our idea of happiness. People in warm climates find their pleasure in sitting still, in going out after the heat of the day is over for a promenade, and in listening to the music, just as we have been doing here. Besides, it has been a pleasure to me to see that you have been happy."

When the summer holidays had passed away, Hugh returned to Rugby, and Lola went back to Cumberland.

IV. AN EXPLOSION

At Christmas Hugh found that things were not so pleasant at home. There was nothing now to take his uncle away from Byrneside, and the dullness of the place told upon him. His outbursts of ill-temper were therefore more frequent than they had been the last holidays Hugh had spent at home. He sat much longer in the dining-room over his wine, after his wife and Hugh had left him, than he did before, and was sometimes moody, sometimes bad-tempered when he joined them. Hugh's own temper occasionally broke out at this, and there were several quarrels between him and his uncle; but there was a savage fierceness in the latter's manner that cowed the boy, and whatever he felt he learned to hold his tongue; but he came more and more to dislike his uncle, especially as he saw that when angry he would turn upon his aunt and speak violently to her in her own language. Sometimes she would blaze out in return, but generally she continued to smoke her cigarette tranquilly as if utterly unconscious that she was spoken to.

So for the next two years matters went on. During the summer holidays Hugh seldom saw his uncle, who was more and more away from home, being now a constant attendant at all the principal racecourses in the country. Even in winter he was often away in London, to Hugh's great satisfaction, for when he was at home there were frequent quarrels between them, and Hugh could see that his uncle habitually drank a great deal more wine than was good for him. Indeed, it was always in the evening that these scenes occurred. At other times his uncle seemed to make an effort to be pleasant with him.

In summer Hugh went away with his aunt for a time, but he

spent a part of his holidays at Byrneside, for of all exercises he best loved riding. His pony had been given up, but there were plenty of horses in the stables, for although William Tunstall did not care for hunting, he rode a good deal, and was an excellent horseman.

"What have you got in the stable, James?" Hugh asked one day on his return from the school.

"I have got a set of the worst-tempered devils in the country, Master Hugh. Except them two ponies that I drives your aunt out with, there isn't a horse in the stables fit for a Christian to ride. They are all good horses, first-rate horses, putting aside their tempers; but your uncle seems to delight in buying creatures that no one else will ride. Of course he gets them cheap. He doesn't care how wicked they are, and he seems to enjoy it when they begin their pranks with him. I thought at first he would get his brains dashed out to a certainty, but I never saw a man keep his seat as he does. He told me once, that when a man had been breaking bronchos—that is what he called them, which means, he said, wild horses that had never been backed— he could sit anything, and that English horses were like sheep in comparison.

"Of course, it is no use saying no to you, Master Hugh; but if you want to go out you must stick to that big meadow. You must mount there, and you must promise me not to go beyond it. I have been letting the hedges grow there on purpose for the last two years, and no horse will try to take them. The ground is pretty soft and you will fall light. You have been getting on with your riding the last three years, and have had some pretty rough mounts, but none as bad as what we have got in the stables now. I shall always go out with you myself with one of the men in case of accident, and I can put you up to some of their tricks before you mount."

Hugh was more than fifteen now, and was very tall and strong for his age. He had ridden a great deal when he had been at home during the summer, and in winter when the weather was open, and had learned to sit on nasty-tempered animals, for these had gradually taken the place of his father's steady hunters; but this year he found that the coachman's opinion of those now under his charge was by no means exaggerated. In spite of doing his best to keep his seat, he had many heavy falls, being once or twice stunned; but he stuck to it, and by the end of the holidays flattered himself that he could ride the worst-tempered animal in the stable. He did not go away this year, begging his aunt to remain at home.

"It is a splendid chance of learning to ride well, aunt," he said. "If I stick at it right through these two months every day I shall really have got a good seat, and you know it is a lot better my getting chucked off now than if I was older. You see boys' bones ain't set, and they hardly ever break them, and if they do they mend up in no time."

His aunt had at first very strongly opposed his riding any of the animals in the stable, and he had been obliged to bring in James to assure her that some of them were not much worse than those he had ridden before, and that a fall on the soft ground of the meadow was not likely to be very serious, but it was only on his giving her his solemn promise that he would not on any account go beyond the meadow that she finally consented. On his return at Christmas he found his uncle at home, and apparently in an unusually pleasant humour. A frost had set in that seemed likely to be a long one, and the ground was as hard as iron.

"I hear, Hugh," his uncle said the second morning at breakfast, "that you are becoming a first-rate rider. I am glad to hear it. Out in the Western States every man is a good rider. You may say that he lives on horseback, and it comes natural even to boys to be able to sit barebacked on the first horse that comes to hand. Of course it is not so important here, still a man who is a really good rider has many advantages. In the first place, all gentlemen here hunt, and a man who can go across any country, and can keep his place in the front rank, has much honour among his neighbours; in the second place, he is enabled to get his horses cheap. A horse that will fetch two hundred if he is free from vice can be often picked up for twenty if he gets the reputation of being bad-tempered. There is another accomplishment we all have in the

West, and that is to be good pistol-shots. As we cannot ride, and there is nothing else to do, I will teach you, if you like."

Hugh accepted the offer with lively satisfaction, heedless of an exclamation of dissent from his aunt. When he had left the room William Tunstall turned savagely upon his wife.

"What did you want to interfere for? Just attend to your own business or it will be the worse for you."

"It is my own business," she said fearlessly. "I like that boy, and I am not going to see him hurt. Ever since you told me, soon after we first came here, that by his father's will the whole property came to you if Hugh died before he came of age, I have been anxious for him. I don't want to interfere with your way of going on. Lead your own life, squander your share of the property if you like, it is nothing to me; when it is spent I am ready to go back to your old life, but I won't have the boy hurt. I have always accepted your story as to how you became possessed of the papers without question. I know that you have killed a score of men in what you call fair fight, but I did not know that you were a murderer in cold blood. Anyhow, the boy shan't be hurt. I believe you bought those horses knowing that he would try them, and believing they would break his neck. They haven't, but no thanks to you. Now you have offered to teach him pistol-shooting. It is so easy for an accident to take place, isn't it? But I warn you that if anything happens to him, I will go straight to the nearest magistrate and tell him who you really are, and that I am certain there was no accident, but a murder."

The man was white with fury, and advanced a step towards her.

"Have you gone mad?" he asked between his teeth. "By heavens!—"

"No, you won't," she interrupted. "Don't make the threat, because I might not forgive you if you did. Do you think I am afraid of you? You are not in California or Mexico now. People cannot be shot here without inquiry. I know what you are thinking of; an accident might happen to me too. I know that any love you ever had for me has died out long ago, but I hold to my life. I have placed in safe hands—never mind where I have placed it—a paper telling all the truth. It is to be opened if I die suddenly and without sending for it. In it I say that if my death is said to have been caused by an accident, it would be no accident, but murder; and that if I die suddenly, without visible cause, that I shall have been poisoned. Do you think I don't know you, and that knowing you I would trust my life altogether in your hands? There, that is enough, we need not threaten each other. I know you, and now you know me. We will both go our own way."

And she walked out of the room leaving her husband speechless with fury at this open and unexpected revolt. Half an hour later his dog-cart was at the door and he left for London. Hugh was astonished when, on his return from a walk down to Gowan's cottage, he found that his uncle had gone up to town.

"Why, I thought, aunt, he was going to be at home all the holidays, and he said that he was going to teach me pistol-shooting."

"Your uncle often changes his mind suddenly. I will teach you pistol-shooting, Hugh. Most Mexican women can use a pistol in case of need. I cannot shoot as he does, but I can teach you to shoot fairly, and after that it is merely a matter of incessant practice. If you ever travel I dare say you will find it very useful to be able to use a pistol cleverly. There are two or three revolvers upstairs and plenty of ammunition, so if you like we will practise in the conservatory; it is too cold to go out. You had better go and ask James to give you some thick planks, five or six of them, to set up as targets. If he has got such a thing as an iron plate it will be better still. I don't want to spoil my picture. The place is forty feet long, which will be a long enough range to begin with."

Half an hour later the sharp cracks of a revolver rang out in the conservatory, and from that time to the end of the holidays Hugh practised for two or three hours a day, the carrier bringing over fresh supplies of ammunition twice a week. He found at first that the sharp recoil of the revolver rendered it very difficult for him to shoot straight, but in time he became accustomed to this, and at the end of a fortnight could put every shot in or close to the spot he had marked as a bull's-eye. After the first day his aunt laid aside her pistol, and betook herself to her favourite hammock, where, sometimes touching her guitar, sometimes glancing at a book, she watched his progress.

At the end of the fortnight she said: "You begin to shoot fairly straight. Keep on, Hugh, and with constant practice you will be able to hit a half-crown every time. In the West it is a common thing for a man to hold a copper coin between his finger and thumb for another to shoot at. I have seen it done scores of times, but it will take you some time to get to that. You must remember that there is very seldom time to take a steady deliberate aim as you do. When a man shoots he has got to shoot quickly. Now, practise standing with your face the other way, and then turn and fire the instant your eye catches the mark. After that you must practise firing from your hip. Sometimes there is no time to raise the arm. Out in the West a man has got to do one of two things, either not to carry a revolver at all, or else he must be able to shoot as quickly as a flash of lightning."

"I don't suppose I am ever going to the West, aunt; still I should like to be able to shoot like that, for if one does a thing at all one likes to do it well."

And so to the end of the holidays the revolver practice went on steadily every morning, Hugh generally firing seventy or eighty cartridges. He could not do this at first, for the wrench of the recoil strained his wrist, but this gained strength as he went on. Before he went back to school he himself thought that he was becoming a very fair shot, although his aunt assured him that he had hardly begun to shoot according to western notions.

Mrs. Tunstall had one day, a year before this, driven over to Carlisle, and, somewhat to the surprise of Mr. Randolph, had called upon him at his office.

"Mr. Randolph," she began, "I do not know anything about English law. I want to ask you a question."

"Certainly, my dear madam."

"If a married woman was to leave a sealed letter in the hands of a lawyer, could he retain possession of it for her, even if her husband called upon him to give it up?"

"It is a nice question, Mrs. Tunstall. If the lawyer was acting

Hugh practises shooting with his revolver.
See page 58.

as the fiduciary agent of a lady he would at any rate see that her wishes were complied with; whether he could absolutely hold the paper against the husband's claim is a point upon which I am not prepared at present to give an answer. But anyhow there are ways of evading the law; for instance, he could pass it on to a third party, and then, unless the husband had been absolutely informed by his wife that she had handed over this document to him, the husband would be powerless, the lawyer would simply declare that he had no such document. Are you asking for your own sake, Mrs. Tunstall, or in the interest of a friend?"

"In my own interest, Mr. Randolph. I have a written paper here. I have not signed it yet, because I believe it is necessary to sign papers in the presence of witnesses."

"It depends upon the nature of the paper, Mrs. Tunstall; but in all cases it is a prudent step, for then no question as to the authenticity can arise."

"And is it not necessary for the witnesses of the signature to read the contents of the document?"

"By no means; they simply witness the signature."

"Well, Mr. Randolph, this is the document I want to leave in safe hands, so that it can be opened after my death, unless I previously request, not by letter, but by word of mouth, that it should be returned to me. I know of no one else to whom I could commit the paper, which is, in my opinion, a very important one; the only question is whether, as you are Mr. Tunstall's solicitor, you would like to take it."

"Frankly, without knowing the nature of the contents, Mrs. Tunstall, I should certainly prefer not to undertake such a charge. Should it remain in my hands, or rather in the hands of our firm—for we may sincerely trust that there would be no occasion for opening it until very many years after my death—it might be found to contain instructions which could hardly be carried out by a firm situated as we are with regard to Mr. Tunstall."

"I see that, Mr. Randolph."

There was a pause, and then the lawyer said: "Will you be going up to town shortly, Mrs. Tunstall?"

"Yes, in the course of a month or so I shall be passing through London with Hugh."

"Will the matter keep until then?"

"Certainly, there is no great hurry about it: but I wish the packet placed in safe hands, where it would be opened in the event of my death, unless I recall it before that."

"In that case, Mrs. Tunstall, I will give you the address of the firm who do my London business. They are an old-established firm of the highest respectability, and the document will be perfectly safe in their hands until you demand it back, or until they hear of your demise. I will give you a letter of introduction to them."

Accordingly when Mrs. Tunstall went up to town the next time with Hugh she called upon the firm of solicitors, whose place of business was in Essex Street, and upon reading Mr. Randolph's letter, which stated that she was the wife of one of his clients, a gentleman of means, she was courteously received, and they at once agreed to take charge of any document she might place in their hands, upon the understanding that if she did not write or call for it, it should be opened when they heard of her death, and its contents, whatever they might be, acted upon.

"You will stand in the position of our client, Mrs. Tunstall, and we will do all in our power to carry out your wishes as expressed in this document, whatever it may be. It is no unusual matter for a will to be left with us under precisely similar circumstances."

"If the packet should be opened under the conditions I name," Mrs. Tunstall said, "you will probably not regret having undertaken its charge, for I can assure you that it may put a considerable amount of business in your hands. But how will you know of my death?"

"Mr. Randolph or his successor would inform us. Of course we shall request him to do so."

"And as soon as he knows of the event," Mrs. Tunstall added, "it is of the utmost importance that the paper should be opened as soon as possible after my death."

"We will request Mr. Randolph to inform us by telegraph

immediately he receives the news. But, pardon me, you look well and healthy, and are young to be making such careful provisions for an event that may be far distant."

"That may or may not be far distant," she said, "but for certain important reasons I wish to be prepared for it at all points. I will now sign it in your presence, Mr. Curtice. I have not yet put my signature to it."

"Very well, Mrs. Tunstall. Two of my clerks shall witness your signature. It may be many years before any question as to the authenticity of the signature may arise; so I shall be a witness also."

The document was a lengthy one, written on sixteen pages of foolscap. Two of the clerks were called in.

"Now if you will turn that last page down, Mrs. Tunstall, so that its contents cannot be seen, you can sign your name and we will witness it." This was done. "Now, Mrs. Tunstall, if you will put a sheet of brown paper over the other sheets, and place your initials on the margin at the bottom, we will put ours, so that no question can arise as to the whole of them forming part of the document signed by you. Now, madam, if you will fold it up and place it in this envelope I will attach my seal. I presume you do not carry a seal?"

"No, sir."

"I think it would be more satisfactory that you should affix a seal of some sort, no matter how common a thing it may be. Mr. Carter, will you go up into the Strand with this lady, and take her to some shop where she can purchase a seal? It does not matter what it is, Mrs. Tunstall; any common thing, with a bird or a motto or anything else upon it. These things are not cut in duplicate, therefore if you seal the envelope in two or three places with it and take the seal away with you, it will be a guarantee to you, should you ever require it to be returned, that it has not been opened. In the meantime I will get a small strong-box similar to those you see round the room, and have your name painted on it. When it is completed I shall put the envelope in it, lock it up, and place it in our strong-room downstairs."

The seal was purchased and fixed, and Mrs. Tunstall took her departure, satisfied that she had left the document in safe hands. Mr. Curtice talked the matter over with his partner. The latter laughed.

"Women love a little mystery, Curtice. I suppose she has got a little property in her own right, and does not mean to leave it to her husband, and is afraid he may get hold of her will and find out how she has left it."

"I don't think it is that," Mr. Curtice said, "although, of course, it may be. I should say she was a foreigner—a Spaniard or Italian; she spoke with a slight accent. Besides, the thing extends over sixteen pages of foolscap."

"That is likely enough if she made the will herself, Curtice. She may have gone into a whole history as to why she has not left her money to her husband."

"Possibly, but I don't think so. You mark my words, Harris, if that packet ever comes to be opened there will be some rum disclosures in it. That woman was no fool, and there is no doubt about her being thoroughly in earnest. She said it was likely to give us some work when it was opened, and I believe her. I will write a letter to Randolph and ask him to give us a few particulars about this client he has introduced to us."

When he received Mr. Randolph's reply, stating briefly the history of Mr. William Tunstall, the husband of the lady he had introduced to them, Mr. Curtice was more convinced than before that the delivery of this packet into his charge was not a mere freak, and offered to bet his partner a new hat that the document was not merely a will, but that it would turn out something altogether unusual.

Mr. Randolph congratulated himself on his forethought, when, a year after Mrs. Tunstall's visit, Mr. Tunstall came into the office.

"I am just on my way up to town," he said. "I wish you would let me have a couple of hundred in advance on the next rents."

"Certainly, Mr. Tunstall. You have already had £200 on them, you know."

"Yes, I know; but I have been a little unlucky lately, and have got an account I want to settle. By the way," he said carelessly, as he placed the bank-notes in his pocket-book, "Mrs. Tunstall asked me to get from you the letter or packet she left in your charge."

"A letter, Mr. Tunstall? I think there must be some mistake. Mrs. Tunstall has certainly left nothing whatever in my charge."

"Oh! I suppose I misunderstood her. I only made up my mind to start a short time before I came off, and did not pay much attention to what she was saying; but it was something about a letter, and she mentioned your name; there were half a dozen commissions she wanted me to execute for her in London, and I suppose they all got mixed up together. I dare say it is of no consequence one way or the other. Well, thanks for the money—now I am off."

"I am very much afraid that William Tunstall is a liar," Mr. Randolph said to himself thoughtfully after his client had left. "He has found out that his wife has entrusted some document or other to someone, and he guessed naturally enough that she had most likely come to me with it, and he played a bold stroke to get it. I do not like the way he has fallen into of spending all his time going about the country to racecourses. I don't believe he has been at home two months this year. Besides, he sounded me last time he was here about raising a few thousands on a mortgage. He is not turning out well. I thought when he first came back that his wanderings had done him no harm. No doubt I had been prepossessed in his favour by his refusal to accept Edgar's offers to divide the rents with him, but I was too hasty. I am afraid there will be trouble at Byrneside. It is very fortunate Edgar put my name in as trustee for his son, so that his share of the property is safe whatever happens to the other; but I hate to see a man of a good old family like the Tunstalls going wrong. I wonder what this mysterious document his wife wanted to leave with me is? It must be something of great importance, or he would never have come to me and lied in order to get it into his hands. It is a queer business."

Hugh did not see his uncle when he was at home for the summer holidays. His aunt seemed to take his absence as a matter of course.

"Don't you expect uncle home soon?" he asked her one day.

"I never expect him," she said quietly.

"I think it a shame he stays away so, leaving you all by yourself, aunt!" Hugh said indignantly.

"I am accustomed to it by this time, Hugh; and, upon the whole, I think perhaps he is better away than here while you are at home. You see you do not get on very well together."

"Well, aunt, I am sure I don't want any rows."

"I don't say you do, Hugh; but still there are rows. You see he is passionate, and you are passionate, and it is very much better you should be apart. As for me, I have always been accustomed to his being away from me a good deal ever since we married, and it does not trouble me at all. I would much rather have you all to myself. Your being here makes it a very pleasant time for me: we ride together, drive together, and practise shooting together. It is all a change to me, for except when you are here I seldom stir beyond the gardens."

Hugh had indeed no doubt that his aunt was more comfortable when his uncle was away, for he heard from Wilson that when Mr. Tunstall was at home there were constant quarrels between him and his wife.

"He ain't like your father, Mr. Hugh. Ah! he was a gentleman of the right sort! Not that your uncle is a bad master. He is hasty if everything is not quite right, but in general he is pleasant spoken and easy to get on with. He is popular with the gentry, though of late they have held off a bit. I hear it said they don't hold to a gentleman spending all his life on the racecourses and leaving his wife by herself. Your aunt is well liked, and would be better liked if she would only go abroad and visit; but she never drives out unless when you are here, and people have given up calling. It is a bad job; but I hope when you come of age, Mr. Hugh, we shall have the old times back again, when the Tunstalls were one of the first families in the county, and took the lead of pretty nigh everything."

"Well, they have five years to wait for that, Wilson. I am just

sixteen now, and I mean when I do come of age and I am my
own master to travel about for a bit before I settle down into a
country squire."

"Well, I suppose that is natural enough, Mr. Hugh, though
why people want to be running off to foreign parts is more than
I can make out. Anyhow, sir, I hope you won't be bringing a foreign wife back with you."

"There is no fear of that"—Hugh laughed—"at least according
to my present ideas. But I suppose that is a thing no one can settle about until their time comes. At any rate aunt is a foreigner,
and I am sure no one could be kinder or nicer than she is."

"That she is, Mr. Hugh. I am sure everyone says that. Still,
you see, there is drawbacks. Her ways are different from the
ways of the ladies about here, and that keeps her apart from
them. She don't drive about, and call, and make herself sociable
like, nor see to the charities down in the village. It ain't as she
doesn't give money, because I know that whenever the rector
says there is a case wants help she is ready enough with her
purse; but she don't go among them or know anything about
them herself. No, Mr. Hugh; your aunt is a wonderful nice lady,
but you take my advice and bring home an English wife as mistress of the Hall."

When he came home for the Christmas holidays Hugh found
his uncle again at home. For a time matters went on smoothly.
Mr. Tunstall made an evident endeavour to be friendly with
him, talked to him about his life at school, asked whether he
wished to go to the university when he left; and when Hugh said
that he didn't see any use in spending three years of his life
there when he did not intend entering any of the professions,
and that he would much rather travel and see something of foreign countries, he warmly encouraged the idea.

"Quite right, Hugh! There is nothing opens a man's mind like
foreign travel. But don't stick in the great towns. Of course you
will want a year to do Europe; after that strike out a line of your
own. If I had my time over again I would go to Central Asia or
Africa, or some place where there was credit to be gained and
some spice of adventure and danger."

"That is just what I should like, uncle," Hugh said eagerly; and looking at his aunt for confirmation, he was surprised to see her watching her husband intently beneath her half-closed eyelids. "Don't you think so, aunt?"

"I don't know, Hugh," she said quietly. "There is a good deal to be said both ways. But I don't think we need settle it now: you have another year and a half at school yet, you know."

Hugh went out skating that afternoon, for it was a sharp frost. As he was passing through the hall on his return he heard his uncle's voice raised in anger in the drawing-room. He paused for a moment. He could not catch the words, for they were spoken in Mexican. There was silence for a moment, and he imagined that his aunt was answering. Then he heard a loud exclamation in Mexican, then a slight cry and a heavy fall. He rushed into the room. His aunt lay upon the hearthrug, his uncle was standing over her with clenched hand.

"You coward, you brutal coward!" Hugh exclaimed, rushing forward, and, throwing himself upon his uncle, he tried to force him back from the hearthrug. For a moment the fury of his assault forced his uncle back, but the latter's greatly superior strength then enabled him to shake off his grasp, and the moment he was free he struck the lad a savage blow across the face, that sent him reeling backwards. Mad with passion, Hugh rushed to the fender, and seizing a poker, sprang at his uncle. William Tunstall's hand went behind him, and as Hugh struck, he levelled a pistol. But he was too late. The blow came down heavily, and the pistol exploded in the air; as the man fell back his head came with terrible force against the edge of a cabinet, and he lay immovable. Hugh's passion was stilled in an instant. He dropped the poker, and leaned over his uncle. The blood was flowing down his forehead from the blow he had given him, but it was the injury to the back of the head that most alarmed the lad. He lifted an arm, and it fell heavily again. He knelt down and listened, but could hear no sound of breathing. He rose to his feet, and looked down, white and trembling, at the body.

"I have killed him," he said. "Well, he brought it on himself, and I didn't mean it. It was the cabinet that did it. Perhaps he is only stunned. If he is, he will charge me with trying to murder him. Well, it is no use my staying here; they will be here in a moment," and he glanced at the door. But the servants at Byrneside were so accustomed to the sound of pistol shots that they paid no attention to it. Hugh picked up the weapon that had dropped from his uncle's hand and put it in his pocket; then glanced at his aunt and hesitated. "She will come round in time," he muttered, "and I can do nothing for her." Then he walked out of the room, turned the key in the door, and took it with him. He went out to the stable, and ordered his horse to be saddled, keeping in the stable while it was being done, so that his white face should not attract notice. As soon as the horse was brought out he leapt into the saddle and galloped off.

V. ACROSS THE SEA

M r. Randolph was at dinner when the servant came in and said that young Mr. Tunstall wished to speak to him; he was in the library, and begged the lawyer to give him two minutes' conversation. Hugh was walking up and down the little room when he entered. The old lawyer saw at once that something was wrong.

"What is it, Hugh, what is the matter, lad?"

"A good deal is the matter, Mr. Randolph; but I don't want you to ask me. I am sure you will be glad afterwards that you don't know. You were a friend of my father's, sir. You have been always very kind to me. Will you give me fifty pounds without asking why I want it?"

"Certainly I will, lad; but in heaven's name don't do anything rash."

"Anything that was to be done is done, Mr. Randolph; please let me have the money at once. You don't know how important it is. You will know soon enough."

Mr. Randolph unlocked his desk without a word, and handed him ten five-pound notes. Then he said: "By the way, I have gold, if you would rather have it. There were some rents paid in this afternoon."

"I would much rather have gold."

Mr. Randolph put the notes in the desk, and then unlocked the safe. "Would you rather have a hundred?"

"Yes, sir, if you will let me have them."

The lawyer handed him a small canvas bag.

"God bless you, sir!" the lad said; "remember, please, whatever you hear, it was done in self-defence."

Then without another word he opened the door and was gone.

"Why, what is the matter, my dear?" Mrs. Randolph exclaimed, as her husband returned to the dining-room. "Why, you are as pale as death."

"I don't know what is the matter exactly," he said. "Hugh has borrowed a hundred pounds of me, and has gone."

"Gone! Where has he gone to?"

"I don't know, my dear. I hope, I sincerely hope he is going out of the country, and can get away before they lay hands on him."

"Why, what has happened?"

"I don't know what has happened. I know things haven't been going on well for some time at Byrneside. I am afraid there has been a terrible quarrel. He begged me to ask him no questions, and I was glad not to do so. The less one knows, the better; but I am afraid there has been a scuffle. All he said was, just as he went out: 'Whatever you hear, remember I did it in self-defence.'"

"But, goodness gracious, Thomas, you don't mean to say that he has killed his uncle?"

"I don't mean anything," the lawyer said. "Those were his words. I am afraid it won't be long before we hear what he meant. If they come to ask me questions, fortunately I know nothing. I shall say no word except before a magistrate, and then my story is simple enough. He came and asked me to let him have £100, and as I was his trustee, and have the rents of his estate for the past five years in my hands, I let him have it as a matter of course. I did not ask him why he wanted it. I saw that he was agitated, and from his manner, and from my knowledge that he and his uncle did not get on very well together, I judged there had been a quarrel, and that he intended to leave home for a while. It was only when he was leaving the room that I gathered there had been any personal fracas, and then from his words, 'It was done in self-defence,' I judged that his uncle had struck him, and that he had probably struck him in return. I hope that is all, my dear. I pray heaven that it may be all."

Hugh had dismounted just outside the town, opened a gate leading into a field, taken off his horse's bridle, and turned the

horse in and closed the gate behind it. Then he had turned up
the collar of his coat, pulled his hat down over his eyes, and made
his way to the lawyer's. He had cooled down now, but still felt no
regret for what had passed. "He would have killed me," he said
to himself, "and I had no thought of killing him when I knocked
him down; anyhow, he brought it on himself. If he is dead, and I
am pretty sure he is, I have no one to prove that it was done in
self-defence; but if he is not dead, he will give his own version of
it when he recovers. I know he is a liar, and in his quiet manner
he would be able to make everyone believe that I had attacked
him without the least provocation. He might even say that I fired
the pistol, that he knocked it out of my hand, and that then I
sprang on him and struck him down with his head against that
cabinet. Either way I shall get years of imprisonment if I am
caught; but I don't mean to be caught if I can help it."

On leaving Mr. Randolph's he proceeded to the railway station, consulted the time-tables, and then took a third-class ticket
to Glasgow. He bought a Bradshaw, and sitting down on a bench
under a light, turned to the advertisements of the sailing of
steamers. By the time he had done that the train came in. It was
a slow one, stopping at every station. He got out at the first station and paid the fare from Carlisle, then walked back to the
town, and took a second-class ticket by the night mail for
London. Arriving at Euston, he walked across to the docks,
whence he had found that a steamer started for Hamburg at
eight o'clock, and he would catch a trans-Atlantic steamer that
started the next day. On his arrival at Hamburg he went to the
steamboat office and took a second-class ticket to New York.
Having done this, he bought at a shop near the wharves a supply of clothes for the voyage, placed them in a cheap German
trunk, and walked on board the steamer.

He was now, he thought, fairly safe from pursuit. The hour at
which he would arrive at the station at Carlisle would be known,
and as the northern train was nearly due, and someone answering to his description had taken a ticket to Glasgow, it would be
at once suspected that he intended to sail by a steamer from that
port. No pursuit could be set on foot before the morning.

Indeed, it was probable that before the police took the matter fairly in hand it would be late in the afternoon. It might then be another day before they picked up the clue that he had gone to Glasgow, and followed him there.

If a steamer had happened to start that morning or the day before, it would be supposed that he had gone by it, and they might telegraph across, and search the ship for him when it arrived at New York. If no steamer had started, and they could obtain no clue to him in Glasgow, they would think that he had gone back to Liverpool, and would make search there, watching all the steamers sailing. They would in any case hardly suspect that he could have gone up to London, across to Hamburg, and caught the steamer sailing from there. Indeed, it would not have been possible for him to do so had he first gone up to Glasgow as they would believe he had done.

As soon as the vessel was fairly under way Hugh looked round. On deck there was no distinction made between second-class emigrants and steerage, but it was easy to distinguish the two classes. The second-class kept somewhat together near the companion leading to their portion of the ship, while the steerage passengers were well forward. The number of the latter was not very large, for the emigrant traffic across the Atlantic was still carried principally in sailing ships. The second-class were composed chiefly of substantial-looking Germans, for the most part farmers going out with a small amount of capital to settle in the West.

There were two or three other young Englishmen, and with one of these, named Luscombe, Hugh struck up an acquaintance before he had been many hours on board. He was a young man of about twenty, and Hugh soon learned from him that he was the son of a large landed proprietor in Norfolk. He had for a few months been in a crack regiment of Hussars, but had gone, as he expressed it, a fearful mucker. His father had paid the greater portion of his debts, but had refused to settle some that he considered debts of honour. Luscombe, therefore, sold out, and was now, as he expressed it, going over to knock about for a bit in the States, till his father took a "sensible view of things." "It was rough on him," he said, "for I had run him up a pretty heavy bill twice before. However, I think it is all for the best. I should never have got out of that line if I had stopped in the regiment. Two or three years' knocking about, and hard work, won't do me any harm; and by that time the governor will be prepared to receive the prodigal son with open arms."

Hugh was slower in giving his confidence. But before the voyage was over he had told Luscombe why he had left England.

"Well, you did quite right, of course," Luscombe said, "in knocking that brute of a fellow down, and if you did split his skull and make your aunt a widow you have nothing to reproach yourself with. Still, I agree with you that it will be more pleasant for you if he gets round, as I dare say he will, or else it will be a long while before you can show up at home. Well, you will know by the time we have been in New York a few days. If the papers the next mail brings out don't say anything about it you may be sure he has got over it. 'A gentleman killed by his nephew' would be a startling heading, and if it is not there, you may go about your work with a light heart."

The voyage was marked by no incident whatever. On arriving at New York Luscombe and Hugh put up at a good hotel for a few days before making a start west. They had agreed to keep together, at any rate for a time. Luscombe was several years older than Hugh, but he saw that the lad had plenty of good sense and a fund of resolution, and knew that he himself was more likely to stick to work in such companionship than he should be by himself. Luscombe's light-hearted carelessness amused Hugh, and though he did not think that his companion was likely to stick very long to anything he took up, he was very glad to have his companionship for a time. Hugh was thankful indeed when the next mail brought a batch of papers of a date a week later than that of his leaving Cumberland, and when a careful examination of the file disclosed no allusion whatever to the event at Byrneside.

"Well, I congratulate you, Hugh," Luscombe said when he told him. "I expected it would be all right. If he had been a good old man you would have killed him, no doubt, but bad old men have always wonderfully thick skulls. Well, now you are ready, I suppose, to make our start to-morrow."

"Quite ready, Luscombe. We are only throwing away our money here."

They had already made many inquiries, and had settled that they would in the first place go down to Texas, and would there take the first job of any kind that offered itself, keeping it until they had time to look round and see what would suit them best. Luscombe, however, said frankly that he thought it probable that sooner or later he should enlist in the cavalry out west.

"I know I shall never stick to hard work very long, Hugh. I have not got my fortune to make, and I only want to pass away the time for a year or two until the old lady and the girls get the governor into a charitable state of mind again. He is a first-rate fellow, and I am not surprised that he cut up rough at last. I expect a few months will bring him round, but I should not know what to do if I went back. I will give myself three years anyhow."

"I am very much in the same position, Luscombe. I shan't go back until I come of age. Then I can snap my fingers at my uncle. I have got a very good trustee, who will look after the estate. I will write to him to-night and let him know that I am all right and very glad to find that uncle has not been killed, and that he may expect me when I come of age, but not before."

On the following morning they took their places in the train, and travelled west, and proceeded to what was then the nearest terminus to their destination—Northern Texas. Travelling sometimes by stage-wagons, sometimes on foot, they arrived at M'Kinney, which they had been told was a young place, but growing fast.

"Well, here we are at last," Luscombe said as they alighted at a one-storied building, on which was a board roughly painted, "The Empire Hotel." "At any rate the scenery is better than it has been for the last two or three hundred miles. There are some good-sized hills. Some of those across the country ahead might almost claim to be mountains, and that is a relief to the eyes after those dreary flats. Well, let us go in and have a meal first, then we will look round. The place has certainly not an imposing aspect."

The meals here, as at the other places where they had stopped, consisted of fried steak, which, although tough, was eatable, and abundance of potatoes and cabbages, followed by stewed fruit. They had arrived just at the dinner hour, and seven or eight men in their shirt sleeves came in and sat down with them. The tea was somewhat better than they had hitherto obtained, and there was, in addition, the luxury of milk. Scarcely a word was spoken during the meal. It was evidently considered a serious business, and the chief duty of each man was to eat as much as possible in the shortest possible time. After the meal was over, and the other diners had gone out, the landlord, who had taken his seat at the top of the table, opened the conversation.

"Are you thinking of making a stay here, gentlemen?"

"Yes, if we can get any work to suit us," Luscombe said.

"It is a rising place," the landlord said as he lit his pipe. "There are two stores and eight houses being built now. This town has a great future before it." Luscombe and Hugh had some difficulty in preserving their gravity.

"It is the chief town of the county," the landlord went on. "They are going to set about the courthouse in a month or two. Our sheriff is a pretty spry man, and doesn't stand nonsense. We have an orderly population, sir. We had only two men shot here last week."

"That is satisfactory," Luscombe said dryly. "We are peaceable characters ourselves. And is two about your average?"

"Well, I can't say that," the landlord said; "that would be too much to expect. The week before last Buck Harris with three of his gang came in and set up the town."

"What do you mean by set up?" Luscombe asked. The landlord looked surprised at the question.

"Oh, to set up a town is to ride into it, and to clear out the saloons, and to shoot at anyone seen outside their doors, and to ride about and fire through the windows. They had done it three or four times before, and as four or five men had been killed the citizens became annoyed."

"I am not surprised at that," Hugh put in.

"The sheriff got a few men together, and the citizens began to shoot out of their windows. Buck Harris and two of his gang were killed and four of the citizens. Since then we have had quiet. And what sort of work do you want, gentlemen? Perhaps I could put you in the way of getting it."

"Well, we wanted to get work among horses," Luscombe said.

The landlord shook his head. "You want to go farther south among the big ranches for that. This is not much of a horse country. If you had been carpenters, now, there would have been no difficulty. A good workman can get his four dollars a day. Then there is James Pawson's woodyard. I reckon you might get a job there. One of his hands got shot in that affair with Buck Harris, and another broke his leg last week. I should say there was room for you there. Madden, that's the man who was shot, used to board here."

"What is your charge for boarding, landlord?"

"Seventy-five cents a day for three square meals; a dollar a day if you lodge as well. But I could not lodge you at present. I must keep a couple of rooms for travellers, and the others are full. But you will have no difficulty in getting lodgings in the town. You can get a room for about a dollar a week."

"Well, let us try the woodyard, Luscombe."

"All right!" Luscombe said. "There is a certain sense of novelty about a woodyard. Well, landlord, if we agree with this Mr. Pawson, we will arrange to board with you, at any rate for the present."

They went down the straggling street until they came to a lot on which was piled a quantity of sawn timber of various dimensions. The name Pawson was painted in large letters on the fence. A man and a boy were moving planks.

"Here goes!" Luscombe said, and entered the gate.

"Want a job?" the man asked, looking up as they approached him.

"Yes. We are on the lookout for a job, and heard there might be a chance here."

"I am James Pawson," the man said, "and I want hands. What wages do you want?"

"As much as we can get," Luscombe replied.

Pawson looked them up and down. "Not much accustomed to hard work, I reckon?"

"Not much," Luscombe said. "But we are both pretty strong, and ready to do our best."

"Well, I tell you what," the man said. "I will give you a dollar and a half a day for a week, and at the end of that time, if you get through your work well, I will raise it to two dollars."

Luscombe looked at Hugh, who nodded. "All right!" he said; "we will try."

Pawson gave a sigh of relief, for hands were scarce. "Take off your coats, then," he said, "and set to work right here. There is a lot to be done."

Luscombe and Hugh took off their coats, and were soon hard at work moving and piling planks. Before they had been half an hour at it there was a shout, and a wagon heavily laden with planks entered the yard. James Pawson himself jumped up on to the wagon, and assisted the teamster to throw down the planks, while the other two carried them away and stacked them. Both of them had rolled up their sleeves to have a freer use of their arms. The sun blazed hotly down, and they were soon bathed in perspiration. They stuck to their work until six o'clock, and by that time their backs were so stiff with stooping that they could scarcely stand upright, and their hands were blistered with the rough wood. Pawson was well satisfied with their work.

"Well," he said, "you move about pretty spry, you two do, and handle the wood quicker'n most. I see you will suit me if I shall suit you; so I will make it two dollars a day at once. I ain't a man that stints half a dollar when I see hands work willing."

"Well, that is not a bad beginning, Luscombe," Hugh said as they went to put on their coats.

"We have earned a dollar, Hugh," Luscombe said, "and we have broken our backs and blistered hands, to say nothing of losing three or four pounds of solid flesh."

"We did wrong to turn up our sleeves," Hugh said. "I had no idea that the sun was so strong. Why, my arms are a mass of blisters."

"So are mine," Luscombe said ruefully, "and they are beginning to smart furiously. They will be in a nice state to-morrow."

"Let us stay at the hotel to-night, Hugh. I feel so tired that I am sure I could never set out to look for lodgings after supper."

The next morning their arms were literally raw. Before starting to work they got some oil from the landlord and rubbed them. "It will be some time before I turn up my sleeves to work again," Luscombe said. "I have had my arms pretty bad sometimes after the first long day's row in summer, but I have never had them like this."

They worked until dinner-time, and then Luscombe went up to Pawson and pulled up his sleeve. "I think," he said, "you must let us both knock off for the day. We are really not fit to work. We daren't turn up our sleeves, and yet the flannel rubbing on them makes them smart so that we can hardly work. Besides, as you said yesterday, we are not accustomed to work. We are so stiff that we are not doing justice either to ourselves or you. If you have any particular job you want done, of course we will come after dinner and do it, but if not we would rather be off altogether."

"Your arms are bad," Pawson said. "I thought yesterday when you were working that, being newcomers, you would feel it a bit. Certainly you can knock off. You ain't fit for it as you are. Take it easy, boys, for a few days till you get accustomed to it. We ain't slave-drivers out here, and I don't expect nothing beyond what is reasonable. I should get my arms well rubbed with oil at once; then to-night wash the oil off and give them a chance to harden, and in the morning powder them well with flour."

As soon as they had had their dinner they went out and found a room with two beds in it, and moved their small kits across there. Then they took a stroll round the town, of which they had seen little, and then lay down in the shade of a thick cactus hedge and dozed all the afternoon. The next morning they felt all the better for their rest. The inflammation of their arms had greatly abated, and they were able to work briskly.

"What do you want with that revolver of an evening, Hugh, when you do not wear it during the day?" Luscombe asked as he saw Hugh put his revolver in his pocket when they went to their lodgings for a wash, after work was over for the day.

"I take off my coat during the day, Luscombe, and whatever may be the custom here I think it ridiculous to see a man at work in a woodyard with a revolver stuck into his pocket at the back of his trousers. At night it is different; the pistol is not noticed under the coat, and I don't suppose there is a man here without one."

"I think one is just as safe without a pistol," Luscombe said. "Even these rowdies would hardly shoot down an unarmed man."

"They might not if they were sober," Hugh agreed; "but most of this shooting is done when men are pretty nearly if not quite tipsy. I heard my uncle say once, 'A man may not often want to have a revolver on him; when he does want a revolver he wants it pretty badly.'"

A few days later they heard at supper that three notorious ruffians had just ridden into the place. "I believe one of them is a mate of Buck Harris, who was shot here three weeks ago. I hear he has been in the bar swaggering about, and swearing that he means to wipe out every man in the place who had a hand in that business. The sheriff is away. He went out yesterday with two men to search for a fellow who murdered a man and his wife somewhere down south, and who has been seen down in the swamps of the East Fork. He may be away two or three days, worse luck. There is the under-sheriff, but he isn't much good by himself. He can fight, Gilbert can, but he never likes going into a row on his own account. He will back up the sheriff in anything he does, but he has got no head to take a thing up by himself."

"But surely," Hugh said, "people are not going to let three men terrorize the whole place and shoot and carry on just as they like."

"Well, mate, I don't suppose we like these things more than anyone else; but I can tell you that when one of the three men is Dutch Sam, and another is Wild Harvey, and the third is Black Jake, it is not the sort of business as anyone takes to kindly, seeing that if there is one thing more tarnal sartin than another, it is that each of them is good to lay out five or six men before he goes under. When things are like that one puts up with a goodish lot before one kicks. They are three as ugly men as there are anywhere along this part of Texas. Any one of them is game to set up a town by himself, and when it comes to three of them together I tell you it would be a game in which I certainly should not like to take a hand. You are new to these parts, mate, or you wouldn't talk about it so lightly. When you have been out here for a few months you will see that it is small blame to men if they get out of the way when two or three fellows like this are on the war-path."

At this moment there was a sound of shouting and yelling with a clatter of horses' hoofs outside. Then came the rapid discharge of firearms, and the three upper panes of glass in the window were pierced almost simultaneously with small round holes in the very centres. Every one bent down over their plates. The next shot might come through the second line of window panes, in which case they would have taken effect among those sitting at the table. Then there was a yell of laughter, and the horses were heard to gallop furiously away.

"That is only their fun at present," one of the men said. "It will be more serious later on when they have drunk enough to be savage."

"I don't see much fun in firing through the windows of a house," Luscombe said.

"Oh, that is nothing!" another put in. "I have seen a score of cowboys come into a place, and half an hour afterwards there wasn't a window-pane that hadn't a round hole in its middle. They will shoot the hats off a score of men; that is one of their favourite amusements. In the first place it shows their skill with the pistol, and in the next it scares people pretty nigh to death, and I have seen the cowboys laugh until they have nearly tumbled off their horses to see a fellow jump and make a straight line into a house. Nobody minds the cowboys; they are a good sort. They are reckless enough when they are on a spree, but they don't really mean to do harm. They spend their money freely, and they hate ruffians like those three fellows outside. If it wasn't for cowboys the bad men, as we call them, would be pretty well masters of Texas. But the cowboys hunt them down like vermin, and I have known them hang or shoot over a dozen murderers and gamblers in one afternoon. They fight among themselves sometimes pretty hard. Perhaps the men on two ranches will quarrel, and then if it happens that a party from one ranche meets a party from the other down in a town, there is sure to be trouble. I remember one battle in which there were over twenty cowboys killed, besides six or eight citizens who happened to get in the way of their bullets."

Just as they had finished the meal a man ran in. "Have you heard the news? Dutch Sam and his party have broken open the door of the under-sheriff's house, pulled him out, and put a dozen bullets into him."

There was an exclamation of indignation. "There," Hugh said, "if the under-sheriff had done his duty and called upon every one to help him to capture or shoot these fellows as soon as they came into the town he wouldn't have lost his life, and I suppose it will have to be done after all."

"The best thing we can do," one of the men said, "is to go round from house to house and agree that every man shall take his rifle and pistol, and take his stand at a window, then we will shoot them down as they ride past."

"But that wouldn't be giving them a fair show," another objected.

"A fair show!" the other repeated scornfully. "Did they give the under-sheriff a fair show? Do you think they give notice to a man before they shoot him, and ask him to draw and be fairly 'heeled' before they draw a trigger? Not a bit of it; and I say we ought to clear them out."

There was a general expression of approval, and after one of the party had opened the door and looked out cautiously to see if the coast was clear, and reported that none of the desperadoes were in sight, the party at once scattered. Luscombe and Hugh stopped for half an hour chatting with the landlord. The latter did not believe that the people would attack the ruffians.

"If the sheriff had been here to take the lead," he said, "they might have acted; but as he is away, I don't think it likely that anyone will draw a bead upon them. You see, no one is sure of anyone else, and he knows that if he were to kill or wound one of them the others would both be upon him. If we had a regular street here with a row of houses running along each side, so that a volley could be poured into them, it would be a different thing; but you see the houses are separated, some stand back from the road, some stand forward; they are all scattered like, and I don't expect anyone will begin. They will be in here presently," he said, "and they will drink my bar pretty well dry, and I don't expect I shall get a dime for the liquor they drink; and that is not the worst of it, they are like enough to begin popping at the bottles, and smashing more than they drink."

"Well, it seems to me a disgraceful thing," Hugh said, "that a place with something like a hundred men in it should be kept down by three."

"It sounds bad if you put it that way," the landlord agreed; "but you must remember that each of these three men could hit every pip on a card twenty yards away; they each carry two revolvers, that is to say, they have got twelve men's lives in their belt, and they are so quick with their weapons that they could fire the twelve shots before an ordinary man could get out his revolver and cock it."

"Why not shut up your place for the night?" Luscombe asked. "Then they couldn't come in and drink your spirits and wreck your bar."

"They couldn't, eh? Why, they would blow the door open with their pistols, and if it was so barred they couldn't get in that way, they would like enough burn the house about my ears. I have known such things done many a time."

"Well, let us get home, Hugh," Luscombe said. "It seems to me the sooner we are quietly in bed the better. As our room is at the back of the house, they may fire away as much as they like without a chance of our being hit."

Hugh put on his hat, and the two started down the street. They had gone but a short distance when the sound of a horse's hoofs was heard.

"Here is one of them!" a voice shouted from an upper window. "Run round to the back of the house, the door is open there. I have heard two or three pistol shots, and he will shoot you down to a certainty."

"Come on, Hugh," Luscombe said.

"You go round, Luscombe, you are unarmed. I am not going to run away from anyone," Hugh said doggedly. "Go on, man, it is no use your staying here, you have no pistol."

"I shan't leave you by yourself," Luscombe said quietly; "besides, here he comes!"

Hugh's hand had already slipped round to his back, and he now had his pistol in his hand in the pocket of his coat. The horseman threw up his arm as he came along, and Hugh saw the glitter of the moonlight on a pistol barrel. Another instant the pistol cracked; but Hugh, the moment he saw it bear on him, dropped on to one knee, and the ball struck the wall just above his head. He lifted his arm and fired, while two other shots rang out from the window. The man threw up his hands and fell back over the crupper of his horse to the ground, and the well-trained animal stopped instantaneously in his gallop, and turning stood still by his side.

"Come on, Luscombe," Hugh said; "the sooner we are out of this the better."

Before, however, they had gone twenty yards they heard the sound of two horses coming up behind them.

"Let us get round the corner of that house, Luscombe. I don't suppose they will pass those men at the windows; if they do, they will be thinking of their own safety as they gallop past and won't notice us."

They had scarcely got round the corner when there was a discharge of firearms, and the reports of the rifles were followed by the quick sharp cracks of revolvers. Then a man dashed past them at a gallop. One of his arms hung by his side, and the reins were loose on the horse's neck.

"I suppose they have killed the other," Hugh said, "and this fellow is evidently hit. Well, let us go on to bed."

Luscombe did not speak until they reached their room. Hugh struck a match and lighted a candle.

"Well, you are a nice lad, Hugh," Luscombe said. "I thought you were always against quarrels, and wanted nothing but to go on with your work peaceably, and here you are throwing yourself into this and standing the chance of being shot, as if you had been fighting ruffians all your life."

"It was he attacked me," Hugh said. "I didn't fire first. I gave him no provocation, and was not going to run away when I was armed. It is you ought to be blamed, stopping there to be shot at when you had no weapon. I call it the act of a madman. Well, there is nothing more to say about it, so let us get into bed."

VI. A HORSE DEAL

After having been at work for a week Hugh and Luscombe found it come comparatively easy to them. Their hands had hardened, and their back and legs no longer ached with the exertion of stooping and lifting planks and beams. They had now got the yard into order: the various lengths and thicknesses of planks piled together, and also the various sized timber for the framework of the houses. Their work was now more varied. The dray had, of course, to be unloaded on its arrival from the mills and its contents stowed away, and as soon as James Pawson found that his new hands could be trusted to see after things he left them pretty much to themselves, going up himself to the mill, of which he was part owner. It now fell to them to keep an account of the outgoings, to see that the planks they handed over to purchasers were of the right lengths and thicknesses, and also to saw the woodwork of the frames for the houses into their required lengths.

All this afforded a change, and gave them an interest in their work, and they came to know a good many, not only of those living in the town, but men who were taking up ground in the neighbourhood, and who came in with their teams for planks and shingles to construct the rough houses which were to shelter them until, at any rate, they got their land under cultivation and things began to prosper. Three months after their arrival Luscombe began to show signs of getting wearied of the work. Hugh was quick to notice it.

"I can see you are getting tired of it," he said one Sunday as they started for a walk to a small ranche three miles away, whose owner had been buying wood for a cowhouse, and had asked them to come over for dinner. "You don't mean me to see it, but I know that it is so."

"I don't know that I am tired, Hugh; but I feel a restless sort of feeling."

"Well, my dear Luscombe, I don't want you to feel that you are in any way bound here on my account. We agreed that from the first, you know. It was a great thing our being together at first; but now the ice is broken we have fallen into the groove, and can either of us shoulder our kits and go where we like in search of a job. We are no longer fresh from the other side of the Atlantic."

"I shall carry out my idea of enlisting," Luscombe said. "There is a military post at Fort M'Kayett. I can strike down by road to Meridian. I can get wagons as far as that, pick up a horse for a few dollars there, and then make my way down until I strike the Colorado River, and, crossing that, bear west, stopping at cattle ranches until I get to the fort. I shall be happier as a trooper than at any other work. Of course the pay is not high, but that does not matter a rap to me; it goes further here than it does at home, and there is not much use for money out on the plains. They say the Indians are very troublesome, and there will be some excitement in the life, while here there is none. I don't like leaving you, Hugh. That is the only drawback."

"Don't let that stop you," Hugh said. "Of course I shall be very sorry when you go; but as you have your plans and I have none, it would come at any rate before long; and, as I have said, now that I have got over the feeling of strangeness, I don't suppose that I shall stay here long after you have left."

The following day Luscombe told his employer that he should leave at the end of the week.

"I am sorry you are going," he said; "but I expected that you would be on the move before long. That is the worst of it out here—nobody sticks to a job. However, I cannot blame you; you have stopped a good bit longer than they generally do. And are you going too?" he asked, turning to Hugh.

"Not just yet," Hugh replied; "but I do think of going in

another week or two. You see, boss, one is not learning anything here."

"That's so. Say, would you like to go up to the mill for a bit? That is different sort of work, and, as you say, you would be learning something. One of the men jammed his hand on Saturday, and won't be fit for that kind of work for some time, so as your mate is going off at the end of the week you can go up there if you like."

Hugh gladly accepted the offer. He would have felt it very dull without Luscombe, but by going to a different sort of work he would feel his companion's departure less hardly. He would have much to learn, and be among new companions, and have much to attend to. So at the end of the week Luscombe set out upon his long journey to Fort M'Kayett, and on Monday morning Hugh started for the sawmill at daybreak in a wagon that had come in on Saturday afternoon with timber. James Pawson had told him that he had spoken to the foreman about him, and the latter would know what to do with him. The team consisted of two fine mules in the shafts and two horses ahead.

"Climb up," the driver said. "We shall go a goodish pace till we get to the hills. That is right—hold on!"

As he cracked his whip the animals started at a trot, and presently broke into a gallop. The road was nothing but a track across the country, and Hugh held on to the seat, expecting every moment to be jerked off. The track was as hard as iron, but the passages of the wagons in wet weather had worn deep holes and ruts in it, and Hugh thought it was a miracle that the wagon did not upset and smash to pieces, as the wheels went down first on one side and then on the other, and the whole framework creaked and quivered with the shock. At the end of about three miles the animals slackened their pace, to Hugh's intense relief.

"That's just their little play," the driver said. "They know they won't get a chance again to-day, and they generally lay themselves down for a gallop where it is good going."

"Do you call that good going?" Hugh asked in astonishment.

"Sartin. Why, it is level ground, and not a watercourse to go over! You don't expect a railway track, graded and levelled, do yer?"

Hugh hastened to say that he entertained no such extravagant ideas.

"This road ain't nowhere, so to speak, real bad," the driver went on; "that is, not for a hill road. I don't say as there ain't some baddish places, but nothing to what I have driven teams over."

The animals had now dropped down into a walk, although so far as Hugh could see, the track was no worse than that which they had been hitherto following.

"The critters are just getting their breath," the driver said as he proceeded to light his pipe. "They have had their fling, and now they are settling down to the day's work. They know as well as I do what they have got before them. Don't you, Pete?"

The mule addressed lifted one of its long ears and partly turned his head round.

"They are fine mules," Hugh remarked.

"You will see bigger than them. Them's Mexicans, and they have wonderful big mules in Northern Mexico. I have seen them standing a hand higher than these. But Pete and Bob are good mules. They would be better if they were a bit heavier when it comes to a dead pull, but except for that I would as lief have them as the biggest."

"Are they better than horses?"

"Better'n horses? You bet! Why, I would rather have a pair of mules than three pair of horses. Why, for steady work and for stay and for strength there ain't no comparison between a mule and a horse. Why, that pair of mules is worth twice as much as the best pair of horses you could find in Texas, except, of course, picked horses for riding. If you pay a hundred dollars for a horse you have paid a long price in this country, but that pair of mules wouldn't be dear at eight hundred for the two of them. There is no trouble with mules: they won't stray far when you turn them out; they won't stampede—not if they are properly trained. Why, there is as much sense in a mule as there is in a score of horses, and the horses know it themselves. If there is a mule turned out among a troop of horses he takes the lead natural, and they will follow him wherever he goes, knowing right well that he has got more sense than they have. Besides, mules seem to get fond of each other, and you don't see horses do that. In a round-up the team horses will just mix up with the others. You don't see two of them keep together or have any sort of friendship; but if there are a pair of mules among the lot you will see them keep together."

"I had an idea that mules were obstinate beasts."

"I won't deny as they have their tempers sometimes, but in most cases it comes from their getting into bad hands. But treat a mule well and he will, in general, do his best. When they once find they have got a job beyond them they ain't going to break their hearts by trying to do it; and if they are treated bad when there is no call for it then they puts up their backs and won't stir another foot, and when they makes up their minds to that you may kill them and they won't do it then; but treat a mule fair and kind and there is no better beast in the world. You know all about it, Pete, don't you?" and he gave the animal a slight flick on the neck with his whip, to which it replied by throwing up its hind quarters and giving a playful kick, which caused Hugh, whose legs were hanging down over the front of the wagon, to withdraw them hastily. "You are a rascal, Pete," the driver said. "Come, now, you have all got your winds. Just sharpen up a bit till you get among the hills."

As if they understood what he said, the mules threw their weight on the traces, broke into a slow trot, and the crack of the driver's whip woke the leaders into activity. This pace was not kept up long, for the ground had now begun to rise. They presently entered a valley between two spurs of the hills, and soon began to mount by a rough road. This became steeper and steeper, and Hugh was glad to get off and walk in front. At times the track they had to cross was bare rock, so smooth and slippery that the animals could scarcely keep their feet and drag up the wagon. Then they wound along on the side of a hill, the ground on one side being so much higher than on the other that it seemed to Hugh that a loaded wagon would infallibly topple over and go rolling down into the valley below. Sometimes they descended sharply into some lateral ravine cut by a stream, and climbed up the other side. The hills now were covered with a growth of small trees and brushwood—the larger timber had already been felled. At last the wagon turned up the bed of a stream running through a rocky gorge.

"Here we are," the driver said; and fifty yards farther they came upon the sawmill—a roughly-built structure, with a water-wheel. A low log hut stood beside it. Beyond, the valley opened out. At the upper end its sides far up the hills were covered with trees, but the woodman's axe had already stripped the lower part of the valley of all its timber trees. A dam had been built across the stream and a leat cut to the water-wheel, which was sunk five or six feet below the level of the ground around it, and the tail-race continued nearly down to the mouth of the gorge, where the water fell again into the old bed of the stream. The wheel was revolving, and the sound of the machinery inside the mill deadened that of the mules and wagon, but a shrill whistle from the driver brought a man to the door. He nodded to Hugh. "You are the new hand the boss spoke of, I suppose? Well, Clarkson, have you brought the things we wanted?"

"Yes, I think the list is complete. I gave it to the old man, and he had all the things on board the first thing this morning. Here they are: six pounds of tea, a barrel of pork, sack of flour, keg of molasses, twenty pounds of sugar. Here is a box of dried apples, and the two cross-cut saws. He will see about a grindstone. He thinks you might make that one last a bit longer."

"It was pretty well worn out when it was put up," the foreman grumbled. "It ain't fit to grind axes on. I told the boss the other day that it had cost him ten times its vally already, because the men couldn't keep a sharp edge on their tools with it."

"Well, you know, Ben, grindstones don't grow down in M'Kinney, and he has got to get them sent out from Missouri."

"If he had to get them from China he might have had one here by this time," the foreman grumbled. "Have you got that bag of iron dogs I wanted?"

"No. There warn't one to be had in M'Kinney. The old man told me to tell you he wrote off on Saturday to Little Rock and told them to express them on."

A negro now came out from the hut and began to carry the provisions in, and Hugh followed the foreman into the mill. There was another man there. One side of the mill was open to a yard behind, in which lay the logs as brought down by the team. These were placed on rollers, and so run into the mill. One end of the log was then lifted by a screw-jack until level with the saw-bench. Here it was packed up, and the jack then taken to the other end. The machinery consisted solely of one large circular saw and of another of smaller size. The water-power would not have been sufficient to drive frame saws, and the whole work had to be done with the circular saws. The mill was not large, but it sufficed for the wants of M'Kinney and the neighbourhood, and two wagon loads of planks were sent down daily. Three axemen, who felled and squared the trees, and a teamster with four horses to drag the balks down to the mill completed the establishment.

Hugh soon found that the work was far more interesting than it had been in the woodyard. It needed a good deal of skill to handle the heavy pieces of timber and get them upon the saw-bench, although they were cross-cut by the woodmen into lengths suitable for planks. Then the great saw cut the balks into planks three inches wide. These were taken to the smaller saw, which ran them down into half, three-quarter, or inch planks, as required. The benches were of a primitive description, the balks being laid on fixed rollers, and the necessary movement given to them by a rope passed through blocks and taken round a shaft, which, as it revolved, wound up the rope and brought the logs forward against the saw.

The noise at first of the saws and of the water-wheel and its machinery almost deafened Hugh, but he soon ceased to notice it. He found that his duties were of a general kind. He assisted in raising the logs to their place and in getting them properly placed on the rollers, and then he helped to fix the blocks and pulleys, to remove the planks as they were cut off, and to work the log back to its place in readiness for another plank to be cut from it. The small saw required one man's constant attention, as the three-inch planks were simply pushed forward by hand against it, being kept in their true position by guides.

"You have got to be careful when you get near the end," the foreman said to him, "or you will find yourself without a finger or two in no time. When you get to within a foot of the end you must not push the plank any farther, but go to the other end of the saw and pull it to you. It is a pretty rough business altogether, but it will only last another few months. There are not enough trees to supply it longer than that. Pawson has bought up another place a bit farther among the hills, and he has ordered better plant than this, and reckons it will be up and ready to run by the time we are done here. This place ain't fit for carrying on much trade. When it was put up two years ago there were but few people about on the plain, and a wagon load a week was about the outside Pawson could get rid of. I have been here from the first. In those days we used to work with our rifles handy, for there was always a chance of an attack by Indians, but the country has grown so much since then that the Indians moved farther north, and don't bother us. Ah! there is Joe's dinner-bell."

Hugh, following the example of the others, went down to the mill-stream and gave his hands a rinse, dried them on a towel hanging from a nail on the door of a hut, and then went in. In five minutes the whole party were assembled, and took their seats on benches beside a long narrow table. The negro cook brought in bowls of pea-soup. This was followed by boiled pork and potatoes, and then came a great dish of dried apples, boiled, with molasses poured over them.

"We get our board up here," the foreman, who had placed Hugh beside him, said. "I suppose the boss told you?"

"Yes, he said I should get forty dollars a month, and my grub."

"That's it. It is better pay than you can get on a farm below, but it is harder work, and lonesome; besides, unless you are careful, you run a pretty good risk of an accident. There have been eight or ten fellows hurt here since we began. It is healthy among the hills, and we don't get fevers, and it is cool enough to sleep comfortably at night even in summer, but in winter it is cold, I can tell you. The old man feeds us pretty well, I must say that for him, and he is as good a boss as there is about here."

Hugh liked the life, the keen mountain air braced him up, and every day he found it more and more easy to do his share of the work of moving the heavy balks. The men as a whole were pleasant fellows, and of an evening Hugh listened with great interest to the stories they told as they smoked their pipes. It was wonderful how many occupations most of them had followed. Two of them had been mining in California before they came down to Texas; one of them had been working with teams across the Santa Fé route; another, named Bill Royce, had been a sailor, had deserted his ship at Galveston, had enlisted and served for three years at a cavalry post west, had deserted again, had worked for two years as a cowboy on one of the Texan ranches, had gone down into Mexico and worked at a ranche there, had come up by sea to Galveston, working his passage, had served as a farm hand for a few months, and then, after various experiences, had come to M'Kinney when there were only three or four houses there.

Another of the men had also worked as a cowboy, but his experience had been but a short one.

"I stopped just a week at it," he said, "and what with being thrown off a horse twenty times a day, and what with the work, and what with the goings-on of the boys, I had enough of it by that time. I had been in one or two Indian fights, and I didn't feel scared then, but those cowboys scared me pretty nigh to death. The way they let off their pistols was a caution. Four or five times, when I was sitting quiet, smoking, bang! and a revolver bullet would knock my pipe into chips, and then they laughed fit to kill themselves when I got up and swore. Then without the least reason, someone, as we were all sitting round the fire, would take it into his head to hit a little bit of flaming wood, then half a dozen others would go at it, and the bits of fire would be sent flying in all directions, and how it was that none of them got killed was more than I could make out. I stood it for the week, and then I weakened. I had got that nervous that I would jump if a fellow moved suddenly, and I concluded that I was not made the same way as the cowboys, and had better quit and take to some other job."

"I reckon you were about right there," Bill Royce said. "Anyone as is thinking of going for a cowboy, had best know how to ride, how to throw a rope, and how to draw his pistol as quick as lightning, before he begins."

The next day Hugh asked the teamster to bring him up from the town a rope, such as the cow-herders used.

"This will do," Bill Royce said, as he examined it. "The cow-boys and Mexicans both use ropes sometimes, but they chiefly make them themselves from strips of raw hide, which they work and grease until they run almost as easy as if they were made of silk. Yes, this is the right length, forty feet. Some men will use fifty, and I have known Mexicans who would throw a sixty-foot length with certainty; but that is quite out of the way; forty feet is the right length. I will splice one end into an eye for you, the other goes through it, and makes a running noose. When you throw it, the loop is three or four feet across. Of course, the better you can throw, the smaller you can have the loop, and the smaller it is the better, for the jerk comes all the quicker before the horse or steer is prepared for it. Now, you see that stump of a young tree sticking up two feet above the ground. Well, you form your loop, and you gather the rest in coils in your hand like this, and you stand, to begin with, twenty feet away, and you cast the loop over the stump—so."

Of an evening, when supper was over, Hugh went out and practised with the rope, and at the end of a month found that he could throw it at a distance of thirty feet with a fair certainty of dropping the loop over the stump. He also took Royce's advice as to the pistol. He had laid it by since arriving at M'Kinney; but he now got a belt similar to those worn by the cowboys, and took to carrying the pistol in it, but unloaded, and at odd moments practised drawing from the belt, levelling it, and pulling the trig-ger with the greatest possible speed. The action seemed simple enough, but he was surprised to find how, with practice, the time taken in doing it diminished, and his fingers came to close upon the handle in exactly the right position almost instantaneously, and as his hand shot out, his thumb drew back the hammer, and his forefinger closed on the trigger. All this he had practised before, more or less, when he had learned to use the weapon in the conservatory at Byrneside, but at that time it had not appeared probable the accomplishment would be of any use. Now he knew that his life might depend upon it, and he came in time to be able to perform it, with, as Royce had said, something of the sleight of hand of a conjurer.

He devoted the whole of his spare time to practising with the pistol and rope, and by the time that summer had gone Hugh was able to throw the rope with certainty over any fixed object within reach, and to draw his revolver with a quickness that astounded Bill Royce.

"I have seen a lot of pistol shooting," the latter said, "since I came out west—cowboys and Mexicans, and horse thieves and such like, but I have never seen one draw as quick as you do, and there are many as draws quick. You shoot fair, but nothing out of the way. There's many a cowboy kin shoot a sight straighter, but for quick drawing you are wonderful, and that is the great thing. When one fellow gets his pistol out, the other has got to cave in."

The valley was now pretty well cleared of its trees, and the party prepared to go down to M'Kinney for the winter. The woodcutters were to move at once to the new location, and to begin to fell trees, and as soon as the snow fell deep the teams would go up and drag them down to the new sawmill, for the timber is hauled down much more easily over the snow than over the rough ground in summer. Thus there would be a big stock in readiness when the thaw came, and the mill began to work in the spring.

Hugh was not sorry when the work of the mill came to an end. He had determined to remain until the season closed, and he was glad he had done so. The time had been by no means lost. He had learned a good deal as to the ways and character of the men with whom he should have to associate. He had from one or other of them picked up a great deal of knowledge about the country, and knew the best places for making a start, the towns from which most of the teams started, and the localities that were best to make for in order to gain the heart of the cattle country. He had learned to throw a rope with enough dexterity to aid him materially in any work he might undertake among cattle or horses, and his constant practice with his revolver gave him a confidence in himself, and in his ability to hold his own in the wild life of the plains and mountains.

In the nine months which had elapsed since he left England he had gained strength, had become manly and self-reliant, and felt that his apprenticeship had been of great value to him. The first thing to do after he came down to M'Kinney, was to look out for a horse. He had been put up to a useful wrinkle in this respect by Bill Royce. "You be careful about any horse trade you make. Bet your boots that any horse that is offered to you here is stolen, and you would get into one of the awkwardest of scrapes if you chanced to go into a district where that horse is known. They don't trouble themselves to ask many questions over a stolen horse. If you buy a horse, the best thing to do is to go before a justice, or the sheriff will do; pay your money before him, and get him to sign his name as a witness to the bargain. His fee will be one or two dollars, and you could not lay out the money better. Men ain't altogether unreasonable even where a horse is concerned, and a paper issued from a sheriff's office certifying that you had bought the horse, and paid a fair price for it, might save your neck from a noose. You may ride a stolen horse all your life, and never happen to light on the place he was taken from; but if you do happen to light on it, you may find yourself in a tight corner."

Hugh put up at the hotel, and having told the landlord that he was on the lookout for a horse, the latter told him one evening, when he returned from a visit to some friends at a farm, that two men had come in an hour before, and had said they had a good horse to dispose of. Bill Royce was sitting in the saloon when Hugh went in.

"I dropped in to see you, Hugh. I saw two fellows come in an hour ago on two likely-looking horses, and they were leading two others, one of which seemed to me as good a bit of horse flesh as I have seen fur a long time. I expect they are on for a trade. The horse is a mustang; I don't expect they come by it honest, but that ain't your business, and you will get it cheaper than if they had. Go slow in bargaining; don't you let out you really want him."

Presently two men came in. They were dressed in broad hats, red shirts, over which they wore jackets with silver buttons, breeches made of a soft leather, and high boots. They wore bright-coloured sashes round the waist.

"They look pretty hard," Bill Royce said quietly; "they may be anything. They are not regular cowboys, but they may have been working on a ranche; they may have been prospecting; they may be horse thieves; they may be regular border ruffians; anyhow, they have got a horse to sell. Maybe they have stole it from a ranche; maybe they have got it from the Indians; maybe they have wiped out its owner. You will be able to tell pretty well by the price they want for it. He would be cheap at two hundred dollars if he is anything like as good as he looks. If they will take anything under that it is because they daren't keep him."

After standing at the bar and talking for some time to the landlord, one of the men came across to Hugh.

"I hear you are looking for a horse."

"Yes, I am wanting to buy one if I find one to suit me at my price."

"I have a horse to trade that would suit anyone, and as to its price, I am ready to let him go a bargain."

"I should like to have a look at him," Hugh said.

"Well, he is in the stable now."

"Yes; but I should want to see him by daylight, get on his back, and try him."

"Look here," the man said. "Me and my mate are pressed for time. Perhaps we have got an appointment with the president, perhaps we haven't; anyhow, we want to go on. We have got two spare horses, and we don't wish to bother with them no further."

"Well, I will look at the horse now," Hugh said, and, accompanied by Bill Royce, he followed the man to the stables. Two horses were standing, ready saddled and bridled, hitched to hooks outside the shed. Inside were two others. One was an ordinary-looking horse, bony and angular. A pack saddle hung on a beam close by. He had evidently been used for carrying baggage. The other was a handsome roan, which snorted angrily as they approached with lanterns.

"That is something like a horse," the man said. "Five years old, strong, and up to anything, clean-limbed, full of courage, and fast."

"He has got a temper," Hugh said, as the horse laid back his ears and made a sudden and vicious snap at the man's hand.

"He is a bit playful," the man said.

"Well, I don't like buying him without trying him," Hugh said. "He may be up to all sorts of tricks, and may kick his saddle over his head. What do you want for him?"

"I tell you what," the man said. "That horse would be dirt cheap at two hundred and fifty dollars, but as I have told you we want to be moving on, and I will sell him for a hundred and fifty. I would rather put a bullet through his head than let him go for less than that."

"Well, let us go back into the saloon and talk it over," Hugh said. "It is a rum way to buy a horse, but I like his looks."

The other man was still standing at the bar when they entered. Hugh, knowing that it would be an unheard-of thing to buy a horse without the ceremony of taking drinks being performed, went to the bar and ordered them for the four. "If I buy that horse," he said, "it will be on one condition. You see I don't know where he has come from. The man you got him from may have stolen him, and I might happen to come across the former owner, and I haven't any fancy for being strung up as a horse thief."

"You don't mean, stranger, to say as we have stolen him?" one of the men said angrily.

"Not at all. It may have gone through half a dozen hands before it came into yours, and yet it may have been stolen. Of course, if you know anyone here who can guarantee that you raised the horse, or have owned him for a couple of years, I shall be quite content; but if you don't, you can hardly expect me to take your word any more than I should expect them to take my word if a party were to ride up to me and accuse me of stealing it. That is right enough, isn't it, landlord?"

"I don't see as there is anything to be said against that," the landlord said. "It is a mighty unpleasant thing in this country to be found riding on the back of a horse that has mayhap been stolen."

"What I propose is this," Hugh went on. "Seeing that these gentlemen are strangers here, I propose that I should call in the sheriff and James Pawson, who is a justice, and that they should witness the sale and give me a signed paper saying that they know me as a resident here, and that I have in their presence bought this horse. I don't think there is anything unreasonable in that. If at any time I am held up for stealing if I can show this paper, and if they doubt it they can write to the sheriff here, and find that it is genuine."

The two men exchanged a few words together in a low voice, and then the one who had shown the horse said, "Well, I reckon that is a fair enough offer. We know we came by the horse honestly, but as we are strangers it is right enough you should be cautious. Bring your sheriff along, and let's be done with it."

"I will fetch the sheriff across," Royce said, "if you go over to Pawson's, Hugh."

In five minutes they returned with the two men. The sheriff looked sharply at the two horse-dealers. They were unknown to him.

"Will you give me my belt, landlord?" Hugh said.

The landlord went out, and returned with Hugh's belt, which had been locked up in his chest since Hugh arrived in the town. The latter counted out 150 dollars in gold.

"Wait a moment," the sheriff said. "I must see the horse first, and see what brand is on him. I cannot describe the horse unless I see him."

Again taking lanterns the party went out to the stable. The horse had been branded with a circle in which was the letter E.

There was no other mark on him. The sheriff brought across with him some official paper, and returning to the bar wrote: "I bear witness to the purchase by"—and he paused—"Hugh Tunstall," Hugh put in—"who is well known to me as having been working for six months in and near the town, of a roan horse branded ⓔ of"—"of Jake Wittingham," the man said—"and to the passing of payment for the same." The sheriff then added his name, writing under it "Sheriff of M'Kinney County," and James Pawson added his signature with the word "Judge."

"That is right and square," the sheriff said. "Now, hand over the money and the trade is done."

"I will throw in the other horse for twenty dollars."

"I will take it," Hugh said; and adding this sum to that he had counted out, handed it over to the men.

"If you will just step over with me, Hugh," the sheriff said, "I will put my official seal to that paper. I have not a doubt," he went on as they left the saloon, "that those two fellows have stolen that horse. They would never have sold him for that money had they come by him honestly. I should have been glad to buy him myself for anything like that price. I don't know the men, and I reckon I know most of the rogues for a hundred miles round here; so that, if it has been stolen, it has probably been brought a good distance. I shouldn't be surprised if there has been murder as well as robbery. If I knew the men I would seize them and have them searched; but as I have never seen them before, and know nothing against them, I cannot do that. I think it is a very good idea of yours getting me in to witness the sale. That horse might get you into serious trouble if you could not prove that you came by it honestly."

He had now reached his house, and proceeded to stamp the document with the official seal. "You may as well put your signature to this," he said, "and I will witness it. Then if there is any question about your being Hugh Tunstall you would only have to sign your name and they would see that you are the man mentioned. That is right; my fee is two dollars."

Hugh gladly paid the money, and putting the document in his pocket returned to the hotel.

"Those fellows have just ridden off," Royce said when he entered. "Pretty hard couple that. I wonder where they got that horse. Nowhere about here, or the sheriff would have known it; a horse like that would be sure to catch the eye."

The next morning Hugh got up early to inspect his purchase. The horse again made hostile demonstrations when he approached it; but, talking to it quietly, Hugh went into the stall, patted and soothed it. When it had quieted down he took the head-rope and led it out into the yard.

"You are a beauty," he said; "there is no mistake about that," and, tying it up to a post, he walked round it. "Well put together, plenty of muscle, fine bone, and splendid quarters. What a hunter you would make if I had you at home!" The landlord came out as he was admiring the animal.

"A mustang," he said; "bigger than they usually run a good bit, and a beauty all over; he is worth double what you gave for him. This is not much of a horse country; if you had him down south you could get three hundred for him any day. I expect those fellows were afraid to take him down there; too well known, I reckon. Look here, I will give you a paper too; and if I were you I would get another from Pawson, saying that you have been working for him at his sawmill, and that he recommends you as a good hand at that work. You can't have too many certificates as to who you are when you are riding on an animal like that in this country. If you want a saddle and bridle, Jim Hoskings has got one to sell; he was speaking to me about it a fortnight ago."

Half an hour later Hugh became the owner of a saddle and bridle. The former was made in the Texan fashion, which closely resembles the Mexican, being very heavy, and with high peak and cantle.

"I hardly see how a man can be thrown off a horse with such a saddle as this," Hugh said as he examined it; "one would be boxed in before and behind."

"Wait till you get on a bad bucking horse," the man said with a smile. "You won't wonder about it then."

Carrying it back to the hotel Hugh saddled his horse and mounted. He felt strange and uncomfortable at first, for the stirrup-leathers were placed much further back than those to which he was accustomed. The stirrups were very large and broad, and the position of the stirrup-leathers rendered it necessary for him to ride almost with a straight leg, so that his grip was with his thighs instead of his knees.

"I shall get accustomed to him in time," he said to himself, "but at present I feel as if I was riding barebacked. Well, I had plenty of practice at that, so I ought to be able to stick on." He rode at a quiet pace down the street, and then he shook the reins, and the horse at once started at a hand-gallop. Hugh was delighted with his pace, which was wonderfully smooth and easy, and returned in an hour fully satisfied with his purchase.

VII. AMONG THE COWBOYS

"Well, now you have got your horses and outfit, Hugh, what air you going to do next?" Bill Royce said, after the rest of the party had got up from breakfast and gone out.

"I don't quite know, Bill," Hugh laughed; "I thought of going teaming, but I am afraid my horse has spoilt me for that."

"Well, so I should say."

"I should like to be my own master for a bit," Hugh went on, "and do some shooting and hunting on the plains, work across to Santa Fé, and then taking anything that turns up. I have got three hundred dollars in cash; that will last me for a long time. But I don't like striking out by myself, I know nothing of the country or the life. What do you say to going with me, Bill?"

"That is just what I have been turning over in my mind," Bill said. "I know the plains powerful well, and have been hunting and shooting there for months. I was saying to myself, as like enough you would be thinking of striking out for a bit afore you settled down again to anything, and you would be wanting someone with you as could put you up to the ropes. I have got pretty sick of working here, but I have spent my money as fast as I have got it, and cannot afford to get an outfit; so I said to myself, if Hugh likes to start me with an outfit I think it would be about square, seeing as he knows nothing of the country, and I could put him straight there. We have worked together for a bit, and I reckon we should get on first-rate. So if that would suit you it would just suit me."

"It suits me capitally, Bill; nothing could be better; it is just what I wanted. I don't suppose I should ever have gone by

103

myself, but with you it would be the very thing to suit me. There's my hand on it."

In another three days their preparations were made. Bill knew of a horse that could be picked up for forty dollars; two rifles were bought, a saddle and bridle for Bill, and saddle-bags for the spare horse. A large stock of ammunition was laid in; fifty pounds of flour, a few pounds of tea and sugar, four blankets, and a few odds and ends, completed the outfit. Royce had already a revolver, and on the morning of the fourth day they started from M'Kinney, striking nearly due south, so as to work round the range of hills. For the first few days they passed occasional settlements, and then struck out across an open country.

"Now we may begin to look out for game," Royce said. "You can shoot, I suppose, Hugh?"

"I have had no practice whatever with the rifle, but I am a pretty good shot with a shot-gun."

"You will soon pick it up, anyhow," Royce said; "anyone who can shoot as you do with a Colt, is sure to shoot pretty straight with a rifle."

For the next four months Hugh and his companion wandered over the plains, and Hugh enjoyed the life immensely. They had directed their course towards the south-west, for winter was setting in when they started, and as the cold is sometimes severe in Northern Texas, they made down towards the Mexican frontier, and there enjoyed delightful weather. They found an abundance of game, and could have shot any number of deer, but they were useless to them, except for food. Herds of wild horses were sometimes seen, and occasionally, in quiet valleys, they came across half-wild cattle, which had strayed away from far-distant ranches. It was strange to Hugh to travel thus at will, to wander freely in whichever direction fancy led them; sometimes passing a week or two without seeing any other human being; sometimes stopping for a night at the camp-fire of a party of cowboys; sometimes bivouacking with a wandering hunter like themselves, or with a ranchman in search of stray animals. During this time their expenses had been next to nothing, their sole outlay being for flour, tea, and sugar, and even these they generally obtained in exchange for venison or other game.

Hugh had learned to use his rope with considerable skill on horseback, for as soon as he got fairly away on the plains he had begun to practise. The first time he tried it upon his companion he would have given him a very heavy fall, had not Bill reined in his horse on to its haunches as soon as the rope fell over his shoulders; for Prince, as Hugh called his horse, was thoroughly up in this work. The instant the rope had been thrown he stopped and braced himself, with his fore-legs extended, to meet the shock, and had it not been for Bill's quickness he would in an instant have been torn from the saddle.

"Thunder!" the latter exclaimed. "Do you want to break my neck, Hugh?"

"I had nothing to do with it!" Hugh protested. "Prince nearly sent me over his head. I had not the least idea of pulling him in, and was perfectly taken aback by his playing me that trick."

"We ought to have thought of it," Bill said. "It was dead sure he would be trained to the work. The idea flashed across me just as the rope came down, and lucky it was so. Well, you will find plenty of other things to practise on as we go along. There are cattle enough running about here without owners, and if you come across a bunch of wild horses you can give chase and rope some of the young ones; and there are coyotes, they will give you plenty of sport that way."

Hugh had used all these opportunities, and had come to throw the noose over the head of a flying animal as well as Bill Royce himself could do, but as yet he was unable to throw the rope round their legs with any certainty. As the spring approached Hugh proposed that instead of carrying out their plan of going to Santa Fé they should for a time take service on a ranche.

"I enjoy this life immensely, Bill, and I should like to become thoroughly up to all the work. At present I am what you call a tenderfoot, and I should certainly like to have a few months among the cowboys."

"Just as well do that as anything else," Bill said. "It is always handy to know that you can hold your own in a round-up and know the ways of cattle, and I tell you that there is plenty to learn. But, mind you, it ain't going to be like this time we've been having. There's no fooling about a cowboy's life: it is just about the hardest life there is. However, it won't be as hard for you as it is for most fellows. You can ride, though there ain't much merit in sitting on that horse of yours. Still, I see you know your way among horses, and you have taught him to come to you when you whistle, and to do pretty nigh everything you want him to; but you will find it a mighty different thing when you get on the back of a broncho. However, it is worth learning to ride a horse that has never been backed. Anyhow, I am with you. I have had a spell at it, and don't mind having another; and there is one thing—you can quit when you like."

"But how about this horse? I should not like to give up Prince."

"Well, you could do as you like about that. Each cowboy has six or eight horses—sometimes he has as many as a dozen—and he just ropes one out of the crowd and rides him as he has a fancy; so you could let Prince run with the rest and use him when you liked, or you could leave him at the headquarters station."

"What do they want such a lot of horses for?" Hugh asked.

"They want them to do the work," Bill said. "A man can go on pretty nigh for ever, but a horse can't. You will find that you can use up six horses in the twenty-four hours, and they want a day to rest before they are fit for work again. Well, they will be starting on their round-up soon, so we may as well head in their direction so as to get taken on before they are full. I was working in the O triangle ranche two years ago; their station ain't above a hundred and fifty miles from where we are. The boss wasn't a bad sort. We may as well go there as to another."

"What do you mean by the O triangle, Bill?"

"That is their brand—a circle in a triangle. We call them always by their brands. They have all sorts of names of their own, but they are never known by them. There is the O triangle, and the double A, and the cross T's, and the diamond square, and the half-circles, and a dozen others. Well, we will head that way to-morrow morning. I don't know that I shall be sorry to be in a crowd again for a bit. It gets lonesome when there are only two of you after a while."

Hugh was beginning to feel this also. Their subjects of conversation had long been exhausted, and after the events of the day's hunting had been discussed there was little for them to talk about as they sat by their fire.

On the evening of the third day they arrived at the headquarters station of the ranche. It consisted of a long, low building, which formed the storehouse and general room. Near it was the manager's house, and behind the barracks for the men. A short distance away was a fence which enclosed fifty or sixty acres of ground. Here were some of the more valuable of the animals: some handsome bulls and a couple of dozen good horses. Three or four wagons stood near the huts, and a number of horses were grazing about over the country. The huts themselves lay in a hollow, down which a small belt of trees extended. A score of men were standing or sitting near the huts, and as many more came out as the newcomers rode up. One or two of these recognized Bill Royce.

"Hello, Bill!" one of them said; "back again! I thought you had got rubbed out. Where have you been all this time?"

"Been down in Mexico, and then back among the settlements, got tired of it and here I am. Been hunting last. This is my mate, gentlemen. He is a good sort, a Britisher, and his name is Hugh. Now you are properly introduced!"

"Glad to see you!" the man said, holding out his hand to Hugh. "Come to pay us a visit?"

"No. I have come to work, if I can get work," Hugh said.

"Oh, there's plenty of work. Well, get off your horse. He is a good un, he is!" Such was evidently the opinion of the rest of the cowboys, for they gathered round and made remarks on Prince's points. "He is too good for this sort of work altogether, leastways for most of it, though he would do well enough for scouting round and hunting for cattle among the foothills. Where did you get him?"

"I bought him at M'Kinney," Hugh said. "Two fellows came along with him and wanted to sell bad, so I got him a bargain."

"I expect he didn't cost them much," the man said. "Well, it is all right as long as you don't fall across the chap he was stolen from. If you do, there will be a good many questions asked, I can tell you. I guess he came from some Mexican ranche down south. You don't often see such a bit of horse flesh about here."

"Here is the boss, Hugh," Bill said; "we may as well speak to him at once"; and they walked together to a man who had just come out from the manager's house.

"Have you got room for two hands?" Bill asked. "I was here a couple of years back; my mate is new at this work, but he can ride and shoot and throw a rope."

"Oh, it's you, Bill, is it? Yes, I can put you both on; I am not quite full yet. Forty dollars a month for you; thirty for your mate till he learns his business."

"That will suit," Bill said. "He won't be long before he gets up to the forty."

"He will find it hard work at first," the manager said; "but he doesn't look as if that would hurt him."

Bill and his companion now rejoined the group of cowboys, while the manager went into the store. Hugh looked with interest at the men who were to be his associates for some time. Their dress was similar to that of all the cowboys he had met while hunting. They wore hats with a very wide, straight brim, and made of a stiff felt almost as hard as a board. Most of them wore a cord of gold or silver mixed with colour round it. All wore flannel shirts, with a handkerchief—which in the majority of cases was of silk—round their throats. Round the waist they wore a Mexican sash of bright colour. Their trousers were either of thick material, or of very soft tanned leather, and over these were chaperajos or Mexican overalls, with a coloured fringe down the outside seam. A few had jackets on, and these had also tufts of coloured fringe on the seams of the arms. They were most of them spare, active men, without an ounce of superfluous flesh. They were quiet in manner, with little of the reckless jollity of the ordinary frontiersman. Hugh was particularly struck with the keen, watchful expression of their eyes, the result of long nights of watching and of days spent on horseback in search of stray animals, and of danger from Indians. All carried a revolver on the hip or hind pocket, had a long knife stuck in their sash, and wore high boots cut away behind at the bend of the knee, but coming several inches higher in front.

Following Bill's example, Hugh unsaddled his horse. "Go off, old boy!" he said, giving him a pat; and Prince walked leisurely away accompanied by his two companions, who always kept near to him.

"We cannot offer you a drink," one of the cowboys said to Hugh. "No liquor is allowed on the ranche. It comes rather hard at first, but it is best for us all."

"I have touched nothing for the last four months but tea," Hugh said, "and don't care for spirits anyway."

"It would be a good thing if none of us did," the other said; "but one must do something when one goes down to a town." Just at this moment a bell began to ring. "There is supper," the man said.

There was a general movement into the large hut. Here long tables were laid out, and dishes piled up with meat, and great platters of potatoes, were ranged along at short intervals. Hugh was gifted with an excellent appetite, but he was astonished at the way in which the food disappeared. The meal was accompanied by a supply of very fair bread fresh from the oven, and tea with milk.

"Ewart keeps a few cows down here," the man next to Hugh said in answer to his remark about his not having seen milk for three months. "Of course we don't get it at the out-stations."

"Who is Ewart?" Hugh asked.

"Oh, he is boss; we don't have any misters out here—one man is as good as another. You have just arrived here at the right time. We have been driving in the horses from the ranche for the last three days, and to-morrow we are going to begin breaking them. Of course a good many of them were ridden last year, but there are a lot of bronchos among them. We have got a broncho-breaker out here."

A broncho, Hugh knew, was a horse that had never been ridden. "How do you do about horses?" he said.

"Well, three or four of those that have been ridden before are told off to each man. Then, if anyone fancies a broncho, he can take him and break him for himself. Then men can swop with each other. You see some men ride better than others. Some men like quiet mounts; others don't mind what they sit on; and you see the best horses are very often the most full of tricks. You ride your horses as you like, but everyone keeps his quietest for night watches. You must have a quiet horse for that, for if your horse was to begin to play tricks he would stampede the cattle, sure."

"I suppose after they have been ridden one season they are quiet enough?" Hugh said.

"Not a bit of it," the man replied. "Some of them seem to get wickeder and wickeder. They get a bit better towards the end of the season, but six months' running wild does away with all that. I would just as soon take my chance with a fresh broken broncho as with one that has been ridden before. They are wilder, you know, but not so cunning. An old horse seems to spend most of his time in thinking what game he shall be up to next, and when you see one walking along as if he had never done anything but walk along all his time, just look out, or you will find yourself six feet up in the air."

Supper over, pipes were lighted, and Hugh listened with great interest to the talk going on around him. Some of the men had been on the ranche all winter; others had been away, some back in the settlements, others in New Mexico, where they had been either loitering away their time in the towns or working on Mexican ranches. Hugh was struck with the quiet way in which they talked, the absence of argument, and the air of attention with which each speaker was listened to. He thought he had never been among a more quiet set of men, and wondered if these could be really the cowboys of whose wild doings he had heard such tales.

Gradually one by one they lounged off to the hut behind, and he and Bill soon went off also. It consisted of one room about sixty feet long. A stove with a huge fire burned in the middle, for the nights were cold. Down both sides and along the ends extended a double row of bunks. In the great majority of these lay blankets, showing that they were occupied. Choosing two empty ones, they placed the blankets and other articles they had taken from their saddles in them, put their belongings under their heads, rolled themselves in their blankets, and were soon sound asleep. The first thing next morning they handed over to the storekeeper the remainder of their flour, tea, and sugar. The value of these was credited to them, and they took out the amount in a couple of pairs of chaperajos, two cowboy hats, and two pairs of high boots, paying the balance in cash; they then joined the cowboys. These were gathered in an enclosure with a very strong fence adjoining the fenced-in ground.

Several cowboys rode off as they entered, and in a quarter of an hour a mob of horses were seen approaching, the men riding behind cracking their whips and yelling at the top of their voices. The gates were opened, and a couple of minutes later the horses rushed in. There were some forty or fifty of them, and of these about two-thirds were branded. In the first place the others were speedily roped both by the head and hind legs. Four cowboys hung on to the ropes while another approached with a heated brand and applied it to the animals' hind quarters, the horses kicking and struggling wildly. As soon as the operation, which lasted but a second or two, was completed the ropes were loosed, and the frightened animals rejoined their companions, who were huddled in a corner of the enclosure.

"Now, each man of No. 1 and No. 2 outfit take one of the horses," the manager said.

Hugh and Bill had the night before been told that they were to form part of No. 2 outfit. Like the others they had their ropes in their hands, and had brought their saddles inside the enclosure. Hugh picked out a horse that struck him as being a good one, and threw his lasso round its neck. One of the cowboys belonging to the other outfit, who was standing by, said: "That is a pretty bad horse, mate. I would take a quieter one if I were you."

"I have got to learn to sit them," Hugh replied; "so I may as well begin with a bad one as a good one."

"All right," the other said, taking hold of the rope, and helping Hugh haul upon it. The animal resisted violently, but the pressure of the rope half-choked him, and he was forced to leave the group and come up to them. "I will hold him," Hugh's assistant said. "Get your saddle and bridle."

There was some difficulty in putting these on, for the animal kicked, plunged, and reared furiously, and it was only when another cowboy threw a rope, and, catching one of its hind legs, pulled it out stiffly behind, that Hugh succeeded in saddling it. "Now, up you go!" the man said. Gathering up the reins Hugh sprang into the saddle, and the two men, as soon as they saw him seated, slipped off the ropes. For a moment the horse stood perfectly still. "Keep his head up," one of the men shouted; but before Hugh could draw in the reins the horse dropped its head to its knees. Then it seemed to Hugh that it doubled itself up, and before he knew what had happened he felt himself flying through the air, and came down to the ground with a crash. There was a shout of laughter from the cowboys, but two or three of them helped Hugh, who for a moment was almost stunned, to his feet.

"That is bucking, I suppose," he said as soon as he could get breath.

"That's bucking, sure enough," one of those who had helped him said.

"Well, I will try again in a minute," Hugh said.

"Take it quietly," the man said good-naturedly. "You fell pretty heavy, and you are shaken up a bit. You'd better hitch him on to the fence, and look about you for a few minutes before you try again."

Hugh thought the advice good, and after fastening up the horse stood watching the man they called the broncho-breaker, who was fighting one of the most vicious of the last year's horses. Had he not seen it, Hugh would not have believed it possible that a horse could go through such performances. He had ridden many vicious brutes at home, and had thought that he knew something of horses, but this was a new experience for him. In the rearing, kicking, and plunging there was nothing novel, and as the horses were much smaller than the English hunters to which he had been accustomed, he felt that if this had been all

"The next jump threw him fairly over the horse's head."
See page 115.

he should have no difficulty in keeping his seat, but the bucking was new to him. To perform it, it was necessary that the horse should be able to get its head down. The moment this was done it sprang straight into the air, at the same moment rounding its back, and this with such a sharp, sudden jerk that it fairly threw the rider into the air.

On coming down the animal kept its legs stiff, so that the jerk to the rider was scarcely less than that of the upward spring, and before he had time to settle himself in the slightest the horse repeated the performance, varying it occasionally by springing sideways, backwards, or forwards. The breaker, or as they were generally called the broncho-buster, kept his figure perfectly upright, with a tremendous grip upon the saddle with his thighs, but depending, as Hugh could see, rather upon balance than upon his hold. The exertion was evidently great. The man's hat had been jerked off, the perspiration stood upon his bronzed forehead. From time to time he dug his spurs into the animal's flanks, and excited it to continue its desperate efforts, until at last the horse was utterly exhausted and stood with its head drooping unable to make another effort. There was a shout of applause from the cowboys looking on.

"Bully for you, Jake! He is a brute, that is, and no mistake."

"I will give him a turn every day for a week," Jake said. "He is worth taking trouble with. I will take him for a gallop to-morrow."

"Do they buck when they are galloping?" Hugh asked the cowboy next to him.

The latter nodded. "Not when they are going at their best pace. They haven't time to do it then, but when they are going at hand-gallop they will do it. They wait until you are off your guard, and then up they go in the air and come down perhaps three yards sideways, and it's fifty to one against your being on their back when they do come down."

"I see how it is done now, though I don't see how I can do it," Hugh said. "But I will try again."

The horse was led out, and Hugh again mounted. This time he was prepared for what was to come, but in spite of the grip with his legs the blow lifted him far above the saddle. It seemed to him that the next buck came before he had fairly descended, for it struck him with the force and suddenness of an electric shock. Again and again he was thrown up, until he felt his balance going, and the next jump threw him fairly over the horse's head, but as he was prepared for the fall it was much less heavy than the first time.

"Well done! well done!" several of the cowboys said as he rose to his feet. "You will do, you will, and make a good rider before long. That will do for to-day; I would not try any more."

"I am going to try it until I can sit him," Hugh said. "I have got to do it, and I may as well go on now before I get stiff."

The broncho-breaker came up to him as, after waiting a minute or two to get his breath, he again prepared to mount.

"Don't keep your back so stiff, young fellow. Just let your back go as if there were no bones in it. I have known a man's spine broke before now by a bucker. Sit easy and lissom. Keep your head, that is the principal thing. It ain't easy when you are being pitched up and down like a ball, but it all turns upon that. Let your legs close on him tight each time you come down, if only for a moment, that saves you from being thrown clean away from him."

Hugh sprang on to the horse, and the struggle again began. It ended like the last, but Hugh had kept his seat somewhat longer than before. Again and again he tried, each time with more success. The fifth time he felt that the horse's action was less sudden and violent, and that it was becoming fatigued with its tremendous exertions. "Now, you brute," he muttered, "it is my turn"; and he dug his spurs into the horse. A spring more violent than any he had yet felt followed the application, and for a minute or two he was almost bewildered by the force and rapidity of the animal's springs; but he was now confident that he was gaining the mastery, and the moment he found that its efforts were decreasing, he again applied the spurs. The response was less vigorous than before, and in five minutes the animal stood exhausted and subdued. A cheer broke from the cowboys who were standing round looking on at the struggle.

"Well done, young fellow! you are the toughest tenderfoot I

have ever seen," one of them said, shaking him by the hand. "I don't believe there are ten men in the camp who would have sat that horse as you have, and you say that it is the very first time you have been on a bucker."

"I have beaten him," Hugh said, "but he has pretty well beaten me. You must help me off my saddle, for I feel as if my back was broken, and that I could not lift my leg over the saddle if my life depended on it."

Two cowboys lifted him from his seat. "That is a hard tussle, mate," the broncho-breaker said, coming up to him, "and you have stuck to it well. You are clear grit, you are. The best thing you can do is to walk about for the next hour; just keep yourself moving, then go and wrap yourself up in two or three blankets and lie down in your bunk for a bit, have a thorough good sweat, and then strip and rub yourself down. Get your mate to rub your back well, and then dress and move about. The great thing is not to get stiff; but you will feel it for a day or two."

Hugh followed the advice, but he found it hard work to do so. He was bruised all over with his falls; he scarce seemed able to put one leg before another, and at every movement a sharp pain shot through the loins, and he felt as if his spine had been dislocated. Still, for an hour he walked about, and at the end of that time felt that his movements were more easy; then he went to the hut, wrapped himself in Bill's blankets and his own, and presently dozed off to sleep. A couple of hours later he woke and saw Bill standing beside him.

"Now, Hugh, you had better turn out and let me give you a rub. Just take off that shirt. I have got a lump of hog's grease here."

Hugh got out of the bunk with some difficulty and took off his shirt. "Now, you lean your hands on that bunk and arch your back; that's it. Now here goes."

For a good half-hour Bill worked at his back, kneading it with his knuckles down both sides of the spine and across the loins. "Now you will do," he said at last. "Put on a dry shirt and come out."

Hugh strolled down to the stockyard. He felt wonderfully better after the rubbing, and was able to walk with far greater ease than before. The scene in the yard was unchanged. Fresh groups of horses had been driven in as fast as the others had been saddled and mounted, and by nightfall each of the cowboys had been provided with three horses. Hugh was greatly amused at the scene, for the spills were numerous, and the shouting and laughter incessant. The next day the work of breaking in the bronchos commenced. One after another they were roped and dragged out of the drove. The bridle was slipped on, and they were then blindfolded while the saddle was put on and fastened. Then Jake mounted. The cloth was drawn off the animal's head, and the struggle commenced. The horses tried every means to unseat their rider, but in vain. Some submitted after comparatively short struggles. Others fought long and desperately. As soon as the first victory was won bars were let down, and the horse was taken for a long gallop across the country, returning home subdued and trembling. Then the process was repeated with a fresh animal.

"How long does he take to break them?" Hugh asked a cowboy.

"Three days generally; sometimes he will ride them four or five times, but three is generally enough. Then they are handed over to us to finish."

"It must take a lot out of them," Hugh said. "It would be better to do it more gradually. You see they are scared nearly to death before they are begun with."

"He cannot afford the time," the man said. "He gets two dollars a horse for breaking them. He will be here for a fortnight, and in that time he will do pretty well a hundred. Then he will go off somewhere else."

"It must be tremendous work for him," Hugh said.

"It is that, you bet. A broncho-buster seldom lasts above two years. They get shaken all to pieces and clean broke up by the end of that time."

As fast as the horses were broken in they were handed over to the cowboys, and Hugh, who had been unable to do any work for two days, then began to break in the lot that were to be his particular property. But he was fond of horses, and could not bring himself to use such violent measures as those which he saw adopted by his companions. The first lesson they taught them was to stand still the moment a rope fell over their necks. The animal was led up to the stump of a tree and then loosed; it at once went off at full speed, but as it did so its owner threw the noose of his rope over its head, and then gave the other end a turn round the stump. The shock was tremendous, the horses being frequently jerked right over on to their backs.

Two or three experiences of this sort were sufficient, and the animal thenceforth learned to stand, not only when a rope was thrown round its neck, but even when the reins were dropped upon it, so that when its master dismounted it remained perfectly quiet until he again mounted and took the reins in his hand, even if he was absent a considerable time. As the teams were to start in a few days on the round-up, Hugh felt that it would be useless for him to attempt to break the horses in by English methods, and he was therefore obliged to adopt those in use by his companions. He modified them, however, to some extent by getting another rope and tying it to his own. He then took only half a turn round the stump, and let the rope run out, at first fast, but checking it gradually until its pressure upon the neck brought the animal half suffocated to a stop.

It took him longer to accomplish his object, but he found that by the end of a week the seven horses had all learned their lessons; each having been ridden for an hour every day. He had had several severe battles with the animal he had first mounted, which was by far the most vicious of them; but the struggle each day had become less severe, as the horse recognized the futility of endeavouring to unseat its master. Hugh had many falls during the schooling, but he was upon the whole well satisfied with the result.

Several of the cowboys had advised him to use the methods they adopted for securing them in their seats upon specially vicious horses. One of these methods was the fastening of a loop of leather to the high pommel. Holding this in the hand, it was wellnigh impossible to be bucked from the saddle, but there was the disadvantage that if the strap broke, nothing could save a rider from a fall far more violent and heavy than that which came from being pitched from the saddle in the ordinary way. Another method was to fasten a strap passed under the horse's belly tightly below each knee; but this, although it held the riders in their saddles, had the serious disadvantage, that in the event of the horse rearing and falling back, or of its falling headlong from putting its foot in a hole, the rider could not free himself, and was almost certain to be crushed under the horse. Others, again, fastened themselves by bringing their feet together, and crossing their spurs, under the horse's belly, a safer measure than the last, but objectionable inasmuch as the spurs when the animal bucked struck him in the belly, and so increased the violence of his action.

Of course the best riders refrained from using any of these methods, trusting only to their leg grip and to balance; and Hugh determined to ride in this way, even if it did cost him a few more falls. He was on excellent terms with the rest of the cowboys. The tenderfoot, as a newcomer is called, is always the subject of endless pranks and annoyance if he evinces the least timidity or nervousness; but if, on the other hand, he shows that he has pluck, determination to succeed, and good temper, he is treated with kindness and cordiality. Hugh's exhibition, therefore, of courage and horsemanship on the occasion of his first attempt at once won their liking and admiration, and all were ready to lend him a hand when necessary, and to give him hints and advice, and he was free from any of the annoyances to which new hands are often exposed. There were several other tenderfeet among the party. Two or three of these got on fairly and soon ceased to be butts; but the rest, before a week was up, found the work altogether too trying, and one after another went off in search of some less dangerous occupation.

VIII. A RATTLESNAKE DIET

Everything was now ready, and one morning four wagons started. The ⚰ was one of the most northern of the ranches, and the four outfits would therefore travel south, searching the whole width of country as they went along. Those from the other ranches would come up from the south, or in from the east, all moving towards a general meeting-place. The range of country which served as common pasturage to some eight or ten ranches was about two hundred miles from north to south, and nearly as much from east to west. The eastern portion of this great tract consisted of plain, sometimes flat and level, but more often undulating. The western portion was broken up into valleys and gorges by the spurs of the great ranges included under the name of the Rocky Mountains.

The cattle of each ranche were as far as possible kept in that portion of the territory nearest their own stations, but during the winter they scattered to great distances in search of better grazing ground or shelter. In the more northern ranges, when snowstorms with violent wind swept down from the north-west, the cattle would drift before it, always keeping their heads from the wind, and feeding as they travelled. Sometimes great herds would thus travel hundreds of miles, until brought up by some obstacle. At this time such things as fences were absolutely unknown on the plains, and when, years after, they came to a certain extent into use, they were, in the regions exposed to snowstorms, causes of terrible disaster; for when a herd drifting before a snowstorm came to one of them, it would be checked, and many thousands of cattle would, when the snow cleared, be found frozen or starved to death in a mass.

Two of the outfits of the ⚘ ranche were to proceed due west, and then to search the ranges among the hills, while the other two were to work the plains. Nos. 1 and 2 were chosen for the former work, and were to keep within twenty or thirty miles of each other, so as to be able to draw together for support should the Indians prove troublesome. It was not until the afternoon that the cowboys mounted, and the men of each outfit, collecting their own horses into a bunch, started for the spot where their wagon was to halt for the night. It had brought up near a stream, and the cook had already lighted his fires and put on his cooking pots when they arrived.

Each outfit consisted of ten cowboys and a man who acted as wagon-driver and cook. The duties of the cook of an outfit were by no means a sinecure, as he had to prepare two meals a day, breakfast and supper, at all times, and dinner for the men whose work allowed them to ride in to it. He had to bake bread, to wash up pots, pans, and dishes, and to cut wood for the fire. In the latter task he was always assisted by the first arrivals at the camping place. The bread was baked in iron pans. The dough was made of flour and water with a mixture of saleratus, which took the place of yeast, and caused the dough to rise. The pans were placed in the wood embers, a quantity of which were piled upon the flat iron lid, so that the bread was baked equally on all sides. Meat was cut into steaks and fried, those of the men who preferred it cutting off chunks of the meat and grilling or roasting them on sticks over the fire.

Once or twice a week there was duff or plum-pudding. The cook was up long before daybreak preparing breakfast, and the men started as soon as it was light. Directly the meal was over, plates, pots, and pans were washed and packed in the wagon, the horses or mules harnessed, and he started for the spot named as the evening camping ground, where he had his fires lighted and the meal well on its way by the time the cowboys arrived. A good deal more meat than was required was cooked at breakfast, and each man, before he started on his day's work, cut off a chunk of bread and meat for his midday meal.

Hugh had ridden Prince, who had been having a very easy

time of it for the last three weeks. The horse had for the first few days kept somewhat apart, and had resented any advances on the part of the strangers. He had now, however, fallen into their ways, and as soon as the saddle was taken off he, like those ridden by the other cowboys, went off at a trot to join the bunch of horses a short distance out on the plain.

"Well, Hugh, how do you think you shall like cattle work?" one of the men, known as Long Tom, asked him, as they sat round the fire after supper was over.

"So far I like it immensely," Hugh replied; "but, of course, I have only seen the smooth side of it. I have not been on night cattle-guard yet."

"Yes, that is the worst part of the work," the man said, "especially when you are short-handed, for then there is only one relief. Of course on a fine night, if the cattle are quiet, there is no hardship about it; but on a dark night, when you cannot see your horse's ears, and the wind is blowing and the rain coming down, and the cattle are restless, it is no joke. I have been a sailor in my time, and I tell you that keeping watch on a wild night at sea isn't a circumstance to it. You know that if the cattle break, you have got to ride and head them off somehow; and I tell you, when you cannot see your horse's ears, and are going at a wild gallop, and know that if he puts his foot in a hole there is no saying how far you may be chucked, and you have got the herd thundering along beside you, you begin to feel that a cowboy's life is not all meat and molasses. There is one comfort, when you do have to ride like that, you have no time to funk. Your blood just boils up with excitement, and the one thing that you think of is to head the herd."

"Shall we place a horse-guard to-night?"

"Yes, there is always a horse-guard when we are away from the station. The horses are more inclined to wander at first than they are afterwards, and ours are a pretty wild lot at present; but I don't think we shall have trouble with them, for we have brought that white jackass along, and the horses are sure to keep round him. There is nothing like a jack for keeping horses quiet. They seem to know that he has more sense than they have. As long as he takes things quietly there is not much fear of their moving."

"Do you think a donkey has more sense than a horse?" Hugh asked in surprise.

"Ever so much," the man replied; "and so have mules, haven't they, mates?"

There was a general chorus of assent. "I had no idea of that," Hugh said. "I should have thought that horses would look down upon a donkey."

"That is where you are wrong," a cowboy called Broncho Harry said. "Trust to jack to find out the best forage and the nearest water. He would manage to pick up a living where a horse would starve. He doesn't get scared and lose his head about nothing as a horse does. If there is a noise, he just cocks one ear forward and makes up his mind what it is about, and then goes on eating, while a horse fidgets and sweats, and is ready to bolt from his own shadow; besides, the horses know that the jack is their master."

"Why, you don't mean to say that a donkey can kick harder than a horse?"

"I don't say he can kick harder, though a mule can, and twice as quick; but a jack does not fight that way, he fights with his teeth. I have seen several fights between stallions and jacks, and the jack has always got the best of it. I remember down at the Red Springs there was a big black stallion with a bunch of mares came down the valley where we camped, and he went at the horses and stampeded them all down the valley. Well, we had a jack with us; he did not seem to pay much attention to what was going on until the stallion came rushing at him, thinking no doubt that he was going to knock his brains straight out with a blow of his fore foot, but the jack went at him with open mouth, dodged a blow of his hoofs, and made a spring and caught him by the neck. He held on like a bull dog. The stallion reared and plunged, and lifted the jack off his feet time after time, but each time he came down with his legs stiff and well apart.

"The stallion struck at him with his fore legs, and cut the skin off his shoulders. Once or twice they fell, but the jack never let go his hold, and he would have killed the stallion, sure, if it had not torn itself away, leaving a big bit of skin and flesh in the jack's mouth. The stallion went up the valley again like a flash, and the jack turned off and went on grazing as if nothing had happened. Jacks don't have a chance in towns; but give them a free hand out on the plains, and I tell you they are just chokefull of sense. But it is getting dark, and I am first on guard, so I must be off."

The other three men who had been told off for guard had each brought in a horse and fastened the ends of their ropes to picket pins driven into the ground, so that they could graze a little and yet be near at hand when the time came to relieve the guard.

"How do you know when to wake?"

"It is habit," Broncho Harry said. "One gets to wake up just at the right time, and if you ain't there within a quarter of an hour of the time you ought to be, you are likely to hear of it. One of the guards will ride in, and talk pretty straight to you, or like enough he will drop his rope round your foot or arm, and give you a jerk that will send you ten yards. When you have been woke up once or twice like that, there ain't much fear of your oversleeping yourself. Ah! there is black Sam's accordion."

Black Sam was the cook, a merry good-tempered negro, and the outfit which secured Sam with the wagon considered itself in luck. Cowboys are very fond of music, and Sam's accordion helped to while away the evening. For the next two hours there was singing and choruses, and then the men rolled themselves in their blankets with their feet to the fire, and the camp was soon asleep.

The next morning at daybreak the cowboys started in pairs; two of them accompanied the wagon in charge of the spare horses, the rest went in various directions to hunt up cattle.

Before nightfall they had collected fifty or sixty cattle, mostly in bunches of threes and fours. At least a third of the number were calves by their mothers' side. Some of them were only captured after a long chase, as they ran with a swiftness far beyond anything of which Hugh could have supposed cattle to be capable.

The cows and steers were for the most part branded, but a few were found without marks. These were, Hugh learned, called mavericks. They were animals that had escaped search at the previous round-up, and it was consequently impossible to tell to what herd they belonged. When the day's work was done these were roped, thrown down, and branded with the ⚿, and became the property of the ranche whose cowboys discovered them.

"There is many a man has become rich by branding mavericks," one of the cowboys said. "It was a regular business at one time. Of course no one could tell whose cattle they were, and when a man had put his brand on them he became the owner; but it was carried on so that the ranche owners all came to an agreement, and any man caught branding cattle with his own brand, except at the regular round-up, got shot. Of course the calves belonged to one or other of the ranches round, and as each ranche sends out a number of outfits to the round-up in proportion to the numbers of its cattle, the present rule is fair enough."

When night fell the cattle were bunched down by the stream by which the party had camped. Six of them were told off on night guard, while three others, of whom Hugh was one, were to look after the horses. Hugh was to take the first watch, and as soon as he had eaten his supper he received his instructions from John Colley, the overseer of the outfit.

"You will have little enough to do," he said. "You have merely got to keep near them, and you needn't even keep on your horse unless you like. As long as they graze quietly leave them alone. If you see two or three wandering away from the rest ride quickly and head them in."

Hugh mounted one of the quietest of his horses and rode out to the bunch a few hundred yards from the camp. At his whistle Prince at once trotted out from the rest and came up to him and took from his hand the piece of bread Hugh had put in his pocket for him.

"Go back to the others, Prince," he said with a wave of his hand; "your business is to eat at present."

The horses were all quiet, and Hugh, when darkness had fairly fallen, was struck with the quiet of the plain. Above, the stars shone through the clear, dry air. Near him were the dark bunch of horses, and he was surprised at the loudness of the sound of their cropping the grass, broken only by that of an occasional stamp of a hoof. He could easily hear the accordion and the singing away back at the camp. When this ceased there came occasionally the crack of a breaking twig as the herd of cattle forced their way through the bushes by the stream on his left, and the songs of the cowboys on watch as they rode in circles around them. The time did not seem long, and he was quite surprised when Bill Royce cantered up and told him his watch was over.

The next day's work was similar to the first, except that, soon after starting, on ascending a slope they saw a small herd of deer some eighty yards away. Before Hugh had time to think, Broncho Harry, who was his companion, had drawn his revolver, and, as the deer bounded off, fired. One of them leaped high in the air, ran fifty yards, and then dropped, while the others made off at the top of their speed.

"That was a good shot," Hugh said. "I should hardly have thought of firing at an object so far distant."

"Oh, these Colts carry a long way," the cowboy said carelessly. "They will carry four hundred yards, though you can't depend upon their shooting much over a hundred. I have seen a man killed, though, at over three hundred; but I look upon that as a chance shot. Up to a hundred a man ain't much of a shot who cannot bring down a deer four times out of five. I don't mean hitting—of course you ought to hit him every time—but hit him so as to stop him. I don't mean to say as the shot would be sure if you were galloping over rough ground, but in a steady saddle you ought not to miss."

On riding up to the deer Broncho Harry dismounted, lifted it on the horse, and lashed it to the back of the saddle. "I am not particularly partial to deer-meat," he said, "but it makes a change to beef."

"I own I prefer beef," Hugh said, "especially after living on venison, as I have been doing, for the last three months."

"I consider bear-meat to be about as good as anything you get in these parts," the cowboy said. "I don't say as it isn't tough, but it has got flavour. I don't want to put my teeth into anything better than a good bear ham. If we have any luck we shall get some up among the hills. Most things are eatable. I lived on rattlers once for a month at a time. I tell you a rattler ain't bad eating."

"Are there many of them out on the plains?"

"A good many," the cowboy said; "but you get them most among the foothills. They like to lie on the rocks in the sun, and I have seen them by dozens on a sunny ledge."

"Do many people get killed by them?"

"Bless you, no. The natives are afraid of them, 'cause, you see, they often go barefoot; but they cannot bite through our thick boots. The only danger is when you lie down, or something of that sort. They are fond of warmth, and if you camp near where they are thick they will crawl down to the fire, and sometimes get into your blanket."

"I suppose their bite is fatal if they do bite."

"Not once in fifty times if you take them right. I have known Mexicans killed by them, but then, a Mexican gives himself away directly and makes no fight for it. Now if we are bitten we just whip out a knife and cut the part out straight, clap a poultice of fresh dung on it, and tie a string round tight above it. Of course, if you have got spirits handy, you pour some in directly you cut it out, and drink as much as you can; but then, you see, we don't often have spirits out here. I was bit once. There." And he pointed to a scar on his right hand, between the little finger and the wrist. "A rattler bit me just on the fleshy part there. I blew his head off with my revolver, and then whipped out my knife and cut the bit out. There wasn't any dung handy, and I had no spirits, so I broke up a revolver cartridge and poured the powder in, and clapped a match to it. It hurt a bit, of course, because it was bleeding, and the powder didn't all flash off at once; but I was all right afterwards. My arm felt numbed for an hour or two, and there was an end of it. Cattle and horses get bit sometimes on the head when they are grazing, and it swells up to pretty well twice its proper size, but they generally get over it in a day or two. No, there is no great danger about rattlers, but if you are in the neighbourhood where they are thick it is just as well to look round before you sit down."

"But how was it you came to live on rattlesnakes for a month?"

"Well, I was up north a bit. I had been looking after a bunch of cattle that had gone up a cañon, when I saw a party of Indians coming my way. Lucky I saw them before they saw me, and you guess I was off the horse pretty sharp. I turned his head up the cañon, and sent him galloping on, and then I sheltered among the rocks. The Indians came up, no doubt to look for cattle. I heard them pass by and then come galloping down again, and I knew they had happened upon my horse. They hunted about that place for two days, but the soft rocks had fallen, and they were piled thick along the foot of the cliffs on both sides, and you may guess I had worked myself down pretty deep in among them.

"I was in too much of a hurry to think of the rattlers as I got in, but I had noticed as I went up what a lot of them there were lying on the rocks, and I thought a good deal about them as I was lying there. Of course I had my knife and pistol with me, but the pistol was no good, for a shot would have cost me my scalp, sure, and a knife ain't the sort of weapon you would choose to use in a tussle with a rattler. When night came I could have shifted, but I guessed I had got as good a place as another, and I might have put my foot into a nest of rattlers in the dark, so I lay there all night and all next day. I slept a bit at night, but all day I kept awake and listened. I could hear the Injuns going about and shoving their lances all about down the holes among the rocks.

"Luckily the place I had got into was just at the foot of the cliffs, and you could not see that there was a hole unless you climbed up there. Well, when night came again I guessed they would give up searching and take to watching. I got out and went a good bit higher up the gorge. I was pretty nigh mad with thirst, and there weren't no water, as I knew of, within wellnigh a hundred miles. I felt sure the Injuns wouldn't come up the valley again, but would keep watch at the mouth, for the hills went up both sides and there was no getting out anywhere 'cept there. Soon as it got light I cut a stoutish stick, tore off a strip of my sash, and tied my bowie to the end. Then I hid up agin there, but so that I could see out a bit. About ten o'clock, as there wur no signs of the Injuns, and the sun wur blazing down fit to frizzle up one's brain, I guessed rattlers would be out. I had got so bad with thirst by that time that I b'lieve, even if I had seen the Injuns, I should have gone out. I had not long to search. I had not gone five yards when I saw a rattler lying on a rock.

"There are two sorts of rattlers; there is the plain rattler and the rock rattler. The rock ain't so big as the other, but he bites just as bad. He saw me coming, but he did not trouble to move. He just sounded his rattles, and lifted up his head as much as to say you had best leave me alone. When I got near him he lifted his head a bit higher, and swish went my stick, and his head flew off him. I picked up the body and went back among the bushes, skinned it, cut it up into chunks, and ate it just as it was. That was the first of them, and I had three or four more before the day was over. That night and next day I remained quiet, except to fill up my larder, and the next night crawled down to the mouth of the valley; and just where it narrowed I could hear Injuns talking. They hadn't lighted a fire; they knew better than that. It would have been just throwing away their lives. So back I went again, for I could not tell how many of the skunks were there. I guessed, perhaps, they would come up the valley again the next day, so I hid again in my old place; and it was lucky I did, for in the afternoon I heard their horses' feet and knew there must have been a dozen of them.

"That night I went down again. I could hear no voices, and I crawled out and out until I was well on the plain, but they was gone. That wur just what I had expected. They had got my water-skin with my horse, and knew well enough that no one could have stood that four days' heat in that valley without dying or going off his head, and as they could see nothing of me they must have thought that I had got into some hole and stuck there till I died. Their own water, too, must have been running short, and they couldn't stay any longer; so off they had gone. I wasn't much better off than I was before. They had driven the cattle away, and as to starting to walk a hundred miles without water the thing wur not to be thought of. I had found there was juice enough in the rattlers to do me; besides, there wur plants growing about that would help me a bit if I chewed the leaves, so I made up my mind that there was nothing else to do but to stop.

"Some of my mates would be sure to get up a hunt for me when they found that I didn't come back. I didn't care so much now that I could light a fire, for I was getting pretty sick of raw rattler. I lit one next morning right up at the head of the valley, choosing a place among the rocks where I could pitch a stone over it and hide the ashes if the Injuns should take it into their heads to pay me another visit. Every morning I cooked enough rattlers for the day, and then took them down and sat among some bushes nigh up at the mouth of the valley, so that I could see if anyone was coming two or three miles away, for I hoped that a deer, or a bear, or perhaps a head or two of cattle might come up, but nary one did I see, though I stayed there a month.

"At the end of that time I saw four mounted figures far out on the plain, and pretty soon made out as they was cowboys. They was riding towards the hills, and you bet I tracked out to meet them pretty slick. They was four men of my own outfit. They had halted for three or four days after I wur lost, and scoured the plains pretty considerable for me. Then they wur obliged to go with the rest to drive the cattle into the station, and as soon as they got there they started out again, making up their minds that they wouldn't go back till they found my body. They reckoned for sure that I had been scalped, and never expected to do more for me than to bury me. They had been four days riding along at the bottom of the foothills searching every valley. They had a spare horse or two with them with water and grub. Yes, that is how I came to live on rattlers for a month, and though I don't say any-thing against them as food, and allow as they make a change to cow's flesh, I have never been able to touch them since."

"That was a close shave," Hugh said. "I suppose people do get lost and die on the plains sometimes."

"Lots of them; but not old hands, you know. A cowboy gets to know which way he is going without looking at a mark. At night he has got the stars to guide him. But tenderfeet often get lost; and when they once lose their bearings there ain't much chance for them unless someone happens to come along. They most all go out of their mind the same day. They run a bit and then drop down, and then run another way and drop again. I tell you there ain't a more awful sight than a man who has been lost for a day or two, and you have got to look out sharp if you come upon one of them, for he is as like as not to shoot you, being altogether off his head, and taking you for an enemy.

"I once came across a chap who was off his head, but who hadn't got weak. He drew his six-shooter when he saw me. It was a long way from a station, and I had no time to fool about, and I didn't want to get shot. He fired once, and the ball went pretty close, so I knew I might chuck away my life by going near enough to rope him. So I fetched out my pistol and took a shot at his ankle, and, of course, down he went. As I expected, he let drop his pistol as he tumbled, and before he could get it again I had ridden up and roped him. Then, of course, it wur easy enough. I tied him tight first, poured a few drops of water into his mouth, fastened him across the horse behind the saddle, and rode with him into the camp. He wur laid up for nigh six weeks with his ankle, but it saved his life.

"Hello!" he broke off, reining back his horse suddenly; "there is a good bunch of cattle right up that dip ahead of us. We are on the wrong side of them now, and if they was to catch sight of us we should have a long ride before we came up to them. We must work round and come down on them from the other side and head them this way, then we shall be travelling in the right direction."

Hugh's eye, less accustomed to search the plains, had not caught the cattle. "How far are they off?" he said.

"About a mile. You go round to the right and I'll go round to the left. When you get to where you think you are behind them stop until you see me; or, look here, you are new at this sort of thing, so we may as well ride together until we get to your station, else we might miss each other and lose a lot of time."

So saying he rode off at full speed, Hugh, who was on Prince, following him. As they went Hugh congratulated himself that he had not started by himself, for riding up and down the undulations, and making a half-circle as they were doing, he very soon lost all idea of direction. After ten minutes' riding the cowboy reined in his horse.

"Now," he said, "they are in the next dip, just about over the line of that bush. I will go a bit farther round and come down on the other side of them. You move on to that bush and wait until you see me coming, and then ride forward. Keep on their flank. That dip lies just about in the line of the camp, so keep them going that way."

Hugh rode until he approached the bush Harry had pointed out, and then sat quiet until he saw the cowboy approaching from the opposite direction. The latter threw up his arm and Hugh moved forward. A few strides of the horse took him to the brow, and there, below him, some forty or fifty cattle were grazing. Broncho Harry was already dashing down the opposite slope. For a moment the cattle stood with heads up and snorts of alarm, and then, as the cowboy uttered a wild yell, dashed off down the hollow. A little behind them, one on each side, rode the two cowboys, and for three miles there was no change in their relative position. Then the speed of the cattle began to abate, but they kept on at a run for another two miles, and then settled gradually into a walk. An hour later the camp was reached.

"There is no occasion to watch them," Broncho Harry said as they arrived within a quarter of a mile of the wagon. "They will go on to the stream and have a drink, and then lie down in the shade of the bushes, or else mix up with the other cattle down somewhere there. They have done enough running for to-day."

"Back early, Harry?" the cowboy who had remained behind to look after the horses said.

"Yes, we have been in luck—got a goodish bunch. Hello, Sam!"

"Hello, Broncho Harry!" the negro replied, putting his head out of the wagon.

"Got any hot water, because we want tea?"

"Not got now, but make him quick. Plenty of fire in the ashes. Not expect anyone back to dinner, only just twelve o'clock."

"Well, here we are, Sam, anyhow. Hand me out a frying-pan; a hot dinner is better than a cold lunch any day. I have brought you in a stag, Sam."

"Dat's good, Broncho, deer's meat better than cow meat."

"Not a bit of it, Sam. It does for a change; but you cannot go on eating it every day as you can beef, unless you have got to, and then one can eat anything."

"Are we going out again after dinner, Harry?" Hugh asked, as they watched the beef frying over the embers of the great fire.

"No, siree, we have done our day's work. We have brought in our bunch, and a good bunch it is. It is just luck that we came on them early, and are back early. If it had been the other way we might not have got back until after dark; maybe we mightn't have got back until to-morrow. After we have done our meal we will go and see if the cattle have settled down quiet, and if they have joined the rest. If they have, we will have a bathe in the stream and then wash our shirts. It will be a good opportunity. One don't get many chances of washing on a round-up."

The cattle were found to have joined those brought in the day before, and the cowboys' programme was carried out.

"You ought to practise with that six-shooter of yours, Hugh; a cowboy ain't thought much of if he can't shoot straight. Look at that tin on the low bough there. That has been there ever since we were here a year ago. I mind that someone stuck it up for a tenderfoot to shoot at; now, you see me knock it off. Jehoshaphat!" he exclaimed, when, as he put his hand on the butt of his pistol, a sharp crack sounded beside him, and the tin fell to the ground. A laugh from Hugh accompanied the shot.

"How in thunder did you do that?"

"The usual way, I suppose," Hugh said. "I drew my pistol, and pulled the trigger."

The cowboy looked him over from head to foot. "I tell you what, Hugh, you are a fraud. You come here as a tenderfoot, and you can sit on a bucking broncho, you've a good notion of throwing a rope, and you can shoot like lightning. Where did you get it all?"

"I have simply practised," Hugh said, smiling at the other's gravity of manner. "I made up my mind to take to ranching some months ago, and I practised with the pistol and rope before I started, and, as I told you, I have been three months hunting."

"It don't seem natural," the cowboy said doubtfully. "I don't say the shot was out of the way, for it wur an easy mark enough

at twenty yards, but it wur the spryness of the shooting that
fetched me."

"That is what I have been specially practising, Broncho. I was
told that the great thing was to be able to draw quick."

"Well, let us see a little more of your shooting." He walked to
the tree and picked up the tin. Hugh put in a fresh cartridge in
place of that he had just fired. "Now I will throw this up, and
you fire at it in the air." Bill Royce had told Hugh that this was
a favourite mark of the cowboys, and not having any tins out on
the plains he had thrown up sods or the head of a stag for Hugh
to fire at. Harry took his place about five yards from Hugh.
"Now," he said. Hugh waited until the tin reached the highest
point and then fired. It flew upward again; the other five shots
were fired in quick succession, and then the tin fell to the
ground. It was a feat frequently accomplished among the cowboys, and Broncho Harry was himself perfectly capable of
accomplishing it, but he was not the less surprised at seeing it
performed by a newcomer to the plains.

"Well, you can shoot. Now let us see you draw; your pistol's
empty, so there ain't no fear of an accident. Just put it in your
belt again. Now stand facing me. We will draw together. Keep
your hand down by your side till I say, Now; then draw, cock,
and pull your trigger. Stop! I will take my cartridges out, there
ain't no use in taking risks, and in a hurry my trigger might go
off too. Now, I am ready—now!"

Broncho Harry rather prided himself on the quickness with
which he could draw, but his pistol was not out of his belt when
the hammer of Hugh's fell, the lad having fired from his hip.

"Waal, I swar!" he exclaimed. "Why, how in thunder did you
do it? I wur looking at your hand, and a'most before I saw it
move there was the thing pinting at me. Why, I am reckoned
pretty slick, and I ain't a spot upon you. Do it again, lad." Hugh
repeated the action. "Waal, that beats me; I can't see how you
do it. Your hand goes up to your hip, thar's a twinkle, and thar's
the pistol cocked and the hammer falling at once; it's like con-
juring! Just do it slow." Hugh showed that as his hand fell on the
pistol his thumb rested on the hammer and his forefinger on the

trigger, while the others closed on the butt, drew the pistol from the belt, and threw the barrel forward.

"It is just practice," he said. "I have been at it for the last six months."

"Waal, young fellow," Broncho Harry said solemnly, "I have been out on the plains for ten years, and I have seen pretty considerable shooting, but I never saw anything that was a circumstance to that. You are all right. You can get into a muss with the worst bad man in Texas just as soon as you like, and you have got him, sure. I wouldn't have b'lieved it if I hadn't seen it; it is a kind of lightning trick. It air useful to be able to back an unbroken broncho, it air useful to throw a rope sartin and sure at full gallop over rough ground, but it air fifty times more useful to be able to draw a pistol like a flash as you do. Waal, let us go back to camp. You don't mind my telling the boys. It would be hardly fair as any of them should get into a muss with you, thinking as they had got a soft thing; and it will keep you out of trouble, for you may be sure as no one is like to be getting up a muss with you when they know it would be sartin death."

"Do as you like, Broncho; but it seems to me that there is no fear of quarrelling, everyone seems to be wonderfully good-tempered, and not to mind a bit what jokes are played upon him."

"That is so, Hugh; people are apt to keep their temper when they know that if they don't someone gets killed; but it won't be always like this. You see we have all been going through the winter, and some of us have been having pretty hard times, and anyhow we are all pleased to be at work again and out on the plains. But you will see that this kind of thing won't last long. When the work gets heavy and men don't get four hours a night in their blankets, and the herds take to stampeding, and one thing and another, men's tempers won't be as they is now; some of them grow sulky, and won't open their lips all day; and others get that crusty that they are ready to jump down the throat of the first man that speaks to them. Then trouble begins, you bet. Besides, when we get farther south, we may come upon Mexican villages, and where there is Mexicans there is spirits, and where there is spirits there is trouble. I tell you, lad, you don't begin to know about a cow-puncher's life yet."

That evening, after the rest of the outfit had returned and supper was over, Broncho Harry said: "I have had about the biggest surprise to-day, boys, that I have ever had. I looked upon Hugh here as a tenderfoot; a good un, but still new to it, and I found out that when it comes to a six-shooter, there ain't a man in the camp, nor in the ranche, and I doubt whether there is in all Texas, as can shoot as he does."

No one expressed a doubt as to the cowboy's assertion, for on the plains to doubt a man's word is a grave insult; but there was a murmur of surprise.

"I don't say as he is the straightest shot," Harry went on; "he is a good shot, although maybe there are plenty who can beat him; but when it comes to quickness of drawing, I never see a man who was a spot to him."

"That's so," Bill Royce put in. "Hugh can shoot straight, wonderful straight; but I have seen men shoot better, and he ain't quite sartin in his shooting when he is going at a gallop, although he'll learn that; but as for quickness—well, I don't know how he does it; his pistol is out before I have time to get a grip of mine."

"Let us see you, Hugh," two or three of the cowboys said simultaneously.

"I have no objection," Hugh said, standing up; "what shall I fire at?"

"Oh, fire at anything. It ain't the aim, it's the quickness Broncho and Bill are talking about."

"Here's a mark I have often seen him fire at when we were out on the plains together." And taking a stick of about the thickness of his wrist from the fire, Bill Royce walked ten or twelve paces away; then he held out the stick, which was blazing at the end.

All eyes were fixed on Hugh, who drew and fired from his hip, and the burning end of the brand flew in fragments. There was an exclamation of astonishment from all present.

"Waal, I never!" Long Tom said. "In course the shot wur nothing from the shoulder, but there ain't many as could do it from the hip; but that ain't so much, it wur the quickness! How on arth did you do it? I had my eyes on your hand, and I don't know how it wur done no more nor a baby. Waal, Hugh, I have never felt like quarrelling with you, and you may take your davie I shall never feel like it now. Waal, I am jiggered!"

The rest all assented with much variety of strange oaths, and then the cowboys' favourite topic having been broached, there was a good deal of talk about shooting, and several exhibitions of skill that surprised Hugh. Long Tom picked a tiny gourd, about the diameter of a penny, from a trailing vine common on the plains, and after giving a stir to the fire to make it blaze up, went ten paces away and held it up between his finger and thumb, and Broncho Harry shattered it with a bullet; then Broncho went the same distance out, turned himself sideways, and Long Tom smashed the bowl of his pipe.

"Would you like to have a try, Hugh?" he asked.

"No, thank you, Broncho! I dare say I might hit the pipe if it were fixed at that distance, but I would not try when it was within three inches of your nose for anything."

"It will come in time, Hugh; it is just nerve; but I wouldn't mind holding it out to you now. I should not be a bit afeard."

Then they sat down to the fire again, and Hugh heard many anecdotes of marvellous shooting. Hitherto he had borne no nickname, being the only one in camp addressed by his simple name; but he found next morning that he had been rechristened, and henceforward he was always addressed as Lightning.

IX. A ROUND-UP

Day by day the herds swelled, and at the end of two months they began to move in the direction of the general rendezvous. Hugh had soon taken his share in the night-guarding of the cattle, and found it fascinating work. He and Broncho Harry generally worked together. The first watch was preferred, because this allowed a fair night's rest to be taken afterwards; but at the same time the work was far harder and more arduous than in the later watches. The cattle were still on their feet when the watch began, and on reaching them the two guards began to ride round and round them, going in opposite directions. For a time the cattle would go on feeding, then, gradually they would lie down, until perhaps all but five or six were on the ground. At this time, however, the slightest noise would bring them on to their feet again, and then groups would try to leave the mass to begin to feed again, and the cowboys had to drive them in.

Upon a dark night they depended more upon their horses' sight than their own, for these would of their own accord leave the close-packed circle and strike out to turn back any animals that had wandered from it. At last, after an hour or two, the herd would all subside, and the cowboys would flatter themselves that their work was done. Then one of the cattle lying outside would leap to his feet with a snort, alarmed, perhaps, by the sudden scamper of an inquisitive jack-rabbit, which, having come up to examine what was going on, had fled at the approach of one of the cowboys. With a loud snort the whole herd would then spring to their feet. Perhaps after a time the herd would lie down again, reassured by the song of the cowboys, who from the time they came on duty always continued to sing, unless they played on a fife or some other musical instrument, which answered as well as the voice.

At other times a sort of general agitation communicated itself to the herd. Those on the outside finding themselves unable to leave the mass owing to the vigilance of their guard, would begin to move along its edge; the motion would spread, and in a short time the whole mass be circling, or, as the cowboys call it, weaving. As this action, unless checked, always terminated in a general stampede, the duty of the cowboys was at once to check it. This could only be done by wedging themselves into the mass, shouting and using their heavy whips to break it up and put a stop to the motion. This was dangerous work, not only from the pressure, but from the sea of horns and angry tossing heads.

Sometimes it would be successful, sometimes it would fail. Above the lowing and bellowing there would be a thunder of hoofs on the side opposite to that on which they were engaged. Then would rise a shout of "They are off!" and the cowboys would edge their horses out of the mass, and, one on each flank, gallop at the top of their speed to head the animals back. As soon as they came near the head of the herd they would yell and shout at the top of their voices, sometimes discharging their pistols in the air, pressing the animals on the flank gradually inward, and so checking the speed of the whole until they at last met in front of the herd. Sometimes they would succeed before two or three miles of ground were passed over; sometimes the wild flight of the herd could not be checked before morning, when they would be thirty or forty miles away from their starting-place.

If unable to stop them, the great aim of the cowboys was to keep them in one body: in that case no great trouble resulted from the stampede. The other men would be out in the morning and the herd would be driven back to its starting-place. But if the herd broke up, as was sometimes the case, and scattered over the country, it might take many days of hard work before they could again be got together. If the night set in wild, so as to render it probable that the cattle would stampede, a third man was placed on the guard. He would aid in keeping them in as long as possible; but if they broke the circle and went off, his duty was to gallop back to camp. The cowboys there would leap to their feet in an instant, run to the horses picketed near, saddled and bridled ready for instant use, throw themselves on their backs, and gallop off at the top of their speed in the direction in which the herd had gone.

Thunderstorms were of not infrequent occurrence, and when the clouds were seen banking up before sunset, and the lightning began to play, the cattle-guard knew that they were in for a troubled night. Long before the storm approached close enough to cause actual alarm among the cattle they would evince signs of uneasiness, the electrical condition of the air seeming to affect them. They might lie down, but it was only to rise again, and the distant roll of the thunder seemed to be answered by their restless bellowing. On such a night it needed no message to the camp to bring up help. As the storm approached, and it became evident by the brightness and rapidity of the flashes that it was going to be an unusually severe one, one by one the men would leave their fire or rise from their couches and go out to their horses, pull up and coil their ropes, leap into the saddle, wrap a blanket round them, and gallop off to the herd, beginning always to sing as they approached it, as otherwise their arrival might stampede the animals.

When the storm came overhead the terror of the cattle rose to the highest point, and the efforts of the whole of the cowboys of the outfit scarcely sufficed to restrain them. The almost incessant flashes of lightning showed a sea of heads and horns, wild eyes, and distended nostrils. The thunder was continuous, and so terrible were some of these storms that Hugh felt grateful to the animals that the trouble they gave, and the incessant efforts and activity required to restrain them, diverted his attention from the terrible war of elements overhead. On such a night it was almost certain that sooner or later the herd would stampede, and once off, the efforts of their guard were directed to keep them together rather than to head them. So long as they remained in a bunch it mattered little whether they were one mile or thirty from the camp.

If headed and held up they would probably start again, and it was less anxious work to gallop by the side of the frightened mass than to hold them in check when once their excitement reached its height. In some respects the ride in such a storm as this was less dangerous than upon a dark, still night, for the lightning flashes showed not only the exact position of the herd, but greatly diminished the chance of serious falls by lighting up the whole configuration of the country, and showing any obstacles in the way. Even a fall, heavy though it might be, would be a trifle in comparison to one occurring while endeavouring to head the herd, for in that case it would entail certain death, as life would be trampled out in an instant by the onward torrent of cattle.

Hugh had by this time come to understand that even twelve horses were by no means too much for the use of each man. Wiry and tough as were the ponies, the men who rode them seemed to be iron. Hugh was frequently in his saddle eighteen hours a day, occasionally twenty, and four or even five horses would be thoroughly done up before his work was over. Had they been fed with grain a smaller number might have sufficed, for unless unusually pressed they could have been ridden again on the following day; but fed entirely upon the dry grasses of the plains they needed a day's rest before they were again fit for work.

The herd increased by another thousand before it reached the general rendezvous of the round-up, for each day six of the men scoured the country lying within ten or fifteen miles of the line of march, and drove in all the cattle met with on their way. At last they reached the stream near whose banks the vast herds driven in from all quarters were gathered. There had been an occasional day's halt on the way to give a needed rest to cattle, horses, and men; but now that the outfit had arrived at the spot indicated before they had left the headquarters station, there was a rest for four days before operations commenced.

The time was employed by the men in washing, overhauling,

and mending their clothes, repairing their saddles, and in sleep. They knew nothing of the position of the other outfits of their own and of the other ranches, but were sure that they all lay within a radius of some twenty or thirty miles—that is to say, all that had as yet arrived. Some had probably come up days before, perhaps weeks; others would not be there for some time; all depended upon the nature of the country to be worked and the distance traversed. There were several other outfits scattered along the banks of the stream above and below them at distances of about half a mile apart, and the overseers of the different ranches were busy making arrangements for the general campaign. Four days after their arrival a cowboy rode in with a letter to the overseer of the outfit. A few minutes later Broncho Harry and four other hands, among whom were Hugh and Bill Royce, were ordered to saddle up and to go down to the central station.

The term order is scarcely a correct one, for cowboys are not men to be ordered. A cowboy is asked to do a thing, and asked in civil terms. The request has all the force of an order, but it is not so conveyed. It is put in the form, "I want you to do so and so"; or, "Will you saddle up and do so and so?" It is just as easy to put it in that form as in any other, and though the cowboy knows that if he does not comply with the request he has got to ride back to the headquarters station and get his money, he does not feel his dignity injured as it would be by a direct order. There are no men more independent than cowboys. They know their value; and a really good man knows, and this was more especially the case at that time, that he has but to ride to the next ranche to get employment. The consequence is that although willing to work to the utmost of his powers in the interest of his employers he by no means regards that employer as a master, but treats even the chief manager on terms of absolute equality, and insists upon being so treated by him in return.

"Broncho Harry," the overseer said, "I want you, Jack Johnson, Bowie Bob, Chunky Royce, and Lightning Hugh to saddle up and ride down to the forks and help in the round-up. The wagon is going to stay here till our herd is called up. There are men from the other outfits there; the boss is there and he will settle about things. Two of the wagons are there, so you will be all right as to grub. I expect you will be there about a fortnight, and then the others will come down and take your place."

"Are we to take down our other horses?" the cowboy asked.

"No. No. 1 outfit will take charge of the cattle as they are cut out and branded. No. 3 will take the next mob. Anyhow, you won't want horses except to take you down there."

"All right!" Harry said, and proceeded to call the other four together.

In a few minutes the horses were brought in and saddled, the blankets rolled up and strapped to the saddles, and the five men chosen, after eating a hasty meal, started for the point named, which was some twenty-five miles distant.

"Now you are going to see some fun, Hugh," Bill Royce, who had got the nickname of Chunky from his short, square figure, remarked as they rode along.

"Yes," Broncho Harry put in, "you will have to look out sharp, Hugh. I tell you it is pretty lively work when you get hold of a six months' calf, and the old savage of a mother is trying her best to hook you. Thar ain't a day that some fellow don't get hurt; but as long as you don't let a cow jam you against the posts it don't much matter. That is what you have got to look to special. A chuck in the air don't much matter, nor being knocked a dozen yards or so, but if you get jammed by one of those brutes against a fence, there ain't nothing to do but to bury you."

Three hours' riding brought them to the forks. Two or three large herds of cattle could be made out far on the plains: another mob could be seen not far from the wooded hollow that marked the course of the stream. Horsemen were hovering round them, and there was a confused mass of animals in what looked to Hugh like a strong stockade near it. A short distance away twelve wagons were drawn up in regular order some fifty yards apart. Columns of light smoke rising near them showed that cooking was going on at each wagon. Quickening the speed of their horses the cowboys rode on until they drew up at the wagon of the ⚕ ranche.

"Howdy, Pete," Broncho Harry said as he leapt from his horse, to a negro who, with a Mexican assistant, was engaged in cooking.

"Howdy, Broncho Harry."

"Where are the boys, and what's new?"

"Dey is out dar," the negro said, waving his hand in the direction of the corral. "Some of dem is working in de herd; some of dem is inside. Irish is in de wagon: him leg broken. New York John got killed three days back."

"That's bad, Pete. How did he manage that?"

"Old cow hooked him—ran horn right through him body. Irish got tossed against posts."

"I suppose there are boys down from the other outfits here, Pete?"

"Yes. Five No. 3, five No. 4. No. 4 came in dis mornin'. Now you come dat make fifteen, and all our own outfit; dat too much for Pete to cook for."

"Well, you have got someone to help you, Pete, so you ought not to grumble."

Pete made a grimace as much as to signify that he did not consider the assistance of the Mexican to be of much account. Between the men of these two races there was a general feud, while the cowboys looked down upon both, and as a rule refused to allow them to work with them except in the capacity of cook.

"Where are our horses, Pete?"

"No. 1 horses over dere," the negro said, pointing to a group of horses out on the plain. "Young Nat looking arter dem."

"Well, we may as well take our horses out there, boys," Broncho Harry said, turning to the others. "It is no use picketing them here; we ain't likely to want them."

"I will ride them out," Hugh volunteered. The others removed their saddles and bridles, and Hugh drove them out to the group on the plain.

"Well, Nat, how are you getting on?" he asked a boy of about fifteen years old who was lying on the ground with his horse's rein over his arm near them.

"Oh, I'm all right," the boy replied; "been here a week, and getting pretty tired of this job, you bet, with nothing to do but just to lie here. Blast all camps, I say!"

"You ought to be at school, you young imp," Hugh laughed.

"I would just as soon be doing that as lying here," the boy said. "It will be all right when I get to be a cowboy, but there ain't much fun about this. Just come in?"

"Yes."

"Who is with you?"

Hugh gave the names.

"Broncho Harry ain't a bad sort," the boy said. "The others ain't of much account."

"You had better tell them so," Hugh said with a smile.

"I would tell them if I thought fit," the boy said angrily. "You don't suppose that I'm afraid of any of that mob?"

"I know you are a very bad man, Nat," Hugh said with assumed gravity, "a very dangerous character in a camp; but I hope you won't do any of them any harm."

"I shan't do them no harm if they don't do me any," the boy said, "but I don't take no sauce from no one."

By this time Hugh had unsaddled Prince, and placing the saddle over his head and carrying the bridle in his hand, nodded to the boy, and started back to the camp, while Prince joined the four horses, which began to graze at a little distance from the rest. Presently two or three of the other horses came over to the newcomers, and after a little snorting apparently recognized them as friends with whom they had been acquainted at the head station, and this fact being established Prince and his companions were allowed to join them.

There were many boys like Nat out on the plains, for the most part lads who had run away from home, and who were now training up to be cowboys, being engaged in day-herding the horses—work that demanded but little skill or attention. They were generally regarded with favour by the outfits to which they were attached, for the cowboys as a rule are silent men, and the liveliness of the boys amused them. These boys generally grew up into the most reckless and dare-devil of cowboys, speedily picking up the worst language and imitating the wildest follies of their companions, and they would have been an unmitigated nuisance in the camps had they not been frequently sternly called to order by men with whom they knew there was no trifling.

It was not until nightfall that the work ceased and the cowboys returned to their wagons. They had been working without a break since daylight, contenting themselves with eating a piece of bread and cold meat standing at their work in the middle of the day.

"Well, boys, come in for a spell?" one of them asked as they came up to the fire where the new arrivals were seated. "We have had a week of it, and it has been a pretty tough job. The cattle are wonderful wild. I suppose the thunder has scared them, and we are pretty sure the Injuns have been chasing them lately by the foothills. Did you see anything of the Reds?"

"No; there were no signs of them in the part we searched."

"There were signs farther south," the other went on. "We came on two places where they had slaughtered a lot of cattle, and we hear they have been making raids down into Mexico, and the troops have been out after them down by the frontier line. Anyhow, the cattle are wilder than usual. You have heard, I suppose, that New York John has been rubbed out?"

"Yes, we heard that, and I have been talking to Irish. He seems getting on all right."

"Irish is a blamed fool. I told him over and over again he would get into trouble if he didn't mind; but nothing could persuade him that there was any difference between the ways of a Kerry cow and a Texas steer, and of course he came to grief. I should have thought that New York John would have known better than to get himself hooked like that; but it were not altogether his fault. He wur holding a calf, and he had his eye on the old cow, who had got her dander up pretty considerable. One of the men had roped her, and New York John naturally thought that she was safe. So he downed the calf, and the brand was clapped to it, and the young un bawls out, and of course the cow made a fresh rush to get at it, and the rope breaks, and she was on New York John afore he could look round."

"But how came the rope to break? A man must be a fool and worse to come down to round-up with a rotten old rope."

"Well, the rope was a new un. You may guess there was a lot of talk over it, and it put our backs up a bit that New York John should get killed that way. The rope wur a new one, there warn't no doubt about that, but it had been cut half through. Who had done it, in course, no one knew. The men were mad over it, and ef they could have found out who had done it he would have swung from the limb of a tree in a squirrel's jump. There were two or three men who had had musses with the chap as the rope belonged to, but no one could say as any of them had cut his rope. Of course it might have been an accident, but no one thought that very likely. However, there it wur. Somebody cut the fellow's rope to spite him, and it cost New York John his life, which was pretty rough on him."

"What is the work for to-morrow?"

"Well, your lot and the men of the other two outfits are to be in the yard. We have got a spell off, except, of course, that we have got to look after our own bunch of cattle."

"How many are there of them?"

"About six thousand I should say. I expect some of us will start driving them up north day after to-morrow."

The next morning Hugh went down to the cattle yard as soon as they had finished breakfast. Day had just broken, and while they were waiting for the herd to be brought up he looked round at the yard. The paling was composed of very strong posts six feet high, placed at intervals of two or three inches apart. It had been built three or four years before, as this place was the most convenient and central upon the plains. A few wagon loads of timber had been taken out there a fortnight before the arrival of the teams, with a gang of men, who took up any posts that showed signs of rottenness and replaced them by others, the various ranches in the round-up performing this duty by turns. The fence enclosed a space of upwards of an acre.

Beside the contingent from the ⌂ ranche some forty or fifty cowboys from the other ranches were gathered within it. Several fires were lighted for heating the brands, and the over-

seer who was in charge of the work for the day divided the men
into parties, each group consisting of representatives of four or
five different ranches. In a short time a great herd was seen
approaching, driven in by a number of mounted cowboys. The
crossbars were removed from the opening that served as a gate
at the upper end of the yard, and the reluctant animals, unable
to withstand the pressure of those behind, poured in. Several
hundreds entered; the bars were dropped again, and the animals enclosed stood in a dense group, stamping the ground, and
threatening an attack as the cowboys approached them.

These all carried their ropes, some holding them in their hands
ready for throwing, while others had them coiled over their left
shoulder, while in their right hands they held their heavy whips.
Those who were to fetch out the calves first approached. Half a
dozen ropes were thrown, and the calves were dragged out, struggling and calling, or, as the cowboys called it, bawling, to their
mothers for assistance. The call was not in vain. The cows rushed
out furiously to the assistance of their calves. As each did so the
cowboy whose comrade was dragging the calf towards one of the
fires shouted out the brand on the cow, and then cracking their
whips, and if necessary using them, they drove the animal back
into the mass and kept her there, while the calf was thrown down
and branded with the same mark as its mother.

Hugh was among those told off to fetch out the calves. He
had had some practice, as many of the mavericks found had
calves by their side, and these as well as the cows had been
branded with the △. Another cowboy assisted him to haul the
calf by main force towards the fire, and held the rope while
Hugh ran up to it. Placing himself beside it he leaned over it,
grasped it by the flank with both hands, and then lifted it and
flung it down on its side. His comrade then ran up and pinned
its head to the ground, while Hugh knelt on its haunches, and
the brander came up with a hot iron and marked it. The iron was
held on long enough only to burn off the hair and slightly singe
the hide, and the mark so made was almost indelible.

In addition to this the calf's ears were cut, each ranche having
its particular mark, such as two long slits and a short one, a

square piece cut out and a notch on either side of it, a semi-circular piece and two notches, a semicircle and a square, &c. These marks were very durable, but even these often became confused owing to the ears getting torn by a rush through thorns, or by the action of a neighbour's horn in a close press or during a stampede. It required but small exercise of strength to throw a calf of three months old; but many of them were eight or nine months and nearly full grown, and it needed a great exertion of strength and a good deal of knack to throw down animals of this size. Once or twice Hugh had narrow escapes, for some of the cows, in spite of the cowboys' whips, burst through them and rushed to the assistance of their calves; but each time the ropes descended over their heads or caught them by their legs, and threw them to the ground before they reached him.

After an hour of this work he was relieved by one of the other men, and took his turn of the lighter work of keeping back the cows. When every calf in the yard had been branded, the gate at the lower end was opened and the animals driven out, while a fresh mob was admitted from the herd. So the work went on until the herd had all passed through the yard, and the calves been branded. Then there was a quarter of an hour's rest while another herd was driven up, and the work recommenced. By nightfall some nine thousand animals had passed through the yard, and nearly four thousand calves had been branded. Begrimed with sweat and dust, the cowboys went down to the stream, where most of them bathed and all had a thorough wash, and then went up to their wagons to supper.

"How do you feel now?" Broncho Harry asked Hugh when he threw himself down by the fire.

"I feel broken up altogether, Harry. My back and loins feel as if I had been beaten to a pulp. I believe I have strained every muscle of my arms, and my hands and wrists are so stiff that I can't close my fingers."

"Yes; calf-chucking is pretty hard work until you get accustomed to it," the cowboy said. "It is knack more than strength, though it needs a lot of strength too when you have got a rampagious ten-months calf in your hands."

"I have not got the knack yet," Hugh said; "and anything over six months I had to have roped by the legs and thrown, but I suppose I shall be able to tackle them in time."

In the case of the cows that had been branded only a year or two before there was no difficulty in recognizing the brand, and so to decide upon the ownership of the calf; but in the case of older cows the brand and ear-marks had in some instances both become so far obliterated that it was difficult to decide what they had originally been. Over these brands there were sharp and sometimes angry disputes among the cowboys belonging to the different ranches. The case was generally settled by the overseer in charge of the day's operations calling upon three cowboys belonging to ranches unconnected with the dispute to give their opinion as to what the marks had originally been. Their decision was accepted by all parties as final, and the cow rebranded as well as the calf.

"What do you do when the brand is so far gone as to make it altogether impossible to say what it was?" Hugh asked.

"It would not get here at all in that state," the cowboy replied. "It would have been rebranded at once by the outfit that first found it just as if it had been a maverick. But in that case, of course, any cowboy could claim the cow as belonging to his ranche if he could convince the others that the old brand was the one used by it. They never brand over the old mark; that must be left as an evidence."

The next day happened to be Sunday, and Hugh felt glad indeed that he had a day on which to recover from his stiffness. Sundays were always kept, except in cases of great emergency, as a day of rest, cowboys taking the opportunity to wash and mend their clothes, to practice shooting with their revolvers, or to run races with their horses. At rounds-up these races afford one of the chief interests to the cowboy, for rivalry between the various ranches runs high, and the men are ready to bet their "bottom dollar" upon the representative of their own ranche.

"Have you ever tried that horse of yours against anything fast, Hugh?" one of his comrades asked.

"No. I am sure he is very fast, but I have never really tried him."

"We were fools not to think of that before," Broncho Harry put in. "We ought to have raced him against some of the others, and have found out what he can do, and then we might have made a soft thing of it. I suppose you wouldn't mind trying him, Hugh?"

"Not at all. But if he is to race, you had better ride him instead of me. I shouldn't say you were much above nine stone and a half."

"I don't know what you mean by your stone," Harry said. "We don't reckon that way out here. I was a hundred and thirty-five pounds last time I weighed at the head station."

"That is two pounds more than I said. Well, I am certainly twenty pounds heavier—I should say twenty-five, and that makes a lot of difference."

"I should think so. Still we had best have a trial, Hugh, before we try to make a match. That is a good horse of yours. I mean the one you first mounted and who played such tricks with you. I should like some day to try him against my best, and see how they go. I dare say you will get him again before the round-up is over."

"What length do you run your races here, Broncho?"

"In general they are short dashes, not above half a mile at the outside, but sometimes a match is made for some distance. Well, when we have had dinner we will trot out into the plain. We must go off a goodish bit, and make sure that none of the boys of the other ranches are within sight."

Accordingly, when dinner was over, Broncho Harry and Hugh went out to the horses. Prince came trotting out as soon as he heard Hugh's whistle, and Broncho Harry soon dropped his noose over the neck of his own horse. They then put on the saddles and bridles which they had brought with them, and went off at a canter across the plains. They ran three or four trials. The result showed that Broncho's horse was quicker in getting off, and that in a quarter of a mile dash there was little to choose between them, but at longer distances than this Prince was, in spite of the greater weight he carried, much the faster.

"That horse can go," the cowboy said admiringly. "I shouldn't mind if there were a pack of Redskins coming behind me if I was on his back. The worst of him is he is so good-looking. If he was ugly to look at we might clean out all the camps, but he looks so good that I am afraid we shan't be able to get much money out of him. Well, now, we won't race him this evening. There are sure to be some matches on, and I will ride my horse. That way I shall find what there is in the camp, and whether there is anything that can beat him as much as your horse can do. Don't you go cavorting about on him; just let him run with the rest of the mob. Then he won't be noticed. There is too much to be got through in this camp for men to take stock of the horses. Then if we keep him dark we can get someone to set up his horse against the best of ours. We will put our boys up to it when we get back, or someone may be blowing about your horse."

There were, as the cowboy anticipated, a number of races run that evening. Broncho Harry beat two other horses, but lost his winnings and more in the third race, when he was beaten somewhat easily by an animal which in point of looks was greatly inferior of his own.

"That is just what I told you, Hugh," he said, when, after unsaddling his horse and sending it off to join its companions on the plains, he returned to the wagon. "I am a blessed fool, for I ought to have known that when that cross T's man offered to back that ugly-looking brute against mine, he wur a sight better than he looked. He just shot off like an arrow at starting. I didn't lose anything afterwards, but I couldn't pick up them three lengths he got in the first forty yards. If we make a match against him we must see that it ain't less than half a mile."

The next morning the work in the stockyards was resumed and continued throughout the week.

X. A RACE

"I don't think, Broncho," Hugh said one evening, "that I should do anything more about that race, if I were you, or if you do, don't lay out any money on it. There is just as much interest in a race if it is for a dollar or two as if all the boys in the outfit piled their money upon it. That horse beat yours pretty easily, quite as easy, I should say, as Prince could beat him for that distance, and I really don't think that Prince would have any pull of him in races of the length you have on here. In a twenty-mile gallop I feel sure he would leave anything in camp behind easily, but I certainly would not race him any long distance of that sort. If I had a troop of Indians after me, Prince would have to do his best whether it was twenty miles or fifty; but I would not press him when it was merely a question of making money on him. Your horse was beaten, and, of course, we none of us like to own that the cross T's men have got a better horse than we have. I am quite willing that Prince should run for the honour of the ranche, but I don't feel at all sure about his winning, and should be sorry to see the boys plank their dollars down heavily upon him."

"All right, Hugh! it is your horse, and I will do as you want; but I should like to take that fellow down a bit. He is one of those fellows as is always blowing. He rather likes to be thought a bad man, and is said to be very handy with his six-shooter."

On Sunday morning after breakfast was over the cowboy in question, with two or three men of the same ranche, came across from their wagon to that of the ⊿ men.

"Have you got anything else that can go in this crowd?" he said, addressing Broncho Harry. "There don't seem any horses worth talking about in the whole round-up. Some of our boys say as how they have seen one of your lot on a likely-looking bay."

"Well, I don't deny he is a good-looking horse," Broncho Harry said, "and can go a bit, but he is slow at starting, and that critter of yours is too speedy for the bay to have a chance of catching him up in a quarter of a mile. Make it a bit over, and I will ride him myself against you if you like."

"I don't care about a half-mile," the man said, "but I will split the difference, if you like; or if you fancy your critter for a long journey, I am open to make a match ten miles out and back, each side to put down two hundred dollars."

"What do you say to that, mate?" Broncho Harry said, turning to Hugh.

Hugh shook his head decidedly. "I wouldn't have him ridden at racing speed twenty miles if there were a thousand dollars at stake," he said; "but if you like to take up the other offer you can ride him."

"Oh! it is your horse, is it?" the cowboy said; "why don't you ride him yourself?"

"Because I ride something like two stone heavier than you do," Hugh said; "and if the horse is going to race he may as well have a fair chance."

"Well, how much shall it be for?" the cowboy said, turning again to Broncho Harry. "I suppose we may as well say the same stake. A hundred dollars a side, I suppose. That won't hurt you, if you fancy the horse."

Two or three of the men broke in together, "Take him up, Broncho, we will all chip in."

"Very well, then, that is settled," Broncho Harry said. "Shall we say five o'clock? I suppose we shall ride the same course as last time. I will go out now and step the distance if you will go on with me."

"All right!" the man said; and they at once proceeded to mark out a distance of seven hundred paces, which they both agreed was somewhere about halfway between a quarter and half a mile. A wand, to which Broncho attached his neckerchief, was stuck up as the winning-post, while a low bush marked the point from which they had started to measure. The news soon spread through the camp, and many of the cowboys of the other ranches strolled in to find out what the △ men thought of their chances, and to see whether they were disposed to back their horse. Hugh, however, persuaded them not to risk their money.

"You see," he said, "my horse didn't beat Broncho's by much."

"No more did the other chap, Hugh; he just jumped two lengths ahead, and after that Broncho held him."

"Yes, I know that," Hugh replied, "but we don't know that he was doing his best."

"That is so," Broncho agreed. "He knew he had got me, and there was no use in giving his horse away. I expect he had got a bit in hand. I don't think it is good enough to bet on. Now let us get this money together."

Twenty of the men put down their five dollars at once; and as the others wished also to have a share, Broncho Harry said, "Well, you three put in your five dollars each, and Hugh and I will make it up to fifty. Like enough they will be laying odds on their horse, especially when they find we won't bet, so that at the last moment I will take them up for this fifty, and if we win we will put it to the stakes and divide up all round."

The proposal was at once agreed to.

Towards the afternoon they found that the ⚔ men were offering three and four to one upon the horse, for the odds had run up rapidly, as none of the other cowboys were disposed to back the △, seeing that the men of that ranche would not bet on their horse. At the appointed hour the two competitors went to the post. There had been several minor races, but these had attracted comparatively little interest; every man in camp, however, had assembled for the purpose of seeing this contest, and they were now gathered near the winning-post. A cowboy belonging to a neutral ranche was to act as starter. The two riders had divested themselves of their heavy boots.

"You must shake him up to begin with, Broncho," Hugh had said to him before he mounted. "He will do his best afterwards. He hates being passed, and when he sees the other ahead of him he will go all he knows."

"Now," the starter said, when the two horses stood side by side in a line with him, "I shall walk on twenty or thirty yards ahead so that you can both see me, then I shall hold up my six-shooter and fire. Don't either of you start till I do. I may fire straight off. I may wait a minute after I have got my hand up. You have got to keep your eyes on me, and when you see the flash then you let them go."

Both men fastened their spurs on to their stockinged feet, and as the pistol went off struck their heels into their mounts, while, at the same moment, Broncho Harry brought down his whip smartly on Prince's quarter. Astonished at this treatment, the animal gave a bound forward and started at full gallop.

There was no occasion for the other man to use his whip; his horse knew what was expected of it, and with its hind legs gathered under it, had been expecting the signal, and was even more quickly away than Prince. It did not, however, gain more than a length. For the first three hundred yards the horses maintained their relative position, but Prince was tugging at his bridle; and his rider, though shouting and yelling as if to urge him to his fullest speed, was yet holding him in. Then the leading horseman, thinking that Prince was doing his best, and feeling certain that he had the race in hand, dug his spurs into his horse, and the animal in a few bounds had added another length to his lead; but Broncho Harry loosened his pull at the reins and let Prince go, and before another hundred yards had been passed his head was level with the other's stirrup.

The ✼ man whipped and spurred, while Broncho Harry sat quiet on his horse, and contented himself by maintaining his present position. When a hundred yards from home he shook his horse up, and slightly touched him with his spur. Almost instantaneously Prince was level with his opponent, and then dashing on ahead passed the flag-post three lengths in advance amidst a loud cheer from the △ men, and from most of the other cowboys; for although few had ventured to back the horse, there was a general feeling of satisfaction at seeing the ✼ man beaten. The latter without a word circled round and rode straight back to his wagon, and the stakeholder handed over the stake and bets, which had both been deposited with him, to Broncho Harry.

"Two hundred and fifty dollars," he said, as he put the roll of notes in his pocket, for the bets had been made at three to one. "I call that an easier way of making money than cow-punching. I can't stand treat, boys, because there is no liquor in camp, but remember I owe you one all round the first time we meet in a saloon."

Returning to camp the division was made, and each of the twenty-five men received his share of ten dollars, together with the money he had staked.

"I shouldn't be surprised, Hugh," Broncho Harry said as they sat round the fire, "if we have trouble with that skunk. He is a bad-tempered lot at best, and he dropped his money heavy, for I hear he put in all the stake himself, and he bet some besides. He took twenty off me last week, but he has dropped pretty well half his season's money. You see if he don't try and get up trouble."

"If he does, leave him to me, Harry."

"I don't want to leave him to you, Hugh. I rode the race, and if he wants fighting, he will get it here; but I am afraid it is likely enough he will try and make trouble with you. He knows that I am a pretty tough hand, but he thinks you nothing but a ten-derfoot, and that sort of fellow always fixes a quarrel on a soft if he gets the chance."

"Well, as you know, Harry, I can take care of myself, and I would much rather it was me than you. I know that you are a good deal better shot than I am, but you know you are not nearly so quick with your weapon. There would be no occasion to shoot, I fancy."

"You are right there, lad; if you get the drop on him, you will see he will weaken directly."

The evening, however, passed off without the defeated cow-boy making his appearance.

"He reckons it wouldn't do," Long Tom said. "You see the hull crowd would be agin him if he were to come and get up a muss because he has been beat in a race. A fellow who runs his horse is bound to look pleasant whether he wins or whether he loses, and a good many of the boys was saying as they never see a worse thing than the way he galloped off after Broncho came in ahead of him. If he was to come down here and make a muss, he knows that for sure the crowd wouldn't stand it, and that if everything wasn't perfectly square, they would come Judge Lynch on him in no time. Now a man may take the chance of being shot in a quarrel; but when, if he ain't shot by one man he is likely to get hung by a crowd, it takes a pretty hard man to run the chances; only, look out for him, Broncho. I believe he has got a touch of Mexican blood in him, although, I dare say, he would shoot the man who ventured to say so, only it is there for all that, and you know a Mexican don't mind waiting months so that he gets even at last."

"That's so," Broncho Harry agreed; "a greaser is about the worst sort of white; that is, if you can call them white. I don't know but I hate them more than Injuns."

On the following morning half No. 1 outfit started north, with a herd of five thousand cattle that had been picked out from those driven in and branded; and Hugh, with his four mates, now took their turn at driving in the herds to the yard. This was much more to Hugh's taste than the previous work had been. He did not mind the work of hauling out and throwing the calves, nor of keeping back the cows, but he hated seeing the calves branded, and still more, the operation of cutting their ears. It was, of course, necessary work, but it was painful to him to share in, and indeed he had generally managed to get Bill Royce to exchange work with him when he was told off to perform these operations.

The herding, on the other hand, was good fun. The animals seemed to have an instinctive repulsion for the stockyard; many of them had been branded there the previous year, and probably recognized the spot. At any rate, there were constant attempts to break away, and it needed all the energy and vigilance of their guard to drive them down to the yard, and still more to keep them there while awaiting their turn to enter it. But more exciting still, and much more dangerous, was the work of those who kept guard at the lower end of the yard. As the animals came out, the calves were half mad with terror and pain, and the cows furious at the defeat of their efforts to succour their offspring, so that it was dangerous work for the men of the various ranches to pick out the animals bearing their brand and to drive them off to the knot of animals gathered at some little distance away under the guard of two of their comrades.

Sometimes the cows made furious charges, which it needed all the agility of horse and rider to avoid; then, as the animal rushed past, a rope would be thrown over its head or under its leg, and an instant later it would come to the ground with a crash. This generally proved sufficient. The cow, when the rope was slackened, rose to its feet in a half-dazed way and walked heavily off, with the evident impression upon its mind that an earthquake had taken place. Hugh was glad when he heard in the middle of the day that the rest of the outfit had arrived with the wagon and all the horses—for he felt that Prince had had enough of it—and he at once galloped off, roped one of his own horses, shifted the saddle on to him, and went back to work.

One or two of the bulls gave a great deal of trouble, charging hither and thither furiously as they came out from the yard. In these cases three or four of the cowboys united, and while one attracted his attention, the others threw their ropes. Some of the bulls had to be thrown half a dozen times before they were subdued.

A few days later the ✗ man, who went by the name of Flash Bill, walked up to the fire round which the cowboys of No. 2 outfit were sitting.

"I have just come across to say I am sorry I rode off that day you beat me, Broncho. I allow it was a mean trick of me, but I was riled pretty considerable; still I oughtn't ter have done it; it wurn't the right thing."

"It wurn't," Harry said; "but now you own up there is an end of it. Sit right down and have a smoke."

For some time the conversation turned upon horses. Two or three other men of the ✗ ranche sauntered up and joined in. Presently Flash Bill turned to Hugh, who had taken no part in the conversation, and said, "Have you a mind to trade that horse?"

"No, I wouldn't sell it at any price," Hugh said. "It exactly suits me, and I should find difficulty in getting another as good."

"Seems to me as I have seen that horse before," the man said. "Had him long?"

"I have had him about eight months," Hugh replied.

"Curious; I seem to know him. Can't think where I have seen him; somewhere out West."

"I bought him at M'Kinney," Hugh said.

"Oh! You bought him, did you?"

"How do you suppose I got him?" Hugh asked shortly.

"Oh! there are plenty of horses out on these plains as never was paid for," Flash Bill said.

"I don't say there are not," Hugh replied. "At any rate, I expect you are a better authority about that than I am."

"What do you mean by that?"

"I mean exactly what I say," Hugh said quietly.

"Do you mean to say as I have been a horse thief?" the man exclaimed furiously.

"I mean to say exactly what I did say," Hugh replied.

"Then you are a liar!" and the man's hand went to his hip. To his astonishment, before his finger had closed on the butt of his pistol, he was looking down the barrel of Hugh's revolver.

"Drop that," Hugh exclaimed, "or I fire!" Flash Bill threw up his hand.

"Now you will take that back," Hugh said.

"I take it back," Flash Bill said sullenly. "You've got the drop on me, though how you did it I don't know. There ain't nothing more to be said. I take it back."

"There is an end of it, then," Hugh said, replacing his pistol in his belt. "You thought you had got a soft thing. You see you've made a mistake."

"You had better git, Flash Bill," Broncho Harry said. "You ain't wanted here. You came over to make a muss, and only I knowed as Hugh could hold his own with you I would have put a bullet into you myself when I saw your hand go to your pistol.

You git, and if you will take my advice, you will git altogether. You can't play the bad man in this camp any longer, after weaking before a young chap as is little more than a tenderfoot."

With a muttered execration Flash Bill got up, and, followed by the men of his own ranche, walked off.

"You did mighty well, considering that it is the first trouble you've been in, Hugh; but you did wrong in not shooting. The rule on the plains is, if one man calls another either a liar or a coward, that fellow has a right to shoot him down if he can't get his gun out first. That's the rule, ain't it, boys?"

There was a chorus of assent.

"You may call a man pretty nigh everything else, and it don't go for much. We ain't chice as to our words here; but them two words, liar and coward, is death, and you would have done well to have shot him. You bet, you'll have trouble with that fellow some day. You'll see he will go now, but you'll hear of him again."

"I could no more have shot him than I could have flown," Hugh said, "for he was really unarmed."

"He would have shot you if he had been heeled first," Long Tom said, "and there ain't a man in the camp but would have said that you had been perfectly right if you had shot him, for it is sartin he came over here bound to kill you. I agree with Broncho. You have done a mighty soft thing, and maybe you will be sorry for it some day. I have heard say that Flash Bill has been a mighty hard man in his time, and I guess as stealing horses ain't been the worse thing he has done, and I reckon he has come back here to work for a bit, because he has made it too hot for himself in the settlements. Well, it's a pity you didn't shoot."

The next morning, as they were saddling their horses, Flash Bill rode past. He had his blankets and kit strapped behind his saddle. He checked his horse as he came up to them. "I give you warning," he said to Hugh, "that I'll shoot at sight when we meet again! You too, Broncho Harry!"

"All right!" Broncho Harry replied. "We shall both be ready for you." Without another word Flash Bill put spurs to his horse and galloped away.

This was the regular form of challenge among the cowboys. Sometimes after a quarrel, in which one had got the drop on the other, and the latter had been obliged to "take back" what he had said, mutual friends would interfere; and if the row had taken place when one or other of the men had been drinking, or when there was no previous malice or dislike between the men, the matter would be made up and things go on as before. If, however, the quarrel had been a deliberate one, and one or other considered himself still aggrieved, he would take his discharge and leave the camp on the following morning, giving his antagonist notice that he should shoot at sight when they next met, and whether the meeting was alone on the plains, in a drinking saloon, or in a street, both parties would draw and fire the moment their eyes fell on each other.

That Flash Bill should have been forced to take back his words by this young hand of the △ ranche was a matter of the deepest astonishment to the camp, and Hugh found himself quite a popular character, for Flash Bill had himself very obnoxious; and with the exception of two or three men of his own stamp in the ✕ outfit, the men of that body were more pleased than anyone else that the bully had had to leave. None were more astonished than the men of the other outfits of the △ ranche. They had heard Hugh addressed as Lightning; but curiosity is not a cowboy failing, and few had given a thought as to how he had come by the appellation. One or two had asked the question, but Broncho Harry had, the night before his party started to the round-up, said to the others, "Look here, boys. If anyone asks how Lightning Hugh came by his name, don't you give him away. They will larn one of these days, and it will be as good as a theyater when he does that gun trick of his. So keep it dark from the other boys."

The few questions asked, therefore, had been met with a laugh.

"It is a sort of joke of ours," Broncho Harry had said to one of the questioners. "You will see one of these days why it fits him."

Hugh was not sorry when the time came for his outfit to start. They had charge of a herd of eight or nine thousand animals all belonging to the ⚠. It was customary for most of the ranches to drive their own cattle, after a round-up, towards the neighbourhood of their station for the convenience of cutting out the steers that were to be sent down to market, or herds, principally of cows and calves, for puchasers who intended to establish ranches in the still unoccupied territory in New Mexico, Colorado, Dakota, and Montana. Some of these herds would have thousands of miles to travel, and be many months upon the journey. Many of the cowboys looked forward to taking service with these herds, and trying life under new conditions in the northern territories.

When the beef herds, and such cow herds as the manager of the ranche wished to sell, had been picked out and sent off, the rest of the cattle would be free to wander anywhere they liked over the whole country until they were again swept together for the round-up, unless other sales were effected in the meantime, in which case parties of cowboys would go out to cut out and drive in the number required. The number of cattle collected at the round-up was enormous, many of the ranches owning from forty to eighty thousand cattle. A considerable number were not driven in at the round-up, as the greater portion of the beef-cattle, which had already been branded, were cut out and left behind by the various outfits, and only the cows and calves, with a few bulls to serve as leaders, were driven in. Nevertheless, at these great rounds-up in Texas, the number of the animals collected mounted up to between two and three hundred thousand.

Two-thirds of the work was over when No. 2 outfit of the ⚠ ranche started.

"Well, I am glad that is over, Bill," Hugh said, as they halted at the end of the first day's march.

"I am not sorry," Bill Royce replied; "it is desperate hard work. All day at the stockyard, and half one's time at night on guard with the herds, is a little too much for anyone."

"Yes, it has been hard work," Hugh said; "but I don't think I meant that so much as that it was not so pleasant in other ways as usual. The men are too tired to talk or sing of an evening. One breakfasted, or rather swallowed one's food half asleep before daylight, took one's dinner standing while at work, and was too tired to enjoy one's supper."

"I reckon it has been a good round-up," Broncho Harry said. "There have been only four men killed by the cattle, and there haven't been more than five or six shooting scrapes. Let me think! yes, only five men have been shot."

"That is five too many, Broncho," Hugh said.

"Well, that is so in one way, Hugh; but you see we should never get on out here without shooting."

"Why shouldn't we?"

"Because we are an all-fired rough lot out here. There ain't no law, and no sheriffs, and no police, and no troops. How in thunder would you keep order if it weren't for the six-shooter? Thar would be no peace, and the men would be always quarrelling and wrangling. How would you work it anyhow? It is just because a quarrel means a shooting scrape that men don't quarrel, and that everyone keeps a civil tongue in his head. There ain't nowhere in the world where there is so little quarrelling as out here on the plains. You see, if we didn't all carry six-shooters, and were ready to use them, the bad-tempered men, and the hard men, would have it their own way. Big fellows like you would be able to bully little fellows like me. We should get all the bad men from the towns whenever they found the settlements too hot for them. We should have murderers, and gamblers, and horse thieves coming and mixing themselves up with us. I tell you, Hugh, that without the revolver there would be no living out here. No, sirree, the six-shooter puts us all on a level, and each man has got to respect another. I don't say as there ain't a lot wiped out every year, because there is; but I say that it is better so than it would be without it. When these plains get settled up, and the grangers have their farms on them, and the great cattle ranches go, and you get sheriffs, and judges, and all that, the six-shooter will go too, but you can't do without it till then. The revolver is our sheriff, and judge, and executioner all rolled in one. No one who is quiet and peaceable has got much occasion to use it."

"I nearly had to use it the other day, Broncho, and I reckon I am quiet and peaceable."

"Waal, I don't altogether know about that, Hugh. I don't say as you want to quarrel, quite the contrary, but you made up your mind before you came here that if you got into trouble you were going to fight, and you practised and practised until you got so quick that you are sure you can get the drop on anyone you get into a muss with. So though you don't want to get in a quarrel, if anyone wants to quarrel with you you are ready to take him up. Now if it hadn't been so there wouldn't have been any shooting-irons out the other night. Flash Bill came over to get up a quarrel. He was pretty well bound to get up a quarrel with someone, but if you had been a downright peaceable chap he could not have got up a quarrel with you. If you had said quietly, when he kinder said as how you hadn't come by that horse honest, that Bill here had been with you when you bought him, and that you got a document in your pocket, signed by a sheriff and a judge, to prove that you had paid for it, there would have been no words with you. I don't say as Flash Bill, who was just spoiling for a fight, wouldn't have gone at somebody else. Likely enough he would have gone at me. Waal, if I had been a quiet and peaceable chap I should have weakened too, and so it would have gone on until he got hold of somebody as wasn't going to weaken to no one, and then the trouble would have begun. I don't say as this is the place for your downright peaceable man, but I say if such a one comes here he can manage to go through without mixing himself up in shooting scrapes."

"But in that way a man like Flash Bill, let us say, who is known to be ready to his pistol, might bully a whole camp."

"Yas, if they wur all peaceable people; but then, you see, they ain't. This sort of life ain't good for peaceable people. We take our chances pretty well every day of getting our necks broke one way or another, and when that is so one don't think much more of the chance of being shot than of other chances. Besides, a man ain't allowed to carry on too bad. If he forces a fight on another and shoots him, shoots him fair, mind you, the boys get together and say this can't go on; and that man is told to git, and when he is told that he has got to, if he don't he knows what he has got to expect. No, sirree, I don't say as everything out in the plains is just arranged as it might be in New York; but I say that, take the life as it is, I don't see as it could be arranged better. There was a chap out here for a bit as had read up no end of books, and he said it was just the same sort of thing way back in Europe, when every man carried his sword by his side and was always fighting duels, till at last the kings got strong enough to make laws to put it down and managed things without it; and that's the way it will be in this country. Once the law is strong enough to punish bad men, and make it so that there ain't no occasion for a fellow to carry about a six-shooter to protect his life, then the six-shooter will go. But that won't be for a long time yet. Why, if it wasn't for us cowboys, there wouldn't be no living in the border settlements. The horse thieves and the outlaws would just rampage about as they pleased, and who would follow them out on the plains and into the mountains? But they know we won't have them out here, and that there would be no more marcy shown to them if they fell into our hands than there would be to a rattler. Then, again, who is it keeps the Injuns in order? Do you think it is Uncle Sam's troops? Why, the Redskins just laugh at them. It's the cowboys."

"It ain't so long ago," Long Tom put in, "as a boss commissioner came out to talk with the natives, and make them presents, and get them to live peaceful. People out in the east, who don't know nothing about Injuns, are always doing some foolish thing like that. The big chief he listens to the commissioner, and when he has done talking to him, and asks what presents he should like, the chief said as the thing that would most tickle him would be half a dozen cannons with plenty of ammunition."

"'But,' says the commissioner, 'we can't give you cannon to fight our troops with.'

"'Troops!' says the chief; 'who cares about the troops? We can just drive them whenever we like. We want the cannon to fight the cowboys.'

"That chief knew what was what. It is the cowboys as keep back the Redskins, it's the cowboys as prevent these plains getting filled up with outlaws and horse thieves, and the cowboys can do it 'cause each man has got six lives pretty sartin at his belt, and as many more as he has time to slip in fresh cartridges for; and because we don't place much vally on our lives, seeing as we risk them every day. We know they ain't likely to be long anyhow. What with death among the herds, shooting scrapes, broken limbs, and one thing and another, and the work which wears out the strongest in a few years, a cowboy's life is bound to be a short one. You won't meet one in ten who is over thirty. It ain't like other jobs. We don't go away and take up with another trade. What should we be fit for? A man that has lived on horseback, and spent his life galloping over the plains, what is he going to do when he ain't no longer fit for this work? He ain't going to hoe a corn-patch or wear a biled shirt and work in a store. He ain't going to turn lawyer, or set up to make boots or breeches. No, sirree. He knows as ten years is about as much as he can reckon on if his chances are good, and that being so, he don't hold nothing particular to his life. We ain't got no wives and no children. We works hard for our money, and when we gets it we spend it mostly in a spree. We are ready to share it with any mate as comes along hard up. It might be better, and it might be worse. Anyway, I don't see no chance of changing it as long as there is room out west for cattle ranches. Another hundred years and the grangers will have got the land and the cowboys will be gone, but it will last our time anyhow."

Hugh was much struck with this estimate of a cowboy's life by one of themselves, but on thinking it over he saw that it was a true one. These men were the adventurous spirits of the United States. Had they been born in England they would have probably either enlisted or run away as boys and gone to sea. They were men to whom a life of action was a necessity. Their life resembled rather that of the Arab or the Red Indian than that of civilized men. Their senses had become preternaturally acute; their eyesight was wonderful. They could hear the slightest sound, and pronounce unhesitatingly how it was caused. There was not an ounce of unnecessary flesh upon them. Their muscles seemed to have hardened into whipcord.

They were capable of standing the most prolonged fatigue and hardship, and just as a wild stag will run for a considerable distance after receiving a wound that would be instantly fatal to a domestic animal, these men could, as he had seen for himself, and still more, as he had heard many anecdotes to prove, sustain wounds and injuries of the most terrible kind and yet survive, seeming, in many cases, almost insensible to pain. They were, in fact, a race apart, and had very many good qualities and comparatively few bad ones. They were, indeed, as Long Tom had said, reckless of their lives, and they spent their earnings in foolish dissipation. But they knew of no better way. The little border towns or Mexican villages they frequented offered no other amusements, and except for clothes and ammunition for their pistols they had literally no other need for their money.

Nothing could exceed the kindness with which they nursed each other in illness or their generosity to men in distress. They were devoted to the interests of their employers, undergoing, as a matter of course, the most prolonged and most prodigious exertions. They were frank, good-tempered, and kindly in their intercourse with each other, as addicted to practical jokes as so many schoolboys, and joining as heartily in the laugh when they happened to be the victims as when they were the perpetrators of the joke. Their code of honour was perhaps a primitive one, but they lived up to it strictly, and in spite of its hardships and its dangers there was an irresistible fascination in the wild life that they led.

XI. A FIRE ON THE PLAINS

After the hard work at the round-up the journey north seemed almost a holiday. Of an evening the cook's accordion was again brought out, and the men sang and, to Hugh's amusement, danced. He thought the proposal was a joke when it was first made, but he soon saw that it was quite serious. He had declined to take part in it, saying that he had never danced since he was a little boy; but it was as much as he could do to restrain his laughter, upon seeing the gravity with which eight of the cowboys went through a quadrille to the music of the accordion. Then followed waltzes, and then some Mexican dances, the entertainment being kept up for a couple of hours.

Dancing, indeed, is one of the favourite amusements of cowboys, and there being no females to dance with they dance with each other, and are so accustomed to do so that it comes to them as naturally as if dancing with women. When, however, they are camped within thirty or forty miles of a Mexican village, it is no unusual thing for a party of half a dozen to ride over to it. Perhaps one has preceded them to make the arrangements. These are simple. The Mexicans are very musical, and there is not a village where men capable of playing upon the mandoline, and perhaps other instruments, cannot be found. An arrangement is made with these and with the landlord of the little inn.

The preparations are not expensive—spirits for the men and a supply of cakes and syrups for the women. The news spreads like lightning, and in the evening Mexican villagers, male and female, in their best attire, from miles round arrive, some in carts and some on horseback. The music strikes up, and the dance is kept up until morning. Occasionally these entertain-

169

ments end with a fray, arising generally from the jealousy of
some young Mexican at the complacency with which his sweet-
heart receives the attentions of a cowboy admirer. But these are
quite the exceptions. The Mexicans know that their hosts will be
off in the morning, and that they shall probably never see them
again, and they therefore put up philosophically with the temporary inconstancy of the damsels of their village.

To the Mexican girls, indeed, these cowboys are veritable
heroes. They have heard endless tales of their courage. They
know that the Indians, who hold their countrymen in absolute
contempt, fear to meet these terrible herdsmen. The careless
way in which they spend their money, their readiness to bestow
their gorgeous silk handkerchiefs, their really handsome and
valuable sashes, or the gold cord of their hats, upon their
favourite partner for the evening, fills them with admiration.
They know, too, that when, as occasionally happens, a cowboy
does marry a Mexican girl, and settles down upon some little
ranche among them, the lot of his wife is greatly easier than that
of those who marry Mexicans, and that she will be treated with
an amount of consideration and courtesy undreamt of by the
Mexican peasant, who, although an humble adorer before marriage, is a despotic master afterwards. It is not surprising, then,
that upon occasions like these the cowboy hosts have a monop-
oly of the prettiest girls at the ball.

Round the camp fires in the evening Hugh heard many tales
of such evenings spent in the villages of New Mexico.

"I had a very narrow escape once," a cowboy known as
Straight Charley said. "There were six of us went up together to
a Mexican village, and we gave a first-rate hop. There was a big
crowd there, and things went on well until there was a muss
between one of our fellows and a Mexican. Jake was rather a
hard man, and we hadn't much fancied his being of our party,
for he was fonder of drink than of dancing, and was quarrelsome
when the drink was in him. I don't know how the muss began,
for I was dancing with as pretty a little Mexican girl as I ever
came across. However, I haven't any doubt as Jake was in the
wrong. The first I knowed about it was that the music stopped,

and then I heard loud voices. I saw a knife flash, and dropped my partner, and was going to run in to stop it, but I hadn't more than thought about it when there was the crack of a pistol. Then knives were out all round, and there was a pretty lively fight.

"It seemed, as I heard afterwards, that when Jake shot the Mexican—and I don't say he had no right to do so when the Mexican had drawn his knife first, for if he had not shot he would have been killed himself—two or three other Mexicans went for him, and, as a matter of course, two of our fellows went for the Mexicans. If they hadn't been all mixed up together the six of us could have cleared the hull lot out, but mixed up like that, and with girls about, our fellows hadn't much show. I was just breaking through to take a hand in the game, when a fellow who had been looking pretty sour at me for some time, jumped on my back like a wild cat, so down I went, and in half a minute my legs and arms were tied tight with their sashes. I didn't try to struggle after I had fallen, for I knew well enough that our fellows had got the worst of it.

"When matters cleared up a bit I found that four Mexicans had been killed, and five or six others pretty badly hurt. Jake and another of our boys were dead; two others had broke out, run to their horses, and ridden away. Another of the boys had been taken prisoner, but he had got two or three knife-cuts before he was knocked down. There was a big hubbub for some time, as you may guess, and then they told us we should be taken to the town in the morning. Well, they took off the sashes, and marched us away to a house at the end of the village. It was a plank house, and built in the same fashion as their adobe huts, with one room behind the other. Of course they had taken our six-shooters and knives away from us, and they shoved us into the inner room, and then a dozen of them sat down to play cards and keep watch in the other.

"The place had been built as a sort of lock-up, and there were heavy bars to the window, just as you see in a good many Mexican houses. They had left our legs free, but had put some ropes round our arms; but we knew that we could shift them easy enough. The Mexicans had shut the door between the two rooms, but we could hear their talk through it, and we heard that, though the thing had been brought on by Jake, there would have been a muss anyhow sooner or later. Two white men had come into the village a fortnight before; they were dressed like cowboys, but I reckon they were horse stealers or outlaws, anyhow they had kicked up a row and shot three men, and rode away, and the Mexicans had seemed to make up their minds that they would take revenge on the next party that came in, whoever they were.

"Well, things looked pretty bad for us. If we had once got inside one of their prisons, the Mexican judges would have made short work of us. The greasers would, of course, have sworn that we had begun the row, and shot down four or five of their people without the least cause, and it would have been a case of hanging, as sure as a gun; so Dave and I agreed that we had got to git somehow. It wur no use talking of fighting, for there was a dozen fellows in the next room, and they had all got their guns along with them. We hadn't got our knives, and there was no chance of cutting our way out. We were talking it over when someone said, 'Are you there, Charley?' at the window. It was one of the boys who had got away. You bet I was there pretty sharp.

"'Here I am, Ginger,' I said. 'How goes it?' 'Pretty bad,' he said; 'Jeffries is cut pretty near to pieces, and I am wounded in half a dozen places, and can scarce crawl. Jeffries is with the horses a mile away. He is too bad to stand. I made a shift to crawl back to see what had become of you. I have been creeping round, and heard the two of you were shut up here, and that you was going to be taken off to-morrow, and would be hung, sure, so I came round to see what could be done; here is my six-shooter if it will be any good to you.' 'No, that won't be any good,' I said; 'there are twelve of them, and they have all got guns; but give me your knife; these planks are pretty thick, but we can cut our way through.' 'I haven't got it,' says Ginger; 'it was knocked out of my belt in the fight, and, worse luck, Jeffries has lost his too. A fellow got hold of his wrist, so he couldn't use his pistol, and he drew his knife, and he was fighting with it, when he got a slice across his fingers which pretty nigh cut them off, and he dropped his knife, and, as luck would have it, just wrenched himself free and bolted.'

"'Well, we must do what we can,' I said; 'but it is hard luck on us. Look here, Ginger, you bring the two horses up to that clump of trees over there; Dave is pretty badly cut about, and cannot run far, but he can make a shift to get over there. If we don't come by an hour before daylight it ain't no use your waiting no longer; you go and pick up Jeffries, and make tracks; but I reckon that somehow we shall manage to come.' 'All right!' says he, and went. 'Now, Dave,' I said, 'you turn over and let me get my teeth at your knots, it is hard if I don't manage to undo them.'

"Sure enough, in five minutes I had loosed a knot, and then the rest was easy. Dave untied me, and we were free so far. 'What next?' says Dave. 'We will have a look round,' says I. Luckily there was a moon, and there was plenty of light to see what was in the room. There was some bits of furniture and bedding, just as they had been left by the people they had turned out to make room for us, but nothing that I could find as would help us to cut our way out. 'Now, Dave,' says I, 'you get to that corner and I will get to this, and just shove against the planks, and see if we can't push the hull side of this shanty out.' Well, it wur too strong for us. It was made of rough boards, pretty strongly nailed. I thought it gave a little, but nothing as would be any good. 'If we could throw ourselves against it both together it might go,' I said; 'but it mightn't, and if it didn't we should have them inside in a moment, and there would be an end to it. What do you say to our burning ourselves out, Dave?'

"'How are we to do that, Charley?' he said. 'Well, I have got my box of matches in my boot, and I suppose you have yours too. Let us pile up some of these wooden things against the two corners; there is plenty of straw in this bed. Before we begin we will hang one of these blankets over the doorway so as to keep the smoke from going through the cracks. I reckon they are all smoking in there, and they won't smell it very quick.' So we made a pile, moving as quiet as we could, standing still when they were not talking much in the next room, and moving whenever they made a row, which was pretty often. 'These things are as dry as chips,' I said, 'and what smoke there is will mostly go out through the window, but I expect that there will be more than we shall like. Here is a big pitcher of water, we will soak these two blankets, and then lie down close to the floor; you cover your head over with one, and I will do it with the other. Now, then!'

"We lit a couple of matches and touched off the straw, and in half a minute there was a blaze up to the roof. Then we lay down by the other wall one on each side of the door, and waited. In about two minutes there was a shout in the next room and a rush, then the door was flung open and the blanket torn down, and such a yelling and cussing as you never heard. The smoke was pretty bad where we was lying, and I reckon that up higher it was as thick as a wall. 'The cursed Americans have lighted the house and smothered themselves,' one of them shouted. Then they rushed out, coughing and choking, and we heard them shouting for water, and there wur as much row as if the village had been attacked by Injuns.

"We waited another three or four minutes, and then Dave shouted, 'I can't stand this no longer.' I had hoped they would have left the outer door open, and that we could have got out that way, but we had heard it shut. I expect someone more cute than the rest suspected we wur inside biding our time. 'Take a long breath, Dave,' says I, 'and don't breathe again until you are out; now jump up and join me.' We joined hands and made a run, and threw ourselves against one corner of the end of the hut. Several of the planks fell, and a couple of kicks sent the rest out, then off we bolted.

"There wur a yell outside, for by this time half the village were there. Luckily the men with guns was mostly round by the door, and when the yells fetched them there was too many women and children about for them to shoot. We went straight on, as you may guess, and we were halfway to the woods before the shooting began, and it wur pretty wild at that. Dave gave out afore he got to the trees, and I had to carry him.

"'This way,' Ginger shouted. I lifted Dave on to a horse, and jumped up behind him, and we wur off just as the Mexicans came running up. After that it wur easy enough. We rode to where Jeffries had been left, got him on to Ginger's horse, and made tracks for the camp. Jeffries died next day, but Dave got over it. That wur a pretty near touch, I reckon."

"It was indeed," Hugh said. "That was a very lucky idea of yours of burning out the corners of the house."

"Some of them Mexicans is cusses," another cowboy put in. "I had a smart affair with them in one of their villages last year. I had rid in with Baltimore Rube. We had been searching some of the gullies for cows, and had run short of sugar and tea. Waal, I was on a young broncho I had only roped two days before, and the critter wur as wild as could be. When we rode in, a lot of them brutes of dogs that swarms almost as thick as their fleas in all these Mexican villages, came barking round, while one big brute in particular made as if he would pin my broncho by the nose, and the pony plunged and kicked till I thought he would have me off. There was a lot of their men standing at their doors smoking, for it wur late in the afternoon, and they wur all back from what they called work. I shouted to them to call their dogs off, but they just laughed and jeered, so I did the only thing as there was to do, just pulled out my six-shooter and shot the dog. Waal, if it had been a man there could not have been a worse sort of row. The Mexicans ran into their houses just as quick as a lot of prairie-dogs when they scent danger, and in a moment were back with their guns, and began to blaze away. Waal, naturally, our dander riz, a bullet chipped the bark off my cheek, and by the way my broncho jumped I knew one had hit him, so Baltimore and I blazed away in return, and neither of us didn't shoot to miss, you bet. We just emptied our six-shooters, and then rode for it.

"Baltimore got a shot in his shoulder. I had one in the leg, and there was two in the saddle. We talked it over and agreed it wur best to say nothing about it. Them Mexicans will swear black is white, and when there is a whole village swearing one way, and only two men swearing the other way, them two has got but a poor show of being believed. So we concluded to leave those parts altogether, and we rode a hundred and fifty miles in the next two days, and then camped for a week till our wounds healed up a bit.

"A fortnight after that we went into the station, and there I happened to light upon one of them rags the Mexicans calls papers, and there sure enough was the account of that business. 'Two cowboys, unknown, rode last week into the quiet village of Puserey, and without the slightest provocation commenced a murderous attack upon its inhabitants, and after killing four and wounding eight men, they galloped off before the inhabitants had time to betake themselves to their arms to defend themselves. A reward of five hundred dollars is offered for their apprehension.' Now, that wur a pretty tall piece of lying; but Baltimore and I agreed it wur best to keep dark about it altogether, for if it wur talked about, it might get to the ears of some of the half-caste Mexicans about the station, and some day or other, when we went into a village, we might find ourselves roped in."

"That is the way," Broncho Harry said indignantly, "us cowboys get a bad name. Now, I dare say that air article wur copied in half the newspapers in the States, and folks as know nothing about it would say, 'Them cowboys is a cuss; they ought to be wiped off the arth right away.' It is always so whenever there is a row between any of us and the Mexicans. They give thar account of it, and we goes away and thinks no more about it one way or the other, and there is no one to show it up as a lie from beginning to end; and I know there's people think we are as bad as the Injuns, if not worse, and that we ride about shooting down people just for amusement. Then all these outlaws and horse thieves and bad men near the settlements dress as much as they can like us, and every murder as they commits, every horse that gits stolen, every man that gits held up and robbed, it is just put down to the cowboys. While if the truth wur known, for every one of these fellows caught or wiped out by the sheriff and their posse, there is twenty gets wiped out by us."

There was a cordial "That is so, Broncho," all round the fire, for the injustice connected with their reputation was a very sore point among the cowboys.

"Well, some day, Broncho," Hugh said, "when I get away from here, for, as you know, I haven't come here to stay, I will take pen in hand and try to give a true account of you and your doings, so that people may see that there are two sides to the question."

"Bully for you, Hugh!" Long Tom said; "just you put it in hot and strong. I tell you it ain't nice if one goes down to the settlements in the winter, when work is slack, to see people look at you as if you wur a wild beast, who is only waiting his chance to hold up the hull town. Why, I have seen women pull their children indoors as I came along, as if I wur a mountain lion, and was meaning to draw my six-shooter on them just for amusement."

"Well," Hugh said, "I must say I heard stories at M'Kinney of cowboys coming down to a town and riding about shooting off the hats of the inhabitants, making targets of the bottles in the saloons, and generally turning the place topsy-turvy. Of course I didn't believe it all."

There was silence round the fire, and then Straight Charley said:

"Well, Lightning, I won't say as you have been altogether deceived as to that, and I won't deny as I have taken part in sprees myself, but you see it don't hurt no one. It is just fun. If we do shoot the heads off the bottles, we pays for them, and it makes one laugh till one can scarcely sit in a saddle to see an old cuss jump when you put a bullet through his stove-pipe hat. It is his fault for wearing such a thing, which is an unnatural invention altogether and should be discouraged."

"We do carry on," Broncho Harry agreed, "thar ain't no denying it. When a man has been out in these plains for six months working worse than a nigger, and that without a drop of liquor, it is natural as he should go in for a high old time when he gits down to a town with money in his pockets; but thar ain't no real harm in it. We know how we can shoot, and that if we fire at a hat there ain't no chance of our hitting the head inside. It just makes things lively for them for a bit, and there is never no trouble, unless anyone is fool enough to take the matter up and make a muss about it."

"I am not saying you do any real harm, Broncho, only you see the people in the towns don't know how well you shoot. If you knock a pipe out of my mouth, as you have done once or twice, I only laugh, because I know there was no chance in the world of your hitting me; but you see they don't all know that. And so when a man finds there are two holes in his hat an inch above his head, he thinks he has had a marvellous escape of being murdered."

"I don't deny as there is something in that," Broncho Harry said reflectively; "but you see it is in their ignorance that the mistake comes in, not in our shooting. Anyhow, you see we have got to do something to amuse ourselves, and we might do worse than just skeer a few storemen, who take it out of us by charging us about double the price they charge anyone else."

Hugh was not convinced by the argument, but he felt that it was of no use to pursue the subject further.

"How do the cows know their calves?" he asked one day, as at the end of a march some of the cows were loudly lowing for their offspring to come to them.

"By smell," Broncho Harry replied promptly.

"You don't see much of their ways here, for the calves are pretty well grown up; but when you are driving a herd, as I have done many a time, made up altogether of cows and young calves, you see a lot of it. Ten or twelve miles a day is as much as you can do with a herd of that sort. What steers there are always go ahead, grazing as they go. The cows will come straggling along next, and then the calves strung out all over the place, and the rearguard have pretty hard work to hurry them up. You see calves have got no sense, and run anywhere—under your horse's legs or anywhere else; while the cows don't pay much attention to them till they get to the end of the march. Then they begin to bawl for their calves to come to them, and the calves begin to bawl for their mothers, and I tell you that for a bit there is such a row going on that you would think the end of the world had come. Two thousand cows and as many calves can kick up a row, you bet, that will wellnigh scare you."

"But don't the calves know their mothers' voices?"

"Not a bit of it; it is just smell and nothing else that brings them together. You would think the cows would know something about the colour of their young uns, but they don't. I have seen a cow that I knew had a white calf run up to a black calf and smell it, then to a brown one, and then to a spotted one, while her own white calf stood bawling fit to kill herself a dozen yards away. It is wonderful how they do find each other at all, and the job often takes them two or three hours. Some of the cows concludes at last that their calves have been left behind, and then off they set, and would go all the way back to the place they had started from in the morning if you didn't stop them. Sometimes they don't find them at all that night."

"But what happens to the calves then?"

"The calves shift for themselves. They run up to other cows which have got their own calves sucking. Each cow will generally let them have a suck or two, and then drive them off, and in that way they get enough to last them on till they find their mothers in the morning.

"There is a good deal of trouble in keeping nightwatch over a herd like that. It isn't that there is any risk of a stampede. A cow herd will never stampede if there are a lot of young calves in it; but they don't settle themselves comfortable to sleep. The calves want to wander about, and the cows who haven't found their young ones keep trying to slip off to take the back track, and you have got to be always on the watch for them. Take it altogether, I would rather drive a beef herd than a cow herd."

After a week's travel they reached the spot that had been fixed upon for the herd to graze. The cowboys' work was now much lighter. Parties of twos and threes could often be spared for a day's excursion up to some Mexican village among the hills, or they would go off for three or four days' hunt among the valleys to pick up any cattle that had evaded search during the round-up. One day, when there were but four of them in camp, two of the party who had been absent a couple of days rode in at full speed, and reported to the head of the outfit that they had seen the light of a fire up north.

"Then there is no time to be lost," Colley said. "Will you two men stop here and look after things? I will ride off with the other four and fight the fire. When the others come back do you start out after us. The last two who come in must stop here. Give us what food you have got, darkey; we may be away four or five days. Directly we have gone set to and cook something for the others."

Hugh and Bill Royce had returned the day before from an expedition among the foothills. Broncho Harry and another cowboy were also in camp. In five minutes the horses were saddled, and they dashed off at full speed.

"It is lucky that the wind is not blowing strong," Colley said, "or we should have the fire down here before we got news of it, and there is no place handy where we could drive the herd. I expects those blessed Injuns lit the fire."

Hugh was very pleased that he was in camp when the news came. He had heard many stories from the cowboys of these terrible fires, and knew that at times they had wrought havoc among the herds, whose only hope of escape lay in reaching a stream wide enough to check the progress of the flames.

After riding twenty miles they could distinguish a faint odour of smoke in the air, and as they gained a crest soon after sunset could see a long line of light in the distance.

"It is a big un," Broncho Harry said, "and no mistake."

They lost no time in getting to work, for the wind was rising, and there was but little time to spare. They had on their way picked out a steer from a bunch they came upon, and had driven it before them, and had also stopped and cut faggots of wood from a clump of bushes in a hollow. A shot from Broncho Harry's revolver brought the bullock dead to the ground, and while Royce lit a fire the others with the long knives proceeded to split the bullock into two portions, dividing it from its head down to its tail.

"Now, Broncho, will you go east with Lightning while Royce and Jake go west? Keep on until you meet some fellows from the other outfits. They are sure to be at work all along the line. If you don't meet any by the time you get to the end of the flames, then work back and fight the fire as you come. I expect the other four men will be up in an hour or two."

Broncho Harry and Royce at once lit two of the long faggots, and fastened the others to their saddles. They then tied the ends of their ropes to the blazing faggots and started. Hugh having been already instructed in his part, fastened his rope to a leg of the half bullock, and mounted his horse—he had not brought Prince this time, as he feared that he might get burned. He waited until Broncho Harry was a quarter of a mile ahead. Already a line of fire was rising in his track, the dried grass catching like tinder as the blazing faggot passed over it. It had already run along a width of twenty feet or so, burning fiercely on the leeward side, and making its way in a thin red line to windward. It was the leeward side that Hugh had to attend to, and galloping his horse along the ground over which the flame had just passed, he dragged the half carcass of the bullock behind him, so that in its course it passed over the line of flame, which its weight and the raw under-surface instantly crushed out. For ten miles he rode on, and then found that Harry had stopped.

"We are beyond the edge of the fire," the latter said. "It is the other side where there is most danger, unless Smith's outfit have got news in time. Waal, we have done our part of the job so far."

Looking back Hugh saw a sea of fire approaching across the plains. The wind was blowing stronger now, and the air was full of smoke and ashes. Far along the track they had come a thin line of fire was advancing against the wind to meet the great wave that was sweeping down towards it.

"We passed some bushes half a mile back," Harry said. "We will ride back to them, and then let the horses go. We shan't want them any more, and they are pretty well mad with fright now."

As soon as they reached the bushes they leapt off, and letting the horses go cut as many boughs as they could carry. Then retiring from the strip of burnt ground, already forty or fifty yards wide, they awaited the flames. Their approach was heralded by burning fragments, and they were both soon at work beating out the flames as fast as they were kindled to leeward of the burnt strip. Single-handed they would not have succeeded, but other cowboys speedily arrived, and along the whole line parties were at work fighting the fire. At times it got such hold that it was only checked by lighting fresh fires to leeward, and crushing them out as had been done at first, and it was thirty hours before the fire was extinguished along that part of the line.

Then the news came that farther west it had burst through, and the cowboys, mounting fresh horses that had been brought up, rode off and joined in the fight there, and it was not until after three days' unremitting effort that the danger was finally subdued. During all this time the men had not a moment's rest. Their food and water had been sent up from the wagons, and a hasty meal was snatched occasionally. When all was done they were blackened with smoke and ashes. Their hair and clothes were singed, and they were utterly exhausted with their efforts. However, they had saved the herds, and were well content with their work; but, as soon as it was over, each man threw himself down where he stood and slept for many hours, watch being kept by some of the last arrivals, for it was by no means improbable that the Indians would swoop down to take advantage of the confusion and drive off cattle.

As soon as the cowboys were roused next morning they rode off to their respective outfits, and Hugh's party on their arrival enjoyed the luxury of a bathe in the stream, near which the wagon of No. 2 outfit was placed. Then, after their change of clothes, they gathered for a comfortable meal.

"Waal, Lightning, that has been a fresh experience for you," Broncho Harry said.

"I am glad I have seen it," Hugh replied; "but I don't want to repeat it."

"This was nothing, Hugh. Four years ago there was a fire here that swept right across the plains; there was a strong wind and no stopping it, and there were over a hundred thousand cattle burned. I suppose some day or other they will be passing laws for putting up fences. If they do, I tell you it will be something like ruin to a good many ranches, for it will prevent cattle from running before the flames. As it is now, their instinct takes them either to a stream or to some high bluff. But if there was fences they would never get away. In the north they lose whole herds in the same way from snowstorms. A herd will drift before snow and wind for hundreds of miles, but if there is anything that stops them they just get snowed up and die. Ranchmen have troubles enough, but if they was obliged to fence it would go far to break up the business.

"Look out, lads, here comes someone galloping into camp. I expect he has got news of the Redskins. I reckoned they would be out on the track of the fire.

"Oh, it's Tom Newport," he said, as the man approached. "Waal, what he says you may take for gospel. He is not one of them fellows who gets hold of the tail-end of a story and then scares the whole country. Waal, Tom, what is it?"

"Just mount up, Broncho, and get all your crowd together. There ain't no time for talking now; I will tell you all about it when we get on the track."

In an incredibly short time the men had all saddled, and were ready for a start, filling their water-skins, and getting from the cook what bread and cold meat remained over from breakfast. "Now, which way, Tom?"

"North-east. I will tell you about it. The Injuns have come down and attacked Gainsford. They have killed five or six men and most of the women and children. They have carried off five or six girls, and old man Rutherford's Rose is among them."

An exclamation of fury broke from several of the cowboys.

"Where is Gainsford? and who is Rutherford's Rose?" Hugh asked.

"Gainsford is a small place just among the foothills south of the Injun country. There are about twenty houses. Rutherford, he wur the first to settle there. We told him over and over agin that it wur to close to the Injuns, and that there would, sure, be trouble sooner or later; but Steve, that is Rutherford, is one of those pesky obstinate cusses who just go their own way, and won't listen to reason from no one. He got a little herd of cattle up in the valley there, and a patch of cultivated land, and he reckoned he wouldn't be solitary long. He was right enough there, for, as I told you, the place grew, and there are pretty nigh twenty houses there now, that is, there wur twenty houses; I don't suppose one is standing now. Rutherford, he wur a cowboy once, and married and settled down there, and Rose is his daughter, and as good a lass as there is west of Missouri. Rutherford's house is free quarters for those of us who likes to drop in. In course we makes it up to him by taking in a deer or a bear's ham, or maybe a few bottles of whisky, if we have been down to the settlement and laid hands on them, and if we come across any mavericks when we are alone, we just brand them R.R., and I reckon Rosie has got two hundred cattle out here, and they will come in mighty handy for her when she chooses a husband."

"Is that often done?" Hugh asked.

"You bet. There are a score and more girls, whose fathers' shanties lie up in the foothills, and who are friends of ours, have got a nice little clump of cattle out on these plains. Of course any man, living near the plains, can turn his cattle out, and there are dozens of private marks. Waal, you see, if a girl only gets twenty branded for her it increases every year, because the calves running with the cows get the same brand put on them; and I have known many a girl when she was married have a little herd of three or four hundred. So, I tell you, it hits us all that Rose Rutherford has been carried away, and we are bound to get her back if it air to be done. When was it, Tom, that it happened?"

"Yesterday evening, 'bout ten o'clock, I wur riding that way and intended to sleep at Steve's, when I saw a light burst up, and then two or three others. I galloped pretty hard, you may guess, but before I got thar it wur over and the Injuns had gone; but I larned from a boy who had been hiding among the bushes, but who came out when he saw me, how it wur. He said he had seen Rose and five or six other girls carried off. Whether old Steve wur rubbed out I don't know. I didn't stop to ask no questions. I knew whereabout your outfit was, and rode straight for it."

"Then the skunks have got sixteen or seventeen hours' start," Broncho said. "There is no chance of our catching them till they are right back into their own country. I reckon we shall have a pretty sharp fight of it before we get them gals back."

XII. AN INDIAN RAID

The cowboys were all mounted on horses that had not been worked for some days—Hugh was on Prince—and they got over the ground at great speed, arriving before sunset at the ruined village. There were three or four men, seven or eight women, and as many children gathered when they rode in. The men had been absent when the attack took place, the women had escaped by seizing their children and rushing out at the backs of the houses and hiding among the rocks and bushes, as soon as the yells of the Indians and the explosion of the firearms burst upon their ears.

"We heard you was coming," one of the men said; "but I fear it is too late; they have got too far a start altogether."

"We didn't waste a minute," Broncho Harry said; "we wur in the saddle three minutes after Tom brought us the news, and we have rode seventy miles since. Tom has done a hundred and forty since last night. Where is Steve Rutherford? has he been wiped out?"

"No; he wur away after a bunch of horses that had strayed. He wur camping out twenty mile away when he saw the light and guessed what it wur; he drove the horses in before him, feeling sure as he would be too late to do any good, but reckoning that they might be useful."

"Good man," Bronco said; "but where is he?"

"He went on alone after them," the man said. "Some of us would have gone with him, but he reckoned he had best go alone; thar wurn't enough of us to fight; he allowed that you boys would be here presently, for the young un here told us as Tom had ridden off with the news. Rube Garston and Jim

Gattling rid off an hour later, and I reckon they will bring a few more up before morning; maybe sooner."

"How many horses are there?"

"Fifteen of the old man's, I reckon. They are in that corral behind his house, and I guess we have got as many more between us."

"Then there are enough to mount us ten and as many more," Broncho Harry said. "Ours ain't good for no more travel to-night. Waal, we will just eat a bit, and then we shall be ready to go on. How many air there of you?"

"Six here."

"Waal, that makes sixteen. I see three of you have got rifles, and four of us have brought rifles along with us. The only question is, which way have the red devils ridden? It air no use our following them if we haven't a clue of some sort. I reckon Steve will be here before long; that is what he has gone for. He would know he couldn't do any good himself, and he would be pretty well sure as we couldn't gather here in any such force as could enter the Injun country afore this evening."

"He took a lantern with him," one of the boys said.

"Yes, that is it. I guess he followed on foot till daylight, then he mounted and went on their trail until he could give a pretty good guess as to where they was heading; then I allow he will come back to tell us; that is how I read it."

"I expect you are right, Broncho. He didn't say much when he started; but when we talked of going with him he said, 'Just you stop where you are, there ain't anything you can do; we can't fight them till we get help. You just wait right here, boys.' It wur rather rough on us, when our gals are being carried off and our wives have been killed, and the hull place ruined; but we knew as Steve knew a sight more about Injuns than we did, and had been many a time into the heart of the Injun country afore they broke out, so we waited. But I tell you, Harry, it wur hard work to sit quiet and know that them murdering villains was getting further away every hour."

"We will have them yet!" Harry said confidently. "If the old man don't ride up in another half-hour we will start. We will follow the trail as far as we can with lanterns. If we get to any place where the trail branches, then there will be nothing to do but to wait for

Steve. Have yer eaten? because if not, yer had best fill up. It air no use starting on such a job as this fasting. We shall have need of all our strength afore we have done, you can bet your boots!"

None of the men had, in fact, eaten anything since the preceding night, but they saw the justice of the advice.

"There is some sheep up behind my place," one of them said. "Like enough they was up on the hills when the Injuns came, but I saw some of them go in there this morning. There ain't no time for cooking now, so we will share your grub, and I will shoot three or four of the sheep and cut them up. They will last us for two or three days."

"That is a good idee; and if there is any flour as hasn't been carried off, you had best make up a few lots of five or six pounds each and tie them up in cloths. They will come in mighty handy. Hello! here are some more of the boys!" A minute later eight more cowboys rode up.

"Hello, Broncho! I thought we should find your crowd here. We have ridden all we knew to be here in time to go on with you—that is, if you are going on."

"We are going on as far as we can, Ike; we are just changing horses. I think there are about enough left to give you one each."

"Have you any news which way the Redskins have gone?"

"Not yet. Old man Rutherford followed 'em up. I expect he will be here soon; if not, we shall meet him. They have got twenty hours' start—that is the worst of it. No, there ain't no chance of overtaking them, that is sartin. What we have got to do is to wipe some of them out, and given them a lesson, and get the girls back again if we can; and we have got to do it quick, else we shall have the hull Injun country up agin us."

"I did not think that they would have done it," another man said. "The old man wur always good friends with the Injuns, and made them welcome when they came along."

"It ain't no good being kind to Injuns," another put in. "There ain't no gratitude in them."

"Injuns air pison!" Broncho said; and a general murmur of agreement expressed that in the opinion of the cowboys this summed up the characteristics of the Redskins.

In a few minutes the newcomers were provided with fresh horses. A spare horse was taken on for Rutherford, and then, headed by the survivors of the raid, the party started three-and-twenty strong. They travelled fast; not that there was any occasion for speed, but because every man was burning with the desire to get at the enemy. After riding about twenty miles they checked their horses, for a fire was seen a short distance ahead.

"That's all right," one of the settlers said. "That will be Rutherford, sure enough. It is just there where the valley forks. He is waiting there for us. He would know we shouldn't want a guide as far as this."

As they came up a tall figure rose from beside the fire.

"Well, Steve, have you tracked them?" Jim Gattling, the youngest of the party from the village, asked eagerly.

"They have gone over the divide into the Springer Valley, have followed that some way, and then through the little cañon, and up towards the headwaters of the Pequinah Creek. I only went through the cañon to see which way they turned, and then made back here. I guessed some of you would be coming along about this time."

"Was they riding fast?"

"No. They halted here for some hours. I reckon they had ridden a long way afore they attacked our place. I saw their fires some time afore I got to them, or I might have walked into them, for I didn't think they would have halted so soon. I tied the hoss up and scouted round 'em, and when they started this morning before daylight took up the trail after them. They weren't travelling very fast. You see they had got about a hundred head of cattle with them, and I reckon they have three or four days' journey before them. As far as I could make out, from what I seed of them, they don't belong to this part at all. Sartin they was going easy, and didn't reckon on being followed. It ain't often they get chased when they are once in the hills. Waal, boys, I am glad to see you, and I thank ye all. It is what I expected from yer, for I felt sure that when you got the news you would muster up."

"We have brought a fresh horse for you, Steve," Jim Gattling said. "We druv in a herd this afternoon, and they changed back there, so we are ready to ride at once."

"That's good, Jim! I was wondering over that, and thinking that if yours had come in from the plains they wouldn't be fit for any more travel to-night, for I knew they was a long way out. Where wur you, Broncho?"

"We wur on Little Creek."

"Ah! that's about sixty miles away from our place. Waal, boys, we may as well go on over the divide and down into the valley; there we had best camp. You will have done a hundred miles by then, and will want sleep. Besides, we mustn't knock the hosses up; they have got their work before them, and maybe we shall have to ride on our way back."

"How many of the skunks are there?"

"Over forty."

"We shan't have much trouble with that lot," Broncho Harry said.

"Not if we catch them before they git to their village, Broncho. But I doubt whether we shall do that."

"Waal, we will fight them, Steve, if there was four hundred of them!" Harry said. "We have come to get your Rosie and the others back, and we are going to do it, you bet."

Rutherford held out his hand and gripped that of the cowboy; then, mounting the horse that had been brought for him, he took his place at the head of the party and led the way.

It was a toilsome journey over the shoulder that divided the two valleys. The pace was necessarily confined to a walk, and it was five hours before they reached the stream upon which they were to camp. Here the horses were turned loose to graze, and the men threw themselves down upon the ground and were soon asleep, for it was now past midnight. With the dawn of day they were on their feet again, a great fire lighted, and some of the mutton cut up and cooked, and some cakes baked. As soon as the meal was eaten they again started.

Hugh had not changed his horse at the village. Broncho Harry told him that it was not likely they would travel for many hours that evening, and he knew that Prince, who had had an

easy time of it lately, could easily do this, and he greatly preferred keeping him, for he felt that upon such an expedition as
this his speed might be of the greatest utility.

A rapid ride of ten miles up the valley took them to the mouth
of the cañon, which came into the main valley at a sharp angle.
It was wide at the entrance, but soon narrowed down into a
gorge from ten to twenty feet wide, with rocks rising precipi-
tously on both sides. It was evident by the smoothly worn face
that in the wet season a tremendous torrent rushed down, filling
it thirty or forty feet deep; but it was perfectly dry now, and for
the most part they were able to ride at a fair pace. Here and
there, however, masses of rock had fallen down from above
since the last rains, and here they had to dismount and allow the
horses to clamber over by themselves as best they could. At such
spots scratches upon the face of the stones showed where the
party they were pursuing had passed on the previous day.

The cañon was upwards of a mile in length, and the valley into
which it led was some hundreds of feet higher than that which
they had left. As soon as they emerged from the pass they put
their horses into a gallop, the track of the party before them
being plainly visible. As they got deeper among the mountains
the scenery became very wild. Forests clothed the hills. Great
masses of rock towered above the valley, and huge blocks of
stone encumbered the route they had to pursue. Sometimes the
track left the bottom and wound up the hillside, passing at times
along the ledges, with precipices above and below. Anxious as
they were to press forward, much of the journey had to be performed at a foot pace, for many of the horses having been
brought up on the plains all their lives were fidgety and nervous
on such unaccustomed ground, and required coaxing and care
to get them along the passes.

They travelled until late in the afternoon and then halted.
The next day's work was of the same character. They were now
high up among the hills, and Steve told them that they were
near the crest of the range.

"We had better stop here," Rutherford said about three o'clock
in the afternoon, as they arrived at a little stream. "We mustn't

knock the critters up; they have done a good days' work already."

"We have gained upon them, Steve," Broncho Harry said. "The traces have been getting fresher."

"Yes, we have gained a bit, but not very much. Their horses would go faster than ours, because they are accustomed to the mountains; but the cattle will have kept them back. Why I stop here is because there is a sort of wall of rock with a passage up through it a mile or two ahead, and though I don't expect they have any idee they are followed, they are like enough to have left a sentry on the top of that wall. It 'ud never do for them to attack us here; we should have no show at all. I want to get my girl back, but throwing away our lives ain't the way to do it. Be careful how you pick the wood for the fires, boys; we mustn't let any smoke go curling up. You have got to see that every bit you put on is as dry as a chip."

"How on earth do the Indians manage to live among these hills?" Hugh asked, after the meal had been cooked and eaten.

"The country is different on the other side," Jim Gattling said. "We are pretty nearly up to the top of the divide now, and on the other side the slopes are much more gradual. They have plenty of ranges where they have got cattle and sheep. But I don't know nothing about the country here. Steve has been over, but there ain't many as has."

"Yes," Rutherford said, "it is as Jim says. There is a wide sort of plateau, with big valleys down to the Canadian. We ain't very far now from the frontier of New Mexico, and from the top of the hills here you can see the Spanish peaks a hundred and fifty miles away. I reckon we may have to go down that side. There are a heap of Injun villages up here, and though we may thrash the lot ahead of us they would gather pretty thick in a short time, and like enough cut us off going back, for they know the tracks better than we do, and their horses would go at a gallop along places where we should have to drag ours. Going down the other way we can ride as fast as they can, and when we once get down in the valley of the Canadian we shall get help at the ranches there."

"That will certainly be the best way, Steve," Broncho Harry said. "We are all ready to fight any number of them on the plains, but it wouldn't be good to be hemmed up among these hills with no chance of help. We could keep them off, I reckon, till we had eaten our boots, but they would make an end of us at last, sure. Have you often been along this line before, Steve?"

"Once. I came across here with a party of Redskins just after the last peace wur made with them, when it was sure that they wouldn't break out again until they had got their presents. I had got a stock of beads, and looking-glasses, and cottons, and such-like, and went up with a couple of mules and traded among them for skins, and worked robes, and moccasins, and Indian trumpery. I sent them back east, and did a pretty good trade with them. But I know the other side well. I was ranching two years down on the Canadian, and we had two or three fights with the Redskins, who was pretty troublesome about that time. There weren't many ranches down there then, and we had to look pretty spry to keep the har on our heads."

"And how do you propose to work it now, Steve?"

"Well, I reckon that if they have got a sentry on them rocks I spoke of he won't stay there after dark, and that the danger will be at the other end of the pass. Like enough, there will be one or two of them there. I reckon the best plan will be for me and Jim Gattling and a kipple of others to go on ahead quiet. If we find any of the skunks there, in course we shall wipe them out. When we have done that the rest can come up the pass. It ain't no place for anyone as doesn't know every foot of the way to come up in the dark; and you must make torches, ready to light up, when one of us goes back with the news that the pass is clear. As soon as we have done with the Redskins, Jim and I will go off scouting. You see we don't know yet what band this is, or how far their village is away. We will follow on the trail, and when the rest get up through the pass they must just wait till we bring them word. I reckon, from their coming by this road, as their place is about fifteen mile from the top of the pass. There is a big village there, and I expect they belong to it. I reckon they are just getting there now, and they will be feasting pretty considerable to-night. It air a pity we ain't handy. However, it cannot be helped. We should risk it all if we was to try to push on afore it got dark."

"Your plan seems to pan out all right, Steve. Who will you take with you?"

"Waal, you and Long Tome may as well come, Broncho, though, I reckon, it don't make much difference, for you all means fighting."

As soon as it became dusk the party again moved forward.

"That's the rock," Rutherford said, pointing to a long dark line that rose up before them. "They can't see us here, and I reckon if there wur a scout there he has moved off before this. Now, do you other fellows take our critters and just move on slowly. You see that point sticking up above the line. Waal, that is on one side of the pass; so you just make for that, and stop when you get there till one of us comes back."

The torches had been prepared during the halt, two or three young pitch-pines having been cut down and split up for the purpose. The four scouts moved off at a quick walk, and the rest of the party picked their way along slowly and cautiously towards the point Steve had indicated. They had some little trouble in finding the entrance to the pass, but when they discovered it they threw the bridles on their horses' necks and dismounted. The time went slowly, but it was not more than two hours before they heard a slight noise up the pass, and a minute or two later a footfall.

"Is that you, Broncho?" Hugh asked.

"No, it air me; but it is all the same thing, I reckon. Jehoshaphat! but I have knocked myself pretty nigh to pieces among them blessed rocks. It air just as dark as a cave; there ain't no seeing your hand."

"Well, is it all right, Tom?"

"No, it ain't gone off right. When we got to the top of the pass there wur two Redskins sitting at a fire. We come along as quiet as we could, but just as we got in sight of them I suppose they heard something, for they both jumped on to their feet and wur out of sight like a streak of lightning. We waited without moving for half an hour, and then they came back again. We could have shot, but Steve reckoned it was too great a risk; so he and Jim undertook to crawl forward while Broncho and me wur to keep ready to shoot if the Redskins made a bolt. It wur a long time, or at least seemed so. The Redskins was restless, and we could see they was on the listen. Waal, at last up they both jumped; but it wur too late. Steve and Jim fired and down they both went, and we came on. The wust of the business wur, that one of their hosses broke loose and bolted. Broncho fired after him. He may have hit him, or he may not; anyhow he went off. So now you have got to hurry up all you know."

The torches were at once lit, and leading their horses the party made their way up the gorge. It was steep and narrow, and encumbered with boulders; but in half an hour they reached the other end. Broncho Harry was awaiting them.

"We have got to move away to the right for about half a mile and stop there. There is a clump of trees, and that is where we are to wait. It air a 'tarnal bad business that air hoss getting away. He is pretty sure to bring the Injuns down on us. Steve ain't going very far. He sez there is another village about three miles from the one he thinks most likely; and when he gets about four miles away from here he will be able to see which way the tracks go, and then he will come straight back to the trees."

"Do you think you hit the horse, Harry?" Hugh asked as they made their way to the clump of trees.

"You don't suppose I could miss a horse if I tried, Hugh. I hit him sure enough, worse luck. If I had missed him it wouldn't have mattered so much. If he came galloping in by himself they might have thought he had got scared at something—by a bar, perhaps—and had just made tracks for the camp. Like enough they would have sent off four men to see if it wur all right; but when the blessed thing turns up with a bullet in his hide, they will know there has been a fight."

"What do you think they will do then, Harry? Are they likely to ride out in force to the gap?"

"They may, and they may not. I should say they won't. I should guess they'll just throw out scouts all round their village and wait till morning. They won't know how strong our party is, and wouldn't take the risk of being ambushed in the dark."

"Perhaps when the horse goes in they won't notice it, especially as they will be feasting and dancing."

"I don't reckon that worth a cent, Hugh. There are safe to be one or two of their boys out looking after the horses; besides, those varmints' ears are always open. They would hear a horse coming at a gallop across the plain half a mile away, aye, and more than that. Directly the boy sees the horse is saddled he will run in and tell them, then they will take it in by the fire and look at it. When they see the mark I have made on it there will be a nice rumpus, you bet. They will know what it means just as if it wur all writ down for them."

Two hours passed, and then the sound of an approaching horse was heard.

"Well, Steve, what news?"

"The horse has gone on straight for the village—the one we thought—and all the other tracks go in that direction. There ain't no chance of taking them by surprise now."

"What do you think they will do, Steve?"

"They will just watch all night, that is sartin, and in the morning two or three will be sent out to scout. There ain't many trees about here, and they will reckon that they can see us as soon as we see them; and those they send out are safe to be on the best horses they have got. In course we could lie down there by the gap and shoot them when they come up; but I don't see as that would do us any good. When they didn't get back it would only put the others more on their guard than ever. If we don't shoot them they will find our tracks here, and take back news how many we are. I tell you, lads, look at it as I will, I don't see no way out of it; and what makes it wuss is, when they take back news that the scouts they left here have both been shot, it will go mighty hard with the captives in the village. I can't see no way out of the kink anyhow. I am ready to give my life cheerful for Rosie, but I ain't going to ask you to give your lives when I don't see as there is any chance of getting her. Do you see any way out of the job, Broncho?"

"I don't, Steve. As you say, there was about forty or fifty of these varmint in the expedition, and we may reckon there will be as many more able to draw a trigger in the village. That makes eighty. Four to one is pretty long odds. If they was out in the plain we might be a match for them, but to attack an Injun camp that's waiting and ready ain't the same thing as fighting in the plains. Half of us would go down before we got in, and there would not be no more chance of the rest of us getting the captives away than there would if they was in the moon. If it hadn't been for this affair of the hoss we might have carried out your plans, and you might have made your way into the village; and there wur just the chance that yer might have got them out and brought them along to some likely place where we was handy; but there ain't no need to talk about that now. They will be guarded that strict that a bird couldn't get to them with a message. That ain't to be thought of. Can any of you boys think of anything?"

No one spoke. Then Hugh said: "I am only a young hand yet, and I don't know that my ideas are worth anything, but I will tell you what they are, and then you can improve upon them perhaps. It seems to me that, in the first place, we ought to leave say four men at the gap. If four Indian scouts come out they ought to shoot or rope three of them, and let the fourth escape. If there were only two of them I would let one get away."

"What should they do that for, Hugh?" Broncho Harry asked in surprise.

"I will tell you directly, Broncho. All the rest of us except the four who are left on watch should start at once and make a big circuit, and come round to the other side of the village, and stop a mile or so away in hiding; at any rate, as near as we can get. Why I propose letting one go is this. Suppose three or four scouts go out and none return, the Indians will be sure that they have fallen in a trap somewhere. They won't know how strong we are, or whether we think of making an attack on their village, and they will stop there expecting us for days perhaps, and then send out scouts again. Now, if one gets back with the news that they saw no signs of us until they got close to the gap, and then three or four shots were fired and his comrades were killed, but he got off without being pursued, it seems to me that they would natu-rally imagine that there was only a small party at the gap—

perhaps three or four men from the village they attacked, who had come out to revenge themselves—and would send out a strong party of their braves at once to attack them. Of course the four men left at the gap would, directly they had done their work, and the Indian was out of sight, mount their horses and make the same circuit as we had done, and join us as quickly as they could. We should be keeping watch, and after seeing the war party ride off we could dash straight down into the village. Half, and perhaps more than half, of their fighting men will have gone, and the others, making sure that we were still at the gap, and that there was no fear of attack, will be careless, and we should be pretty well into the village before a shot was fired."

"Shake, young fellow!" Steve Rutherford said, holding out his hand to Hugh. "That air a judgematical plan, and if it don't succeed it ought ter."

There was a general chorus of assent.

"It beats me altogether," Steve went on, "how yer should have hit on a plan like that when I, who have been fighting Injuns off and on for the last twenty years, couldn't see my way no more than if I had been a mole. You may be young on the plains, Lightning, fur so I have heard them call yer, but yer couldn't have reasoned it out better if yer had been at it fifty years. I tell you, young fellow, if I get my Rosie back agin it will be thanks to you, and if the time comes as yer want a man to stand by yer to the death yer can count Steve Rutherford in."

"And Jim Gattling," the young settler said. "Rosie and me wur going ter get hitched next month, and it don't need no talk to tell yer what I feels about it."

"Which of us shall stay, and which of us shall go?" Broncho Harry said. "You are the only man as knows the country, Steve; so you must go sartin. Long Tom and me will stay here if you like. You can give me the general direction of the village, and I expect I can make shift to come round and join you. Besides, there will be your trail to follow. I don't reckon they will send out those scouts till daylight. Anyhow, we won't start before that, and we are safe to be able to follow your trail then. Who will stop with us? Will you stay, Hugh?"

"No!" Hugh said decidedly; "I will go with Steve. I am not a very sure shot with the rifle."

"You can shoot straight enough," Broncho Harry said.

"Well, perhaps it isn't that, Harry; but so far I have had no Indian fighting, and though I am quite ready to go in and do my share in a fight, I tell you fairly that I couldn't shoot men down, however hostile, in cold blood."

"All right, Hugh. You shan't stay with us. When you know the Injuns as well as we do, and know that mercy ain't a thing as ever enters their minds, and that they murders women and children in cold blood, and that if they do take a prisoner it is just to torture him until he dies, you won't feel that way."

"I will stay with you, Broncho," Jim Gattling said. "I have just seen my house burnt and the best part of my stock carried away, and a dozen or more of my friends killed or scalped, and you bet I would kill a Redskin at sight just as I would put my heel on a rattlesnake."

Another of the party also volunteered to stay at the gap.

No further words were necessary. The party mounted.

"That is where the village lies, Broncho; just about under that star. It is about fifteen mile, as I told you, on a straight line. We shall keep over there to the right, and in a couple of miles we shall get to where the ground falls, and will travel along there. You can't be wrong if you keep down on the slope. There air no chance then of your being seen. I don't know just where we shall turn off. There are several dips run down from above, and we shall follow one of them up when I reckon we have got a mile or two beyond the village. So keep a sharp lookout for our trail there. You needn't bother much about it before, because you can't miss the way; but look sharp at the turnings. I would drop something to show you where we turn off, but if any Injun happened to come along he would be safe to notice it. When you guess you have ridden far enough keep a sharp lookout for the place where we turn off, and then follow the trail careful. It is rolling ground, that side of the village, and I reckon we kin get within half a mile of it. There ain't much fear of their wandering about, and any scouts they have out won't be on that side. So long!"

Steve Rutherford led the way. "There ain't no need to hurry," he said. "We have got plenty of time, and I reckon that when we get a bit farther we will dismount and lead the horses. They have had pretty hard work coming up the hills, and I tell you they are likely to want all their speed to-morrow, and some of them will have to carry double if we can't manage to get hold of a few of the Injun ponies."

Accordingly, after riding for half an hour, the party dismounted, and led their horses for a long distance. This was a novel exercise to the cowboys, for it is rare for one of them to walk a hundred yards. A horse stands ever ready at hand, and if it be only to go down to the stream hard by to fetch a bucket of water the cowboy will always throw his leg over his horse. But all felt the justice of Steve's remarks. They knew that they had at least a hundred-mile ride before they could hope to meet friends, and that the pursuit would be hot. It was therefore of vital importance that the horses should start as fresh as possible. After three hours' walking they mounted again, and continued their way until Steve Rutherford said that he thought they had gone far enough now. The moon had risen at two o'clock, and its light had enabled them to travel fast since they had remounted. Turning up a hollow they followed it for about two miles, and then found they were entering a hilly and rugged country.

"Here we are," Steve said. "The village lies at the foot of these rocks. I don't know how far along it may be, but I am right sure that we have got beyond it. Now, boys, you can sleep till daylight. I will keep watch, and see that none of the horses stray."

In a very few minutes all was quiet in the little valley, save for the sound of the horses cropping the short grass. At the first gleam of daylight Rutherford stirred up one of the sleepers.

"I am going to scout," he said. "When the others wake tell them to be sure not to stir out of this dip, and to mind that the horses don't show on the skyline. The Injuns will be keeping their eyes open this morning, and if they caught sight of one of them critters it would just spoil the hull plan."

Rutherford was gone two hours. Long before his return all the men were up and about. Bill Royce had gone a little farther up the valley, which narrowed to a ravine, and, climbing the rocks cautiously, had taken a survey of the country.

"No signs of the village," he said when he returned, "and no signs of Injuns as far as I can see. So I think, if we go up to the head of this gulch, it'll be safe to make a fire and cook the rest of our meat. There ain't no more than enough for one more feed. After that I reckon we shall have to take to horse flesh. Now, half of us will go up and cook, and the other half keep watch here. We may have Steve coming back with twenty Redskins on his track."

Just as they had fried their meat Steve returned.

"We are about three miles from the village," he said, "but keeping along at the foot of the hills we can get to within half a mile of it safe. Beyond that it is a chance. What are you doing?"

"Cooking."

"Well, one must eat, but the sooner we get on the better. We want to watch how things go."

As soon as the meal was finished the party mounted, and, keeping close to the foot of the hill, rode on till Steve said, "We cannot go beyond that next bluff; so turn up this gulch. I looked in, and there is good feed for the horses there. You had better look round when you get in to see as there ain't no bar or nothing to scare the horses, and two of yer had best stay on guard here at the mouth. Ef one of them critters wur to get loose and to scoot out below there our lives wouldn't be worth a red cent. Now, Stumpy, you and Owen and me will go up over there. From among them bushes just at the foot of the rock we can see the camp, and we will take it by turns to keep watch. If you others will take my advice you will all get as much sleep as you can till we come for you, but mind, keep two on guard here."

"Can I come with you, Steve?" Hugh asked. "I don't feel like sleep at all."

"You can take my place, Lightning," Royce said. "I ain't in no hurry to look at the Injuns. I expect I shall see plenty of them afore we have done."

XIII. RESCUED

Steve Rutherford, the settler Owen, and Hugh made their way along at the foot of the steep rocks, keeping among the fallen boulders, stopping at times, and making a close survey of the plains to be sure that no Indians were in sight, before moving further.

"That is the point," Steve said presently; "from among those rocks we can get a view of the village. You must keep your head low, Lightning, and not show it above the rocks. They will be keeping a sharp lookout, and like enough they would make out a lizard moving at this distance."

When they reached the point they made their way with extreme care to the highest boulders, and then, lying down, looked through the interstices between them. Hugh started as he did so, for although the Indian village was nearly half a mile away, the mountain air was so clear that it did not seem a quarter of that distance. Its position was well chosen; the hill rose almost perpendicularly behind it, defending it from an attack on that side, while in front and on both sides the ground sloped away and was clear of brushwood or inequalities that would afford shelter to assailants. Trees stood in and around it, affording shade during the heat of the day. A number of horses were grazing close to the village, with half a dozen Indian boys round them, in readiness to drive them in at the shortest notice. Smoke was curling up from the top of the wigwams, and through the trees many figures of men and women could be seen moving about.

"How long do you think it will be, Steve, before their scouts get back again?"

"Another hour, I should guess; I expect they started at daybreak. Anyhow, they had gone before I got here. I reckon they wouldn't travel fast going there; in the first place they would scout about and look for signs of an enemy, and in the second they wouldn't want to blow their horses, for they might have to ride for their lives any moment. I should give them four hours, a good two and a half to get there, and something over an hour for one of them to get back again. He may be here in half an hour, he may not be here for an hour; it will be somewhere between one and the other."

Twenty minutes passed, and then Steve exclaimed, "Here he comes!" The other two caught sight of the Indian at the same moment, as first his head and shoulders, then the whole rider and horse, appeared on the crest of a rise some four miles away. He was as yet invisible from the village, but in a few minutes they could perceive a stir there, and three or four warriors ran out from the village, leaped on to their horses, and galloped out to meet the returning scout. They saw them join him, and, sweeping round without a check, accompany him, and in ten minutes they reached the village. A minute later a mournful wail sounded in the air.

"They know it now," Steve said; "they are just about beginning to feel as we do. It is all very well as long as they go out, and murder and burn, and come back with scalps, but they don't like it when the game is played on them."

"When will they start out again, do you think, Steve?"

"Not yet awhile, they are going to talk; Indians never do anything without that. There, do you see, there ain't a man among the trees; there are some women and children, but nary a warrior. You may be sure that they are gathering for a great council; first of all the scout will tell his story, then the chiefs will talk. It will be another hour at least before there is a move made."

"Oh, I do hope our plan won't fail!" Hugh said.

"I don't think that there is much chance of it," Owen put in. "They are bound to do something. Their scout can only report that, so far as he saw, there was not more than four men, and as they did not chase him he expects they have no horses. They never can leave it like that. They are bound to go out and see about it, otherwise they know they couldn't go out in twos or threes without the risk of being ambushed, just as the scouts were; besides, they lost the two men they left behind, and maybe one, maybe three, this morning, and they are bound to have vengeance. Oh, they air safe to go!"

An hour later a sudden succession of wild yells were heard.

"Thar's their war cry," Steve said; "the thing is settled, and they air going." A few minutes later the Indian boys were seen driving the horses in towards the village, and then a number of warriors ran out.

"There air a good lot of them," Steve said, in a tone of satisfaction. "They was sure to go, the question wur how many of them. It will be a strong party anyhow."

The Indians were soon seen to be mounting. "Now we can count them," Steve said. "Five-and-thirty."

"I couldn't tell within four or five," Hugh said; "they keep moving about so, but I should say that that was about it."

"Yes, five-and-thirty," Owen agreed. "You have the youngest legs, Lightning, you scoot across as hard as you can run and tell them to get ready; Steve and I will see them fairly off, and then we will come in. Don't let them move out of the hollow till we join you; there ain't no special hurry, for we mustn't attack till the band have got four or five miles away. If they heard the guns they would be back agin like a torrent."

Hugh did as he was told. As he ran down over the crest into the dip he gave a shout of satisfaction at seeing Broncho Harry and the three men who had remained with him; they had arrived a few minutes before.

"Well, Harry, we saw all had gone right, as only one of their scouts came back."

"Has it drawn them?" Harry asked.

"Yes; a band of five-and-thirty started five minutes ago."

"Bully for us!" Harry said. "Then we have got them all right now. I expect there ain't above thirty fighting men left in the village, and, catching them as we shall, they won't have a show against us."

"How did you get on, Harry?"

"It wur just as you reckoned, lad; three of 'em came out. They were very scarey about coming close; they yelled to their mates, and in course got no answer; then they galloped round, one at a time, getting nearer and nearer, but at last they concluded that the place was deserted, and rode up. We let them get so close that there wur no fear of our missing, and then we shot two of them; the other rode for it. We fired after him, but took good care not to hit him, and as soon as he had gone we ran to the wood where we had left our ponies, and came on here pretty slick. There wur no difficulty in following your trail; we reckoned that we should have to come pretty fast to be here in time, as it wur three or four miles further for us to go than the Injun would have, and he wouldn't spare his horse flesh. Still we was sure it would be an hour at least before they was ready to start, more likely two. Jim Gattling wur flurried a bit; natural he wouldn't like not to be with the others when they went in to rescue Rosie. So it seems we air just in time with nothing to spare. But here comes Steve."

By this time all had been got ready for a start. Horses had been brought up, saddles looked to, girths tightened, and blankets strapped on. A hearty greeting was exchanged between Steve and the party just arrived.

"We will give them another ten minutes afore we start," Steve said. "Now, we had better settle, Broncho, as to what we should each do when we get in, else there may be confusion, and they may tomahawk the prisoners before we find them."

"Yes, that is best," Broncho agreed. "Now, look here; our crowd will do the fighting, and you and your fellows jump off as soon as you get in, and search the wigwams. You will know just where to go; the prisoners are safe to be in a wigwam close by that of the principal chief; he will keep them close under his eye, you may bet your life. And mind, boys, let us have no shooting at squaws or kids. We have come out to rescue the women they have carried off, and to pay out the men for the work they did, but don't let us be as bad as they are."

There was a general assent from the cowboys, but two or three of the men who had come with them grumbled, "They have killed our wives and children, why shouldn't we pay them back in the same coin?"

"Because we are whites and not Redskins," Broncho Harry said. "Look here, Steve; we have come here to help you, and we are risking our lives pretty considerable in this business, but afore we ride into that village we are going to have your word that there ain't going to be a shot fired at squaw or child. Those are our terms, and I don't think they are onreasonable."

As a chorus of approval went up from the rest of the cowboys, and as the others were well aware that what they said they meant, they unwillingly assented.

"That is right and square," Broncho Harry said. "You have all given your promise, and if anyone breaks it, I begin shooting, that is all. Now it's about time to be moving, Steve."

The men swung themselves up into their saddles. "Now, boys, quietly until we get in sight of the village, and then as fast as we can go."

But all were eager for the fight, and the pace gradually quickened till they came within sight of the village. Then they charged down upon it at full gallop. They had gone but a short distance when they heard the cry of alarm, the yells of the Indians, shouts and orders, screams of women and children, and the barking of the village dogs. Shots were fired, but to Hugh's surprise these ceased before the cowboys reached the village.

"The skunks are bolting," Broncho Harry exclaimed. "Keep round the trees, No. 2 outfit, and straight across the plain after them. They may have got some of the girls."

It was, however, less than two minutes from the moment the assailants had been seen to that when they burst into the village. The Indians, taken altogether by surprise at the appearance of a foe from a quarter from which no danger had been apprehended, and seeing a band of the dreaded cowboys dashing down at a gallop, caught up their arms, and then, in obedience to the orders of the chief left behind in charge of the village, dashed out to their horses, mounted, and rode off. Their leader had seen at once that there was no hope of resistance. The assailants were nearly equal in number to the fighting men left

"All safe, Father," cried Rosie."
See page 207.

in the village, they would be armed with those terrible pistols that were the dread of the Indians, and they had all the advantage of a surprise. There was nothing to do but to ride off to the main body.

For a moment the thought of killing the prisoners before starting had crossed his mind, but there was no time to run to the wigwam in which they had been placed, and he saw too that their death would entail that of the Indian women and children. These had been no less speedy in their movements than the men, and at the first cry of danger the women had seized their infants and, followed by the boys and girls of the village, had fled along the foot of the cliff till they reached a spot where, although steep, it was accessible. Here a path, winding among boulders and hidden by bushes, led up to the top of the cliff. This had been constructed by the boys of the village at the time the Indians first established themselves there, for the purpose of enabling its occupants to make their escape in case of a sudden attack by superior forces.

Steve and his party were astonished when, as they dashed into the village, they found the place almost deserted. A few old men stood at the entrances of their wigwams, and four or five aged women were assembled in front of one standing near the centre of the place; and as the cowboys and settlers galloped up, five white women ran out from the wigwam to meet them, with cries of joy.

"All safe, Rosie?" Steve Rutherford shouted as he rode up.

"All safe, father"; and a cheer burst from the rescuers as they leapt from their horses and crowded round the girls. These had all friends or relations among the party.

"Three of you let off your rifles one after the other," Steve said, the instant he had embraced his daughter. "I told Broncho as he rode off that should be the signal that we had got them all. Then some of you had better ride as hard as you can after them. You may be wanted, though I don't expect the Indians will stop. Tell Broncho he had best come back again, there ain't no time to lose. The rest of you scatter and put a light to these wigwams. There is all the things they stole from us scattered among them, and all their skins and things, not worth much, perhaps, but a lot to them. Look into the huts and see there ain't no babies left in them. Where are all the women and children, Rosie?" But Rosie was at that moment much too occupied with Jim Gattling to hear him.

"Never mind that now, gal," Steve said, striding up to them; "there will be time enough for fooling when we get out of this. Whar are the women and children?"

"I don't know, father. We know nothing about it. We were in the wigwam and suddenly heard shouts and screams, and then almost directly everything became quiet, and then these old women opened the door and made signs to us to come out, and as we did we saw you charging in among the trees."

"Where are the squaws and children?" Steve asked one of the old women in her own language. She looked vacantly at him as if she did not understand. "Bah! that's no use," he said; "I might have known that. Scatter about, boys; see if you can't find some of them. They can't have gone out on to the plain, that is sartin. They can't have got up this cliff—not here. Perhaps thar's a cave somewhere. Scatter along and search. Go right along some distance each way, thar may be some path up somewhere.

"What does it matter about them, Steve?" one of the settlers asked. "We agreed there wurn't to be no killing of squaws or kids."

"I don't want to kill them," Steve said. "I am just so pleased at getting my girl and the others back that I don't feel like hurting anything; what Broncho and me reckoned on was to take some of the chiefs' wives and children along with us as hostages. If we had them with us we reckoned they would not attack us on our way back. I tell you, boys, it may just make the difference of our scalps to us."

Not another word was needed, and all, with the exception of a few of the friends of the rescued women, scattered on the search. It was ten minutes before they found the concealed path. The man who discovered it ran back to Rutherford. "I have found the place, Steve; it is away three or four hundred yards to the left there. Just at the end of the clump of trees there are some bushes against the face of the hill. It didn't look as if there could be any way up, but I pushed through them, and, sure enough, there was some steps cut in the rock. I went up them, and round a sharp angle there was a sort of gap in the cliff. You couldn't see it from the plain, and a path went straight up there."

"That air bad news, Owen. They have got a quarter of an hour's start, and it ain't no sort of use our going after them. Waal, there is nothing to do but to ride for it. I wish Broncho's party was back."

"They air just coming back," a man said. "I have been to the edge of the wood to look after them. They are galloping back, and will be here in a few minutes."

By the time Broncho Harry and his party rode into the village the wigwams were all in flames. The men who had set fire to them had brought out the meat they had found inside. There were several quarters of deer, and a quantity of beef, doubtless the produce of animals belonging to the herd they had driven off. They were satisfied that the burning of the wigwams would be a heavy loss to the Indians, for they had found many piles of skins and robes stored up to be used in barter for guns and horses. Indeed, the whole belongings of the tribe, except their cattle, were destroyed, together with, what perhaps would be even more severely felt, the scalps taken from their enemies in many a fight and massacre. A few words acquainted the new-comers with what had taken place, and they were delighted to find that they had arrived in time to save the women from the fate that awaited them.

"Did you hear the rifle shots, Broncho?"

"Nary one. We was having a skirmish with the Redskins. They showed fight at first till they saw the rest of the boys coming out. We chased them two miles, and killed six of them. Then we thought it best to come back, for we could see that a couple of the best mounted had been sent straight off as hard as they could go after the first lot. We should not have chased them as far as we did, but we wanted to rope five of their horses for the women. As soon as we had done that we took the back track. Have you caught some of the squaws, Steve?"

"No, worse luck, they had all cleared out afore we got here. There was nary a soul in the village except these old men and women."

"But where on earth did they get to?"

"It took us a quarter of an hour to find out, and then one of the men lit on it pretty nigh by accident. Right along the cliff thar is some steps cut in the rock. They are hidden by bushes, and up above them is a sort of gap in the rock with a path up it. You can't see it from the plain at all. No doubt that is the principal reason why they fixed their village here. It gave them a means of escape if they were attacked."

"Waal, if you haven't got no hostages, Steve, there ain't another minute to waste here. You see we had figured on them hostages. I see you have got some meat; that is good. Waal, are you all ready? because if so, let's git."

Three minutes later the party rode away from the burning village, the women mounted on the Indian horses.

"Thar's our cattle," Steve said, pointing to a herd out on the plain, "but it ain't any use thinking of them now."

"You bet," Broncho Harry replied. "There ain't no thinking about horns or hides at present. It is our own har we have got to think of."

"You think they will catch us up, Broncho?" said Steve.

"I don't think nothing at all about it. They are just as sure to catch us up as the sun is to rise. We have got every foot of a hundred miles to go, and the horses have been travelling hard for the last three days. By this time those fellows as have galloped on ahead are pretty nigh their main party, if they haven't overtook them before this. They had no call for speed, and would be taking it easy. You can't reckon much more than ten miles start. Still, when they catch us they won't be more than three to one.

"There was thirty-five went out, you said, Steve, and another twenty-five in the second lot. That brings them up to sixty, which is pretty nigh three to one.

"Well, three to one ain't such great odds even if they wur to come down and fight us in a body; but I reckon they would not do that. They are more likely to make a surround of it. They would know that we should have to leave pretty near half our number to guard the women, and the rest wouldn't be strong enough to charge them. Besides, it ain't only sixty we have got to reckon with. Like enough half a dozen of them started, as soon as we turned back, to the other villages of the tribe. You may reckon we shall have two or three hundred of them coming along in our track in an hour or two. Don't you make any mistake about it, Steve; we shan't get away, and we have got to fight. Now, you know the country, and what you have got to reckon up is, where shall we fight? You can't calkilate on above fifty miles, and if you say forty it will be safer. A few of the horses might get a bit further than that, but taking them all round, and reckoning they have been going hard for the last few days, forty is the longest we can calkilate on afore we hear the Redskin yells behind us."

"The Two Brothers are about forty miles from here," Steve Rutherford said.

"Ah! I have heard of them. They are two buttes close together, ain't they?"

"Yes. We should be safe enough there if all the Redskins in creation was attacking us. They might starve us out, but they could never climb up. One of the Brothers there ain't no climbing up at all. It stands straight up all round, but the other has got a track up. I have seen cattle on the top."

"Do you know the way up, Steve?"

"Yes. I was with a party that came out from the Canadian looking up cattle that had strayed. We didn't find many of the cattle. The Injuns had got them, you may be sure; but we stopped at the foot of the buttes, and did some hunting for a day or two. Three or four of us climbed up. It ain't a road you would choose to drive a team down, and I should not have thought that cattle could have climbed it if I hadn't been told they did so. Still, it is good enough for us."

There was no attempt to gallop at full speed, the horses being kept at a canter, the pace to which they are most accustomed.

"There," Steve said, pointing to the lower country ahead of them, for they had since starting been gradually descending— "there are the Brothers."

"They don't look far away," Hugh, who was riding beside him, remarked.

"I guess they are near fifteen miles, Lightning."

"I should have said five if I had been asked," Hugh said.

"I wish they was only five. I expect before we get halfway to them we shall hear the Injuns behind us."

"Yes, Broncho has been telling me what you think of it. Well, there is one thing, if we get to those buttes first we can keep the whole tribe at bay."

"Yes, lad, as far as fighting goes; but there is one thing agin us."

"Water?" Hugh asked.

"You have hit it. I don't say as there mayn't be some water up there. I reckon there is, for they told me the cattle would stay up there for some time without coming down. There weren't no cattle when I was there, and I didn't see no water, but it may be at times there is some. The top of the place seemed to me lowest in the centre—not a great deal, perhaps, maybe not more than three or four feet—and if there is any hole in the middle there may be water there. I wurn't thinking of it at the time, and didn't look for it. Maybe in the rains it gets filled up, and there is enough to last the cattle some time. Everything depends on that."

"I have been thinking," Hugh said, "that if I were to ride straight on I might get through to the next ranche. My horse is a first-rate one, and I am sure he could do the distance."

"If he had started after a couple of days' rest he could carry you a hundred miles, I don't doubt. There ain't nothing out of the way in that. I have ridden as much a score of times; but you see, lad, he has not had much rest and not much time to eat since we started. You rode him out from your camp and then on to the first halting-place; that made eighty or ninety mile. Next day we made sixty, I reckon. Then he was going all yesterday till we halted before we went up through the pass, and he kept on going till a good bit past midnight. We may not have done more than fifty or sixty mile, but he got no feeding till we got into that dip about two o'clock this morning.

"If you only had the horses after you that the Indians rode

down to Gainsford I should say your horse would carry you as well as theirs would; but it won't be so. You bet your life, that mob we saw outside the village was a fresh one. The fust thing they would do when they got to camp in the afternoon would be to send some of the lads off to the grazing grounds with the horses they had ridden, and to fetch in a fresh lot. Besides that, as I told you, there will be others of the tribe coming up and jining in the chase. Scores of them. They will all be on fresh mounts, and they will be just on the best ponies they have got, for they will guess that we are heading for the Canadian. No, no, lad! it'll never do. They would ride you down sartin.

"Another thing is, whoever goes has got to know every foot of the country, to travel at night, and to be able to find his way to the nearest ranche. That job will be mine, I reckon. I know more of the Injun ways than anyone here, and if anyone can do the job I can. Besides, it is my place. You have all gone into this affair to get my Rosie out of the hands of the Redskins, and it is my duty to get you out of the scrape. Listen!"

The whole party checked their horses simultaneously as the air brought to their ears a long, quavering yell, and looking back they saw against the distant skyline a confused body of horsemen.

"Two miles good, ain't it, Broncho?"

"About that, I should say, Steve; and we have got twelve to ride. Now, then, let the ponies know they have got to do some work."

The shouts of the riders, the tightening of the reins, and a touch of the spur told the horses what was required of them, and they sped along at a very different pace to that at which they had hitherto travelled.

"We are all right, I think," Long Tom said to Hugh. "They have been riding a good deal faster than we have, and I don't think they will gain on us now—not anything to speak of. We shall be at the buttes long before they catch us, though you see when one party is chasing another they have got a great advantage."

"How do you mean, Tom? I don't see what advantage they have."

"They have this advantage, Lightning. All horses ain't the same. Some can go a lot faster than others. Some can keep on ever so much longer than others. There are some good and some bad."

"Of course there are, Tom, but that is the same with both parties."

"Sartin it is, lad, but you see the party that is chasing go at the speed of their fastest horses; waal, not of their fastest, but the speed that the most of them can keep up. Those who are badly mounted drop in the rear and are left behind; the others don't consarn themselves about them. Now, it is just the contrairy with the party that is chased. They have got to go at the pace of the slowest horse among them. They can't leave one or two of their mates to the marcy of the Redskins: they have got to keep together and to fight together, and, if must be, to die together. There is a lot of difference among the horses in this crowd. We just took what we could git when we started; thar wurn't no picking and choosing. Thar wur one apiece for us good or bad. The pace we are going ain't nothing to that horse of yours, but you'll soon see that some of the others can't keep it up, and then we shall have to slow down to their pace."

"I didn't think of that, Tom. Yes, I see, a party that pursues has an immense advantage over one that flies, providing, of course, they are greatly superior in numbers. If not, there will be a time when the best-mounted men could no longer ride at full speed, because if they did they would be inferior in numbers to those they chased when they came up to them."

"That is reasonable, lad, and if those Redskins behind us are only the lot from the village, that will bring them up a bit. They know well enough they can't lick us, if they ain't pretty nigh three to one, and so they will want their whole crowd up, and they won't be able to travel at the speed of their best horses. That is why I said that we shall beat them easy. It ain't really them, it is the bands from the other villages that we have got to fear. I don't know this kintry, and I don't know where the other villages are; but I shouldn't be surprised any moment to see bands cutting in from the right or left. Some of the Injuns would ride straight off there, and they will have heard the news as soon or sooner than the band that went after us to the rocks. They will guess the line we should take, and will all be on fresh horses. That is what I am thinking of all the time."

"I suppose Steve knows?" Hugh said.

"He knows. He ain't said much, but he dropt behind an hour ago, and said to me, 'Keep a sharp lookout on both sides, Tom; that is where the danger comes in.'"

For the next five miles the pursuers did not appear to gain.

"Can't we take it easy, Steve?" Jim Gattling asked. "Some of the horses are beginning to blow a bit. There ain't more than seven miles now between us and the buttes. We might let them walk for five minutes now to get their wind again."

Steve turned in his saddle and looked round at the horses. Wiry little animals as they were, many of them were showing signs of distress.

"We will go a little bit easier," he said, "just a little. When we get to that brow a mile ahead we shall get a better view. Then we will see about it."

The horses were pulled in a little, but still kept at a gallop until they got to the top of the ascent. From this point there was a smooth and regular fall right down to the valley from which rose the buttes six miles away.

"Now you have got to ride for it and no mistake," Steve said sharply. "There they come both ways. That is just what I was afeard of."

An exclamation of something like dismay broke from many of the men, for two bands of Indians were seen, one on each hand, riding, like themselves, for the buttes. The one to the left was perhaps a mile away, but considerably in advance of them. That on the right was perhaps twice as far, and was, like themselves, just beginning to descend the long incline.

"We shall pass the crowd to the right," Broncho Harry said, "but the others will cut us off, sure."

"That is so, Harry," Steve said quietly. "But there is one thing, there ain't above forty or fifty of them, while that crowd to the right are twice as strong. If they had been first, it would have been all over with us. Well, don't travel too fast, lads. We can't pass ahead of that lot to the left, but there is no fear of the crowd to the right. Just go at the pace we are going now. Look here, what has got to be done is this: we have got to keep together with the women in the middle of us. We have got to go right through them. Now nine of you have got rifles, you keep next to the gals. The moment we have got through the Injuns, you ride with them straight on to the foot of the butte. I must go with you, because I know just where the path starts, and no one else does. The moment you get there you jump off the ponies, take post among the rocks, and open fire on the Injuns. You, Broncho, with the rest of them, directly we are through, you turn again and charge them. Just check them for about a minute, that will be enough; then you ride in and we will cover you with our rifles."

"That is about it," Harry replied. "Now, boys, you all hear. You with the rifles go straight on. And look here, empty your six-shooters into them as you charge—the more you wipe out the better. Then the rest of you with me just give a yell to scare them, and then close with them again. Don't you empty your six-shooters at first, but keep your fire till we are through them; it is mighty hard if the others, with six shots apiece, don't clear the way for us. You must bear in mind that you will want every shot after we are through, so don't throw away one. Don't you bother about the advance crowd with the women. I will keep my eye on them, and when I see they are ready I will give a yell, and then we will ride for it together."

The Indians saw that they had it in their power to cut off the whites from the buttes, and they no longer rode at the headlong speed at which they were going when first perceived, but slackened down their pace. They could, if they had chosen, have brought on the fight at some distance from the buttes, but they had no motive for doing so. They saw the large party coming from the other side, and preferred to delay the contest till the last moment in order that their friends should be near at hand. Steve remarked with satisfaction that they did not attempt to outride his party.

"The fools," he said to Broncho Harry, "they won't be there above a hundred yards before us, and won't get above one shot each before we are on them. If they had known their business they would have ridden fit to kill their horses till they got there, and then jumped off and run up that path and held it. We should have lost half our number at least fighting our way up. In fact, with the women with us, we couldn't have done it."

Scarce another word was spoken as the party galloped on. Mile after mile had been passed, and the buttes were now towering up in front of them. When within half a mile of the foot the riders gradually fell in to the places assigned to them. Those with rifles went in front, then the women, then the men with revolvers only. The small party of Indians kept on until within a hundred and fifty yards of the foot of the buttes, then they halted and turned. The whites were at the moment some two hundred yards behind them. The great party of Indians on the right were about half a mile away. The Indians in front did not await the shock of the whites, knowing that the impetus of the latter would give them an advantage, but raising their war cry dashed forward to meet them, discharging their rifles as they came.

Not a shot was fired by the whites until the two lines were within twenty paces of each other, then the revolvers of the ten men in front cracked out sharply. Several of the Indians fell. Then there was a crash as the lines met, and then for a moment a confused medley—the Indians fighting with tomahawk and spear, the whites with their deadly revolvers. The conditions were too unequal. There was not one among the band of whites who could not rely with certainty upon his aim, and as in a close line, boot touching boot, they pressed on, the Indians melted like snow before them. It seemed to Hugh but a moment from the time the fight began till the path before them to the buttes was open.

"Forward!" shouted Steve. "We are through them, boys."

As Hugh dashed on he heard Broncho Harry's shout, the cracking of the revolvers, and the yell of the Indians. The women were riding abreast with them now.

"Never mind the gals," Steve shouted. "All tumble off together."

It was but a few seconds before the first band threw themselves from their horses and took up their post behind boulders and bushes. As they dismounted Steve gave a loud shout, and almost at the same moment the party that had fought under the leadership of Broncho Harry wheeled round and rode towards them. Had there been only the Indians that had tried to bar their way to reckon with, there would have been no need for them to seek refuge at the buttes. Half their number had fallen under the bullets of the front line of the whites as they fell upon them. The charge of Broncho Harry's detachment had completed the effect of the blow. The whole conflict had only lasted half a minute, but in that time the deadly six-shooters had wrought terrible havoc with the band of Indians. Less than half of them went galloping back to meet their advancing friends, and several of these were leaning over their saddles evidently badly wounded. Over twenty lay together at the spot where the two parties had met. A few of the horses stood quietly beside their dead owners, the rest were careering wildly over the plain. A loud cheer broke from both parties of the whites as Broncho Harry's band rode in and dismounted.

"That has been a pretty tight race," Long Tom said, "but we beat them handsome."

"Tom, do you all stow away your horses and ours as snug as you can among the rocks and trees, then take your places down here. We will get a bit higher up so as to get a wider range for our rifles, but we haven't time for that now, we must just give this other crowd a hint that we have got rifles and can use them. Now, boys, take steady aim at that clump of Redskins. Don't throw away a shot. There is nothing like straight shooting for skeering a Red. Here goes"; and Steve, taking a steady aim, fired, while his companions followed his example.

XIV. SURROUNDED BY REDSKINS

The large band of Indians had checked their horses some five hundred yards from the foot of the buttes as they saw the survivors of the party in front galloping back to them, and realized that the whites had gained shelter. Some of the more impetuous spirits had, however, ridden on, and were some distance in advance when the rifles of the defenders cracked out. Four of the Indians fell from their horses, three others were wounded, and these, with their companions, wheeled round and rejoined the main body, who now, at the order of their chief, fell back, and were, a few minutes later, reinforced by the band that had followed on the footsteps of the fugitives.

"Now, boys, we can go up to the top; but first let us see how we stand. Has any gone down?"

"Yes, there are two missing," Long Tom said. "I saw two of the first line go down as we charged them."

"John Spencer wur killed," Jim Gattling said. "He wur riding next to me."

"Boston wur the other," Broncho Harry said. "I wur riding in a line with him behind, and saw him go back ker-plumb. I knew he wur hit through the head by the way he fell."

Four other men were, it was now found, wounded, and one of the women had been hit in the shoulder with a rifle ball.

"The Redskins ain't no account with their rifles on horseback," Long Tom said. "Let them lie down and get their piece on a log and they can shoot pretty straight, but it's just throwing away lead to try to shoot with a rifle from a horse. I never knew more than two or three whites who was anyway sartin with their pieces when their horses was on the move. A six-shooter's worth ten rifles on horseback. A fellow kin gallop and keep his arm straight, but when it comes to holding out a long tube with both arms, and your pony going on the jump, it stands to reason there ain't no keeping the thing straight. If those Redskins had hurried up and dismounted, and steadied their rifles on their saddles, I reckon they might have wiped out half of us before we reached them. Waal, Steve, you and the women, and best part of the others, may as well get up to the top; but Broncho and me, and two or three of the boys, will stop down here and look after the horses. Lightning, you may as well stop down here with a kipple of other fellows with rifles, so as just to give them a hint to keep at a distance, otherwise they will be sending their lead up while the others are getting to the top."

But the Indians showed no signs of any intention of harassing them for the present. They knew that the rifles in the hands of the defenders carried farther and straighter than their own. They had suffered heavy losses already, and were in no way disposed to do anything rash. They knew that there was no occasion for haste, and no fear of the fugitives attempting to make their escape. After some consultation they drew further off into the plain, and in a short time smoke could be seen ascending at several points.

"There ain't no occasion to wait down here no longer," Long Tom said. "The Injuns know well enough that they can't take this place, not at least without losing a hundred men; and it ain't Redskin fashion to throw away lives, special when they know they have only got to wait to do the job without any fighting at all. So let us go up."

The path was comparatively easy for three-quarters of the way to the summit of the buttes. It seemed that on this side either the rock had crumbled away in past ages so as to make a gradual slope, or else water or wind had thrown up a bank against it. The height of the butte above the broad valley would be about three hundred feet, and the slope was covered with trees and undergrowth, until it terminated abruptly at the face of a wall of rock fifty feet from the summit. At one point only this wall was broken by a sort of gap or cleft some three feet wide at the bottom, and slanting as steeply as the roof of a house. The bottom was worn almost smooth by the rains of centuries and by the feet of cattle, and Hugh had to sling his gun behind him and use both hands to grasp the irregularities of the rock on either side to get up. On reaching the top he found that the summit was almost flat, a couple of hundred yards in length, and as many feet in width. It was covered with grass, and several trees, some of considerable size, were scattered about over the surface.

"Well, Bill," he said as Royce came up to him, "have you found any water?"

"Yes, there is a rock pool in the centre there by that big tree. There is water enough for us and the horses for maybe a week. Enough for us without the horses for a month or more."

"What are you going to do? Bring the horses up here?"

"We haven't settled that yet. I reckon we shall bring the best of them up anyhow."

"I suppose there is no possible place the Indians can get up except by that gap?"

"Nary one, everywhere else the rock goes straight down to the plain. There ain't no way, except by flying, to get up here if you don't come by this gap. Anyhow we shall bring the horses a good long way up the slope; it is a long line along the bottom there, and the Redskins might crawl up in the night, and we should pretty nigh all have to keep guard. Steve says that though where we came up the ground wur smooth enough, it ain't so over the rest of the slope, but that, what with the boulders and the undergrowth and thorns, it is pretty nigh impossible to get up through the trees anywhere else. He expects that it's been water washing down the earth and sand through that gap that has filled up between the boulders, and made it smooth going where we came up. So we will bring up the horses, and get the best of them up here, and tie the others just below the gap. We can take them down water in our hats if we decide to keep them, or get them up to-morrow if we like. Anyhow, all we shall want will be to keep four men at watch down below them."

"I should have thought it best to bring them all up at once, Bill; what is the use of leaving them below?"

"Waal, Hugh, there ain't grass enough to bring them all up

here, and every morning we can take them down and let them graze below. There air no fear of the Injuns coming close to drive them off, and if they tried it, the critters would come up the path again of their own accord, except those we took from the Indians. They can get a good lot of sweet grass under the trees down thar, and as long as they get that they can do pretty well without water. Thar, do you see thar are two or three more lots of Indians coming down to join the others. They'll have three hundred of them down thar before long."

"It don't make much difference how many of them there are, if they dare not attack us," Hugh said.

"That's where you are wrong, Hugh," Broncho Harry, who had now joined them, said. "The more thar are of them the closer watch they can keep to see that none of us gets away, and the more thar are of them the bigger the party must be that comes to rescue us. You may be sure that they have scouts for miles and miles off, and if they get news that there is a party coming up, they will just leave a guard to keep us here, and go down and fall on them."

"I didn't think of that, Harry. Yes, it will need a very strong party to bring us oft. But perhaps they will get tired and go."

"Don't you bet on that, Hugh. Ef thar air one thing an Injun never gets tired of, it's waiting. Time ain't nothing to them. Them chaps can send out parties to hunt just as if they wur in their own villages. The boys will bring them down corn, and gather their firewood for them, and as long as we are up here, they will stop down thar, if it was six months. They know how many of us thar are here. Lots of them must have been up here at one time or another, and knowing the time of year, and how much rain has fallen lately, there ain't no doubt they can calkilate pretty well how much water there is in this pool. They will know that we shall keep our horses as long as we can, and they will reckon that three weeks at the outside will see the end of the water. As for food, of course, we are all right. We have got the horses to eat, and horse is pretty nigh as good as cow beef. I would just as soon have one as the other. A young broncho's a sight tenderer than an old cow any day."

Hugh now took a turn round the edge of the butte. It was, as

Royce had said, a mass of rock rising perpendicularly from the plain. It was separated from the other butte by a gap a hundred and fifty feet wide. It was clear that they had once formed one mass, for between them was a rocky shoulder connecting them. This was very steep on both sides, narrowing almost to a razor edge at the top, where it joined the butte on which they were standing. This edge was fifty feet below the top, but it rose as it retreated from it, and on the opposite side reached up to a level with the plateau.

A fire had already been lighted on the top of the butte, and over this the women were cooking some of the meat they had brought from the Indian village, and in a short time the whole party except two, who were placed on sentry to watch the movements of the Indians, gathered round it.

"Waal, boys," Steve said when the meal was finished, "I reckon that thar ain't no time to lose, and that I had best start to-night. There ain't no denying that we air in a pretty tight fix here, and it won't be easy to get a force as can fight their way through that crowd. I reckon I shall not be able to gather over fifty cowboys on the Canadian, and so I'll have to ride to the nearest fort and get the troops to help. That air about two hundred miles from the Canadian. It ull take me three days to get there after I leave the ranches. It ull take four at the very least before the troops will get down there. You can't reckon less than a week. I shall be two days getting down to the ranches, as there won't be any travelling by day. So you see if I start to-night, you can't reckon on seeing us back afore ten days at the earliest."

"That will be about it, Steve. I don't see as you can do without the troops noway. Waal, we can hold out a fortnight easy. We must put the horses on mighty short allowance of water, so as to make it last a fortnight. If we find it running out quicker'n we expect, we must kill off half the animals. It don't matter about them a bit, ef you come up strong enough to thrash the Redskins without our help. Yes, I think you had better go to-night. You are as likely to get out to-night as any night, but you'll have to look mighty sharp, Steve, for you may bet your life them Injuns will be as thick as bees round the butte."

"How do you mean to go, Steve?" Hugh asked.

"Tie the ropes together, Lightning, and get lowered down over the edge."

"I have been looking at the ridge that runs from this butte to the other," Hugh said, "and it struck me that if you were lowered down on to it you might get along on to the other butte. Of course two others would be lowered with you, and then you could be let down from the farthest side of the other butte. You said nobody had ever been on it, and anyhow the Indians are not likely to be as thick over there as they would be round this one."

"Thunder! You are right again, Lightning. I will go and have a look at it at once. It will soon be getting dark; Broncho, do you and Long Tom go along with me. We will lie down afore we get to the edge. You may be sure that there are plenty of sharp eyes watching all round, and if they was to see us standing there, and looking at that ledge of rock, they might guess what we had in our minds. While we are away, the rest of you might go down and get up the ponies."

It took some time to lead all the horses up the slope. Prince and four others were brought up to the plateau, but it was necessary to tie strips of blankets under their feet to enable them to get sufficient footing to climb up through the gap.

"I shouldn't have thought that cattle could have come where horses can't," Hugh said.

"Cattle can climb pretty nigh anywhere," the cowboy he addressed replied. "I have seen cattle climb places where you would have thought that nothing but a goat could get to. You see their hoofs are softer than horses', and get a better hold on rocks. But horses could get up here easy enough if they weren't shod. They don't have a fair show with shoes on."

By the time the horses had been brought up, night had fallen. Four men were told off as a guard; two of them took up their post halfway down the slope; two went down to its foot. No attack was anticipated, for the Indians would be sure that a sharp watch would be kept, and there would be no chance whatever of their making their way up to the summit unobserved. Hugh was not with the first party on watch, and joined the crowd round the fire.

"What time are you going to start, Steve?"

"As soon as it gets quite dark. Thar ain't no good in waiting. They air on watch now, and they will be on watch all night, so thar is no difference that way, and the sooner I goes, the farther I will git afore morning. It is settled that if I am caught to-night, Jim Gattling will try next; ef he goes down too, Broncho Harry will try. After that you can settle among yourselves."

"I will volunteer to be next," Hugh said. "Another couple of days and Prince will be ready to do anything. If I was to try I should start on his back and take my chance. The Indians cannot have many horses as fast as he is, and if I can get through safely, they may ride as hard as they like. There won't be many who can catch me anyhow, and if they came up one at a time, I have my revolver and can hold my own. I shouldn't like to try to-night, for many of their horses are fresh, and Prince wants at least twenty-four hours before he is fit for work again; but if you like to give up your attempt to-night, Steve, I will try to-morrow night."

"No, no, lad, we will do as we have planned. You might do it, and you might not. More likely you would not, for like enough you would run agin a dozen of them going out, and would get a lasso dropped over your shoulders afore you saw or heard them. Besides, you are young, lad. You have got your life afore you. I am getting on, and Rosie will have Jim to look after her, so it don't make much matter along of me."

An hour later it was perfectly dark. Steve had left his hat lying on the edge of the rock exactly above the ridge, when he had visited it with Harry and Long Tom. Several of the ropes were knotted together; while this was being done, Steve withdrew with his daughter and Jim Gattling from the fire, and was absent five or six minutes. He came back by himself.

"I am ready," he said. "Goodbye to you all! I hope as I'll see you all agin afore long." He shook hands with them all round, and then, taking up his rifle, walked away without looking round, followed by Broncho Harry and Long Tom, the latter saying to Hugh and two others, "You come too. We shall want you to lower the last of us down, and to hoist us up again."

The hat was soon found. All three men took off their boots.

Broncho Harry tied those of Steve together by a short piece of rope and slung them over his shoulder, and he and Tom left their revolvers and belts behind them.

"Now we are ready," Harry said; "mind, Steve, as you go down you keep your face to the rock, so that that gun of yours shan't strike it; you can't be too keerful, you know." A loop was placed round Steve's shoulder under the arm. "You lie down, Hugh, with your face over the edge, then Steve can tell you if we are one side or other of the ledge. It looked plumb down from here, but it mayn't be."

Harry had, rather to Hugh's surprise, taken up his blanket as he left the fire, but he now saw the object; it was partly folded and laid over the edge so as to prevent any chance of the rope touching a rock and being cut by it.

"Now, Tom and I will hold it out a bit beyond the face," Harry said; "and you two do the lowering away. Now, Steve."

Steve knelt down at the edge and lowered himself until the strain came on the rope. This Broncho and Tom held out as far as they could, and the other two steadily lowered it. It was so dark that Hugh could not see the ridge, and presently lost sight of Steve. Soon, however, he heard his voice, "About a foot more to the right." A few seconds later the strain on the rope ceased.

"Are you all right, Steve?" Hugh asked.

"Yes, I am astride of it; it is wider than I thought it was. Now I will move on; you can let Broncho down as soon as you like."

The other two men were lowered, and then there was a long silence. It was no easy matter, Hugh knew, to crawl along the ridge, for it was by no means even. The great danger was that there might be loose pieces which would be dislodged and go clattering down below. When, however, ten minutes had passed without any sound being heard, the watchers felt sure that the three men must have gained the opposite summit. There was nothing now to do but to sit down and wait. At the end of an hour and a half, Hugh, who was again leaning over listening intently, heard a voice below him, "Lower down that other rope, Hugh, we are both here."

The short rope was lowered, for the long one had been taken

by them to lower Steve from the other butte, and in a short time Broncho and Long Tom stood beside them.

"I think the old man has got safe off," Broncho Harry said. "We have stood over there listening all this time and ain't heard a sound. There are plenty of the varmint about. You hear that barking of prairie-dogs and hooting of owls? That's them letting each other know where they are; they are thick everywhere, I guess, round the foot of this butte, but we didn't hear them on the other side, and I reckon there ain't many of them there anyhow. Steve must have got beyond them by this time. That wur a first-rate idea of yours, Hugh; he never would have got through if we had lowered him off here; but it wasn't no joke getting along that ridge in the dark, I can tell you. We air all accustomed to balance ourselves in the saddle, and so made a shift to get across; but in some places the rock wur pretty nigh as sharp as a knife."

"Do you think that there is any chance of a night attack, Broncho?"

"One never can answer for the varmint, but I don't reckon as they are like to try it; they know they couldn't get up to the top, and all they could hope for would be to kill some of the horses and cut off the men on watch. It wouldn't be worth risking many lives to do that; besides, it ain't a nice place to climb in the dark. They can crawl along out on the plain without making more noise than a snake would do, but that is a different thing to climbing up among bush and rock in the dark. They couldn't reckon on doing it without being heard. No, Hugh, it may be that one or two of the young bucks wanting to distinguish themselves and thirsting for scalps, may crawl up and see if they can catch anyone napping down below there, but I reckon that is all, and that ain't likely to be tried to-night. They are all out there trying to make sure that no one gets away. That is their first consarn; besides, like enough the chiefs will try in the morning to get us to surrender, and it wouldn't do for any young brave to make a venture on his own account, until it is sartin that they ain't going to get us without fighting; still, I wouldn't say that when it comes to your turn to be on guard, Lightning, it would be altogether safe for you to put your rifle down and take an hour's sleep."

"Well, I am not likely to try that experiment anyhow, Broncho."

"No; I didn't guess as you was. I only said as it wouldn't be safe. I don't think Steve put enough men on guard. I am going to talk to the others about it. I reckon we ought to divide into two guards, say ten on each watch; four down below, four up with the horses, two up here at the top of the path. We shan't have much to do all day, and can sleep as much as we like. Steve is an old Injun fighter, and he knows better than we do what the chances air, still there ain't no good taking risks."

"I quite agree with you, Broncho. Now that Steve has got safe away we know we shall get help before very long; and it would be foolish to run any risk merely from want of care. I would go even further and let fifteen men be on watch at night, and let five sleep and keep lookout during the day."

"That would be no better, lad, that would be worse, for it is difficult to keep awake the whole night, especially if night after night passes without an alarm."

By this time they had reached the others, and there was much rejoicing when it was heard that Steve Rutherford had got safe away.

"Do you feel sure, Harry, that they might not have caught him and killed him without any noise?" Rosie asked anxiously.

"Sartin. Steve's last words was: 'I shall keep my six-shooter in my hand, and if they riddle me with arrows, Broncho, I will fire a shot or two before I drop, don't you fear about that.' And he would do it. Besides, it ain't in Injun nature to kill an enemy without setting up a yell over it. A Redskin's like a hen laying an egg; he has got to boast of it loud enough for all the world to hear. No; you needn't be a bit afeard, gal. Your father has got off safe, and by this time I reckon he is ten miles away."

Harry then made the proposal that half the men should be always on guard, to which they at once agreed, and six of them, taking up their arms, left the fire without further words, and started to take up their post on the slope.

"Now, Rosie, you shall give us a pan of tea and a bit of meat, and then the sooner we are all asleep the better. We shall want to use our eyes when it is our turn on watch."

At twelve o'clock they were on their feet again, and went down the hill. "Now, Harry," said Long Tom, "Lightning and you and me will go along to the bottom; three others keep about fifty yards behind us, two up below the horses, and two on the top here."

As they took their places, and the men they relieved returned to the summit, Long Tom said: "Listen to the calls, Lightning; the Redskins have heard us moving and are warning each other to look sharp. I reckon they are as thick as peas all round here, for they know that if one of us tries to make a bolt on horseback it is here he must start; but they can hardly suppose that we are such fools as that comes to. Now you move away five or six yards to the right and post yourself behind a rock. You have got to keep your eyes in front of you to see if you can see anything moving in the grass; and you have got to listen for any sound over there to the right, in case any of the Redskins should try to crawl up through the bushes to circumvent us. I'll go to the left, and Broncho kin take the middle of the path."

Hugh took up his post and maintained a vigilant watch; he was much more afraid of an attempt on the part of the Indians to crawl up on the right than of an attack in front, and listened intently for the slightest sound of moving leaves on that side, for he knew that the Indians would not be likely to break the smallest twig in their progress. In front of him he could discern the expanse of the plain stretching out; there were a few low bushes here and there, and at times, to his straining eyes, it seemed that some of the dark masses moved, but he knew that this might be only fancy. Hour after hour passed. Presently Harry stole up to his side. "Day will be breaking in an hour, Hugh, keep a sharp lookout now; they will try it, if they try it at all, just as the sky begins to lighten."

All, however, remained quiet, and Hugh felt in no slight degree relieved as the light stole gradually up the eastern sky, and he felt that Harry's anticipations were incorrect, and that no attack would be made. As soon as the sun rose the sentries were relieved, and the party on watch retired to the crest, for from there a view over the whole of the plain was obtainable, and it was impossible for the Indians to crawl up towards the buttes without being seen. Two hours later a party were seen approaching from the main Indian camp; they stopped five hundred yards away; then two Indians advanced and held up their arms to show they had left their rifles behind them.

"I thought they would be wanting to have a talk this morning," Broncho Harry said. "I suppose two of us had better go down to meet them."

"You and Jim Gattling had better go, Broncho."

"No," Jim said; "Rason had better go with you, Broncho; he speaks a little of their language, and I don't; it is not likely either of the chiefs speak English."

"All right!" Broncho said; "it is as well to understand what they say, though we know well enough that nothing will come of it. Put your six-shooter in your pocket, Rason, they will have their tomahawks and knives hidden about them somewhere; half a dozen of the rest had better come down the slope. It ain't likely they will make a rush, but when they find we won't agree to their terms they may turn nasty."

Hugh watched the meeting from the top of the butte. It lasted about ten minutes, and then the envoys separated and returned to their respective parties. The result was clear enough, for when the Indian chiefs reached their followers they raised a defiant war cry, which was taken up all over the plain.

"Just as I expected," Harry said. "The Redskins always like to have a talk before they begin to fight, even when they know well enough that nothing can come of it."

"What was their proposals?"

"They said that they knew we could hold out for a time, but that the water would soon be finished, and we must give in then. We had stolen the white women out of their camp, and had killed their young men; but if we would give up the women and surrender our arms and ammunition they would let us depart free."

"What did you say, Broncho, in return?"

"I said that we was very comfortable up here, and that if we had taken the women, they had stolen them away from us. As to our arms, we thought they was more useful in our hands than they would be in theirs; but that if they would go back to their villages we would promise to do them no further harm until they troubled us again."

"Who were the chiefs, Harry?"

"One was the Eagle; he is a big chief. I have often heard of him. The other was the Owl. I fancy the Eagle is the fighting chief, and the Owl the counsellor. He is a crafty-looking beggar. The Eagle is a fine tall Redskin, a sort of chap I shouldn't care about having a hand-to-hand fight with, with knives and toma-hawks. He told us it wur no use our hoping for assistance, for that none could come to us, and unless we could fly we could not get through his young men; and that even if we could, our scalps would be hanging in their lodges long before we could get down to the ranches. I said he might have our scalps if he could take them; but that if he did it would be off dead bodies, for as long as one of us had strength to draw trigger, he would not get up on to the butte. That was all. He knew well enough what the answer would be. He wanted to see, I fancy, how we took it, and whether we were in good heart. It wur just a game of bluff, and neither of us wur going to show our hands."

That night Broncho Harry's party went first on watch, and were relieved at twelve o'clock. The Indians had remained quiet all the day, and Harry said to Hugh as they returned up the hill after being relieved, "I shouldn't be surprised if they try and attack before morning. In the first place, they have been won-derful quiet all day; and in the next place, I reckon that when the chief said he acknowledged that we could hold the place, he just meant to give us the idee that he didn't mean to attack, and wur only going to starve us out. In course they will do that after-wards, but I think they will try one rush first. I tell you what, Hugh, we will set to work now and get the rest of the horses to the top. They can't pick up much where they are now, and they may as well be out of the way if there is a fight."

The ten men soon got the horses up on to the plateau and then lay down to sleep. The morning was just breaking when the crack of a rifle was heard, and it was followed instantly by a score of others and an outburst of fierce yelling; every man sprang to his feet and ran to the top of the path. "Hugh, do you and two others take your place on the edge of the rock on the right of the gap. Tom, you and Stumpy and Rason, take your places on the left and kiver us as we fall back, if we have to, as is like enough. Come on with me the rest of you."

Standing on the edge of the cliff, Hugh saw the flashes bursting out rapidly among the rocks and trees at the foot of the slope, and soon perceived that they were mounting upwards. A crowd of Indians must have thrown themselves suddenly forward and established themselves in cover, and they were now fighting their way up. The defenders had fallen back, for the answering flashes were halfway up the slope. The rattle of musketry was incessant, but far above it rose the yells of the Indians. The whites fought silently.

It was still too dark to make out the figures, and Hugh and his companions remained inactive.

"Our men are falling back, Bill," he said presently to Royce, who was standing a few yards away on the other side of the gap.

"They are sure to do that," Royce replied. "I guess there are two hundred Injuns down there, and though it is difficult for them to make their way through the bushes, they will do it. You will see our fellows will soon be up here."

Five minutes later, indeed, three or four figures were seen coming up the path. "Who are you?" Hugh shouted.

"It is all right," one of them called out. "There air too many for us, and Broncho has ordered us to fall back, and help you cover the rest."

Gradually the flashes of the defenders' rifles ceased to spurt out from among the rocks, and died away altogether. Then at full speed the men dashed up the pathway, followed closely by a number of leaping figures. Then the rifles of those along the edge of the rock cracked out. There was a chorus of cries and yells, and the pursuers bounded in among the rocks and bushes again, and their rifles flashed out angrily. Rason fell backwards, shot through the head, and a cry on the other side of the gap showed that at least one was hit there.

"Lie down," Hugh shouted, "and fire over the edge."

In a minute the whole party were gathered on the crest. The

daylight was now broadening rapidly; but not one of the assailants could be seen, though the puffs of smoke from behind rock and bush showed how thickly they were gathered.

"Will they try a rush, do you think?" Hugh asked Broncho, who had taken his post beside him.

"I don't think so," Harry said. "I expect they didn't reckon on finding so many men on guard on the slope, and thought they might carry it with a rush and get here afore we was ready for them, and before it wur light enough for us to shoot straight. They can't gather thick enough among the rocks down thar to give them a chance of making a big rush."

Apparently this was also the opinion of the Indians, who soon learned that it was dangerous to show their position by firing, for every shot was answered instantly, and several were killed as they raised their heads to fire from behind the rocks. The firing, therefore, gradually ceased.

"Now we are just as we was before," Harry said. "It wur sartin we couldn't hold the slope if they made an attack. The only thing is, they are nearer for a rush in the dark than they was afore. There ain't no fear of their trying it as long as it is light. Six will be enough to keep guard at present. We will talk over what is best to be done."

Six men were picked out as a guard, the rest assembled in council. "We have got to block up that gap somehow," Harry said. "If they make a rush in the dark we may kill a lot of them; but the chances are, they will get up. It seems to me that we had best kill half the horses and pile them up down near the mouth. That will make a breastwork, and will stop their bullets."

There was a general chorus of assent. Then Hugh said, "That seems a very good idea, Harry, but I should think that it would be better if we were to make that breastwork halfway up the gap, and to cut off some big arms of these trees and pile them in front of it. If we were to pretty well fill up the gap with boughs it would be very difficult to get through, and a couple of us behind the breastwork with six-shooters would prevent them from clearing it away, especially as the others could fire down from above on them."

"That's it," Broncho Harry said. "That will make us as safe as if there wur no gap at all. Bully for you again, young un! Let us set to work about it at once."

There was not a hatchet among them, and it took them the whole day to cut off five or six stout boughs of trees with their bowie-knives. However, it was done at last. The boughs were dragged along until near the mouth of the gap and then dropped into it, the butt-ends inwards, Broncho Harry and two or three of the others going down into the gap and arranging them so that a dense screen was formed outwards with the boughs and leaves. One or two shots came up from the bottom of the slope, but these were harmless, and the guard took care that no one was able to fire from a direct line with the gap from anywhere near the summit. At last the boughs were all in position, and a dense hedge filled the gap twelve feet high.

"We can spare the horses," Harry said. "They can't get through that hedge with us above them. They will never even try it. They see as we are up to something by their firing, but I don't suppose they can make out what it is. Like enough one of them will crawl up after it gets dark to see, and when he reports what we have done they will know that the game is up as far as taking the place by storm is consarned."

From this time forward no attempt was made to renew the attack. The Indians still held the slope, for shots were occasionally fired whenever one of the defenders came near enough to the edge to allow his head to be seen, otherwise all was quiet. As soon as the meat brought up was finished, one of the Indian horses was killed, and Hugh found that its flesh was by no means bad eating. The water was carefully husbanded, horses as well as men being placed on the smallest possible allowance. The horses too were picketed so as to prevent them from grazing at will, and the grass was cut and supplied to them in small bundles, mixed with leaves from the trees. With good management it was agreed that they would be able to hold out for a fortnight without difficulty.

XV. WITH THE WAGON TEAMS

Soon after daybreak on the twelfth day the watch, which had now been carefully kept up for some days, reported that two Indians were galloping at full speed up the valley. A cheer broke from the defenders of the butte, for they doubted not that these brought news of the approach of a relieving party. When the horsemen arrived at the main encampment out on the plain a stir was immediately visible, and in two or three minutes the Indians were seen running out to the horses grazing on the plain beyond, while loud yells rang through the air.

"Those who have got rifles had better come to the edge," Long Tom shouted. "All these fellows who are here will be scooting out on the plain in a minute. We must stop a few of them anyhow."

A minute or two later scores of Indians dashed out from the trees at the foot of the buttes, and ran towards their encampment. The whites at once opened fire, but a running man far below is a difficult mark, and not a single shot took effect.

"You don't call that shooting," Broncho Harry said indignantly.

"It is all very well, Harry," Hugh said, "but a brown spot three hundred feet below you, and as many yards away, isn't an easy mark."

"Waal," Harry said, "it can't be helped. Now we will get ready to go out to lend a hand to our friends. Let us have a couple of ropes; we will tie them to the branches one by one and haul them up. There is no fear of an attack. Now look here, Jim, you and your lot had best stop here to guard the women, and we will sally out. There are five of you; that will be plenty."

The man on watch now gave a shout. "I can see them," he said.

"How many of them?"

"I guess there is about eighty. There is a thick clump in the middle, I reckon that they are the soldiers; and thirty or forty riding loose, I allow they are cowboys."

"That is just about the right number," Harry said; "if there was more of them the Indians wouldn't fight. I don't know as they will now, but seeing as there must be three hundred of them, I expect they will try it. Now, then, up with these branches."

In a quarter of an hour the branches were all hauled out of the gap. While this had been going on the women had given a feed and a good drink of water to the horses, for there was no occasion any longer to husband their resources. The animals were now saddled and led down through the gap. By this time the Indians were all mounted, and were moving in a close body across the plain to meet the advancing foe.

"Now, Jim," Broncho Harry said, "you stand on the edge, and when you see the fight begin you wave your hand. We can't make a start until they are at it, and we shan't be able to see down below there."

The cowboys made their way down to the plain and then mounted. They sat for ten minutes with their eyes fixed upon Jim Gattling. Presently he waved his arm, and with a shout they started at a gallop. As soon as they were fairly out on the plain they heard the sound of firearms, and after galloping half a mile came suddenly in view of the combat. The Indians had boldly closed with the troops and cowboys, who were now driven together. A desperate hand-to-hand conflict was raging. Swords flashing in the sun, waving tomahawks, and spears could be seen above the mass. The cracking of revolvers was incessant, and a light smoke hung over the conflict.

"They are hard at it, boys," Long Tom exclaimed; "now don't shout until we are on them. They are too busy to notice us. Keep well together, and we shall go through them like a knife."

Not a word was spoken as they galloped down upon the scene of conflict. When they were within a hundred yards a cry of warning was raised, and some of the Indians faced round; but in a moment, with a loud shout, the band of cowboys charged down upon them and cleft their way into the mass, horse and rider rolling over under the impetus of the onslaught. The deadly six-shooters spoke out, while the Indians fell thickly around them; and in a minute they had joined the whites in the centre of the mass. There was a shout of welcome, and then the officer commanding the troops cried:

"Now is your time, lads; press them hard, give it them hot!" and the united party attacked the Indians with fresh vigour.

Up to this time there had been little advantage on either side. Many more of the Indians had fallen than of the whites, owing to the superiority of the latter's weapons, especially the revolvers of the cowboy section. Still, their great superiority in numbers was telling, and when the six-shooters were emptied the cowboys had no weapons to oppose to the spears and tomahawks of the Indians. The sudden attack from the rear, however, had shaken the Redskins. In the momentary pause that had ensued many of the cowboys slipped fresh cartridges into their pistols, and in a short time the Indians began to give ground, while the less courageous of them wheeled about their horses' heads.

War Eagle and some of the chiefs fought desperately; but when the former fell, cut down by one of the troopers, a panic spread among his followers, and as if by a sudden impulse they turned and fled. The pursuit was a short one, for the horses of the rescuing force were jaded with the long journey they had performed; those of the party from the butte were weakened by hunger, while the ponies of the Indians had been doing nothing for days, and speedily left them behind. After hearty congratulations by the rescuers, and sincere thanks by those whom they had relieved from their peril, the party returned to the scene of conflict. Four troopers and two cowboys had fallen, and a score had received wounds more or less serious; while on the part of the Indians over thirty lay dead. Graves were dug for the fallen whites, the wounds of the others were bandaged up, and they then proceeded to the butte, at whose foot the women, and the settlers who had been left to guard them, had already gathered, they having hurried down as soon as they saw the plain covered with flying Indians.

Steve had returned with the rescuing party, and had been severely wounded in the fight, a blow from a tomahawk having cut off one of his ears, wounded his cheek, and inflicted a terrible gash on his shoulder. He was, however, in the highest spirits.

"I shan't look so purty, my dear," he said to his daughter, who burst into tears at the sight of his injury, "but then I was not anything uncommon afore, and I haven't any thought of going courting again. Waal, we have given the Injuns a smart lesson."

When the handshaking and congratulations ceased, the captain commanding the cavalry held a consultation with Steve and some of the cowboys as to the advisability of following up the victory and attacking the Indians in their own villages.

"I should not feel justified in doing it unless I was pretty certain of success. The commandant of the fort gave me orders to rescue this party, and I have done so; but he said nothing about engaging in a regular campaign with the Indians."

"I shouldn't try, captain," Steve said. "I reckon they haven't half their force here to-day—no, nor a quarter—for they reckon to put a thousand fighting men in the field. They didn't guess as any of us had got off to get help, and knew that they had plenty here to keep us caged upon the butte. Another thing is, the cowboys with us air all employed on the ranches, and although they came off willing to rescue the women, and pay the Injuns off for that murdering business at our settlement, I reckon they will want to be off again to their work. But even with them we ain't no match for the forces the Redskins can collect, so if you will take my advice, captain, you won't waste a minute, for thar is no saying how soon they will be down on us again, and if they did come the fight to-day wouldn't be a sarcumstance to the next."

"You are right," the officer said; "it would be folly to risk anything by waiting here. I suppose you are all ready to start."

"I reckon so," Steve said; "the horses have all been brought down from the hill."

The officer at once gave orders to mount.

While this conversation had been going on, Hugh, who was occupied in giving Prince a good feed from the grain the soldiers had brought for their horses, saw one of the troopers staring at him.

"Hullo, Luscombe!" he exclaimed, "who would have thought of seeing you here?"

"I thought I couldn't be mistaken, Hugh," the other exclaimed as they grasped each other's hands; "but you have changed so much, and widened out so tremendously in the eighteen months since I left you, that for a moment I wasn't sure it was you. Well, this is luck, and it is quite a fluke too. I was getting heartily sick of doing duty at that wretched fort, where one day was just like another, and there was nothing in the world to do except cleaning one's traps, when a letter arrived from the governor. I told you the old boy was sure to give in sooner or later, and he sent me money to get my discharge and take me home. I was just going to the commanding officer to make my application when Rutherford rode into camp. It was evidently something very important, for his horse fell dead as he drew rein. So I waited to hear the news, and found that our troop was ordered to mount instantly to ride to the rescue of a party of settlers and cowboys who were besieged by the Indians.

"You may guess I dropped my letter into my pocket and said nothing about it. We have done a good deal of scouting, and had two or three paltry skirmishes with the Indians, but nothing worth talking about; and this seemed, from what Rutherford said, to be likely to be a regular battle, and so, you see, here I am. It has been a jolly wind-up for my soldiering. And to think that you should be one of the party we have ridden something like three hundred miles to rescue! Now tell me all about yourself."

At this moment the trumpet to saddle sounded.

"I will tell you as we ride along," Hugh said. "I don't suppose there will be any particular order kept on our way back."

Five minutes later the whole party were cantering down the valley. They did not draw rein until late in the afternoon, and then halted on the banks of the Canadian. A strong cordon of sentries was posted that night, but there were no signs of

Indians, and the next day the party reached one of the ranche stations.

During the two days' march and at the camp Hugh and Luscombe had kept together, the latter having obtained permission from his officer to fall out of the ranks, upon his telling him that one of the cowboys was an old friend who had come with him from Europe.

"I shall be off in a month or two," Luscombe said when they parted that evening. "I expect there are formalities to be gone through here just as there are in England. You are quite sure there is no chance of your going home with me?"

"Quite sure. I have another three years to stop out here yet, and then I can go back and claim my own. I wrote to Randolph, my trustee, you know, to tell him I am alive and well, and very glad that I did not kill that uncle of mine, and saying that I shall return when I am of age, but not before. What do you mean to do, Luscombe?"

"I am going to settle down," Luscombe said. "I can tell you a year's work as trooper in one of these Yankee forts is about enough to make a man sick of soldiering. I have eaten the bread of adversity, and very hard bread it is too, and there is mighty little butter on it. I am going in for fatted calf when I go back, and am quite prepared to settle down into a traditional squire, to look after fat beeves, become interested in turnips, and to be a father to my people. Well, anyhow, Hugh, you will let me know when you come back to England. You know my address; and as soon as you have kicked that uncle of yours out, and have squared matters generally, you must come straight to me. You will be sure of the heartiest welcome. The governor is a capital old boy, and if he did cut up rusty, the wonder is he didn't do it long before. My mother is a dear old lady, and the girls—there are two of them—are first-rate girls; and the youngest, by the way, is just about the right age for you. She was fourteen when I came away."

Hugh laughed.

"I shall very likely bring home an Indian squaw or a Mexican, so we won't build on that, Luscombe; but when I go back to

England you shall hear of me, and I accept the invitation before-hand."

On the following morning the party broke up. The troops started back for the fort. Steve Rutherford and the cowboys rode for a time south-west, and then worked their way over the foothills and came down into the plains of Texas, and after a week's travel returned to the village from which they had started. It had already begun to rise from its ruins. Wagon-loads of lumber had been brought up from below, and there was no lack of willing hands from other scattered settlements to aid in the work of rebuilding the houses. Little attention was paid to the party as they rode up from the plains, for it was not on that side that a watch had been kept up for their return, and indeed the eyes of the survivors had almost ceased to turn towards the mountains, for hope had wellnigh died out, and it had been regarded as certain that the whole party had been cut off and massacred by the Indians.

As soon, however, as the news spread that there were women among the approaching troop, axes, saws, and hammers were thrown down, and there was a rush to meet them. The scene was an affecting one, as mothers clasped daughters and women embraced their husbands, whom they had never thought to see again. The cowboys were pressed to stay there for the night, but they refused, as they were anxious to return to the ranche, from which they had been absent more than three weeks. Fortunately, the busy season was almost over when they left, and they knew that there were enough hands on the ranche to look after the cattle during their absence. On the way back Broncho Harry said to Hugh:

"I expect, Hugh, a good many of us will be getting our tickets before long. They don't keep on more than half their strength through the winter. What are you thinking of doing? If you would like to stop on I will speak to the boss. I reckon I shall have charge of an outfit this winter, and can manage for you and Stumpy."

"Thank you very much, Broncho, but, as I have told you often, I don't want to stop. I have had a season's life as a cowboy, but I have no idea of sticking to it, and mean to have a try at something else. I intend to go back to England when I am twenty-one. I have some property there, and have no need to work. I got into a scrape at home with the man who is my guardian, and don't care about turning up until he has no longer any authority over me."

"Waal, you know your own business, Lightning. It is a pity, for in another year you would make one of the best hands on the plains."

"If I were to stay for another year I expect I should stay for good, Harry. It is a hard life, a terribly hard life; but it is a grand one for all that. There is nothing like it in the way of excitement, and I don't wonder that men who once take to it find it very difficult to settle down to anything else afterwards. Therefore, you see, it is just as well to stop before one gets too fond of it. I know I shall always look back upon this as the jolliest time of my life, and I am lucky to have gone through it without having been damaged by a cow, or having my neck broken by a broncho, or being shot by an Indian. Royce has made up his mind to go with me, and as soon as we get our discharge we shall make our way to New Mexico, and perhaps down into Arizona; but of course that must depend upon other things."

Upon reaching the station they found that, as Harry had predicted, hands were already being discharged. The manager said, when they went to him and told him that they wished to leave, "Well, I had intended to keep you both on for the winter; but of course if you wish to go, there is an end of it, and there are so many anxious to be kept on that a man in my position feels almost grateful to those who voluntarily afford vacancies."

There were very hearty adieus between Hugh and Royce and Broncho Harry, Long Tom, and the others who had been their close companions for months. Then they mounted and rode off from the station. They had heard from a man who had just arrived that a large wagon-train was on the point of starting from Decatur for Santa Fé. It was composed of several parties, who had been waiting until a sufficient force was collected to venture across the Indian country. There were several wagon-trains going with supplies for the troops stationed at the chain of forts along the line. Others had goods for Santa Fé; while a third was freighted with machinery and stores for mining enterprises farther south in New Mexico.

It took Royce and Hugh a week to traverse the country to Decatur, and on arriving there they heard that the teams had started two days before. They waited a day at Decatur to buy a pack-horse and the necessary stores for their journey, and then set out. In two days they overtook the train, which consisted of forty wagons. Learning which man had been selected as the leader of the party, they rode up to him.

"We are going to Santa Fé," Royce said. "We are both good shots and hunters, and we propose to travel with you. We are ready to scout and bring in game, if you will supply us with other food."

"That's a bargain," the man said briefly, by no means sorry at the addition of strength to the fighting force. "I reckon you will earn your grub. They say the Injuns air on the warpath."

"They are right enough there," Royce said. "We have been engaged in a fight with a band of the Comanches who made a raid down on a little settlement named Gainsford, killed a score of settlers, and carried off five women. We got together a band from the ranche we were working on and went after them, and we had some pretty tough fighting before we got through."

"Waal, you will just suit us," the man said. "I hear pretty near all the tribes are up, but I doubt whether they will venture to attack a party like this."

"I don't think they will if we keep together and are cautious," Royce said. "You have forty wagons; that, at two men to a wagon, makes eighty."

"That's so," the other agreed; "and what with cooks and bosses and one thing and another, we mount up to pretty nigh a hundred, and of course every man has got a rifle along with him."

"That makes a strong party," Royce said, "and with the advantage you will have of fighting from the cover of the wagons, I don't think the Redskins would dare to attack you. We have got a pack animal along with us, as you see, with our blankets and things. We will hitch him to the tail of one of the wagons."

The man nodded.

"I have got four teams here of my own," he said, "and a spare man who cooks and so on for my outfit, so you may as well jine in with that. They air the last four wagons in the line."

The journey occupied six weeks. They kept at first up the west fork of the Trinity River, crossing a patch of heavily timbered country. Then they struck the main fork of Brazos River and followed it for some distance; then took the track across to the Rio Pecos. It led them by a toilsome journey across an elevated and arid country without wood or water, save that which they obtained at the headwaters of the Double Mountain River and from four small streams which united lower down to form the north fork of the Colorado River.

From this point until they reached the Pecos, a distance of over a hundred miles, there was no water. At ordinary times caravans would not have followed this route, but would have kept far to the north. But they would have been exposed to attacks by the Comanches and Utes, so in spite of their strength they thought it prudent to follow the longer and safer route. With a view to this journey across the desert each wagon carried an empty hogshead slung behind it. These were filled at the last springs, and the water, doled out sparingly, sufficed to enable the men and animals to subsist for the five days the journey occupied, although the allowance was so small that the sufferings of the cattle were severe. Up to this time Hugh and Royce had succeeded almost daily in bringing a couple of stags into camp, but game was scarce in this parched and arid region, where not only water was wanting, but grass was scanty in the extreme, and the only sustenance for deer was the herbage of the scattered bushes.

They therefore rode with the caravan, and aided it as far as they could. The wagons, which were of great size, were generally drawn by twelve oxen or mules, and in crossing the deep sand it was sometimes necessary to use the teams of two wagons to drag one over the sandhills. Sometimes even this failed to move them, and the mounted men fastened their ropes to the spokes of the wheels, and so helped to get the wagons out of the holes into which they had sunk.

"I would rather run the risks of a fight with the Indians," Hugh said to Royce on the last day of their journey across the plain, "than have to perform this frightful journey. The heat is simply awful, and I feel as if I could drink a bucket of water."

"You will get plenty of water to-night, Hugh. The Pecos is a good big river. I believe the animals smell it already. Look how hard they are pulling. The drivers crack their whips and shout as usual, but the beasts are doing their best without that. We have been very lucky that we have had no sandstorms or anything to delay us and confuse us as to the track. Waal, we are over the worst of the journey now; except the Guadalupe Pass there ain't much trouble between the Pecos and El Paso. Once there we are on the Rio Grande all the way up to Santa Fé."

Towards the afternoon the ground became harder, and the animals quickened their pace almost to a trot, straining at the ropes with heaving flanks, while their tongues hanging out and their bloodshot eyes showed how they were suffering. An hour before sunset a shout broke from the men as, on ascending a slight rise, the river lay before them. The instant they reached its bank and the animals were loosed, they rushed in a body into the stream and plunged their nostrils deeply into the water, while the men, ascending the banks a short distance, lay down at the edge of the stream and satisfied their thirst. Five minutes later all had stripped and were enjoying a bath.

Hugh had been much struck with the difference between the teamsters and the cowboys; the former did not wear the chaperajos or leather overalls with fringed seams, or the bright silk neck handkerchiefs or flat-brimmed hats of the cowboys. Their attire was sober rather than bright. They wore soft hats, with slouched brims, and great cow-hide boots. There was none of that dashing, reckless air that characterized the cowboys, or the quick alertness that showed the readiness to cope with any emergency that might occur. Nor in the camp at night was there any trace of the light-hearted gaiety which showed itself in song, laughter, and dance in the gatherings round the cowboys' fires. They were for the most part silent and moody men, as if the dull and monotonous labour in which they were engaged, and the months of solitary journeying, with nothing to break the silence save the cracking of the whips and the shouts of encouragement to the animals, had left their mark upon them. Hugh and Royce agreed cordially that, with all its dangers and its unmeasured toil, they would infinitely prefer the life of a cowboy, short as it might be, to that of a teamster, even with the prospect of acquiring a competence upon which to settle down in old age.

Two days' halt was made on the banks of the Pecos to rest the footsore animals. Then the journey was recommenced, the river crossed at a shallow ford, and its banks followed until, after three days' journey, a small stream running in from the west was reached. Hence the route lay due west to El Paso. The country was flat until they reached the Guadalupe range of hills, which they crossed by a winding and difficult pass, each wagon being taken up by three teams. Then, skirting the Alimos Hills, they crossed the Sierra Hueco by the pass of the same name, which was far easier than that of Guadalupe, and then one long day's march took them down to Fort Bliss, which stands on the Rio Grande, facing the town of El Paso. They had now arrived at the borders of civilization. Mexican villages and towns and United States posts were scattered thickly along the course of the river all the way from El Paso up to Santa Fé.

"What air you thinking of doing, young fellow?" the head of the party asked Hugh as they sat by the fire of the encampment a short distance out of El Paso. "You see we shall kinder break up here. I go wit my teams to the forts along the river, and then strike out east to the outlying posts. About half my freight is ammunition and such like. Waal, then, pretty nigh half the wagons go up to the mines. They have powder, tools, and machinery. One or two stay here. They bring hardware and store goods of all sorts for this town; the rest go up to Santa Fé. Now what air you thinking of doing? You can make up your mind to stay here, or you kin go up to Santa Fé. You told me you had a fancy for jinin' some prospecting party and going out west into

Arizona. I doubt whether you will find anyone much bent on that job at present, seeing as how the Injuns is stirring, though I don't know that makes much difference, seeing they is always agin anyone going into what they calls their country.

"Anyhow, the miners will all have to work with a pick in one hand and a rifle in the other. You have got the Apaches here, and they air wuss than the Comanches. The Comanches have had to deal with western hunters and pioneers, and know that there ain't much to be got out of them but lead, so beyond stealing cattle they've got into the way of being mostly quiet, though now and agin they break out, just as they have at present. Now the Apache has had to deal all along with Mexicans, and he has pretty good reason for thinking that he is a much better fighter than the white man. He has been raiding on the Mexican villages for hundreds of years, burning and killing and carrying off their women and gals, and I guess thar is a pretty good sprinkling of Mexican blood in his veins, though that don't make him better or wuss, as far as I know. Still, take them altogether, they air the savagest and hardest tribe of Redskins on this continent.

"However, if you like to go prospecting among thar hills and to run the risk of losing your scalp, that is your business; but if you do, this is the place to start from, and not Santa Fé. There is gold pretty nigh everywhere in the valley of the Gila, and that lies a bit to the north-west from here. At any rate, it seems to me that this is the place that you are most likely to fall in with parties starting out. But let me give you a warning, lad. You will find this town is pretty nigh full of gold miners, and you won't find one of them who won't tell you that he knows of some place that's a sartin fortune up among the hills. Now, don't you believe them. Don't you go and put your money into any job like that. If you find a party being got up, and others think it good enough to jine, of course you can chip in, but don't you go and find the money for the whole show."

"There is no fear of that," Hugh laughed. "I had about five-and-twenty pounds when I went on to the ranche, and I have got that and six months' pay in my belt. That won't go far towards fitting out an expedition."

"No, it won't," the teamster agreed. "It will be enough for you to be able to chip in with others, but, as you say, not to stand the whole racket. Waal, what do you think?"

"I am very much obliged to you for your advice," Hugh said, "and I think we can't do better than stay about here for a bit at any rate. What do you say, Royce?"

"It is all one to me," Royce replied; "but there is no doubt that El Paso is as good a place as any, if not better, for looking round."

"Then that is settled, Bill; and to tell you the truth, I have had pretty nigh enough riding for the present, and shan't be sorry for a fortnight's rest."

"Same here," Bill said. "I feel as if I was getting part of the horse, and should like to get about on foot for a bit so as to feel that I hadn't quite lost the use of my legs."

Accordingly the next morning they bade goodbye to their comrades of the last two months, and mounting, rode into El Paso.

It was a town of some size, and purely Mexican in its features and appearance. The inhabitants almost all belonged to that nationality, but in the street were a considerable number of red-shirted miners and teamsters. Hugh and his companions rode to one of the principal haciendas, and handed over the three horses to a lounging Mexican.

"They have been fed this morning," Royce said. "We will come in and give them some corn in two hours."

"I will see after Prince," Hugh said, patting his horse's neck. "Don't you be afraid that I am going to leave you to the care of strangers. We have been together too long for that, old boy."

They then went into the hotel, and ordered a room and breakfast.

"I don't care much for this Mexican stuff with its oil and garlic," Royce said as they had finished the meal.

"Don't you? I call it first-rate. After living on fried beef and broiled beef for over a year, it is a comfort to get hold of vegetables. These beans were delicious, and the coffee is a treat."

"It isn't bad for one meal," Royce admitted reluctantly, "but you'll get pretty sick of Mexican cookery after a bit, and long for a chunk of plain beef hot from the fire."

"Perhaps I shall," Hugh laughed, "but I think it will be some little time first. Now let us take a stroll round the town."

It was all new to Hugh. He had seen the Mexican women in their native dress in the villages among the hills, but here they indulged in much more finery than the peasant girls. The poblanas were all dressed in gay colours, with a scarf or rebozo over their heads, with gold pins and ornaments in their glossy black hair, and with earrings, necklaces, and generally bracelets of the same metal. No small share of a peasant's wealth is exhibited on the persons of his womankind. They wore short skirts, generally of red or green, trimmed with rows of black braid, while a snow-white petticoat below and a white chemisette partly hidden by a gay handkerchief over the shoulders completed the costume. They were almost all barefooted, but Hugh observed that their feet and ankles were exceedingly small and well formed, as were their hands and plump brown arms.

Here and there were a good many of the upper class half shrouded in black mantles, wearing the Spanish mantilla, worn so as partly to conceal the face, though it needed but the slightest movement to draw it aside when they wished to recognize anyone they met. Most of these were on their way to a church, whose bell was pealing out a summons, and carried their mass book in one hand and a fan in the other. Many a look of admiration was bestowed by the merry peasant girls upon Hugh as he walked along. He was now eighteen and had attained his full height, and his life on horseback gave an easy and lissom appearance to his tall, powerful figure. His work among the cattle had given to his face something of the keen, watchful expression that characterizes the cowboys, but not to a sufficient extent to materially affect the frank, pleasant look that was his chief characteristic.

His grey eyes, and the light-brown hair with the slight tinge of gold in it, typical of the hardy north-country race, were very attractive to the dark-skinned Mexicans. He and his companion had both donned their best attire before leaving camp, and this differed but slightly from that of the Mexican vaqueros, and though sufficiently gay to attract general attention elsewhere, passed unnoticed at El Paso. The western cowboy was not an unusual figure there, for many of those discharged during the winter were in the habit of working down upon the New Mexican ranches and taking temporary employment with the native cattle raisers, by whom their services were much valued, especially where the ranches were in the neighbourhood of those worked by white cowboys. These in any disputes as to cattle with the Mexican vaqueros were accustomed to carry matters with a high hand. But the white cowboys in Mexican service were just as ready to fight for their employers' rights as were those on the American ranches, and the herds were safe from depredation when under their charge.

There were many priests in the streets, and, numerous as they were, they were always saluted with the deepest respect by the peasant women.

"It is wonderful how much women think of their priests," Royce observed philosophically. "Back east it used to make me pretty well sick, when I was a young chap, to hear them go on about their ministers; but these Mexican women go a lot further. There is nothing they wouldn't do for these fat padres."

"No. But they are not all fat, Royce," Hugh said. "I acknowledge they look for the most part plump and well-fed, and upon the best of terms with themselves, as well they may be, seeing how much they are respected."

"They have got a pretty easy life, I reckon," Royce said contemptuously. "They have to say mass two or three times a day, sit in a box listening to the women's confessions, and fatten upon their gifts and offerings."

"At any rate, Royce, the people here are religious. See, there are as many peasants as peasant women going into that church. Whatever may be said about it, religion goes for a good deal more in a Catholic country than in a Protestant. It is a pity there is not more religion among the cowboys."

"How are we to get it?" Royce protested. "Once or twice a year a minister may arrive at a camp and preach, but that is about all. We always give him a fair show, and if any fellow wur to make a muss it would be worse for him. I don't say as cowboys don't use pretty hard language among themselves, but I will say this, that if a minister or a woman comes to camp they will never hear a swear word if they stop there a week. No, sir. Cowboys know how to behave when they like, and a woman might go through the ranches from end to end in Texas without being insulted."

"I know that, Royce. The point is, if they can go without using what you call swear words when a woman is among them, why can't they always do so?"

"It is all very fine to talk, Hugh; but when you get on a bucking broncho that sends you flying about ten yards through the air, and you come down kerplump, I never seed a man yet as would pick himself up and speak as if he wur in a church. No, sir; it's not in human nature."

When they got back to the hotel Hugh observed that questioning glances were cast at them by several men who were lounging about the steps. Royce observed it also.

"What have those fellows got in their heads, I wonder?" he said. "Do they reckon we are two bad, bold men who have been holding up some Mexican village, or do they take us for horse thieves? There is something wrong, Hugh, you bet."

"They certainly didn't look friendly, Royce, though I am sure I don't know what it is about. You haven't been winking at any of their women, have you?"

"G'ar long with yer!" Royce laughed. "As if any of them would look at a little chap like me while I am walking along of you. If there has been any winking it's you as has done it."

"I am quite innocent, Royce, I assure you. Still there is something wrong. Well, let us go and see that the horses are fed."

There were five or six men in the yard. They were talking excitedly together when Hugh and his companion came out of the hotel, but they were at once silent, and stood looking at them as they crossed the yard and went into the stable.

"Thar's something wrong," Royce repeated. "If my horse wur as good as yours, Hugh, I should say let's settle up quietly and ride out and make a bolt; but they would overtake me in no time."

"That would never do, Royce. I don't know what their suspicions are, but they would be confirmed if we were to try to escape, and if they overtook us the chances are they wouldn't give us much time for explanations."

"You are right there, Hugh. The Mexicans hates the whites. They know that one of us can lick any three of them, and it riles them pretty considerable. They don't give a white man much show if they get their hands on him."

"Well, it is no use worrying about it, Royce. I suppose we shall hear sooner or later what it is all about."

Passing through the hotel they took their seats at some tables placed in the shade in front of the house, and there sat smoking and talking for some time.

"If those fellows round the door keep on looking at us much longer," Royce said, "I shall get up and ask them what they mean."

"Don't do that, Royce. It would only bring on a fight; that is no use here."

"Waal," Royce said doggedly, "I haven't got to sit here to be stared at, and some of them fellows is going to get wiped out if they go on at it."

"We are sure to hear before long, Royce. See, there is a knot of four or five fellows in uniform at the other end of the square. I suppose that they are a sort of policemen. I have seen them looking this way. You will see they are going to arrest us presently, and then, I suppose, we shall hear all about it."

"I wish we had Broncho Harry and the rest of our outfit here," Royce said. "We would clear out the whole town."

Half an hour later there was a clatter of horses' hoofs, and two gentlemen, followed by half a dozen Mexican vaqueros, rode into the square and made straight for the hotel. Simultaneously the guardians of the peace moved across the square, and there was a stir among the loungers at the entrance to the hotel.

"The affair is coming to a crisis, Royce!"

One of the Mexicans was an elderly man, the other a lad sev-

enteen or eighteen years old. The latter dismounted and
entered the hotel. In two minutes he reappeared and spoke to
the other, who also dismounted, and after a word or two with
one of the men belonging to the hotel, and a short conversation
with the leader of the party of civil guards, advanced to the table
at which Hugh and Royce were sitting. He saluted them as they
rose to their feet. Hugh returned the salutation.

"Señors," he said courteously, in very fair English, "you have,
I understand, just arrived here, having accompanied a wagon-
train across the deserts from Texas."

"It is perfectly true, señor," Hugh replied. "Is there anything
unusual in our doing so?"

"By no means," the Mexican said. "The matter that concerns
me is that one of you is riding a horse which belonged to my son,
Don Estafan Perales."

"You mean the bay?"

The Mexican made a gesture of assent.

"I purchased that horse at M'Kinney, a small town in the
north-east of Texas."

"May I ask who you purchased it from?"

"Certainly, señor. It must have passed from the hands of your
son before it was offered for sale to me. I bought it from two
men whom I had never seen before."

A little crowd had gathered behind the Mexican, and at this
answer there were exclamations of "A likely story that!" and
"Death to the horse thieves!" Two men in mining costume, the
one a tall, powerfully-built man some fifty years old, the other
small and of slight figure, with snow-white hair, who had just
strolled up, separated themselves from the rest and ranged
themselves by Hugh's side, the big man saying in Mexican:

"Softly, señores, softly. You ain't neither judges nor jury on
this case, and me and my mate is going to see fair play."

"There is no intention, señor, of doing anything unfair," the
Mexican said. "The matter is a simple one. These strangers have
just ridden in here with a horse belonging to my son. He started
from here with three servants and a party going to Texas. This
was upwards of eighteen months ago. He had business at New

York. His intention was to spend a few weeks in Texas hunting, then to proceed to the nearest railway station and take train to New York. From the time he started we have never heard from him. Some members of the party he accompanied have long since returned. It seems that he accompanied them until they had passed the Bad Lands, and then left them to carry out his intention of hunting. We have never heard of him since. He certainly has never arrived at New York. And now that these strangers arrive here with his horse, which was recognized as soon as it entered the stables, I have a right to enquire how they obtained it."

"Surely, señor," Hugh said. "The men from whom I bought it were, as I said, strangers. They were two very doubtful-looking characters, and as they appeared very anxious to sell the horse, and were willing to part with it considerably under its value, my opinion was that undoubtedly they had not become possessed of it honestly. My friend here was with me at the time, and the only terms upon which I would purchase it and a pack-horse they had also to sell, were that they should give me a formal receipt signed in the presence of the sheriff and judge, in order that, should I at any time come across the owner of the animal, I should be in a position to prove that I at least had come by it honestly. That receipt I have here"; and taking a small leather letter-case from his pocket he produced the receipt. "There are the signatures, señor, and the official stamps of the writers, and you will see that they testify also to their personal knowledge of me as a resident of the town. I may add that it is certain that had I been an accomplice of the thieves I should have taken good care not to bring the horse to a locality where he would be at once recognized."

The Mexican glanced through the paper. "That is perfectly satisfactory, señor, and I must apologize for having for a moment entertained suspicions of you. Explain this, Carlos," he said to his son. "I would have further talk with these gentlemen."

The young Mexican translated in his own language the effect of what had passed, and the little crowd speedily dispersed, several having walked away as soon as the two miners sided with the accused, as a fray with four determined men armed with revolvers was not to be lightly entered upon. The miners were also turning away when Hugh said to the Mexican, "Excuse me a moment, señor."

"Thank you greatly," he went on, turning to the miners, "for siding with us. We are strangers here. Will you let us see you again, and have a talk with you? At present, as you see, this gentleman, who has lost his son, who has most probably been murdered by these horse thieves, wants to question me. Do me the favour to come in this evening and drink a bottle of wine with us, when we can again thank you for your aid."

"There are no thanks due," the bigger of the two men said. "Me and my mate knew nothing of the affair, but seeing two of our own colour facing a lot of these Mexikins we naturally ranged up alongside of you to see fair play. But as you are strangers, and we have nothing particular to do, I don't mind if we come in and have a talk this evening. Eh, mate?"

The little man nodded, and the two walked off together. Hugh then turned to the Mexican.

"Now, señor, we are at your service."

"Señors," he said courteously, "my name is Don Ramon Perales. My hacienda lies three miles away; this is scarcely a place for quiet conversation. I am anxious to learn all particulars that you can give me as to the men from whom you bought the horse. May I ask if you would mount your horses and ride back with me?"

"With pleasure, señor," Hugh said. "Our time is entirely our own, and I can readily understand your anxiety to hear all you can about this matter."

XVI. A MINING EXPEDITION

In a few minutes Hugh and Royce remounted and joined the two Mexican gentlemen, and set out, with the party of vaqueros riding behind them.

"You came in with quite a strong force, Don Ramon," Hugh said smiling.

"It might have been necessary," the Mexican replied. "I could not tell with whom I had to deal. Our guard do not care very much about risking their skins, especially when it is a question of Texan cowboys, who have, if you will excuse my saying so, a terrible reputation, and can use their pistols with a skill that is extraordinary. I could not guess that I had to do with gentlemen."

"There is nothing that way about me, señor," Royce said abruptly. "I am a cowboy, or a teamster, or a miner, or anything that comes to hand, but nary a claim to be a gentleman."

"My friend is a good fellow, señor, in every way," Hugh said, "and is my staunch and true friend. I myself am an Englishman who has come out to enjoy the hunting and the rough life of the plains of the West for a few years before settling down at home."

"And now, señor," the Mexican said with a bow, "will you let me begin to question you, for I am full of anxiety as to my unfortunate son? I feared before that he was lost to us; I fear now even more than before, for I am sure that he would never have parted with his horse, which he had reared from a colt and was much attached to. These men from whom you bought it, were they known in that locality?"

"No," Hugh replied. "Wherever they came from they did not belong to that corner of Texas, for neither the judge nor the sheriff had ever seen them before. Had they known that they

256

were bad characters they would have arrested them and held them until an owner was found for the horse; but as they knew nothing against them they did not feel justified in doing so."

"Will you describe them to me?" the Mexican said.

"They were men of between thirty and forty. From their attire they might have been hunters. They were dressed a good deal like your vaqueros: they wore chaperajos with red sashes round their waist, and flannel shirts. They had jackets with silver buttons, which you don't see much among our cowboys on the plains, and broad, soft, felt hats. I should say that one was a half-breed—that is to say, half Mexican, half American. Both had black moustaches, and what I should call hang-dog faces."

"I have no doubt, from your description," Don Ramon said, "they were two men who joined the caravan a day or two before my son left it. These men said they were hunters, and I was told that my son engaged them to accompany him while he was hunting, to act as guides, and show him the best places for game. They were described to me by some of the party that returned here, and I feared at the time that if evil had befallen him it was through them. Now that you tell me they sold you his horse, I feel but too certain this was so."

"They seemed to have ridden fast and far. Their own horses and the bay were in fair condition, señor, but the pack-horse was very poor. The men were evidently in great haste to get away, and I should judge from this that if, as you fear, they murdered your son and his three servants, they probably did it at the last camping place before they arrived at M'Kinney. Had they done it when far out on the plains there would have been no good reason why they should have been in so much haste; but if it had been but a short distance away they might have feared that someone might find the bodies and organize a pursuit at once."

"Why should they have delayed so long if their intention was murder?" the younger Mexican asked.

"That I cannot say, Don Carlos. They may have fallen in with other hunters after leaving the caravan, and these may have kept with them all the time they were out on the plains, and they may have had no opportunity of carrying out their designs till the party separated; or again, your brother's attendants might have been suspicious of them, and may have kept up too vigilant a watch for them to venture on an attack before. But this watch may have been relaxed when the journey was just at an end, and it seemed to them that their fears were unfounded."

"That is the most likely explanation," Don Ramon said. "They were three picked men; two of them were hunters, the other my son's body-servant. It is likely enough that the hunters would have kept alternate watch at night had they suspected these fellows. Those two were to have remained in charge of the horses at the town where my son took rail, and to await his return there; the other man was to accompany him to New York. My son had an ample supply of gold for his expenses, and I fear it was that rather than the horse that attracted the scoundrels."

They were by this time approaching a large and handsome building, standing in extensive grounds. As they halted before it a number of *peóns* ran out and took the horses. Prince had quickened his pace as he neared the house, and had given a joyful neigh as of recognition. When Hugh alighted, the horse, as usual, laid his muzzle on his shoulder to receive a caress before turning away, and then, without waiting for one of the *peóns* to take his rein, walked away towards the stables.

"I see he is fond of you, señor. You have been a kind master to him."

"I love horses," Hugh said, "and Prince, as I have called him, has been my companion night and day for eighteen months. We have hunted together, and roped in cattle, and fought Indians, and divided our last crust together."

Don Ramon led the way into the house, and then into a room where an elderly lady and two young ones were sitting. They rose as he entered.

"What news, Ramon?" the elderly lady asked.

"Such news as there is is bad, Maria. These caballeros, Don Hugh Tunstall and——" (he hesitated and looked at Royce, with whose name he was not acquainted). "Bill Royce, without any Don!" the cowboy put in. The Mexican repeated the name—"have been good enough to ride over here with me, in

order that you, as well as I, might question them as to what they
know of our son. Unhappily they know little. We were not mis-
informed. Don Hugh has indeed our son's horse, but he bought
it, as he has proved to me, from two strangers, who tally exactly
with the description we have received of the two hunters who
left the caravan with our son. I feared all along that these men
were at the bottom of whatever might have befallen Estafan. I
fear now that there is no doubt whatever about it. Caballeros,
this is my wife, Donna Maria Perales. These are my two daughters, Dolores and Nina."

For an hour Hugh and his companion remained answering
the questions of Donna Perales; then Hugh rose, feeling that
the ladies would be glad to be alone in their grief, for the confirmation of their fears respecting Don Estafan had brought
their loss back to them freshly. Don Ramon and his son accompanied them to the door.

"I pray you," the former said, "that if at any time you come
upon the villains you give them in custody. I and my son will
make the journey to appear against them, however far it may be."

"You need not trouble on that score," Royce said. "If we meet
them, I warrant you we can manage their business without any
bother of judge or jury. They will have a cowboy trial, and after
the evidence Hugh and I can give, you may be sure that a rope
will very soon settle their affair."

"I must ask you, Don Ramon," Hugh said, "to lend me a horse
back to the town, and to send a vaquero with me to bring it
back."

"But why, sir?" the Mexican asked in surprise. "You have your
own horse."

"No, señor, Prince is not mine. He was your son's, and is
yours. A man who buys stolen property is liable to lose it if he
meets the proper owner, and when I bought Prince for half his
value I knew that I was running that risk."

"No, señor Englishman. I do not say that a man who has lost
his horse has not the right to reclaim it wherever he may find it.
That is, if he happens to be in a place where the law is
respected, or if not if he happens to be with the strongest party;

but in the present case I could not think of depriving you of the horse. It is evident that he has found a good master, and that you stand in his affections just as my son did; besides, if you will pardon my saying so, the horse is more to you than it is to me. There are many thousands of horses running wild on my estates, and although my son used to assert that there was not one which was equal to his horse, there are numbers that are but little inferior, for our horses are famous. They are mustangs crossed with pure Arab blood, which my grandfather had selected and sent over to him, regardless of cost. Pray, therefore, keep the bay. May it carry you long and safely! It will be a real pleasure to my wife and myself to know that poor Estafan's favourite horse is in such good hands. I have also," he said courteously to Royce, "taken the liberty of ordering my *peóns* to change the saddle of the horse you rode to one more worthy of being a companion to the bay. It is of no use for one man to be well mounted if his comrade does not bestride a steed of similar swiftness."

Hugh and Royce warmly thanked Don Ramon for his kindness. The horses were brought round, and that of Royce fully bore out the commendation of the Mexican.

"We hope to see you again to-morrow," Don Ramon said as they mounted. "You will always be welcome guests here."

"And you will not forget," Don Carlos said in a low tone, "if you ever meet those men."

"That has been a fortunate adventure," Royce said as they rode off. "I have often wondered whether we should ever fall upon the original owner of your horse, and pictured to myself that we might have a bad time of it if we did. It isn't everyone who would have accepted that receipt of yours as proof."

"No; I always felt that myself, Royce. Well, that sorrel of yours is a splendid animal, and really worthy to go with Prince. I often wished you had a mount as good as mine, for my sake as well as your own, for there is no doubt of the truth of what he said. When two friends are riding together their pace is only that of the slower horse."

"That is so," Royce agreed. "So there is some Arab blood in them. I have often talked over the bay in the camps. We all

The meeting in the Inn Garden at El Paso.
See page 262.

agreed we had never seen so good a mustang. There are good mustangs, but they are never a match for a really first-rate States horse, and yet we could not see any signs of such a cross in Prince. He wur mustang, but there seemed more whipcord and wire about him than a mustang has. I have heard say that the mustangs are the descendants of Spanish barbs, and that the barbs were Moorish horses."

"Yes, that is so, Royce. The barb is related to the Arab, but is not, I believe, of such pure blood; it is a coarser animal; and if Don Ramon's grandfather brought over some pure Arabs of first-rate strain they would, no doubt, greatly improve the mustangs."

"Waal, Hugh, if we ever do meet those two murdering villains, I reckon their chances of getting away from us ain't worth mentioning."

The reception on their return to the hotel was very different to that they had before experienced. They had been visitors at Don Ramon's hacienda, and Don Ramon was the richest proprietor in the district of El Paso. After they had finished supper that evening, and were enjoying coffee and cigars at a table placed with others in a garden behind the hotel, the two miners who had stood by them in the morning came up and took seats beside them. "You had a pretty rough welcome this morning at El Paso," the big man said. "But, by the way, I do not know what to call you. My own name is Sim. I am generally known as Surly Sim. My friend's name is Frank; I generally call him the doctor."

"My name is Bill," Royce said; "and out on the plain the boys call me Stumpy, which don't need any explanation. My mate's name is Hugh, and he has got the name of Lightning."

"Ah! and why is that, may I ask?" the white-haired little man said.

"Well, it is because of one of his accomplishments, doctor. He has got the knack of drawing a pistol that sharp, that almost before you see his hand move you are looking down the tube of a pistol."

"A very useful accomplishment," the little man remarked, "always supposing that it is not used too often, and that it is only used in self-defence. I am a peaceful man myself," he went on, "and have a horror of the use of firearms."

His companion laughed.

"Now you know that that is so, Sim," the little man said earnestly.

"Waal, doctor, I don't go for to say that you are quarrelsome, and ef anyone said so in my hearing I should tell him he wur a liar. But for a peaceable man, doctor, and I don't deny as you are peaceable, I don't know as thar is a man in the mining regions who has used his weapon oftener than you have."

"But always on the side of peace, Sim," the little man said earnestly. "Please to remember, always on the side of peace."

"Yes, in the same way that a New York policeman uses his club, doctor."

"Well, I can assure you I don't often use what you call my accomplishment," Hugh said. "I practise it so that I may be able to defend my life if I am attacked, but except in a fight with a band of Comanches, I have only once had occasion to draw my pistol."

"And he weakened?" Sim asked.

"Yes, I had the drop of him. There was nothing else for him to do."

"And what are you doing at El Paso?"

"You are too abrupt, Sim, much too abrupt," the little man said deprecatingly.

"Not at all, doctor. If it is anything they don't want to tell they won't tell it. If it isn't, we may be useful to them."

"We have no particular object in view," Hugh said. "I am an Englishman; but not a rich Englishman, who comes out to buy ranches, or to speculate in mines. But I have come rather to pass three or four years in seeing life on the Western plains than to make money. I worked for six months in M'Kinney, had three or four months' hunting, and then worked six months as a cowboy; and I thought that, for a change, I should like to come this way and see something of mining adventure in New Mexico or Arizona. My mate here has been with me for nearly two years, and has thrown in his fortune with mine."

"There is adventure enough, and more than enough, in mining down thar in Arizona. The doctor and I have been at it for some years. We haven't made a penny, but we have saved our scalps, so we may be considered lucky."

"I was told," Hugh went on, "that El Paso was the most central place to come to. My idea was that I might find some party setting out on a prospecting expedition, and that I might be able to join it."

"It ain't a good time for prospecting expeditions," Sim said. "Even on the Upper Gila the mining camps is all on guard, knowing that any day the Apaches may be down on them, and it would want a man to be wonderful fond of gold for him to go out prospecting down in Arizona."

"I don't care much for gold," Hugh laughed, "though I don't say I should object to take my share if we hit on a rich lode. I should go for the sake of the excitement, and to see the life."

"Well, at other times you might find any number of people here in El Paso who would be glad enough to take you out on such an expedition," the doctor said. "You ask the first man you meet, Mexican or white, and he will tell you that he knows of a mine, and will take you to it if you will fit out an expedition."

"You are exceptions to the rule, doctor."

"No, I don't say that," the doctor replied, though his companion gave a growling protest.

"Oh, yes, we know of a mine!" he went on, not heeding the growl. "At least we believe we do, which is, I suppose, as much as anybody can say; but we are like the rest, we say that it is better to stay at El Paso and keep our scalps on, even if we are poor, than to go and throw away our lives in looking for a mine. We have been out working for the last six months on a mine in the Gila Valley on shares with six others. We weren't doing so badly; but the Mexicans who were working for us got scared and wouldn't stay, so we have given it up and come down here. Some day or other when things settle down again, I suppose the mine will be worked, but it won't be by us. We are looking out for someone who will buy our shares, but I don't suppose anyone will give five dollars for them, and they would be right. The thing paid in our hands, but it wouldn't pay in Mexicans'. They are poor shiftless creatures, and have no idea of hard work. We should have given it up anyhow, even without these Indian troubles, which don't make much difference, for the Apaches are always ready to come

down when they see a chance. It is always war between them and
the whites. But we were there six months, and six months are
about the outside Sim and I ever stop anywhere."

"When you go prospecting, do you often get any hints from
the Indians as to where gold is to be found?"

"Never," Sim Howlett said. "The Injuns are too lazy to work
theirselves, and they know that when the whites get hold of gold
they pour down in numbers. I believe they do know often where
there are lodes. I don't see how they can be off knowing it, for a
Redskin is always keeping his eyes on the move. Nothing escapes
him, and it would be strange if, wandering about as they do, and
knowing every foot of their country, they didn't notice gold when
it is there to see. Besides, they have got tales handed down from
father to son. In old times they had gold ornaments and such like,
but you never see them now. They know well enough that such
things would draw the whites. Sometimes a Redskin will tell a
white who has done him some great service where there is a lode,
gold or silver or copper, but it don't happen often. Besides, most
times the place lies right in the heart of their country, and for all
the good it is, it might as well be in the middle of the sea. Of
course, if it was gold, and the metal was found in nuggets, and a
horse load or two could be got in a month, it might be done; but
not when it comes to settling there and sinking shafts and mining;
that can't be done until the Apaches are wiped out."

"But are there such places as that, Sim?"

"Waal, there may be, but I have never seen them. The doctor
and me have struck it rich many a time, but not as rich as that.
Still, I reckon there are places where the first comer might
gather a big pile if the Redskins would but let him alone for a
month."

"I suppose you are absent some time on one of these expeditions? Do prospectors generally go on foot or horseback?"

"They in general takes a critter a piece, and two others to
carry grub and a pick and shovel; sometimes they go two
together, but more often one goes by hisself. In course where
two men knows each other and can trust each other, two is kind
of handier than one. We shouldn't like to work alone, should we,

doc? But then, you see, we have been twelve years together. Sometimes a man finds his own outfit. Sometimes he goes to a trader in a town; and if he is known to be a good miner and a straight man, the storekeeper will give him a sack of flour and a side of bacon, and such other things as are required, and then they go partners in what is found. Sometimes this goes on for months, sometimes for years; sometimes the trader loses his money, sometimes he makes a fortune. You see there are plenty of places as ain't in what you may call the Indian country, but somehow or other it do seem as if the Redskins had just been put down where the best places is, so as to prevent the gold being dug. In Arizona some big finds have been made, but nobody's any the richer for them. The Redskins is always on the lookout. Often an exploring party never comes back. Sometimes one or two come back with the news that the others have all been wiped out; but what with the awful country and the want of water, and the sartainty of having to fight, and of sooner or later being surprised and scalped, there ain't many men as cares about following the thing up."

"I suppose you know of such places, Sim?"

"Waal, maybe we do," the miner said cautiously. "Maybe we do; eh, doctor?"

The little man did not reply, but sat looking searchingly at Hugh. When he did speak it was not in direct answer to the question.

"I like your face, young fellow," he said. "It reminds me of one I have seen somewhere, though I can't say where. You look to me as if you were downright honest."

"I hope I am," Hugh said with a laugh.

"You may bet your boots on that," Bill Royce said. "He is as straight a man as you will find in Texas."

"And you are out here," the other man went on, "part for pleasure, part just to see life, and part, I suppose, to make money if you see a chance?"

"I have never thought much of making money," Hugh replied, "although I should certainly have no objection if I saw a chance; but I have never thought of doing more than keeping myself."

"And he has been with you, you say, nigh two years?" and he nodded at Royce. "And you can speak for him as he does for you?"

"That I can," Hugh said warmly. "We have worked together and hunted together, we have been mates in the same outfit, and we have fought the Comanches together, and I can answer for him as for myself. He gave up his work and went with me, not because there was any chance of making more money that way than any other, but because we liked each other."

"Well, Sim," the little man said, "it seems to me that these two would make good mates for that job of ours."

"Waal, doctor, you know I leave these things to you. I kinder feels that way myself towards them, and anyhow I don't see as there can't be no harm in setting it afore them, seeing as there ain't no need to give them the indications. But I reckon there is too many about here to talk on a matter like that. Waal, it comes to this," he went on, turning to Hugh, "if you air disposed to make a jint expedition with us, and ain't afeard neither of roughing it nor of Redskins, you meet us to-morrow three miles outside the town on the South Road, and we will talk to you straight."

"That is just what would suit me," Hugh said; "and you, Royce?"

"It is all the same to me, Lightning. If you are for an expedition you know you can count me in."

"Good night, then," Sim Howlett said, rising. "We have sat here quite long enough talking together if we mean to do anything. I reckon there is a score of these Mexikins have been saying to themselves afore now, What can those two miners and them cowboys be a-talking together about? and when a Mexikin begins to wonder, he begins to try and find out; so we are off. Three miles out on the South Road at nine o'clock to-morrow morning. About half a mile past a village you will see a stone cross by the road. There is a path turns off by it, you follow that, and you will come across us afore you have gone two hundred yards."

"What do you think of it, Royce?" Hugh asked when they were alone.

"Don't think nothing of it one way or the other. Most of them miners have got some tale or other. However, they seem to me straight men."

"I feel sure they are," Hugh said. "The big one looks an honest fellow. I don't so much understand the little one, but evidently he is the head of the party. He is a curious little fellow with his white hair and gentle voice. He doesn't look strong enough for such a life as they lead, but I suppose he is able to do his share or they would never have been working twelve years together. At any rate I came here to see something of life among the mines, and this seems as good a chance as we are likely to have."

The next morning they breakfasted at seven, and at half-past eight saddled their horses and rode out. They found their two companions of the previous night at the appointed place. As the miners saw them approaching they turned off the path and preceded them to a Mexican hut, and there waited for them to come up.

"Good morning!" the doctor said as they dismounted; "there is no fear of our being overheard here. The Mexican who lives here has often been up with us among the hills, and started for the town a quarter of an hour ago, when we told him we had a rendezvous here. Now, if you will hitch your horses up and sit down on these maize stalks we can talk comfortably. A year ago, when Sim and I were working in a gulch among the mountains, we heard a call in the distance. We went to see what it was, and found a man who had dropped down, just worn out and famished, after he had given the cry that fetched us. He had been shot in four or five places, and we saw at once that his journey was nearly over.

"We carried him to our fire and brought him round, and did all we could for him for three weeks; then he died. He told us he had been one of a party of six who had been prospecting in the hills west of the Lower Gila. One of them had learned, from an Indian he had helped in some way, of a place where the bed of a stream was full of gold. They found it; but the next morning they were attacked by the Apaches, who had, I expect, been following them all the time. Two of them were killed at once, the others got upon their horses and rode for it. Three of them were shot down, but this man was well mounted and got off, though they chased him for three days. He lost his way; his horse fell dead, but he struggled on until he saw the smoke of our fire and made us out to be whites.

"Before he died he told us how the place could be found. He said there was no doubt about the gold, and he had three or four nuggets in his pockets, weighing two or three pounds each. He said he had had lots of bigger ones, but had chucked them all away to lighten his horse. Well, it is a long journey. It will take us all a month, I reckon, to get there. We cannot go straight—the Apaches would have us to a certainty—but must go north into the Moquis country, and then down again from that side. We have been minded to try it ever since, but luck has been bad with us, and, besides, two men wouldn't be enough for such a journey.

"It ain't every one Sim and I would care about going with, but we have both taken a fancy to you. We saw you stand up straight before that crowd of Mexicans; besides, we know it wants good grit for that cowboy life. Now this is the offer we make. We have got two horses, and we can buy two pack-horses, but we can't go further than that. You have got two out-and-out horses; we saw you ride in yesterday afternoon. You will want another pack-horse, and you will have to provide the outfit: say two bags of flour, two sides of bacon, ten pounds of tea, and a couple of gallons of spirits; then there will be sugar and some other things.

"We shall also want a small tent. Now if you like to join us on these terms you can. There is plenty of gold for us all. But mind you, it will be no child's play. The journey from the Moquis country there will be terrible; and there is the chance, and a pretty big chance it is, I tell you, of a fight with the Redskins. We may never find the place. We have got pretty good indications, but it is not an easy matter to find a place among those mountains. Still, there it is. If you get there and back you will each have a horse load of gold; if you don't, you will leave your bones there. What do you say to it?"

Hugh looked at Royce. "I reckon we kin take our chances if you kin," the latter said. "At any rate, mates, you will find as we can take our share in whatever comes."

"Then that is agreed," the doctor said. "Now about preparations.

It will never do for you to be buying the things here; for if we were seen to start off together we should be followed, sure enough; it would be guessed at once we had told you of something good. We must not be seen together again. We will get our pack-horses and load up, and go as if we were undertaking a job on our own account, and camp up somewhere twenty miles away, and stop there a week. After we have gone you can get your outfit and move off and join us. Sim and I have been talking over whether it will be a good thing to take José—that is the man here—with us, instead of buying baggage horses. He has got four beasts. He could ride one himself, and the other three, with the one you have, would make up the number. José can be trusted; besides, we should not tell him where we were going, but we should have to say it would be a long journey and a dangerous one. He is a widower, with one child, and these horses are his only possession, and I think he would want their value put down before he started, say seventy-five dollars apiece for them and their saddles, that is three hundred dollars. You wouldn't buy them for less. So as far as money goes it would come to the same thing. You will get it back again if José and the animals come back; but if we all do come back, three hundred dollars would be nothing one way or the other. Then comes the point, would it be worth while to take him? There would be one more mouth to feed, but that does not go for much; there would be one more rifle in case we had to fight, and José has plenty of courage. I have seen him in a fix before now. He would look after the beasts and leave our hands free; and his pay would cost nothing, for if we got there he would help us gather and wash the gold."

"What is the drawback, then?" Hugh asked.

"The drawback is, that if we have to ride for it he might hinder us."

"There ain't much in that, doc.," Sim Howlett put in. "Our horses are pretty good, though they ain't much to look at, but the horses our mates here have got would leave them standing, and I don't know that José's best is much slower than ours; besides, when you are working among those mountains speed goes for nothing. A horse accustomed to them would pick his way among the rocks faster'n a racehorse. Ef we are attacked there running won't be much good to us. Ef we get fairly out from the hills with the gold and the 'Paches are on our trail, why, we then must trust to cunning, and our mates here can ride clear away."

"We shan't do that, Sim," Hugh said. "If we throw in our lot with you we shall share it to the end, whatever it is."

"Waal, that is all right, lad; but there are times when stopping to fight is just throwing away your life without doing no good. The doctor here and me ain't men to desart mates; but when a time comes where it ain't no sort of good in the world to fight, and when those mates must get rubbed out whether you stick by them or not, then it is downright onreasonable for anyone as can get clear off to throw away his life foolish."

"Well, anyhow, Sim," Hugh said, "it seems to me that it will be best to take José and his horses with us. It will, as you say, leave our hands free, and it will make the journey much more pleasant, and will add one to our strength. Well, that would cost, you say, three hundred dollars; how much will the rest of the outfit cost?"

"Three hundred at the outside," the doctor said. "We have been reckoning it up. Of course we have all got kits, and it's only grub and ammunition we have got to buy, and two or three more shovels, and some pans for washing the sand, and another pick or two, and a couple of crowbars. Three hundred dollars will get as much grub as the four pack-horses will carry, and make a good proper outfit for us. Will your money run to that?"

"Hardly," Hugh said, "that's just about what we have got between us. We had each six months' pay to draw when we left the ranche, and I had some before. I think we are about twenty dollars short of the six hundred."

"That is plenty," the doctor said. "If you put in four hundred, Sim and I can chip in another two hundred, as we shan't have to buy pack-horses; so we have plenty between us. We shall see José to-night and talk it over with him, and if he agrees he will come to you and bring a document for you to sign, saying that if he does not return in six months, the three hundred dollars are to be paid over for the use of his child; then he will go with you to a priest and put the paper and the money in his hands; then you can hand him over your pack-horse, he will take charge of it; then, if you will give us a hundred dollars, we engage to get the outfit all provided. When it is all done we will let you know what day you are to meet us, and where. You see we are asking you to trust us right through."

"That is all right," Hugh said. "We are trusting you with our lives, and the dollars don't go for much in comparison."

"That is so," Sim Howlett said. "Waal, there is nothing more to say now. You had best ride back to the town and give yourself no more trouble about it. You will hear from us in a few days, or it may be a week. We shall buy half the things and send them on by José, and then get the others and follow ourselves. It would set them talking here if we was to start with four loads. There is some pretty bad men about this place, you bet."

"Well, we shan't have much for them to plunder us of," Hugh said.

"Four laden horses wouldn't be a bad haul, but it ain't that I am afraid of. If there wur a suspicion as we was going out to work a rich thing, there is plenty of men here would get up a party to track us, and fall on us either there or on our way back. There are two or three bands of brigands upon the mountains, and they are getting worse. There have been several haciendas burned and their people killed not many miles from El Paso. Parties have been got up several times to hunt them down, but they never find them; and there is people here as believe that the officers of the *guárda* are in their pay. They have come across us more than once when we have been prospecting. But they don't interfere with men like us, because, firstly, we haven't got anything worth taking, anyway nothing worth risking half a dozen lives to get; and in the next place, ef it got known they had touched any of our lot, the miners would all join and hunt them down, and they know right enough that would be a different thing altogether to having to deal with the Mexikins."

Five minutes later Hugh and Royce were on their way back to El Paso.

XVII. CARRIED OFF

The next morning, in accordance with the promise they had given Don Ramon, Hugh rode out to the hacienda, Royce saying that they were too great swells for him, and he would rather stop quietly at El Paso; "besides," he said, "most likely José will come this morning, and I will stop and fix up that business with him." Hugh did not try to dissuade him, for he had seen that Royce was ill at ease on the occasion of his first visit.

On reaching the hacienda he received a hearty welcome from Don Ramon and his family, and Don Carlos rode with him over a part of the estate, where a large number of *peóns* were engaged in the cultivation of tobacco, maize, and other grain.

"If you have time, Señor Hugh, you must go with me to see our other estates; our principal one lies twenty leagues to the south. We have five hundred square miles of land there, and big herds of cattle and droves of horses, but I suppose you have seen enough cattle."

"Yes; there is no novelty about that," Hugh replied. "How many have you?"

"There and in other places we have somewhere about a hundred and fifty thousand head; as to the horses, we don't know; they are quite wild, and we drive them in and catch them as they are wanted. We have about a score of our best here, but these are the only animals we keep here except bullocks for the plough and the teams to take the crops down to market."

"I hear you have been rather troubled with brigands lately; have you any fear of them?"

"The scoundrels!" the young man exclaimed passionately; "it is a disgrace that they are not hunted down. Yes, they have been

very daring lately, and my father and several of the other hacien-
deros have written lately to the authorities of Santa Fé com-
plaining of the inactivity of the police here. I have tried to
persuade my father to move down to our house at El Paso until
the bands have been destroyed; but he laughs at the idea of danger. We have twenty armed *peóns* sleeping in the outhouses, and
twelve male servants in the house, and indeed there is little
chance of their attacking us; still, one cannot but feel uncomfortable with ladies here.

"There are a hundred troops or so stationed in the fort on the
other side of the river, and they have joined two or three times
in the search for the brigands, but of course they are too far off
to be any protection to us here; besides, they are not of much
use among the mountains. The officer in command is fonder of
good wine than he is of the saddle. It is a difficult thing to rout
out these brigands; half the peasantry are in alliance with them,
and they get information of everything that is going on, and even
if we knew of their hiding-places, there would be little chance
of our taking them by surprise. However, sooner or later, I suppose, we shall have them. There is a large reward offered for
their capture; someone is sure to prove traitor at last. It is always
the way with these bands, someone thinks himself ill-used in the
division of the booty, or takes offence with the leaders, or something of that sort, or is tempted by the reward, and then we get
them all; if it wasn't for treachery, the country would soon
become uninhabitable."

His host would not hear of Hugh returning that evening to El
Paso, but sent a *peón* in to tell Royce that he would not return
until next day. Hugh spent a delightful evening; the young ladies
played on the mandoline, and sang with their brother. The soft
light, the luxurious appointments, and the ripple of female talk,
were strange and delightful after so long a time among rough
surroundings; and it was with great reluctance that he mounted
his horse and rode back on the following morning. He found on
arrival that his comrade had arranged the matter with José, and
had deposited the money with the priest. As he was standing
chatting to him at the door of the hotel, a ragged Mexican boy

ran up, placed a scrap of paper in Hugh's hand, and at once darted away.

"It is from the doctor," Hugh said, opening it, and then read as follows: "I have something particular to say to you; it must be private; when you have received this, stroll quietly through the town as if you were only looking at the shops; go down to the river and follow it up till you hear three whistles, then come to them; you had better come alone. The Doctor."

"I wonder what the little man has got to say, Royce?"

"Dunno," the other said. "I suppose you had better go and see. You have got your six-shooter anyhow?"

Hugh obeyed his instructions and walked along the river bank till he heard the whistles; they came from a small clump of bushes standing apart from any others. As he approached it he heard the doctor's voice. "Look round and see if there is anyone in sight."

"No one that I can see," Hugh replied.

"Then come in."

Hugh pushed his way through the bushes.

"Why, what is the matter, doctor?" he asked, surprised at all these precautions.

"I will tell you. Sit down there. It is just as we fancied it might be. I told you that we might be watched. These confounded Mexicans have nothing to do but watch, and they have found out what we are after."

"How did they learn that, doctor?"

"Well," the doctor said reluctantly, "my mate has but one fault, he will sometimes go in for a drink. It's not often, but just occasionally, once perhaps every few months. It has always been so ever since I have known him. Well, last night it came over him. He thought it would be a long while before he would have a chance again, I suppose; he is not quarrelsome when he drinks, but you may be sure I always go with him so as to take care of him. So yesterday evening, seeing that he had made up his mind for it and was not to be turned, I went with him to a little wineshop near where we lodge. There were half a dozen Mexicans in there drinking and talking, and as they stopt talking directly we went in, I saw we were not wanted. But I noticed more than that. I saw two of them glance at each other, and though I could not recollect I had ever set eyes on them before, I saw they knew us.

"We hadn't any money on us beyond what was wanted to pay for the liquor, so though I didn't like the look of them I was not uneasy. We sat down and called for some liquor, and I managed to say to Sim, 'These chaps know us, Sim; don't you go drinking.' He nodded. We drank for a bit, at least he did, I don't touch spirits. Then, talking carelessly out loud, we, in whispered asides, made out a plan. We agreed that we should quarrel, and I should go out, and that he should seem to go on drinking until he got drunk and stupid, and then like enough he might hear something. So we carried that out.

"As soon as he had drunk his glass he called for another, and then another. I got up a row with him, and told him he was always making a beast of himself. He said he would drink if he chose, and wouldn't be interfered with by anyone. Then I got nasty, and we had a big row, and I went out. Then Sim went on drinking; he can stand a lot more than would floor most Mexicans. They got into talk with him, and he could see they were trying to pump him as to what we were going to do, but you bet he didn't let much out. Then he got gradually stupid, and at last rolled off the seat on to the ground. For a bit the Mexicans went on talking together, and then one of them crept over and felt his pockets, and took the few dollars he had in them out. That convinced them he was dead off to sleep, and they went on talking.

"What he gathered was this: the fellows were the spies of one of these bands. They had noticed you particularly when you came in, because it seems their captain was in the town and rec-ognized your horse, and told them he didn't like your being here, and they were to watch you sharp. They were in the crowd when there was the row about the horse, and they saw us hav-ing our talk with you. They followed you out to the Don's and back again, and when you rode out in the morning to meet us they sent a boy after you, and he kept you in sight and tracked you up to the hut, and then crawled up close and overheard what we were saying. They sent off word at once to their chief, and we are to be followed by two men; when they have traced us to the place, one is to ride back to some place where a dozen of them will be waiting to attack us on our way back."

"That is bad," Hugh said; "what is to be done?"

"This has got to be put a stop to," the doctor said calmly, "though I don't see how yet. At any rate Sim and I think we had better not hurry, a few days won't make any difference, and something may occur. He picked up from their talk that the villains had something else in hand just at present—some stroke from which they expect to make a lot of money—but they talked low, and he couldn't catch much of what they said. Maybe it will go wrong, and the country may be roused and hunt them down, and if so you bet we will be in it; we have got chances enough to take in this job as it is, and we don't want to reckon on brigands; not that there is much fear of them now that we know their plans, we have only got to ambush the men they send after us. Still, we ain't going to take any chances. The fellows may follow direct; they are sure to choose someone who knows the mountains well, and they may judge by our direction the course we are taking and go by other paths; they would know pretty well we are not the sort of people to fool with. Still, it is better to wait a little while and see if there is a chance of putting a stop to it here. It is not that we are feared of the skunks; if we could not throw them off our trail, we could fight them anyway, but one don't want to have them on one's mind; we have got plenty of things to think about without them."

"O yes! I think it much better to stay here for a bit, doctor. There is no hurry about a start on our expedition, and I should certainly like to take a share in routing out these bandits, especially as, from what you say, it seems that the men at their head are the fellows who murdered Don Ramon Perales' son, and sold me his horse. I wonder which hacienda it is that they are meaning to attack!"

"Yes, it is a pity Sim didn't manage to find that out; we would have caught them then."

"Have you any idea how strong the band is?"

"They are not often over twenty," the doctor replied. "Twenty is enough for their work, and if there were more the shares of the plunder would be too small; but, as I said, they have got friends everywhere, and could probably gather thirty or forty more if they knew the troops were going to attack them. A Mexican is always ready on principle to join in if there is a chance of getting a shot at an American soldier."

"I suppose you have not the least idea in what direction these fellows have their headquarters?"

"Well, I have some sort of an idea, at any rate I know of one place where there is a party who don't care about being interfered with by strangers. Two or three months ago, when Sim and I were away about forty miles over to the north-west, we were in a village just at the mouth of a bit of a valley, and the girl who waited on us at the little wineshop whispered in my ear when the landlord's back was turned, 'Don't go up the valley.' Well, we were not thinking of going up the valley, which was only a sort of gulch leading nowhere, but after that we thought that we would have a look at it. We took a goodish round so as to get above it, and looked down, and we saw a house lying among some trees, and lower down, near the mouth of the valley, made out two men sitting among some rocks on the shoulder.

"The sun shone on their gun barrels, but that didn't go for much, for the Mexicans out in the country pretty well always go armed. We watched them for a couple of hours, and as they didn't stir we concluded they were sentries. The girl wouldn't have given us that warning unless there had been something wrong, and I expect that house was the headquarters of one of these gangs."

"What made her do it, I wonder, doctor?"

"That I can't say, Lightning. It is never easy to say why a woman does a thing. She may have thought it a pity that Sim and I should get our throats cut, though I own that wouldn't be a thing likely to trouble a Mexican girl. Then she may have had a grudge against them; perhaps they had shot some lover of hers, or one of them may have jilted her. Anyhow, there it was, and if we hear of any attack of brigands upon a hacienda, we will try that place before going any further. And now, lad, you had better be going back. I shall lie here quiet for an hour or two in case there should be anyone watching you, as is likely enough."

Hugh returned to the hotel and told Royce what he had heard.

"That will suit me," Bill said. "I am death on border ruffians, and if ever I see two of them it wur them fellows as sold you the horse at M'Kinney. And so it's their intention to follow us and wipe us out, and get our swag? Waal, maybe it will be the other way. If I was you, Lightning, I would ride over to Don Ramon's this evening, and give him a hint to be on his guard. There is no reason why it should be his place they have got in their mind more than any other. But the fact that they stole the son's horse, to say nothing of killing him, might turn their thoughts that way. If you do a fellow one injury, I reckon that like as not you will do him another. I don't know why it is so, but I reckon it's human nature."

"I will ride over at once," Hugh said.

"I wouldn't do that, Hugh. You don't know who may have been watching you, and if it is known that you had been meeting the doctor quiet, and the doctor is a mate of Sim's, and Sim was in that wineshop, they will be putting things together, and if you ride straight over to Don Ramon now, they will think it is because of something the doctor has been saying to you. Then if it should chance as that is the place they are thinking of, it air long odds that Sim and the doctor get a knife atween their shoulders afore bedtime. You go quietly off in the cool of the evening, just jogging along as if you was going to pay a visit of no particular account. They ain't got no interest in us, except as to this expedition to find gold, and they won't consarn themselves in your movements as long as I am here at the hotel and the others ain't getting ready to make a start. They have learnt all they want to learn about our going."

Just as the sun was setting, Hugh set out. It was dark when he reached Don Ramon's hacienda. After chatting awhile with Don Ramon, his wife and son—the two girls, their father said, being somewhere out in the garden—Hugh said quietly to the Mexican that he wanted to speak to him for a moment in private. Don Ramon lighted a fresh cigarette, and then said carelessly: "It is a lovely evening, we may as well stroll outside and find the girls. I don't suppose they know that you are here." Don Carlos followed them into the broad verandah outside the house.

"Your son can hear what I have to say," Hugh said in reply to an enquiring look from Don Ramon, and then reported the conversation that Sim had overheard. Father and son were both much excited at the statement that the horse had been recognized.

"Then poor Estafan's murderers are somewhere in this neighbourhood!" the don exclaimed. "That is the part of the story that interests me most, señor. As to attacking my hacienda, I don't believe they would venture upon it. They must know that they would meet with a stout resistance, and El Paso is but three miles away. Daring as they are, they would scarcely venture on such an undertaking; but I will, of course, take every precaution. I will order four men to be on guard at night, bid the others sleep with their arms ready at hand, and see that the shutters and doors are barred at night. But the other matter touches us nearly. If Estafan's murderers are in the province we will hunt them down if I have to arm all the vaqueros and *peóns*, and have a regular campaign against them.

"You were quite right not to mention this before my wife; she and my daughters had better know nothing about it. By the way, I wonder where the girls are; they are not generally as late as this. I suppose the evening has tempted them; it is full moon to-morrow." He raised his voice and called the girls. There was no reply. "Carlos, do you go and look for them, and tell them from me to come up to the house; and now, señor, we will have a cup of coffee."

In a quarter of an hour Carlos returned. "I cannot find them, father. I have been all round the garden calling them."

Don Ramon rose from his seat and struck a bell on the table. "They must have gone up to their rooms," he said, "without coming in here." When the servant appeared, he said, "Rosita, go up to the señoritas' room, and tell them that Don Hugh Tunstall is here."

"They are not there, señor. I have just come down from their rooms."

"What can have become of them, Carlos?" Don Ramon said.

"I have no idea, father; they had Lion with them. He was asleep here when they called him from outside, and I saw him get up and dash through the open window."

"I can't understand it," the don said anxiously, "for the evening is cold; besides, they would scarcely go outside the garden after nightfall."

"They might be down at Chaquita's cottage, father."

"Oh, yes! I didn't think of that, Carlos," Don Ramon said. "Yes, they are often down at their old nurse's. Rosita, tell Juan to go down to Chaquita's cottage and beg the young ladies to return, as I want them."

In ten minutes the servant came back.

"They are not there, señor; they left there just as it was getting dark."

"Surely there is nothing to be uneasy about, Ramon!" his wife said. "The girls are often out as late as this on a moonlight evening. They are sure to be about the garden, somewhere."

"But Carlos has been round," Don Ramon said. "Well, we will go and have another look for them. Followed by the two young men, he stepped out on to the verandah. "Carlos," he said, "go round to the men's quarters and tell them your sisters are missing, and that they are all to turn out and search. I don't like this," he said to Hugh, after his son had left. "I should have thought nothing of it at any other time, but after what you have just been telling me, I feel nervous. Now, let us go round the garden."

They traversed all the walks, Don Ramon repeatedly calling the girls' names. They were joined in their search by Don Carlos and a number of the men. "They are certainly not in the garden," Don Ramon said at last. "Now, let us go down towards Chaquita's cottage; they may either have followed the road on their way back, or have come along a bypath to the garden. We will go by the path, and return the other way."

The path lay through a shrubbery. Just as they entered it, a man met them running.

"Well, what is it, Juan?" Don Ramon asked as he came up and he could see his face by the light of the torches some of the men were carrying.

"I don't know, señor, but we have just come upon some fresh blood on the path."

With a cry of alarm Don Ramon ran forward with his son and Hugh. Fifty yards farther they saw two of the men standing with torches in the middle of the path.

"Here is blood, señor," one of them said. "We passed it without noticing it on our way to the cottage; we were not examining the ground; but on our way back the light of the torches fell upon it."

Don Ramon stood staring in speechless horror at a large patch of blood on the path. "There has been a struggle here," Hugh said, examining the ground. "See! there are marks of large feet. Some of them have trod in the blood. See, Don Carlos!" and he pointed to a line of blood drops leading to one of the bushes.

"Search, Hugh," the young man groaned. "I dare not."

Hugh motioned one of the men with a torch to follow him. The father and son stood gazing after them as they entered the bushes. A moment later Hugh called out:

"It is the dog, señors, there is nothing else."

An exclamation of joy broke from the two Mexicans. They were at least relieved of the overpowering dread that had seized them at the sight of the blood, and at once joined Hugh. The dog, a fine Cuban bloodhound, was lying dead, stabbed in a dozen places.

"What can it mean, father?" Don Carlos said in a low voice.

"I can hardly think," the Mexican said, passing his hand across his forehead.

"I am afraid, señor, it is too evident," Hugh put in. "This is the explanation of what my friend heard. The brigands did not intend to attack the hacienda. They have carried off your daughters, and the hound has died in their defence."

"That must be it," Don Ramon exclaimed in the deepest anguish. "Oh, my poor girls, how can it have happened?"

"I expect they were in hiding here," Hugh said, "and sprang up suddenly and seized and gagged the señoritas before they had time to scream. The hound doubtless sprang upon them, and, as you see, they killed it with their knives."

"What is to be done?" Don Ramon asked hopelessly.

"The first thing is to follow the path down to the road," Hugh said; "probably they had horses somewhere. Will you tell the men to go along cautiously with their torches near the ground."

Don Carlos gave the order in Mexican. One of the party, who was the chief hunter at the hacienda, went a little ahead of the others with a torch. He stopped a short distance before he reached the junction of the path with the road, which they could see ahead of them in the moonlight.

"Here are fresh marks of horses' hoofs," he said. "See," and he held the torch above his head and pointed to the bushes, "twigs have been broken, and there are fresh leaves upon the ground. The horses must have been hidden here. Do not move until I examine down to the road." He went forward alone, and returned in two or three minutes. "There are faint tracks from the road to this point; they came along at a walk. There are deep ones down to the road, and along it; they went off at a gallop. There were six of them."

"What is to be done, señor?" Don Ramon said to Hugh. "My brain seems on fire, and I cannot think."

"I should imagine your daughters can be in no immediate danger, señor," Hugh said quietly. "The brigands have doubtless carried them off in order to wring a heavy ransom from you. They must have got two hours' start, and I fear pursuit would be useless to-night, though I would send three of the men accustomed to tracking on at once to follow their traces, and to learn the direction they have taken after leaving here. Of course it will be for you to decide whether you will go down to the town and see the alcalde, and obtain a posse of men to join your vaqueros in a search for them, and then to cross the river to the fort and get the help of the troops, and scour the whole country; or whether you will wait until you hear, as you doubtless will, from the brigands."

"Let us go back to the house," Don Ramon replied; "we must think it over. We must not do anything rash, or we might endanger their lives." The news had reached the house before they arrived there. Donna Maria was completely prostrated with grief, the women were crying and wringing their hands, and the wildest confusion prevailed. Don Ramon had by this time recovered himself, and sternly ordered silence. He then proceeded to the room where his wife had been carried, and endeavoured to assure her that there was little fear for their daughters' lives, for the brigands could have no purpose in injuring them, and had only carried them off for the purpose of exacting a ransom.

"What do you really think had best be done, my friend?" Don Carlos asked Hugh when they were alone together. "Of course, whatever ransom these villains ask must be paid, although I have no doubt it will be something enormous. But it is terrible to think of the girls being even for an hour in their hands, especially when we feel sure that these men are the murderers of my brother."

"I should say," Hugh replied, "that whatever they demand must be paid. It will not do to risk the señoritas' lives by doing anything as long as they are in their hands. But I should advise that the moment they are free we should fall upon these scoundrels and exterminate them, and recover the ransom. I think that I have a clue to the place where they are likely to be taken. One of my miner friends was speaking to me of a place that would be likely to be used for such a purpose. He could lead a party there. But it would never do to attempt it while the ladies are in their hands. You may be sure that a careful watch will be kept, and at the first alarm the villains might murder them. We will hear what your father says when he returns, and if he thinks, as I do, that we can attempt nothing until he receives some communication from the brigands, I will ride back to El Paso and consult my friends there."

Don Ramon on his return said that he was strongly of the opinion that it would risk the girls' lives were any movement made until he heard of them. As he could be of no utility Hugh rode over to El Paso, Don Carlos saying that he would let him know the instant they received any communication from the brigands, but that he should anyhow see him in the morning, as he should ride over with his father to report the matter to the authorities. It was past ten o'clock when Hugh reached the hotel. It happened to be a festa, and the square was full of people, and the cafés and wineshops open. Royce was in the bar-room of the hotel.

"Royce, do you know where Sim and the doctor are likely to be found?"

"I saw them sitting in front of the wineshop in the corner of the square, not more than ten minutes ago."

"Come along with me, then, Bill."

"But I thought we weren't to be seen with them?" Royce said.

"There can be no reason against it now," Hugh replied. "They have learned all they wanted to learn about it, and know that we are going together. At any rate our meeting would seem to be accidental."

"Is anything up, Hugh?" Royce asked as they made their way through the crowd in the square. "You look troubled."

"I will tell you directly, Bill."

"There they are. They are still at the same table, Hugh."

There were two empty chairs at the table. Hugh nodded carelessly to the doctor and Sim, and sat down beside them.

"After what you told me this morning, doctor, there can be no harm in our being seen together. I want to talk to you badly. There are too many people about here. Do you mind both coming down to the river? We can talk as we go."

Directly they were out of the square he told the three men what had happened.

"Carried off those two young ladies!" Royce exclaimed. "By thunder, that is too bad! What is to be done, boys?"

"Let us wait until we know all about it," Sim replied; while the doctor said, in his quiet way, "This has really got to be put a stop to. Let us wait until we are down by the river. We must hear all this quietly, Lightning. Four men can't talk as they walk."

They soon gained a quiet spot away from the houses.

"Now tell us how it came about," the doctor said, "and while we are talking each of you keep his eyes and ears open. We have behaved like fools once, and let ourselves be overheard. We won't do it again."

Hugh told the whole story of the girls' abduction, and stated the determination arrived at by Don Ramon, not to attempt a pursuit, but to pay whatever ransom was demanded, and then to hunt the brigands down.

"That is all very well," the doctor said; "but when they have once got the money, and you may be sure that it will be a very big sum, they will divide it and scatter; and there won't be one of them in the district twelve hours after the girls are given up."

"But what is he to do, doctor?" Sim Howlett said. "He daren't move till he gets the gals. They would cut their throats sure if he did."

"My idea was, Sim," Hugh said, "that if this is the work of the band in that house the doctor was telling me about this morning, we could be in hiding near it; and directly the men who take the girls back to their father return with the ransom, we could fall upon them, destroy the whole band, and get back the money."

"We should want a big force to surround the place," Sim replied; "and there would be no getting it there without being seen. You bet there are a score of them on the lookout, and their friends would bring them word, long before we got there, of such a force being on the way. Besides, there is no surety that it is the place where the gals are, and, even if it is, the hull band may leave when they send the gals away. They may scatter all over the country, and meet again at night fifty miles off. Another thing is, you may bet your boots there will be a lot of trouble about handing over that ransom, and they won't give 'em up until after they have got the money."

"I see that there are all sorts of difficulties before us, Sim, but I am sure you and the doctor will see some way out of it. I am deeply interested in rescuing these poor girls, and we are all interested in this band being wiped out before we start."

"Have you any plan at all?" the doctor asked. "You have had longer time to think this over than we have."

"Well, doctor, my idea was that we could start to-night and

get to some place among the hills, where we could hide our horses a mile or two from this house where we suppose they are. We should lie quiet there to-morrow. The next evening we should make our way down, and try and ascertain for certain whether they are there, and see whether it is possible to carry them off.

"Of course that couldn't be attempted unless we are absolutely certain of being able to protect them. If we could get them out without being seen, we might try to do it. If it is not certain we could do that, and get off without being seen, I should say one of us should ride back next morning to Don Ramon and get him to bring up twenty or thirty of his men, or if not, a body of troops from the fort. We should guide them at night to a point as near the house as it would be safe for them to get. Then we four could crawl down to the house. The moment we are in a position to protect the girls, that is to say if we can get into the room where they are kept, we will fire a pistolshot out of the window as a signal. Then we shall have to make as good a fight of it as we can till the others come up to help us.

"You may be sure that the brigands will be all pretty well occupied with us, and the other party will be able to surround the house, and then rush in to our assistance."

"That looks a good plan, by thunder!" Sim Howlett said. "What do you say, doctor?"

"Well, I think it might be worked somehow on those lines," the doctor agreed. "I don't think there is much danger for the ladies, because, if the brigands did come upon us when we were scouting, some of them would attack us, and the rest would carry the ladies off to some other hiding-place. I don't say if they were surrounded and saw no chance of escape they mightn't kill them out of revenge, but they would never do that until the last thing, because they would reckon, and truly enough, that as long as they are in their hands they have got the means of making terms for themselves. But to one thing I agree anyhow. Let us get our horses and start at once. Don't let us go together. We will meet at the first crossroad a mile to the west of the town. No one is likely to notice us going out. There are plenty of people who have come in from the country to this festa; besides, just at present they won't be watching us. They know what our plans are, and that we don't intend to start for another week, and they won't be giving a thought to us until this affair of the girls is settled. What do you say, Sim?"

"That is right enough," Sim said; "but we must be careful about the roads, doctor. Like enough they will have a man on every road going anywhere near the place, and perhaps miles away."

"Yes, we must make a big circuit," the doctor agreed. "Strike the hills fifteen or twenty miles away from their place, and then work up through them so as to come down right from the other side."

"Shall I get some provisions at the hotel?" Hugh asked.

"No; we will attend to that. There are plenty of places open, and we will get what is wanted. Now, do you and Bill go back by yourselves; we will follow in a minute or two."

XVIII. THE BRIGANDS' HAUNT

By daybreak on the following morning Hugh and his three companions were far among the hills. They had halted an hour before, and intended to wait until noon before pursuing their journey. They had already been eight hours in the saddle, and had travelled over sixty miles. They had halted in a little valley where there was plenty of grass for the horses, and after cooking some food lay down and slept until the sun was nearly overhead. Fortunately, the two miners had traversed the country several times, and were able to lead them across the mountains, where otherwise it would have been impossible to find a way.

After four hours' riding, on emerging from a valley the doctor said:

"There, do you see that village three miles away? That is the village where we stopped. The gorge in which the house lies runs from the village in this direction. You cannot see it here: it is a sort of cañon cut out ages ago by the water. The sides are nearly perpendicular; but at the upper end the bottom rises rapidly, and, as far as we could see from the spot from which we looked at it, there is no difficulty in getting down there. As you see, there are woods lying back to the left. We have got to come down at the back of them, and there is no chance of our being seen even if they have got men on the lookout on the high ground above the house. They will be looking the other way; they can see miles across the plain there. Of course they have no reason to believe that anyone knows of their haunt; still, they are always on the lookout against treachery."

"Well, let's go on at a trot now, doctor. We shall be in the wood before sunset."

When they reached the trees they dismounted, and led their horses until they perceived daylight through the trunks on the opposite side.

"Now we will finish the remainder of our dinner," the doctor said, "and talk matters over. We are about half a mile now from the end of the valley, and it is another half-mile down to the house. Now, what are we going to do? Are we all going, or only one?"

Hugh was silent. These men understood matters better than he did.

"Only one, of course," Sim Howlett said. "The others can come on to the top of the valley so as to lend a hand if he is chased; but it would be just chucking away lives for more than one to go. Well, it is either you or me, doc."

"Why?" Hugh asked. "I am quite ready to go, and I am sure Bill is too. Besides, this question of the young ladies is more my affair than yours, since you do not know them, and I certainly think I ought to be the one to go."

"There is one reason agin it, Lightning," Sim said. "What you say is true, and if it came to running you could leg it up a good bit faster than the doc. or me; but that don't count for much in the dark. It is creeping and crawling that is wanted more than running. The reason why the doc. or I must go is, you don't speak Mexican, and we do. It ain't likely that the young ladies will be seen out in the verandah, and one can't go and look into each of the windows till we find the right one. We have got to listen, and that way we may find whether they are there, and if we are lucky, which room they are in. So you see it is for one of us to go."

"I shall go, Sim," the doctor said quietly. "I can walk as light as a cat. I haven't above half as much bulk to hide as you have, and I am cunning while you are strong, and this is a case where cunning is of more use than strength. So it is settled that I go; but you may as well give me your six-shooter. I may want twelve barrels."

"I shall be sorry for the Mexicans if you use them all, doc.," Sim Howlett said, handing over his pistol to the doctor. "I would rather go myself; but I know when you have once made up your mind to anything it ain't no sort of use argying."

"That's right," the doctor said, putting the weapon into his belt. "Well, there is just time for a pipe before I start. The sun has been down nearly half an hour, and the moon won't be up over those hills there for another hour, so we shall have it dark till I get well down into the valley, and the moon won't be high enough to throw its light down there afore I am back again."

"A wonderful man is the doctor!" Sim Howlett said when, with noiseless step, he had made his way down into the upper end of the ravine. "You wouldn't think much of him to look at him. But, you bet, he has got as much grit as if he was ten times as big. See him going about, and you would say he might be one of them missionaries, or a scientific chap such as those as comes round looking after birds and snakes and such like. He sorter seems most like a woman with his low talk and gentle way, and yet I suppose he has killed more downright bad men than any five men on this side of Missouri."

"You don't say so!" Hugh said in surprise.

"Yes, sir, he is a hull team and a little dog under the wagon, he is. He ain't a chap to quarrel; he don't drink, and he don't gamble, and he speaks everyone fair and civil. It ain't that; but he has got somethin' in him that seems to swell up when he hears of bad goings-on. When there is a real bad man comes to the camp where he is, and takes to bossing the show, and to shooting free, after a time you can see the doctor gets oncomfortable in his mind; but he goes on till that bad man does something out of the way—shoots a fellow just out of pure cussedness, or something of that kind—then he just says this must be put down, and off he goes and faces that bad man and gives him a fair show and lays him out."

"You mean he doesn't fire until the other man is heeled, Sam?"

"Yes, I mean that."

"Then how is it he hasn't got killed himself?"

"That is what we have said a hundred times, Lightning. He has been shot all over, but never mortally. One thing, his looks are enough to scare a man. Somehow he don't look altogether arthly with that white hair of his—and it has been the same colour ever since I have known him—floating back from his face. He goes in general bareheaded when he sets out to shoot, and the hair somehow seems to stand out; not a bit like it does other times. I heard a chap who had been a doctor afore he took to gold digging say his hair looked as if it had been electrified. Then he gets as white as snow, and his eyes just blaze out. I tell you, sirree, it is something frightful to see him; and when he comes right into a crowded saloon and says to the man, as he always does say in a sort of tone that seems somehow to frizz up the blood of every man that hears it, 'It is time for you to die!' you bet it makes the very hardest man weaken. I tell you I would rather face Judge Lynch and a hundred regulators than stand up agin the doctor when his fit is on; and I have seen men who never missed their mark afore shoot wide of him altogether."

"And he never misses?" Royce asked.

"Miss!" Sim repeated; "the doctor couldn't miss if he tried. I've never known his bullet go a hair's-breadth off the mark. It always hits plumb in the centre of the forehead. If there is more than one of them, the doc. turns on the others and warns them: 'Git out of the camp afore night!' and you bet they git. He gives me a lot of trouble, the doc. does, in the way of nursing. I have put it to him over and over again if it is fair on me that he should be on his back three months every year, 'cause that is about what it's been since I have known him. He allows as it ain't fair, but, as he says, 'It ain't me, Sim, I have got to do it; I am like a Malay running a-muck'—them's chaps out somewhere near China, he tells me, as gets mad and goes for a hull crowd—'and I can't help it'; and I don't think he can. And yet you know at other times he is just about the kindest chap that breathes. He is always a-nussing the sick and sitting up nights with them, and such like. That is why he got the name of doctor."

"He isn't a doctor really then?" Hugh asked.

"Waal, Lightning, all that's his secret, and ef he thinks to tell you, he can do it. I know he is the best mate a man ever had, and one of the best critters in God's universe, and that is good enough for me. I reckon he must be somewhere down among them Mexikins by this time," he went on, changing the subject abruptly.

"I almost wish one of us had gone with him," Royce said, "so that if he should get found out we might make a better fight of it."

"He ain't likely to get found out," Sim said quietly, "and ef he does he kin fight his way out. I don't know what way the doctor will die, but I allowed years ago that it weren't going to be by a bullet. I ain't skeery about him. Ef I had thought there wur any kind of risk, I would have gone with him, you bet."

It was two hours before the doctor suddenly stood in the moonlight before them. They had been listening attentively for some time, but had not heard the slightest sound until he emerged from the shadow of the ravine.

"Well, doctor, are we on the right scent?"

"The girls are there, Sim, sure enough. Now let us go back to the wood before we talk. We have been caught asleep once on this expedition, when we thought we were so safe that we needn't be on the watch, and I don't propose to throw away a chance again." They went back without another word to the wood. As soon as they reached it the doctor sat down at the foot of a tree, and lighted his pipe; the others followed his example.

"Well, there was no danger about that job," he began. "It seems not to have struck the fools that anyone was likely to come down from this end of the gulch. Down at the other end they have got two sentries on each side up on the heights. I could see them in the moonlight. I reckon they have some more at the mouth of the valley, down near the village; but you may guess I asked no questions about it. I saw no one in the gulch until I got down close to the house. It is as strong a place as if it had been built for the purpose. It stands on a sort of table of rock that juts out from the hillside; so that on three sides it goes straight down. There is a space round the house forty or fifty feet wide.

"On the side where the rock stands out from the hill they have got a wall twelve feet high, with a strong gate in it. On that side of the house they have bricked all the windows up, so as to prevent their being commanded by a force on the hillside above them, and all the windows on the ground floor all round are bricked up too. I expect the rooms are lighted from a courtyard inside. So you see it is a pretty difficult sort of place to take all of a sudden. I could hear the voices of five or six men sitting smoking and talking outside the door, which is not on the side facing the hill, but on the other side. I guessed that when the house was built there must have been steps up from that side, for there is a road that runs along the bottom of the valley; so I crawled up and found that it was so. There had been a broad flight of steps there; they had been broken away and pulled down, still they were good enough for me. There were one or two blocks still sticking out from the rock, and there were holes where other blocks had been let in, and I made a shift to climb up without much difficulty till I got my eyes level with the top.

"The moon hadn't risen over the brow, still it was lighter than I liked; but one had to risk something; so I first of all pulled myself up, crawled along the edge till I got round the corner, and then went up to the house and examined the windows on the other side, and then got back to the top of the steps and began to listen. I soon heard the girls were there. They had brought them straight there after they had carried them off. A man had started early the next morning with a letter to Don Ramon demanding ransom. He was expected back some time to-night. They had had news that so far the don was taking no steps to raise the country, though the news of the girls being carried off was generally known. I didn't hear what the sum named for the ransom was; but the men were talking over what they should each do with their share of it, and they reckoned that each would have seven or eight thousand dollars.

"Well, there wasn't anything new about this. The matter of interest to us was which was the room where the girls were. As the journey would have been of no sort of use if I could not find that out, there was nothing to do but to get up again and crawl along to the house. I had reckoned that I should most likely want my rope, and had wound it round my waist. There was a guard at the gate, so it was one of the sides I had to try.

"I had learned from what the men said that most of the gang were away scattered all over the country down to El Paso, so as to bring news at once if there was any search for the girls going on. The chief and his lieutenant were down in the village, and would ride in with the messenger who brought down Ramon's answer. There was a guard inside the house, because the men at the fire said it was time for two of them to go and relieve them; but I guessed that otherwise the house was empty. I threw my rope over a balcony and climbed up, opened the fastening of the window with my knife, and went in. Everything was quiet. I felt my way across the room to a window on the other side. I opened that and looked down into the courtyard. Two or three lanterns were burning there, and I saw two men sitting on a bench that was placed across a door. They were smoking cigarettes, and had their guns leaning against the wall beside them. There was no doubt that was the room where the girls were.

"It was on the opposite side of the courtyard to that where I was standing—that is, on the side of the house facing down the valley,—and was the corner room.

"I had learned everything I wanted now, so I had nothing to do but to shut the window, slide down the rope, shake it off the balcony, and come back again; and here I am."

"Well done, doctor! You have succeeded splendidly. But what a pity we didn't all go with you. We could have cleared out that lot and rescued the girls at once."

"You might not have gone as quietly as I did," the doctor said. "Four men make a lot more noise than one, and at the slightest noise the seven men at the door would have been inside, the door bolted, and the first pistol shot would have brought in the guard at the gate, the four sentries on the height, and I expect as many more from the mouth of the valley. It would have been mighty difficult to break into the house with nine men inside and as many out; besides, it would never do to run risks; and even if we had done it, and hadn't found the girls with their throats cut, we should have had to fight our way up the valley to the horses, and a bullet might have hit one of them. No, no; this is a case where we have no right to risk anything. It's for the don to decide what is to be done. Now we know all about it, and can lay it before him. Lightning, you had better saddle up and ride with me. You must go, because he knows you, and will believe what you tell him. I must go, because he will want me to guide the force back here, so as to avoid any chance of their being seen on the way. The horses have done eighty miles since this time yesterday, so it's no use thinking of starting to-night. Besides, there is no hurry. We will be off in the morning."

After breakfast Sim was about to saddle the doctor's horse, when Royce said:

"The doctor had better take my horse. He is miles faster than his own."

The girths were tightened. The doctor, as he mounted, said to Sim: "You will keep a sharp lookout over the house, and reckon up how many go in and come out. I expect if the don writes to say he will pay the money, a good many of those outside will come here."

"We will keep our eyes open, doctor."

"It may be two or three days before you hear of us, Sim."

"There is no hurry, doctor. There will be a lot of talk about how the ransom is to be paid afore anything is done."

"Do you mean to go back the same way we came?" Hugh asked the doctor as they rode off.

"No, there is no occasion for that. We will ride thirty miles or so along the foot of the hills, east, and then strike straight by road for El Paso. It is about nine o'clock now. We shall be there by five o'clock. We won't go in together. I will wait on the road and come in by some other way after dark, or, what would be better, put up at José's. You had better not go up to the don's until to-morrow morning. Were you to go up directly you returned, the scoundrels who are watching both you and the don might suspect that your journey has had a connection with his business."

Next morning Hugh arrived at Don Ramon's, having obtained another horse at the hotel. "Why, where have you been, Señor Hugh?" Don Carlos exclaimed as the servant showed him into the room where they were at breakfast. "When I rode with my father into the town to give the alcalde notice, I went to the hotel and found that you were out. We sent over there three times yesterday and the day before, but they knew nothing of you. You had taken your horse and gone out the evening you returned, and had left no word when you would come back. We have been quite anxious about you, and feared that some harm had befallen you also. We were quite sure that you would not have left without telling us of your intentions."

"No, indeed," Hugh said. "I should have been ungrateful indeed for your kindness if I had left you in such terrible trouble; but before I tell you what I have been doing, please let me know what has happened here."

"About midday, the day after my daughters had been stolen," Don Ramon said, "a horseman rode up. I saw him coming, and guessed he was the man we were expecting. He was shown in here, and Carlos and myself received him. He handed me a letter. Here it is. I will translate it:

"'Señor Don Ramon Perales,—If you wish to see your daughters alive, you will, as speedily as possible, collect two hundred thousand dollars in gold and hand them over to the messenger I will send for them. When I receive the money your daughters shall be returned to you. I give you warning, that if any effort is made to discover their whereabouts, or if any armed body is collected by you for the purpose of rescue, your daughters will at once be put to death. Signed Ignatius Guttiero.'"

"And what did you reply, Don Ramon?"

"I wrote that it would take some time to collect so great a sum in gold, but that I would send up to Santa Fé at once, and use every effort to get it together in the shortest possible time. I demanded, however, what assurance I could have that after the money was paid my daughters would be returned to me. To that I have received no answer."

"No, you could hardly get one before this morning," Hugh said. "You look surprised, señor; but we have found out where they are hidden."

"You have found that out!" the others cried in astonishment.

"My companions and I," Hugh said; "indeed, beyond riding a

good many miles, I have had but little to do with the matter. The credit lies entirely with the two miners I spoke to you of, with whom I was going shortly to start on an expedition to a placer they know of."

He then related the reason why the miners had suspected where the gang of brigands had their headquarters, and the steps by which they had ascertained that the girls were really there; and then explained the scheme that he and the doctor had, on their ride down, arranged for their rescue.

Don Ramon, his wife, and son were greatly moved at the narrative. "You have, indeed, rendered us a service that we can never repay," Don Ramon said; "but the risk is terrible. Should you fail it would cost you your lives, and would ensure the fate of my daughters."

"We are in no way afraid about our own lives, Don Ramon; there are not likely to be more than twenty of these scoundrels there, and if we were discovered before we could get to your daughters we could fight our way off, I think. In that case, seeing that there were only four of us, they certainly would not throw away their prospect of a ransom by injuring their captives. They would suppose that we had undertaken it on our own account as a sort of speculation, and though, no doubt, they would remove your daughters at once to some other place, they would not injure them. You see, our plan is that the force we propose shall be at hand, shall not advance unless they hear three shots fired at regular intervals. That will be the signal that we have succeeded in entering your daughters' apartment, and that they are safe with us; in that case you will push forward at once to assist us. If, on the other hand, you hear an outbreak of firing, you will know that we have been discovered before we reached your daughters, and will retreat with your force silently, and return to El Paso by the same route by which you went out, and you would then, of course, continue your negotiations for a ransom."

"At any rate," Don Carlos said, "I claim the right of accompanying you. It is my sisters who are in peril, and I will not permit strangers to risk their lives for them when I remain safe at a distance. You must agree to that, señor."

"I agree to that at once," Hugh said. "I thought that it was probable that you would insist upon going with us; it is clearly your right to do so."

"It must not be attempted," Don Ramon said gravely, "if in any way I can recover my daughters by paying the ransom. The risk would be terrible, and although two hundred thousand dollars is a large sum, I would pay it four times over rather than that risk should be run. The question is, what guarantee the brigands will give that they will return their captives after they have received the money. I shall know that soon; we will decide nothing until I receive the answer."

"Would it not be well, señor, for you to go over to arrange with the officer in command of the fort for twenty or thirty men to start with you at a moment's notice? If you decide to make this attempt to rescue your daughters the sooner we set about it the better, that is, if you intend to take troops instead of a party of your own men."

"I have already seen the commandant," Don Ramon said; "he is a personal friend, and rode over here directly he heard the news, and offered to place the whole of his force at my disposal should I think fit to use it."

At this moment a servant entered, and said that a man wished to see Don Ramon. The Mexican left the room, and returned in a minute with a letter. It was brief: "Señor, if you want your daughters back again you must trust us; we give no guarantees beyond our solemn pledge. You will tell my messenger on what day you will have the money ready, and do not delay more than a week; he will come again to fetch it. See that he is not followed, for it will cost your daughters their lives if an attempt is made to find out where he goes. Your daughters will be returned within twenty-four hours of your sending out the money."

"We will try your plan, señor," Don Ramon said firmly. "I would not trust the word of these cut-throats, or their oaths even, in the smallest matter, and assuredly not in one such as this. What shall I say in reply to this letter?"

"I should write and say that, although their conditions are

hard, you must accept them, but that you doubt whether you can raise so large a sum of gold in the course of a week, and you beg them to give ten days before the messenger returns for it; and you pledge your honour that no attempt whatever shall be made to follow or to ascertain the course he takes."

Don Ramon wrote the letter, and took it down to the hall, where the messenger was waiting, surrounded by servants, who were regarding him with no friendly aspect.

"There is my answer," Don Ramon said as he handed the letter to the man. "Tell your leader I shall keep my word, and that I trust him to keep his."

"Now, Señor Hugh, will you give me the details of your plan. How do you propose that the troops are to be close at hand when required without their presence being suspected?"

"The doctor's idea was this, señor. That you should this morning send a letter by a servant to the commandant. Will you tell him that you believe you have a clue to your daughters' hiding-place, but that everything depends upon the troops getting near the spot without suspicion being excited. Will you beg him to maintain an absolute silence as to any movements of the troops until to-night, and to issue no orders until the gates are shut and all communication closed. Will he then order an officer and twenty men to be ready at four o'clock in the morning to start under the guidance of a miner who will to-night arrive at the fort bearing your card.

"This will, of course, be the doctor. Request the officer to place himself absolutely in his hands. Our plan is that they shall keep the other side of the river, travel some thirty miles up, and then halt until nightfall. At that point they would be as far off from the brigands' hiding-place as they are here, and if the fact that a detachment has started becomes known to the friends of the brigands, it will not be suspected that there is any connection between their journey and the affair with your daughters. After nightfall they will start again, cross the river, and meet you and myself at one o'clock, near the village of Ajanco. Thence we shall go up into the hills, rest there all day, and come down upon the gulch where the brigands' haunt lies."

"That sounds an excellent plan, señor; but how do you propose that we shall get away without being noticed to-morrow evening?"

"The doctor and I agreed that the best plan you could adopt would be to ride over and see your banker the first thing in the morning. That will seem perfectly natural. Then in the evening, after dark, you and Don Carlos should again ride down to him. You will naturally take at least four of your men down with you as a guard. You will leave your horses with them when you enter the banker's. You will then pass through his house, and at once leave by the back entrance, wrapped in your cloaks. You will then proceed to a spot half a mile out of the town, where Juan, who you say knows the country, will be waiting with your horses, and I also will be there.

"The people who are watching you—and you will certainly be watched—will naturally suppose that you are at the banker's. At ten o'clock he will come to the door and tell your men to return home with your horses and to bring them back at ten in the morning, as you and your son will sleep there. Even should anything be suspected—which is hardly likely—the scoundrels would have no clue whatever as to the direction you will have taken, as, at any rate, you will have had two hours' start before they can begin to think that anything is wrong."

"That is a capital plan, señor. You keep on adding to our already deep obligations to you."

Everything was carried out in accordance with the arrangements. Hugh returned at once to El Paso, and in the evening the doctor mounted his horse and rode to the fort. The next day passed quietly, and as soon as it became dark Hugh went out to the stable, saddled his horse without seeing any of the men about the yard, and rode off in the direction of Don Ramon's, and then, making a circuit of the town, arrived at the spot where Juan was waiting with the horses. They had been placed in a thicket a short distance from the road so as to be unobserved by anyone who might happen to pass. Hugh took his post close to the road, and an hour later Don Ramon and his son came up. The horses were at once brought out, and they mounted and rode off, Juan riding ahead to show the way.

They maintained a fast pace, for at one o'clock they were to meet the troops at the appointed place. They arrived a quarter of an hour before the time, and ten minutes after the hour heard the tramping of horses. The doctor was riding ahead, and halted when he came up to the group.

"Has all gone well, Lightning?" he asked.

"Excellently, as far as we know."

"This is Lieutenant Mason, who is in command of the troops," the doctor said as a figure rode forward. "Lieutenant Mason, this is Don Ramon Perales."

"You are punctual, señor," the officer said. "I have orders to place myself and my men entirely at your disposal. I think we had better have half an hour's halt before we go further. We have ridden fast, and you must have ridden faster, as your guide told me you were not to leave El Paso until eight o'clock, and I presume we have a good deal farther to go to-night."

"Another twenty miles," the doctor said. "The moon will be getting higher, and we shall want all her light. It will do no harm if we halt an hour, lieutenant, and eat our supper while the horses are eating theirs."

During the halt the doctor had a long talk with Juan, who came from this part of the country, and knew it well. When they mounted, instead of riding through the town, they struck off by a by-path before they reached it.

Three hours later they were deep among the hills, and then again halted, after turning off from the track they had been following, into a ravine. The girths were loosened, and the horses allowed to graze, and the men, wrapping themselves in cloaks or blankets, were soon asleep, a sentry being placed at the entrance to the ravine. At ten o'clock all were on their feet. Fires were lighted and breakfast cooked, and then, following mountain paths, they rode until two in the afternoon, at which time they reached the valley from which the party had before made their way down to the wood near the ravine. At dusk they again mounted and rode on to the wood. They were met at the edge of the trees by Sim Howlett and Royce.

"I was expecting you to-night, boys," Sim said. "We looked out for you last night, but didn't reckon as you could possibly do it."

"Have you any news of my daughters?" Don Ramon asked eagerly.

"Nary a word," Sim replied. "Bill and me have never had our eyes off the house from sunup to sundown. Lots of fellows have come and gone on horseback. Of course we cannot answer for what has been done after nightfall, but we reckon there is about thirty men there now, not counting those they may have in the village and the sentries down by the mouth of the valley. I calkilate the best part of the gang is there now. The chiefs would like to keep them under their eye. They will think the only thing they have got to be afraid of is treachery. I suppose matters stand as they did when you left, doc.?"

"Just the same. We four and Don Carlos are to go on and get at the ladies. When we are in there safe three pistol shots are to be the signal. Then Don Ramon and the soldiers are to come down and surround them."

Don Ramon had been very anxious to accompany the party, but the doctor had positively refused to take him with them. "It would add greatly to our risks," he said, "and do no good. If we can get to your daughters, Don Ramon, we five can keep the fellows at bay until you come up, easily enough. I believe we could thrash the lot, but it is no good taking chances; but anyhow, we can keep them off. I would rather have gone without your son, but as Lightning has passed his word, there is nothing more to be said. On a job like this the fewer there are the better. Each man after the first pretty nearly doubles the risk."

By this time the troopers had dismounted and fastened their horses to the trees. Meat, that had been cooked in the morning, and biscuits were produced from their haversacks. When the meal had been eaten the soldiers lit their pipes, while their officer proceeded with Hugh and the others to the lower end of the wood and walked on to the head of the ravine.

"There are the lights!" Hugh said. "Ah! I see they have lighted a fire on the terrace, Bill."

"I expect they are pretty crowded in the house," Bill said; "but they go in to sleep. Sim and I have been down near the house twice, and though we were not quite close we were able to make pretty sure that except one sentry there and another at the gate, the rest all go in."

"How far are we to go down?" the officer asked.

"Well, I would rather you did not go down at all," Sim Howlett said. "You can get down there from here in ten minutes after you start if you look spry, and I am desperately afraid some of your men might make a noise, which they would hear certain if everything was quiet. There is no fear of their being heard when the firing once begins down there; but if one of them fell over a rock and his gun went off before we had done our part of the affair, there would be an end of the whole business."

"That is what I think, Sim," the doctor agreed. "We have said all along we might get the ladies out by ourselves, but again we mayn't be able to get them off at all. But we can defend them easy enough if we can get into their room. Five minutes won't make any difference about that, and it is everything to avoid the risk of noise until we get at them. If they discover us before we get there we just fall back fighting. They will think that we are only a small party, and the ladies will be none the worse."

"If you think that is the best way we must agree to it," Don Ramon said; "but we shall have a terrible time until we get to you."

"Don't you be afeard," Sim Howlett said. "The doctor, me, Lightning, and Bill could pretty well wipe them out by ourselves, and we reckon on our six-shooters a sight more than we do on the soldiers."

XIX. A FIGHT AND A RESCUE

Soon after sunset the five men started. The doctor was of opinion that it was better not to wait until the brigands had retired to rest.

"Of course we cannot begin operations," he said, "until all is quiet; but as long as the men are sitting round the fires smoking and singing they will keep a very careless guard, and any noise we make will pass unobserved. When they once get quiet the sentries will begin to listen, but until then we might almost walk up to their fires without being observed."

It was necessary to move slowly and cautiously, lest they should fall over a rock or stump; but the doctor led the way and the others followed close behind him. Twenty minutes' stealthy walking took them to the spot whence the doctor had before reconnoitred the house. A fire blazed on the terrace, and some fifteen men were sitting or lying round it. The light fell upon bottles and glasses. One of the party was playing upon a mandoline and singing, but few of the others were attending to him, a noisy conversation plentifully sprinkled with Spanish oaths being kept up.

"The room where your sisters are confined," the doctor said to Don Carlos, "is round the other side of the house. I did not mean to begin until all were asleep, but they are making such a noise down there that I do think it will be best to move at once, and if possible to let your sisters know that we are here. So we will work quietly round to that side; they had no sentry there last time, but they may have to-night."

After twenty minutes of cautious movement, they reached the foot of the rock on which the house stood. The doctor had

brought out from El Paso a small grapnel and rope. The former
had been carefully wrapped round with strips of cloth so as to
deaden any sound. It was now thrown up, and at the second
attempt became firmly fixed above.

"Do you mount first, Lightning," he said to Hugh. "When you
get up lie quiet for a minute or two. When you have quite
assured yourself that all is clear give the rope a shake. We others will come up one by one. Let each man when he gets to the
top lie down."

Don Carlos followed Hugh, and the others soon joined them.

"You see that light there," the doctor said to Don Carlos.
"That is your sisters' room. As I told you, the windows on the
ground floor are all blocked up, but three or four bricks have
been left out just at the top of each, for the sake of light and air.
Now, Sim and you had better go together; he will stand against
the wall, and if you climb on to his shoulders I think you can just
about reach that hole, pull yourself up, and look in. I need not
tell you to be as silent as possible, for there may be someone in
with them. If they are alone tell them what we are going to do.
See whether there are any bars inside the brickwork. I am afraid
there are sure to be, the Spanish houses most always have bars
to the lower windows. Royce, you and I will go to the right-hand
corner of the house; you go to the left, Lightning. If you hear
anyone coming give a low hiss as a warning, then we must all lie
down close to the wall. It is so dark now that unless a man kicks
against us he won't see us. If he does touch one of you, he is
likely to think that it is one of his own party lying down there for
a sleep; but if he stoops over to see who it is, you have got either
to stab him or to grip him by the throat, so that he can't shout.
Now, I think we all understand."

The five men crawled cautiously to their respective stations.

"Now, young fellow," Sim said to Don Carlos, "if, when you
are mounted on my shoulders, you find you cannot reach the
hole, put your foot on my head. You won't hurt me with them
moccasins on. Directly you have got your fingers on the edge
give a little pat with foot to let me know, and I will put my
hands under your feet and help hoist you up. You can put a big-

gish slice of your weight on me; when I am tired I will let you know. I will lean right forward against the wall—that will help you to climb up. Now!"

When he stood up on Sim's shoulders the young Mexican found that he could reach the opening. Getting his fingers firmly upon it, he gave the signal, and with Sim's aid had no difficulty in raising himself so that he could look into the room. Two candles burned upon the table, and by their light he could see the girls stretched on couches.

"Hush, girls, hush!" he said in a low voice. "It is I, Carlos! Silence, for your lives!"

The two girls sprang to their feet. "Did you hear it, Nina?" the elder exclaimed in a low voice.

"Yes; it was the voice of Carlos. We could not both have been dreaming, surely!"

"I am up here at the opening," Carlos said. "We are here, girls, a party to rescue you; but we must get in beside you before we are discovered, or else harm might come to you. Wait a moment," he broke in, as the girls in their delight were about to throw themselves upon their knees to return thanks to the Virgin, "I am being held up here, and must get down in an instant. I can see that there is a grating to the window. Is it a strong one?"

"Yes, a very strong one."

"Very well; we will saw through it presently. Do you keep on talking loudly to each other to drown any noise that we may make. That will do, Sim; you can let me down now."

"Now, young fellow," Sim said as soon as Don Carlos reached the ground, "you go along and tell Bill Royce to come here and help. The doctor will go on keeping watch. Then go to the other end and send Lightning here, and you take his place. He is better for work than you are."

Sim was soon joined by Royce and Hugh. He had already set to work.

"These bricks are only adobe," he said. "My knife will soon cut through them."

In a very few minutes he had made a hole through the

unbaked bricks. "Señoritas," he said in Mexican, "place a chair against this hole and throw something over it, so that if anyone comes it won't be observed."

The men worked in turns with their keen bowies, and in half an hour the hole was large enough for a head and shoulders to pass through.

"Now for the files, Lightning. You may as well take the first spell, as you have got them and the oil."

It took two hours' work to file through the bars. Just as the work was finished Sim said, "You had better fetch the lad, Lightning. Send him through first."

"Don't you think, doctor," Hugh said when they were gathered round the hole, "that we might get the girls off without a fight at all?"

"I doubt it," the doctor said. "The men have just gone in except two who are left as sentries, and the night is very still. They would be almost sure to hear some of us, and if they did the girls might get shot in the fight. Still, it might be worth trying. As soon as you get in, Don Carlos, begin to move the furniture quietly against the door."

All this time the girls had been singing hymns, but their prudence left them as their brother entered the room. They stopt singing abruptly and threw themselves into his arms with a little cry of joy. Almost instantly there was a loud knock at the door.

"What are you doing there? I am coming in," and the door was heard to unlock. Carlos threw himself against it.

"Fire the signal, doctor!" Sim exclaimed, as he thrust Hugh, who was in the act of getting through the hole, into the room; as he did so three shots were fired outside. The instant Hugh was through he leaped to his feet and ran forward. The pressure against the door had ceased, the man having, in his surprise at the sound of the shots, sprung back. Hugh seized the handle of the door so that it could not be turned.

"Pile up the furniture," he said to Don Carlos. "Get into the corner of the room, señoritas; they will be firing through the door in a moment."

By this time a tremendous din was heard in the house. As yet none of the brigands knew what had happened, and their general impulse was to rush out on the terrace to hear the cause of the shots. The doctor had followed Hugh closely into the room, the hole being large enough to admit of his getting through without any difficulty. Royce followed immediately, and, as he got through, Sim Howlett's pistol cracked out twice, as the sentries ran round the corner of the house, their figures being visible to him by the light from the fire. Then he thrust himself through the opening. The instant he was through he seized one of the cushions of the couches and placed it across the hole by which he had entered. Several attempts had been made to turn the handle of the door, but Hugh held it firmly, while the doctor and Carlos moved the couches and chairs against it.

"Here, doctor, you watch this hole; I will do that work," Sim said.

They worked as silently as possible, and could hear through the opening at the top of the window the sound of shouts and oaths as a number of men ran past on the terrace. Then one voice shouted angrily for silence.

"There is no one here," he said. "Martinez, go in and fetch torches. What has happened? What have you seen, Lopez?"

"I have seen nothing," the voice replied. "I was lying close to the door when Domingo, who was on guard at the señoritas' door, said something, then almost directly three shots were fired outside. I jumped up and unfastened the door and ran out. Martos and Juan, who were on guard outside, were just running across. I heard two more shots fired, and down they both fell. I waited a moment until all the others came out, and then we ran round the corner together. As far as I see there is nobody here."

"Mille demonios!" the first speaker exclaimed; "it must be some plot to get the girls away. Perez, run in and ask Domingo if he heard any sounds within. Open the door and see that the captives are safe."

There was a pause for a minute, and then Perez ran out.

"Domingo cannot open the door," he said. "They are moving the furniture against it, and the handle won't turn; he says there must be something wrong there."

"Fool! What occasion is there to say that, as if anyone could not see there was something wrong. Ah! here comes the torches. Search all round the terrace, and ask whoever is on guard at the gate whether he has heard anything. We will see about breaking down the door afterwards."

There was a pause, and then the men came back again.

"There is no one on the terrace. Nobody has been through the gate."

Then there was a sudden, sharp exclamation. "See here, Vargas, there is a hole here. The bricks have been cut through." A fresh volley of oaths burst out, and then the man in authority gave his orders.

"Perez, do you and Martinez take your post here. Whether there is one or half a dozen inside they can only crawl out one at a time. You have only got to fire at the first head you see. The rest come inside and break open the door. We will soon settle with them."

"That is much better than I expected," the doctor said. "We have gained nearly five minutes. Now let them come as soon as they like. Bill, will you stop at this end and guard this cushion. When the fight begins they may try to push it aside and fire through at us. Let the upper end lean back a little against this chair. Yes, like that. Now, you see, you can look down, and if you see a hand trying to push the cushion aside, put a bullet through it; don't attend to us unless we are badly pressed and call for you."

There was now a furious onslaught made on the door from the outside, heavy blows being struck upon it with axes and crowbars.

"Now, Sim, you may as well speak to them a little," the doctor said. "When you have emptied your Colt, I will have a turn while you are loading."

The noise of the blows was a sufficient indication to Sim where the men wielding the weapons were standing. He had already recharged the two chambers he had emptied, and now, steadily and deliberately, he fired six shots through the panels of the door, and yells and oaths told him that some of them had taken effect. There was a pause for a moment, and then the assault recommenced. The wood gave way beneath the axes and the door began to splinter, while a number of shots were fired from the outside. The doctor, however, was stooping low, and the others stood outside the line of fire, while Bill at his end was kneeling by the cushion. The doctor's revolver answered the shots, and when he had emptied his pistol Hugh took his place. By the furious shouts and cries without there was no doubt the fire was doing execution.

But the door was nearly yielding, and, just as Hugh began to fire, one of the panels was burst in. The lock, too, had now given, the piece of wood he had jammed into it having fallen out. The Mexicans, however, were unable to force their way in owing to the steady fire of the besieged, who had extinguished their candles, and had the advantage of catching sight of their opponents through the open door, by the light of the torches without. The besieged shifted their places after each shot, so that the Mexicans fired almost at random.

For ten minutes the fight had raged, when there was a sudden shout, followed by a discharge of firearms without. A cheer broke from the defenders of the room, and a cry of despair and fury from the Mexicans. The attack on the door ceased instantly, but a desperate struggle raged in the courtyard. This went on for three or four minutes, when the Mexicans shouted for mercy and the firing ceased. Then Don Ramon's voice was heard to call, "Where are you? Are you all safe?" There was a shout in reply. Then the furniture was pulled away and the splintered door removed, and as Don Ramon entered, his daughters, who had remained quietly in the corner while the fight went on, rushed into his arms.

The success of the surprise had been complete. The man on guard at the gate had left his post to take part in the struggle going on in the house, and the officer in command of the troops had gained the terrace unobserved. He at once surrounded the house, and the two men outside the opening had been shot down at the same moment that he, with a dozen of his men, rushed into the courtyard and attacked the Mexicans. None of these had escaped. Eighteen had fallen in the house, four had been killed outside, and twelve had thrown down their arms, and were now lying bound hand and foot in charge of the troops.

No sooner had Don Ramon assured himself that his daughters were safe and uninjured, than he turned to their rescuers and poured out his hearty thanks. They were not quite uninjured. Bill had escaped without a wound; Don Carlos was bleeding from a pistol ball which had grazed his cheek; Sim Howlett's right hand was disabled by a ball which had taken off his middle finger, and ploughed its way through the flesh of the forearm; Hugh had a bullet in the shoulder; the doctor's wound was the only serious one, he having been hit just above the hip. One of the soldiers had been killed, and five wounded while fighting in the courtyard. Leaving Don Ramon and his son to question the girls as to what had befallen them, and to tell them how their rescue had been brought about, the others went outside.

"Let's have a blaze, lieutenant," Sim said. "Most of us want dressing a bit, and the doctor is hit very hard. Let us make a good big fire out here on the terrace, then we shall see what we are doing. We were in a smother of gunpowder smoke inside."

The officer gave an order, and the soldiers fetched out billets of wood from the store and piled them on the fire on the terrace, and soon a broad sheet of flame leaped up.

"Now, then, let us look at the wounds," Sim went on. "Let us lift you up and make you a little comfortable, doctor. I am afraid that there is no doing anything with you till we get you down to the town. All you have got to do is to lie quiet."

"And drink, Sam."

"Ay, and drink. I am as thirsty myself as if I had been lost on an alkali plain. Bill, will you get us some drink, plenty of water, with just a drop of spirit in it; there is sure to be plenty in the house somewhere."

Royce soon returned with a large jar of cold water and a bottle of spirits.

"Only a few drops of spirits, Sim, if you don't want to get inflammation in that hand of yours."

"What had I better do for it, doctor?"

"Well, it will be better to have that stump of the middle finger taken out altogether. I could do it for you if I could stand and had a knife of the right shape here. As it is, you can't do better than wrap your hand up in plenty of cloths, and keep them wet, and then put your arm in a sling. What's yours, Lightning?"

"I am hit in the shoulder, doctor. I don't think that it is bleeding now."

"Well, you had better get Bill to bathe it in hot water, then lay a plug of cotton over the hole, and bandage it up; the doctor at the fort will get the ball out for you as soon as you get down there. He is a good man, they say, and, anyhow, he gets plenty of practice with pistol wounds at El Paso."

Royce did his best for his two friends. Then they all sat quietly talking until the young officer came out from the house.

"We have been searching it from top to bottom," he said. "There is a lot of booty stowed away. I want you to have a look at the two leaders of these scoundrels; they have both been shot. Don Ramon said that he believed they were the murderers of his son, and that two of you might recognize them if they were, as you did a horse trade with them."

Hugh and Royce followed him to the other side of the house, where the bodies of the brigands who had fallen had been brought out and laid down. Two soldiers brought torches.

"I have no doubt whatever that these are the men," Hugh said after examining the bodies of the two leaders, who were placed at a short distance from the rest.

"Them's the fellows," Royce said positively. "I could swear to them anywhere."

"They are notorious scoundrels," the officer said, "and have for years been the scourge of New Mexico. They were away, for a time, two years ago. We had made the place so hot for them that they had to quit. We learned that from some of their gang whom we caught. They were away nearly a year; at least they were quiet. I suppose they carried on their games down in Texas, till they had to leave there too; and then, thinking the affair had blown over, they returned here. There has been a reward of ten thousand dollars for their capture anytime for the last five years. Properly that ought to be divided between you, as it is entirely your doing that they have been caught; but as the reward says death or capture, I suppose my men will have to share it with you."

"That is right enough," Sim Howlett said. "It will give us three or four hundred dollars apiece, and that don't make a bad week's work anyhow. When are you thinking of starting back, lieutenant, and what are you going to do with this house here?"

"I shall set fire to the house after we have got everything out of it. I guess it has been a den of brigands for the last ten years. I have sent four men down to keep guard at the mouth of the valley, and I expect we shall get all their horses in the morning. They must be somewhere about here. The prisoners will ride their own, and that will leave us twenty or more for carrying down the best part of the plunder. There is a lot of wine and other things that they have carried off from the haciendas that they plundered. I will send those down in carts with an escort of four of my men."

"Then I think we had better get a bed in one of the carts, and send my mate here down upon it. He has got a bullet somewhere in the hip, and won't be able to sit a horse."

"We will send him off the first thing in the morning," the officer said. "There is one of my own wounded to send down that way too."

"I will go with them as nurse," Sim said. "Get the cart to go straight through without a halt, lieutenant. The sooner my mate is in the hands of your doctor the better."

"I will see about it now," the lieutenant said; "no time shall be lost. I will send a sergeant and four men down to the village at once to requisition a cart and bring it here. It will be much better for them travelling at night. I will tell the men I send as escort to get hold of another cart in the morning and send them straight on."

"Thank you, lieutenant. That will be the best plan by far."

Don Ramon now came out from the house, and joined the group.

"In the name of my children, their mother, and myself, I thank you most deeply, señors, for the noble way in which you have risked your lives for their rescue. Had it not been for you, God knows whether I should have seen my daughters again, for I know that no oaths would have bound those villains, and that when they had obtained the ransom they would never have let my daughters free to give information that would have led to their capture. I shall always be your debtor, and the only drawback to my pleasure is that the three of you have been wounded."

"The doctor here is the only one wounded seriously," Sim Howlett said. "My hand and arm will soon heal up, and the loss of a finger is no great odds anyway. I don't suppose Lightning's shoulder will turn out worse than my arm. As for the doctor, he is hit hard, but he has been hit hard so many times, and has pulled through it, that I hope for the best."

"Señor Hugh," Don Ramon said, "it was indeed a fortunate day for me when I questioned you concerning my son's horse, for it was to your advice and to your enlisting your friends on my behalf that I owe it chiefly that my daughters are with me this evening. I must leave it to their mother to thank you as you deserve."

Two hours later the doctor and one of the wounded soldiers were placed on a bed laid at the bottom of a cart, and started under the escort of two soldiers, Sim Howlett accompanying them. As the girls had expressed the greatest disinclination to remain in the house where they had been prisoners and where so much blood had just been shed, they with the rest of the party returned with a sergeant and six soldiers carrying torches up the valley to the wood, where the horses had been left. Here two fires were soon blazing, and the girls were not long before they were asleep, wrapped in blankets that had been brought up from the house.

The following morning Hugh and Royce handed over their horses for the use of the girls, who were both accomplished horsewomen, and, mounting the horses of Sim and the doctor, they started with Don Ramon, his son, and daughters. Fifteen miles before they got to El Paso they passed the cart with the wounded men, and Hugh said he would ride into the fort to ensure the doctor being there when they arrived. Royce and he accompanied Don Ramon and his party to the gate of the hacienda, which they reached just at sunset. The Mexican was warm in his entreaties to Hugh to become his guest until his wound was healed, but he declined this on the ground that he should be well cared for at the fort, and should have the surgeon always at hand.

"I shall be over the first thing in the morning to see you," Don Carlos said. "I shall want my own face strapped up, and I warn you if the doctor says you can be moved I shall bring you back with me."

Royce accompanied Hugh to the fort. The commandant was highly gratified when he heard of the complete success of the expedition, and still more so when he learned that the two notorious brigands for whom he and his troopers had so often searched in vain were among the killed. Hugh was at once accommodated in the hospital, and the surgeon proceeded to examine his wound. It was so inflamed and swollen with the long ride, he said, that no attempt could be made at present to extract the ball, and rest and quiet were absolutely necessary. Two hours later the cart arrived. The doctor was laid in a bed near that of Hugh, the third bed in the ward being allotted to Sim Howlett. The doctor's wound was pronounced by the surgeon to be a very serious one.

It was some days before, under the influence of poultices and embrocations, the inflammation subsided sufficiently for a search to be made for the bullet in Hugh's shoulder. The surgeon, however, was then successful in finding it imbedded in the flesh behind the shoulder bone, and, having found its position, he cut it out from behind. After this Hugh's progress was rapid, and in a week he was out of bed with his arm in a sling. The doctor, contrary to the surgeon's expectations, also made fair progress. The bullet could not be found, and the surgeon, after one or two ineffectual attempts, decided that it would be better to allow it to remain where it was. The stump of Sim's finger was removed the morning after he came in, and the wound had almost completely healed by the time that Hugh was enabled to leave the hospital, a month after entering it.

Don Ramon and his son had ridden over every day to enquire after the invalids, and had seen that they were provided with every possible luxury, and he carried off Hugh to the hacienda as soon as the surgeon gave his consent to his making a short journey in the carriage. Donna Maria received him as warmly as if he had been a son of her own, and he had the greatest difficulty in persuading her that he did not require to be treated as an invalid, and was perfectly capable of doing everything for himself.

For a fortnight he lived a life of luxurious idleness, doing absolutely nothing beyond going over in the carriage every day to see how the doctor was going on. Hugh saw that he was not maintaining the progress that he had at first made. He had but little fever or pain, but he lay quite and silent, and seemed incapable of making any effort whatever. Sim Howlett was very anxious about his comrade.

"He don't seem to me to try to get well," he said to Hugh. "It looks to me like as if he thought he had done about enough, and was ready to go. If one could rouse him up a bit I believe he would pull round. He has gone through a lot has the doctor, and I expect he thinks there ain't much worth living for. He just smiles when I speak to him, but he don't take no interest in things. Do you get talking with me when you go in, Lightning, and asking about what we have been doing, and I will tell you some of the things he and I have gone through together. Maybe that may stir him up a bit."

"How long have you known him, Sim?"

"I came across him in '49. I came round by Panama, being one of the first lot to leave New York when the news of gold came. I had been away logging for some months, and had come down at the end of the season with six months' money in my pocket. I had been saving up for a year or two, and was going to put it all in partnership with a cousin of mine, who undertook the building of piers and wharves and such like on the Hudson. Well, the first news that met me when I came down to New York was that Jim had busted up, and had gone out west some said, others that he had drowned hisself. I was sorry for Jim, but I was mighty glad that I hadn't put my pile in.

"Waal, I was wondering what to start on next when the talk

about gold began, and as soon as I larned there were no mistake about it I went down to the wharf and took my passage down to the isthmus. I had been working about three months on the Yuba when I came across the doctor. I had seen him often afore we came to speak. If you wur to see the doctor now for the first time when he is just sitting quiet and talking in that woman sort of voice of his and with those big blue eyes, you would think maybe that he was a kind of softy, wouldn't you?"

"I dare say I might, Sim. I saw him for the first time when he came up with you to take my part against that crowd of Mexicans. There didn't look anything soft about him then, and though I was struck with his gentle way of talking when I met him afterwards I knew so well there was lots of fight in him that it didn't strike me he was anything of a softy, as you say."

"No? Waal, the doctor has changed since I met him, but at that time he did look a softy, and most people put him down as being short of wits. He used just to go about the camp as if he paid no attention to what wur going on. Sometimes he would go down to a bit of a claim he had taken up and wash out the gravel, just singing to himself, not as though it wur to amuse him, but as though he did not know as he wur singing, in a sort of curious far-off sort of voice; but mostly he went about doing odd sorts of jobs. If there wur a man down with the fever the doctor would just walk into his tent and take him in hand and look after him, and when he got better would just drift away, and like enough not seem to know the man the next time he met him.

"Waal, he got to be called Softy, but men allowed as he wur a good fellow, and was just as choke-full of kindness as his brain would hold, and, as he walked about, any chap who was taking his grub would ask him to share it, for it was sartin that what gold he got wouldn't buy enough to keep a cat alive, much less a man. Waal, it was this way. I got down with fever from working in the water under a hot sun. I hadn't any particular mates that time, and wur living in a bit of a tent made of a couple of blankets, and though the boys looked in and did any job that wur wanted I wur mighty bad and went off my head for a bit, and the first thing I seen when I came round was Softy in the tent tend-ing me. Ef he had been a woman and I had been his son he couldn't have looked after me tenderer.

"I found when I began to get round he had been getting meat for me from the boys and making soups, but as soon as I got round enough to know what was going on I pointed out to him the place where I had hid my dust, and he took charge of it and got me what was wanted, till I picked up and got middling strong again. As soon as I did Softy went off to look after someone else who was bad, but I think he took to me more than he had to anyone else, for he would come in and sit with me sometimes in the evening, and I found that he wurn't really short of wits as people thought, but would talk on most things just as straight as anyone. He didn't seem to have much interest in the digging, which wur about the only thing we thought of; but when I asked him what he had come to the mining camps for, if it wasn't to get gold, he just smiled gently and said he had a mission.

"What the mission wur he never said, and I concluded that though he was all there in other things his brain had somehow got mixed on that point, onless it wur that his mission was to look after the sick. Waal, we were a rough lot in '49, you bet. Lynch law hadn't begun, and there wus rows and fights of the wust kind. Our camp had been pretty quiet ontil someone set up a saloon and gambling shop, and some pretty tough characters came. That was just as I wur getting about again, though not able to work regular. It wurn't long before two fellows became the terror of the camp, and they went on so bad that the boys began to talk among themselves that they must be put down; but no one cared about taking the lead. They had shot four fellows in the first week after they came.

"I hadn't seen Softy for ten days. He had been away nussing a woodman as had his leg broke by the fall of a tree. I was sitting outside my tent with a chap they called Red Sam. We had a bottle of brandy between us, when them two fellows came along, and one of them just stooped and took up the bottle and put it to his lips and drank half of it off, and then passed it to the other without saying by your leave or anything. Red Sam said, 'Well, I'm blowed!' when the fellow who had drunk whipped out his bowie—six-shooters had hardly come in then—and afore Red Sam could get fairly to his feet he struck him under the ribs. Waal, I jumped up and drew my bowie, for it wur my quarrel, you see. He made at me. I caught his wrist as the knife was coming down, and he caught mine; but I wur like a child in his arms. I thought it wur all over with me, when I heard a shout, and Softy sprang on the man like a wild cat and drove his knife right into him, and he went down like a log.

"The other shouted out an oath and drew. Softy faced him. It wur the strangest sight I ever seen. His hat had fallen off, and his hair, which wur just as white then as it is now, fell back from his face, and his eyes, that looked so soft and gentle, wur just blazing. It came across me then, as it have come across me many a time since, that he looked like a lion going to spring; and I think Buckskin, as the man called himself, who had often boasted as he didn't fear a living thing, was frighted. They stood facing each other for a moment, and then Softy sprang at him. He was so quick that instead of Buckskin's knife catching him, as he intended, just in front of the shoulder and going straight down to the heart, it caught him behind the shoulder, and laid open his back pretty near down to the waist.

"But there wur no mistake about Softy's stroke. It went fair between the ribs, and Buckskin fell back dead, with Softy on the top of him. Waal, after that it wur my turn to nuss the doctor, for no one called him Softy after that. He wur laid up for over a month, and I think that letting out of blood did him good and cleared his brain like. When he got well he wur just as you see him now, just as clear and as sensible a chap as you would see. Why, he has got as much sense as you would find in any man west of Missouri, and he's the truest mate and the kindest heart. I have never seen the doctor out of temper, for you can't call it being out of temper when he rises up and goes for a man; that is his mission. He has never got that out of his head, and never will ontil he dies.

"He can put up with a deal, the doctor can; but when a man gits just too bad for anything, then it seems to him as he has got a call to wipe him out, and he wipes him out, you bet. You don't

want lynch law where the doctor is: he is a judge and a posse all
to himself, and for years he was the terror of hard characters
down in California. They was just skeered of him, and if a downright bad man came to a camp and heard the doctor wur there,
he would in general clear straight out agin. He has been shot
and cut all over, has the doctor, and half a dozen times it seemed
to me I should never bring him round agin.

"It ain't no use talking to him and asking him why he should
take on hisself to be a jedge and jury. When it's all over he always
says in his gentle way that he is sorry about it, and I do think he
is, and he says he will attend to his own business in future; but
the next time it is just the same thing again. There ain't no holding him. You might just as well try to stop a mountain lion when
he smells blood. At such times he ain't hisself. If you had once
see him you would never forget it. There wur a British painting
fellow who wur travelling about taking pictures for a book. He
wur in camp once when the doctor's dander rose, and he went
for a man; and the Britisher said arterwards to me as it were like
the bersek rage. I never heard tell of the berseks; but from what
the chap said I guessed they lived in the old time. Waal, if they
wur like the doctor I tell you that I shouldn't like to get into a
muss with them. No, sir."

"Do you know what the doctor's history is, Sim?"

"Yes, I do know," he said, "but I don't suppose anyone else
does. Maybe he will tell you some day if he gets over this."

"Oh! I don't want to know if it is a secret, Sim."

"Waal, there ain't no secret in it, Lightning; but he don't talk
about it, and in course I don't. It is a sort of thing that has happened to other men, and maybe after a bit they have got over it;
but the doctor ain't. You see he ain't a common man: he has got
the heart of a woman, and for a time it pretty nigh crazed him."

XX. THE AVENGER

Hugh told the coachman to go back to the hacienda, and to return for him late in the afternoon, and then went in with Sim. The doctor smiled faintly as Hugh sat down beside him and asked how he was getting on.

"I am getting on, lad," he said. "I reckon I shall be there before long."

Hugh affected to misunderstand him.

"You must pick up strength," he said, "or we shall never carry out that expedition among the Apaches, you know."

"If you wait for that you will wait a long time," the doctor said quietly.

"I hope not," Hugh said cheerily. "By the way, Sim, you told me you would tell me some of your adventures in the early days of California. I am interested in that, because I had an uncle there. He was ten years or so out there."

"What was his name, Lightning?" Sim asked.

"His name was Will Tunstall."

An exclamation burst from both his hearers.

"Your uncle!" Sim exclaimed. "Waal, that beats all, and to think that we should have been all this time together and never known that. Is your name Tunstall too?"

"Yes, Hugh Tunstall."

"To think now, doctor!" Sim said; "and we never knowed him except as Hugh or Lightning, and he is Will Tunstall's nephew. Why, lad, Bill—English Bill we called him—was a mate of ours, and a better mate men never worked with."

"You are like him, lad," the doctor said in a voice so different from that in which he had before spoken that Hugh quite

322

started. "I thought you reminded me of someone, and now I know. It was English Bill. He was just as tall and as straight as you are, and laughed and talked just as you do. I wonder, Sim, we didn't notice it at once. Well, well, that is strange!"

Hugh was greatly surprised. It was indeed strange that he should have met these two mates of his uncle. Stranger still that they should have entertained such evident affection for a man who seemed to differ in character so widely from them. He was surprised, too, at the doctor's remarks about his resemblance to his uncle, for he could see no likeness whatever.

"Well," he said, "I should have had no idea that I was like my uncle. I think you must have forgotten his figure. He is tall and muscular certainly, but he is much darker than I am, and, I think, altogether different."

The doctor and Sim looked at each other with astonishment.

"There must be some mistake," Sim said. "Do you say your uncle is alive now?"

"Certainly I do," Hugh replied, in turn surprised.

"Ah! then, it isn't the same man," Sim said. "Our Bill Tunstall was killed ten years ago. It is odd, too; Tunstall ain't a common name, at least not in these parts. If you had ever said your own name before I should have noticed it, and asked you about it; but Royce always called you Lightning, or Hugh, and one may know men here for years by the name they have got without ever thinking what name they might be born with."

"Is Tunstall a common name in England, Lightning?" the doctor asked.

"No, I don't think so, doctor. I never met any others. We came from the north of England, from Cumberland."

"So did English Bill," Sim said. "Never heard tell of a chap that came out from there of that name, a tall, straight, strong fellow like you? He must have come out before you wur born, though, of course, we didn't know him for years afterwards."

"My uncle came out before I was born," Hugh said; "but I never heard of anyone else of the same name doing so; still, if your friend is dead, of course it isn't the same, for my uncle is alive. At least he was two years ago. He is strong, and active, and well knit; but he is not as tall as I am by two inches, I should say."

"Lift me up in bed, Sim," the doctor said excitedly. "How long ago did your uncle return?"

"Over six years ago," Hugh replied, surprised at this strange excitement upon the part of a man who, ten minutes before, had seemed to have no further interest in anything.

"Six years ago, Sim! You hear that; six years ago?"

"Gently, doctor, gently; what are you driving at?" Sim asked, really alarmed at his mate's excitement.

The doctor paid no attention to him. "And he had been a great many years away? Went away as a boy, and when he came back was so changed they wouldn't have known him?"

"Yes, that was so," Hugh said, more and more surprised.

"You hear that, Sim? you hear that?" the doctor exclaimed sharply.

"I hear it, mate, but do you lie down. You are not strong enough to be exciting yourself like this, though I am blamed if I can see what it is about."

"What did he go home for?" the doctor asked, still unheeding Sim.

"He went home because my father had died, and he came in for a considerable property, and he was one of my guardians."

"Do you hear that, Sim?" the doctor cried in a loud shrill voice that was almost a scream; "do you see it all now?"

"Just you run and call the surgeon, Lightning; the doc.'s going clear off his head."

"Stop!" the doctor said, as Hugh was about to hurry off. "If Sim wasn't that thick-headed he would see what I see. Give me a drink."

Hugh handed him a glass of lemonade, which he tossed off.

"Now, then, Sim, haven't I told you this young fellow was like someone, though I couldn't mind who. Don't you see it is our mate, English Bill?"

"Yes, he is like him," Sim said, "now you name it. He is a bit taller, and his figure is loose yet, but he will widen out ontil he is just what Bill wur."

"Like what his uncle was," the doctor broke in; "don't you see, Sim, his uncle was our mate?"

"But how can that be, doctor? Don't you hear him say as his uncle is alive in England, and didn't we bury poor Bill?"

"You've heard Hugh say what his uncle came home for. What was Bill going home for, Sim?"

"Ah!" Sim exclaimed suddenly, as a light flashed across him, "it was just what Lightning has been saying. His brother was dead, and he was going home to be guardian to his nephew; and because he had come into an estate."

"Quite so, only he never went, Sim, did he?"

"No, certainly he never went, doc. There is no doubt about that."

"But somebody did go," the doctor said, "and we know who it was. The man who killed him and stole his papers."

An exclamation of astonishment broke from Hugh, while Sim exclaimed earnestly:

"By thunder, doctor, but you may be right! I reckon it may be as you say, though how you came to figure it out beats me. That must be it. We never could make out why he should have been killed. He had money on him, but not enough to tempt the man as we suspected."

"Suspected? No! the man we knew did it," the doctor broke in. "You see now, Lightning, how it is. It was known in camp that our mate had come into an estate in England. He said goodbye to us all and started, and his body was found a few miles away. We felt pretty sure of the man who had done it, for he was missing. He was a gambler. Bill had been pretty thick with him for some time, and I allow the fellow had got the whole story out of him, and knew the place he was going to, and knew where it was, and had wormed a whole lot out of him that might be useful to him. Then he killed him, and wasn't seen any more in these parts. I searched for him for a year up and down California, and Nevada, and New Mexico, and down into Northern Mexico, but I never came across his track. If I had got as much as a sign which way he had gone, I would have hunted him down all over the world; but there was not a sign from the day he had left the camp. Nobody ever heard of him again. I found out he had a wife down in Southern California, a Mexican girl, and I went down there to hunt her out, but she had gone too—had left a few days after he had disappeared. Now we are on his track again, Sim. I guess in a week I will be up, and you and I will go straight off with this young fellow to England, and see this thing out. Lay me down now. I must be quiet for a bit. Take Lightning out and talk it over with him, and tell the cook to let me have some strong soup, for I have got to get out of this as soon as possible."

"Can all this be true, Sim, do you think?" Hugh said; "or is the doctor light-headed? Do you think it is possible that the man who murdered my uncle is the one who has taken his place all these years?"

"It is gospel truth, Lightning. At least it is gospel truth that your uncle was murdered here, for there can't be no doubt that your uncle Bill Tunstall and our mate is the same man; but I can't say whether the one as you thought is your uncle is the one that killed him. Your description is like enough to him. Tell me a little more about him."

"He is rather dark, with a moustache but no whiskers; he has a quiet manner; he is slight, but gives you the idea of being very strong. He has very white well-made hands. He shows his teeth a little when he smiles, but even when I first knew him I never liked his smile; there was something about it that wasn't honest. And he brought over with him a Mexican wife."

"That's him," Sim said in a tone of conviction; "you have just described him. He has a light sort of walk like a cat, and a tigerish way with him all over. There ain't a doubt that is the man. And what is the woman like?"

"She has always been very kind and good to me," Hugh said. "No aunt could have been kinder. I am awfully sorry for her, but I hated the man. That was why I left England. I came into the room one day and found that he had knocked his wife down, and I seized him. Then he knocked me down, and I caught up the poker. I was no match for him then in strength. Then he drew a pistol, but I hit him before he could aim; and as he went down his head came against a sharp corner of a piece of furniture, and

I thought that I had killed him, so I bolted at once, made my way to Hamburg, and crossed to New York. That is how I came to be here."

"Has he got much of the property, lad?"

"He has got what was my uncle's share," Hugh replied. "Now that I know who he is I can understand things. I could not understand before. If I had died before I came of age he would have had the whole of the property. He used to get the most vicious horses he could find for me to ride, and I remember now, when we were in Switzerland together he wanted to take me up mountains with him, but my aunt wouldn't let me go. Then he offered to teach me pistol-shooting, but somehow he dropped that, and my aunt taught me herself. I think she must have stopped him. Thinking it all over now, I feel sure that he must have intended to kill me somehow, and that she managed to save my life. There were often quarrels between them, but she didn't seem to be afraid of him. I think that she must have had some sort of hold over him."

"Waal, there is one thing," Sim said after a pause; "I believe this here discovery has saved the doctor's life. He had made up his mind that he had done with it, and wasn't going to try to get better. Now, you see, he is all eagerness to get on this fellow's scent. If he had been a bloodhound he could not have hunted the country closer than he did for that thar tarnal villain. He had an idee it wur his business to wipe him out, and when the doctor gets set on an idee like that he carries it out. It will pull him round now, you see if it don't."

"I do hope so, indeed, Sim," Hugh said warmly. "The doctor is a wonderful fellow, and if it hadn't been for him we should never have arrived at this discovery. Well, I am glad. Of course I am sorry to hear that my uncle was murdered, but as I never saw him that does not affect me so much; but I am glad to hear that this man whom I hated, a man who ill-treated his wife and who spent all his time at horse-racing and gambling, is not my uncle, and has no right to a share in the property that has been in our family for so many years. I only hope that this excitement will not do the doctor any harm."

"I am sure that it will do him good," Sim said confidently; "but it wur strange to see a man who looked as if he wur just dying out wake up like that; but that has always been his way; just as quiet as a woman at most times, but blazing out when he felt thar wur a great wrong, and that it wur his duty to set it right. I can tell you now what I know about his story. Now he knows you are English Bill's nephew he won't mind your knowing. Waal, his story ain't anything much out of the way. There are scores who have suffered the like, but it didn't have the effect on them like it did on the doctor.

"He is really a doctor trained and edicated. He married out east. He wur a quiet little fellow, and not fit to hustle round in towns and push hisself forward; so he and his wife came round and settled in Californy somewhere about '36. Thar wurn't many Americans here then, as you may guess. He settled down in the south somewhere a hundred miles or so from Los Angeles. He had some money of his own, and he bought a place and planted fruit trees and made a sort of little paradise of it. That is what he told me he lived on, doctoring when it came in his way. There wur some rich Mexicans about, and he looked after most of them; but I guess he did more among the poor. He had four children, and things went on peaceable till '48. Then you know gold was discovered, and that turned Californy upside down.

"It brought pretty nigh all the roughs in creation there. They quarrelled with the Mexikins, and they quarrelled with the Injuns, and there was trouble of the wust kind.

"There was gangs of fellows as guessed they could make more money by robbing the miners than they could by digging for gold, and I reckon they was about right; and when they warn't robbing the miners they was plundering the Mexikins. Waal, I never heard the rights of it, the doctor never could bring hisself to talk about that, but one day when he had been twenty miles away to visit a patient, he came back and found his place burned down, and his wife and the four children murdered. He went off his head, and some of the people as knew him took him down to Los Angeles, and he wur a year in the madhouse thar. He wur very quiet. I believe he used ter just sit and cry.

"After a time he changed. He never used to speak a word, but just sot with those big eyes of his wide open; with his face working, as if he seen an enemy. Waal, after a year he got better, and the Mexikins let him out of that madhouse. Someone had bought his place, and the money had been banked for him. He took it and went off. He never got to hear who the gang wur as had been to his house. I think the idee comes to him ever since when he comes across a really bad man, that he wur one of that lot, and then he goes for him. It is either that, or he believes he has got a sort of special call to wipe out bad men. As I told you, he is always ready to do a kindness to anyone, and ef he has killed over a score or more of the wust men in Californy, I guess he has saved five times as many by nussing them when they are ill, only he will never give them medicine. One of his idees is that if he hadn't gone on doctoring, he wouldn't have been away when that gang came to his house, and that is why he will never do anything as a doctor again. He is just a nuss, he says, and nothing more.

"Now, don't you go for to think, Lightning, that the doctor is the least bit mad, because he ain't, and never have been since I first knew him, and I should like to see the man as would say that he wur. He is just as sensible as I am; that ain't saying much; he is ten times as sensible. He always knows the right thing to do, does the doctor, and does it. He air just an ornary man, with heaps of good sense, and just the kindest heart in the world, only when thar is a regular downright bad man in the camp, the doctor takes him in hand all to hisself."

"But, Sim, I thought you were going about this gold business, this placer, directly the doctor was able to move."

"That has got to wait," Sim said. "Maybe some day or other, when this business of yours is over, I may come back and see about it; maybe I won't. Ef the doctor is going to England with you, I am going; that is sartin. Besides, even if I would let him go alone, which aren't likely, maybe his word wouldn't be enough. One witness wouldn't do to swear that this man who has stepped into your uncle's shoes ain't what he pretends to be; but if thar is two of us can swear to him as being Symonds the gambler, it'll go a long way. But you may have trouble even then. Anyhow, don't you worry yourself about the gold mine. Like enough we should all have been wiped out by the Redskins ef we had tried it. Now I will just look in and see how the doctor is afore you go."

Sim returned in two minutes, saying that the doctor had drunk a bowl of soup, and had told the orderly who brought it that he was going to sleep, as he wanted to get strong, being bound to start for a journey in a week's time.

As the carriage was not to return until late, Hugh started to walk over to Don Ramon's, as he wanted to think over the strange news he had heard.

"Your friend is better, I hope," the señora said as he entered, "or you would not have returned so soon."

"He is better, señora. We have made a strange discovery that has roused him up, and given him new life, while it has closely affected me. With your permission I will tell it to you all."

"Is it a story, Señor Hugh?" the younger girl said. "I love a story above all things."

"It is a very curious story, señorita, as I am sure you will agree when you hear it; but it is long, therefore I pray you to make yourselves comfortable before I begin."

As soon as they had seated themselves, Hugh told the story of the flight of his uncle as a boy, of his long absence and return; of the life at home, and the quarrel that had been the cause of his own flight from home; and how he had that day discovered that his companions in their late adventure had been his uncle's comrades and friends; and how, comparing notes, he had found that his uncle had been murdered, and that his assassin had gone over and occupied his place in England. Many exclamations of surprise were uttered by his auditors.

"And what are you going to do now, señor?"

"I am going to start for home as soon as the doctor is well enough to travel. I should have been willing to have first gone with them upon the expedition upon which we were about to start when your daughters were carried off, but Sim Howlett would not hear of it."

"I intended to have had my say in the matter," Don Ramon said, "and have only been waiting to complete my arrangements. I have not hurried, because I knew that until your companion died or recovered, you would not be making a move. I am, as you know, señor, a very wealthy man, wealthy even for a Mexican, and we have among us fortunes far surpassing those of rich men among the Americans. In addition to my broad lands, my flocks and herds, I have some rich silver mines in Mexico which alone bring me in far more than we can spend. The ransom that these brigands set upon my daughters was as nothing to me, and I would have paid it five times over had I been sure of recovering them; but, you see, this was what I was not sure of, and the fact that they had not asked more when they knew how wealthy I was, in itself assured me that they intended to play me false, and that it was their intention to keep them and to continue to extort further sums.

"You and your friends restored my daughters to me. Now, Señor Hugh, you are an English gentleman, and I know that you would feel the offer of any reward for your inestimable services as an insult; but your three companions are in a different position, two are miners and one is a vaquero. I know well that in rendering me that service, there was no thought of gain in their minds, and that they risked their lives as freely as you did, and in the same spirit, that of a simple desire to rescue women from the hands of scoundrels. That, however, makes no difference whatever in my obligation towards them.

"My banker yesterday received the sum in gold that I directed him to obtain to pay the ransom, and I have to-day given him orders to place three sums of twenty-five thousand dollars each at their disposal, so that they need no longer lead their hard and perilous life, but can settle down where they will. I know the independence of the Americans, señor, but I rely upon you to convince these three men that they can take this money without feeling that it is a payment for their services. They have given me back my daughters at the risk of their lives, and they must not refuse to allow me in turn to make them a gift, which is but a small token of my gratitude, and will leave me still immeasurably their debtor."

"I will indeed do my best to persuade them to accept your gift, Don Ramon, and believe that I shall be able to do so. The doctor is a man of nearly sixty, and Howlett is getting on in years, and it would be well indeed for them now to give up the hard life they have led for so long. As to Bill Royce, I have no doubt whatever. I have heard him say many a time that his greatest ambition is to settle down in a big farm, and this will enable him to do so in a manner surpassing anything he can ever have dreamt of."

"And now, señor, about yourself. What you have just told us renders it far more difficult than I had hitherto thought. We have talked it over, I, my wife, Carlos, and my daughters. I knew that you were a gentleman, but I did not know that you were the heir to property. I thought you were, like others of your countrymen, who, seeing no opening at home, had come out to make your way here. What we proposed was this. To ask you whether your inclinations had turned most to cattle breeding or to mining. In either case we could have helped you on the way. Had you said ranching, I would have put you as manager on one of my largest ranches on such terms that you would in a few years have been its master. Had you said mining, I would have sent you down to my mine in Mexico there to have first learned the nature of the work, then to have become manager, and finally to have been my partner in the affair. But now, what are we to do? You are going home. You have an estate awaiting you, and our intentions have come to nought."

"I am just as much obliged to you, señor, as if you had carried them out," Hugh said warmly, "and I thank you most deeply for having so kindly proposed to advance my fortunes. Had I remained here I would indeed have accepted gratefully one or other of your offers. As it is I shall want for nothing, and I can assure you I feel that the small share I took in the rescue of your daughters is more than repaid by the great kindness that you have shown me."

The next day Hugh explained to two of his friends the gift Don Ramon had made them. Bill Royce, to whom he first spoke, was delighted. "Jehosaphat!" he exclaimed, "that is some-

thing like. I thought when the judge here paid us over our share
of the reward for the capture of those brigands, that it was about
the biggest bit of luck that I had ever heard of; but this beats all.
That Don Ramon is a prince. Well, no more ranching for me. I
shall go back east and buy a farm here. There was a girl
promised to wait for me, but as that is eight years ago, I don't
suppose she has done it; still, when I get back with twenty-five
thousand dollars in my pocket, I reckon I shan't be long before
I find someone ready to share it with me. And you say I can walk
right into that bank and draw it in gold?"

"Yes, you can, Bill, but I shouldn't advise you to do it."

"How am I to take the money, then, Lightning?"

"The bank will give you an order on some bank in New York,
and when you get there you can draw the money out as you like."

Sim Howlett received the news in silence. Then he said:
"Waal, Hugh, I don't see why we shouldn't take it; as Don
Ramon says it isn't much to him, and it is a big lump of money
to us. I would have fought for the gals just as willing if they had
been *peóns*; but seeing as their father's got more money than he
knows what to do with, it is reasonable and natural as he should
want to get rid of the obligation to us, and anyhow we saved him
from having to pay two hundred thousand dollars as a beginning
and perhaps as much as that over and over again, afore he got
them back. We had best say nothing to the doctor now his mind
is set on one thing, and he is going to get well so as to carry it
out; when that job is over it will be time enough to tell him
about this. I am beginning to feel too stiff for work, and the doc.
was never any good that way, and he is getting on now. I shall be
able to persuade him when the time comes, and shall tell him
that if he won't keep his money, I shall have to send back mine.
But he is too sensible not to see, as I do, that it is reasonable on
the part of the don, and if he don't want it hisself, he can give it
to a hospital and share mine with him. I reckon we shall hang
together as long as we both live; so you can tell the don it is settled, and that though we had no thought of money, we won't say
no to his offer."

Now that the doctor had made up his mind to live, he recovered with wonderful rapidity, and in a fortnight was ready to travel.

Hugh took leave of Don Ramon and his family with great regret; they were all much affected at parting with him, and he was obliged to promise that if ever he crossed the Atlantic again he would come and pay them a visit. Prince went back to his old stable, for the party were going to travel down the Rio Grande by boat. At Matamoras, the port at its mouth, they went by a coasting steamer to Galveston, and thence by another steamer to New York. Here Royce left them, and the other three crossed by a Cunarder to Liverpool. The quiet and sea voyage quite restored the doctor, who was by far the most impatient of them to get to the journey's end. They had obtained a complete rig-out of what Sim called store clothes at New York, though Hugh had some difficulty in persuading him to adopt the white shirt of civilization.

On arriving Hugh wrote to Mr. Randolph saying that he had news of very great importance to communicate to him, but that he did not wish to appear at Carlisle until he had seen him, and therefore begged him to write and make an appointment to meet him at Kendal on the third day after he received the letter. The answer came in due time. It was short and characteristic: "My dear Hugh, I am delighted to hear that you are back in England again. You behaved like a fool in going away, and an even greater one in staying away so long. However, I will give you my opinion more fully when I see you. I am very glad, for many reasons, that you have returned. I can't think what you want to say to me, but will arrive at Kendal by the train that gets in at 12 o'clock on Thursday next."

When Mr. Randolph got out of the train at Kendal, Hugh was awaiting him on the platform.

"Bless me! is this you?" he exclaimed, as the young fellow strode up to him. "You were a big lad when you left, but you are a big man now, and a Tunstall all over."

"Well, I have been gone nearly three years, you see, Mr. Randolph, and that makes a difference at my age. I am past nineteen."

"Yes, I suppose you are, now I think of it. Well, well, where are we to go?"

"I have got a private sitting-room at the hotel, and have two friends there whom I want to introduce you to; when I tell you that they have come all the way with me from Mexico to do me a service, they are, you will acknowledge, friends worth having."

"Well, that looks as if there were really something in what you have got to say to me, Hugh; men don't take such a journey as that unless for some strong reason. What are your friends? for as I have no idea what you have been doing these three years, I do not know whether you have been consorting with princes or peasants."

"With a little of both, Mr. Randolph; one of my friends is a Californian miner, and as good a specimen of one as you can meet with; the other is a doctor, or rather, as I should say, has been a doctor, for he has ceased for some years to practise, and has been exploring and mining."

"And they have both come over purely for the sake of doing you a service?" Mr. Randolph asked, elevating his eyebrows a little.

"Simply that, Mr. Randolph, strange as it may appear to your legal mind. However, as this is the hotel where we are putting up you won't be kept much longer in a state of curiosity.

"Sim and Doctor, this is my oldest friend and trustee, Mr. Randolph. Mr. Randolph, these are my two very good friends, Doctor Hunter and Mr. Sim Howlett." In the States introductions are always performed ceremoniously, and the two men shook hands gravely with the lawyer. "I said, Mr. Randolph," Hugh went on, "that they were my good friends. I may add that they were also the good friends of my late uncle, William Tunstall."

"Of your late uncle, Hugh! What are you thinking about? Why, he is alive and well; and more's the pity," he muttered to himself.

"I know what I am saying, Mr. Randolph. They were the dear friends of my late uncle, William Tunstall, who was foully murdered in the town of Sacramento, in California, on his way to San Francisco, in reply to your summons to return to England."

Mr. Randolph looked in astonishment from one face to another as if to assure himself that he heard correctly, but their gravity showed him that he was not mistaken.

"Will Tunstall murdered in California!" he repeated; "then who is it that——"

"The man who murdered him, and who, having possessed himself of his letters, and papers, came over here and took his place; a gambler of the name of Symonds. My friend obtained a warrant from the sheriff at Sacramento for his arrest on this charge of murder, and for upwards of a year Dr. Hunter travelled over California and Mexico in search of him. It never struck them that it was anything but a case of murder for the money he had on him. The idea of the step Symonds really took, of personating the man he had murdered, never occurred to them. We met in New Mexico, and were a considerable time together before they learned that my name was Tunstall, for out there men are known either by their Christian names or by some nickname. Then at once they said they had years before had a mate of the same name, and then gradually, on comparing notes, the truth came out."

"Well—well—well—well!" Mr. Randolph murmured, seating himself helplessly in a chair; "this is wonderful. You have taken away my breath; this is amazing indeed; I can hardly take it in yet, lad. You are sure of what you are saying? Quite sure that you are making no mistake?"

"Quite certain. However, the doctor will tell you the story for himself." This the doctor proceeded to do, narrating the events at Cedar Gulch; how the murder had been discovered, and the body identified; how a verdict of wilful murder against some person unknown had been returned by a coroner's jury; how he and Sim Howlett had gone down to Sacramento, and how they had traced the deed to the gambler Symonds.

"There can be no doubt," Mr. Randolph said when he concluded, "that it is as you say, and that this man is William Tunstall's murderer."

"And we shall be able to bring him to justice, shall we not?" Hugh asked. "That was why I wanted you to meet me here, so that we could arrange to arrest him before he had any suspicion of my return."

"Ah! that is a different thing altogether, Hugh. The evidence of your two friends, and the confirmation that can doubtless be obtained from Sacramento as to the existence of the gravestone erected to William Tunstall, and of the finding of the coroner's court, will no doubt enable us to prove to the satisfaction of the courts here that this scoundrel is an impostor. But the murder case is different.

"In the first place you would have to bring forward the charge, and give your evidence in the United States, and obtain an application for his extradition. British law has no jurisdiction as to a murder committed in a foreign country. Having set the United States authorities in action, you would return here and aid in obtaining an order from a magistrate here for that extradition; the evidence of your friends would doubtless be sufficient to induce a magistrate to grant such an order, then he would be taken over to the States, and, I suppose, sent down to California to be tried there. Your friends here will be best able to judge whether any jury out there would convict a man for a murder committed eight or ten years ago, unless the very strongest evidence was forthcoming.

"It would be next to impossible to obtain the evidence of those people, the waiters and others, from whom your friends gleaned the facts that put them upon the trail of Symonds, and without that evidence there is no legal proof that would hang a man. Morally, of course, there would seem to be no doubt about it. He and you were in the mining camp together, he knew the object for which Will Tunstall was leaving for England, and that he was entitled to considerable property on arriving here. He followed him down to Sacramento, or at any rate he went down at that time. They were together drinking; there your uncle was found murdered; this man appeared here with the letters that your uncle carried, and obtained possession of the estate.

"It is a very strong chain of evidence, and were every link

proved might suffice to hang him here; but at present you have no actual proof that Symonds ever was in Sacramento with him, or was the man he was drinking with; and even could you find the waiters and others, it is very unlikely that there would be anyone to identify him after all this time. Symonds' counsel would argue that there was no proof whatever against his client, and he would, of course, claim that Symonds knew nothing about the murder, but that he afterwards obtained the papers from the man who really committed the murder, and that the idea of coming over to England and personating Tunstall then for the first time occurred to him. So I think you would find it extremely difficult to get a verdict out in California merely on the evidence of these two gentlemen, and of my own that he was possessed of a letter I wrote to Tunstall. But in any case, if you decide to have him arrested on the charge of murder, you will have to go back to California to set the law in motion there, to get the State authorities to apply to the supreme authorities of the United States to make an application to our government for his arrest and extradition. You must do all this before he has any idea that you have returned, or at any rate before he knows that you have any idea of his crime; otherwise he will, of course, fly, and we shall have no means of stopping him, and he might be in Fiji before the application for his arrest was received here."

Hugh and his companions looked helplessly at each other. This was an altogether unexpected blow. They had imagined they had but to give their evidence to ensure the arrest, trial, and execution of William Tunstall's murderer.

The doctor's fingers twitched, and the look that Sim Howlett knew so well came into his eyes. He was about to spring to his feet when Sim touched him.

"Wait, doctor," he said. "We will talk about that afterwards."

"Then what do you advise, Mr. Randolph?" Hugh asked after a long pause.

"I should say that for the present we should content ourselves with arresting him on the charge of impersonation, and of obtaining possession of your uncle's estate by fraud. I think the proof we now have, in the evidence of these two gentlemen, and in this copy of the finding of the coroner's jury, will be quite sufficient to ensure his conviction, in which case he will get, I should say, seven years' penal servitude—perhaps fourteen—for although he will not be charged with that offence, the conviction that he murdered your uncle in order to obtain possession of the estate cannot but be very strong in the mind of the judge. Yes, I should think he would give him fourteen years at least. We may, of course, want some other evidence that can be obtained from Sacramento, such as an official copy of the record of the proceedings at the coroner's inquest; but that would be a matter for counsel to decide. My own opinion is, that the evidence of these two gentlemen that the William Tunstall who corresponded with your father, received my letter informing him of the will, and left the mining camp on his way to England, and was murdered on his way to Sacramento, was the real William Tunstall, will be quite sufficient.

"It is a very lucky thing for you, by the way, Hugh, that there were provisions in your father's will, that if William Tunstall died without issue his half of the property came back to you, for that clause has effectually prevented him from selling his estate, which he would have done long ago had it been possible to do so. To my knowledge he has tried over and over again, and that clause has always prevented it. He has raised a little money on his life interest, but that will of course have no claim on the estate now. Now, what do you say? It is for you to decide. In the one case you will have an enormous amount of trouble, and you may finally fail in getting an American jury to find this man guilty of the murder; and in any case, if they do find him so, they will not execute him for a murder committed so long ago, and it is probable that he will get off with imprisonment for life, and may be acquitted altogether. On the other hand, if you have him arrested at once here, on the charge of impersonation and fraud, he is morally certain of getting a sentence which, at his age, will be pretty nearly equivalent to imprisonment for life."

"I certainly think that is the best plan," Hugh agreed. "Don't you think so?" he asked, turning to the others.

"I think so," Sim Howlett said at once; and even the doctor, though less readily, agreed.

Since his last illness he had changed a good deal. He had no longer fits of abstraction, and was brighter and more cheerful than Sim Howlett had ever seen him before. The loss of blood and the low fever that had brought him to death's door had apparently relieved his brain of a load that had for years oppressed it.

"Let it be so," he said reluctantly. "Had we met out in the West it would have been different; but as it is, perhaps it is best."

Late that evening the party proceeded to Carlisle, and early the next morning Mr. Randolph went with the others to one of the county magistrates, and, after laying all the facts before him, obtained a warrant for the arrest of John Symonds *alias* William Tunstall.

"I must congratulate you, Mr. Tunstall," the magistrate said to Hugh after he had signed the warrant, "upon your discovery. This scoundrel has been a disgrace to your name. He has been for years a consorter with betting men and blacklegs, and stands in the worst odour. It is said that he has mortgaged his life interest in the estates and completely ruined himself."

Mr. Randolph nodded. "Yes, I believe he is pretty well at the end of his tether, and at any moment he might be turned out of Byrneside."

"Well, there is an end to all that," the magistrate said, "and the men who have proved themselves even sharper rogues than he is, will be disappointed. I am sorry for the person who has passed as your aunt, for I know that she is spoken well of by the people in the neighbourhood, and I fancy she has had a very hard time of it with him; but of course she must have been his accomplice in this impersonation of your uncle."

"I am sorry for her, very sorry," Hugh said. "She was always most kind to me, and I have reason to believe that she did all in her power to protect me from him. You see at my death he would have inherited the whole property, and we now know that he was not a man to stick at anything. I am sure that she acted in fear of him."

"I have private reasons for believing so too," Mr. Randolph said; "for, unless I am greatly mistaken, she has deposited a document that, in case of her death, would have exposed the whole plot, in the hands of some legal friends of mine. However, we will not occupy your time any longer, but will start at once with a couple of constables to execute this warrant."

Returning to Carlisle Mr. Randolph secured the services of two constables, and hiring vehicles they started at once for Byrneside. On arriving there Mr. Randolph said to the servant, "Announce me to Mr. Tunstall. Do not say that I am not alone." Following him closely they went across the hall, and as he opened the door and announced Mr. Randolph the others entered. The man was standing on the hearth rug. The woman looked flushed and excited. They were evidently in the midst of a quarrel. Symonds looked up in angry surprise when the party entered.

"Do your duty," Mr. Randolph said to one of the constables.

"John Symonds, I arrest you under a warrant on the charge of impersonation and fraud."

A deep Mexican oath burst from the lips of the man, then he stood quiet again.

"Who dares bring such a charge against me?" he asked.

"I do," Hugh said, stepping forward; "and these are my witnesses, men who knew you at Cedar Gulch, and who identified the body of my murdered uncle."

"Traitress!" Symonds exclaimed in Mexican, and in an instant his arm was stretched out and there was a report of a pistol. "And she sent you out!" he exclaimed, turning to Hugh, but as he was in the act of again raising his arm there was the report of another pistol, and he fell shot through the brain.

The others stood stupefied at the sudden catastrophe, but the doctor said quietly: "I saw his hand go behind him, and knew he was up to mischief. I ought not to have waited, it is always a mistake to wait in these cases."

Hugh sprang forward towards the woman who had been kind to him, but she had fallen back in her chair. The gambler's bullet had done its work; it had struck her on the temple, and death had been instantaneous.

The excitement in the county when the news spread of what had taken place at Byrneside was great indeed, and the revelations made before the coroner's jury greatly added to it. They returned a verdict that "Lola Symonds had been wilfully murdered by John Symonds, and that the latter had come by his death at the hands of Frank Hunter, who had justifiably shot at and killed him while opposing by armed means the officers of the law, and that no blame attaches to the said Frank Hunter."

When all was over, Hugh was warmly congratulated by the gentlemen who had come in to be present at the inquest, upon his recovery of the whole of his father's estate, and upon his escape from the danger he had certainly run at the hands of the murderer of his uncle. He was much affected by the death of the woman he still thought of as his aunt, and the document that she deposited at the lawyers' in London showed how completely she had acted under fear of her husband, and that she had knowingly risked her life to save his.

The doctor and Sim Howlett remained for a fortnight with him at Byrneside. He had urged upon them to make it their home for a while and to settle near him; but at the end of that time the doctor said to him one evening: "Sim and I have talked matters over, Hugh, and we have made up our minds. I have heard from him that we are each the owners of twenty-five thousand dollars. I should not have taken it had I known it at the time, but I should not like to hurt the don's feelings by sending it back now, and perhaps it will do more good in my hands than in his. So Sim and I are going back to California. We shall buy a place near the spot where I lived many years ago—Sim tells me he has told you the story—and there we shall finish our days. When we die the money will go to charities. That is our plan, lad. We shall find plenty to help, and what with that and a little gardening our time will be well occupied, and Sim and I will have plenty in the past to look back upon and talk about."

And so a week later they sailed. Hugh went with them to Liverpool and saw them off, and then travelled for a time on the Continent, for Byrneside was repugnant to him after the tragedy that had been enacted there.

On his return he went down to Norfolk and stayed for some time with Luscombe, and the visit was so pleasant that it was repeated whenever he happened to be in England.

Three years later he crossed the Atlantic again. He traversed the States more easily now, for the railway across was almost completed. After spending a month in California with the doctor and Sim Howlett, whom he found well and happy, he visited Don Ramon at El Paso. There had been changes here, for both Don Carlos and his two sisters were married, and all insisted upon his being their guest for a time.

His first visit after his return to England was again to Norfolk. It was a short but important one, and on its termination he went back to Byrneside to give orders for many changes and alterations that were to be made with all speed in view of the coming of a new mistress. It had for some time past been apparent to Luscombe that the remark he had laughingly made years before on the banks of the Canadian was likely to bear fruit, and that his sister Phillis constituted no small portion of the attraction that brought Hugh down to Norfolk. Indeed, before leaving for the States Hugh had chatted the matter over with him.

"Of course you have seen, Luscombe, how it has been. I shall be three-and-twenty by the time I get back, which is quite young enough for a man to talk about marriage. As soon as I do I shall ask Phillis."

"Just as well to wait, Hugh. It seems to me that you and Phillis pretty well understand each other; but I don't see any use in engagements till one can fix a date for the marriage, and as you have made up your mind to go on this trip, it will save you both a lot of trouble in the way of writing to leave it alone until you come back. It is a horrid nuisance to keep on writing letters when you are travelling. Besides, you know, the governor has strong ideas against early marriages, and will think you quite young enough then, and so I should say leave it as it stands."

And so Hugh had left it; but it is doubtful whether he had left Phillis quite in ignorance of what would be said on his return. At any rate no time was required by her before giving an answer to the question when it was put, and two months later the marriage took place. Many as were the presents that the bride received, they were thrown completely into the shade by that which arrived as a joint gift from Don Ramon and his family a few days before the wedding, being sent by their order from Tiffany's, the great jeweller of New York. It consisted of a case of jewellery of extraordinary value and magnificence, and was, as Mr. Luscombe, senior, remarked, suitable rather for a princess of royal blood than for the wife of a Cumberland squire.

The return of Mr. and Mrs. Tunstall after the termination of their honeymoon to Byrneside was hailed with great rejoicing by the tenantry, who were happy to know that the old state of things had at last returned, and that a resident landlord with an English wife would in future be established in the family mansion.